BANJO

Books by Claude McKay

SONGS OF JAMAICA

SPRING IN NEW HAMPSHIRE

HARLEM SHADOWS

HOME TO HARLEM

BANJO

GINGERTOWN

BANANA BOTTOM

A LONG WAY FROM HOME

HARLEM : NEGRO METROPOLIS

SELECTED POEMS

BANJO

A Story without a Plot

BY

CLAUDE McKAY

A Harvest/HBJ Book
Harcourt Brace Jovanovich, Publishers
New York and London

Harvest edition published by arrangement with Hope McKay Virtue and Harper & Row, Publishers.

ISBN 0-15-610675-2

Printed in the United States of America

DEFG

For Ruthope

CONTENTS

THIRD PART

FIRST PART

I. The Ditch

HEAVING along from side to side, like a sailor on the unsteady deck of a ship, Lincoln Agrippa Daily, familiarly known as Banjo, patrolled the magnificent length of the great breakwater of Marseilles, a banjo in his hand.

"It sure is some moh mahvelous job," he noted mentally; "most wonderful bank in the ocean I evah did see."

It was afternoon. Banjo had walked the long distance of the breakwater and was returning to the Joliette end. He wore a cheap pair of slippers, suitable to the climate, a kind much used by the very poor of Provence. They were an ugly drab-brown color, which, however, was mitigated by the crimson socks and the yellow scarf with its elaborate pattern of black, yellow, and red at both ends, that was knotted around his neck and hung down the front of his blue-jean shirt.

Suddenly he stood still in his tracks as out of the bottom of one of the many freight cars along the quay he saw black bodies dropping. Banjo knew box cars. He had hoboed in America. But never had he come across a box car with a hole in the bottom. Had those black boys made it? He went down on the quay to see.

The fellows were brushing the hay off their clothes. There were four of them.

"Hello, there!" said Banjo.

"Hello, money!" replied the tallest of the four, who was just Banjo's build.

"Good night, money. What I want to know is ef you-all made that theah hole in the bottom a that box car? I nevah yet seen no hole in the bottom of a box car, and I've rode some rails back home in the States."

"P'raps not. They's things ovah heah diffarant from things ovah theah and they's things ovah theah diffarant from things ovah heah. Now the way things am setting with me, this heah hole-in-the-bottom box car is just *the* thing for us."

"You done deliver you'self of a mouthful that sure sounds perfect," responded Banjo.

"I always does. Got to use mah judgment all the time with these fellahs heah. And you? What you making foh you'self down here on the breakwater?"

"Ain't making a thing, but I know I'd sure love to make a meal."

"A meal! You broke already?"

"Broke already? Yes I is, but what do you know about it?" asked Banjo, sharply.

"Nothing in particular, ole spoht, cep'n' that I bummed you two times when you was strutting with that ofay broad and that Ise Malty Avis, the best drummer on the beach. Mah buddies heah bummed you, too, so if youse really broke and hungry as you say, which can be true, 'causen you' lips am as pale as the belly of a fish, just you come right along and eat ovah theah." He pointed to a ramshackle bistro-restaurant on the quay. "We got a little money between us. The bumming was good last night."

"This is going some, indeed. I gived you a raise yestidday and youse feeding me today," said Banjo as they all walked toward the bistro. "I don't even remember none a you fellahs."

" 'Cause you was too swell dressed up and strutting

fine with that broad to see anybody else," said the smallest of the group.

They were all hungry. The boys had been sleeping, and woke up with an appetite. Before them the woman of the bistro set five plates of vegetable soup, a long loaf of bread, followed by braised beef and plenty of white beans. Malty called for five bottles of red wine.

Banjo got acquainted over the mess. The shining black big-boned lad who bore such a contented expression on his plump jolly face and announced himself as Malty Avis, was the leader and inspirer of the group. His full name was Buchanan Malt Avis. He was a West Indian. His mother had been a cook for a British missionary and from the labels of his case goods, for which she had had a fondness, she had taken his Christian names. The villagers dropped Buchanan and took Malt, which they made Malty.

Malty's working life began as a small sailor boy on fishing-boats in the Caribbean. When he became a big boy he was taken by a cargo boat on his first real voyage to New Orleans. From there he had started in as a real seaman and had never returned home.

Sitting on Malty's right, the chestnut-skinned fellow with drab-brown curly hair was called Ginger, a tribute evidently, to the general impression of his make-up. Whether you thought of ginger as a tuber in reddish tropical soil, or as a preserved root, or as the Jamaica liquid, it reminded you oddly of him. Of all the English-speaking Negro boys, Ginger held the long-term record of existence on the beach. He had lost his seaman's papers. He had been in prison for vagabondage and served with a writ of expulsion. But he had destroyed the writ and swiped the papers of another seaman.

Opposite Ginger was Dengel, also tall, but thin. He

was a Senegalese who spoke a little English and preferred the company of Malty and his pals to that of his countrymen.

Beside Dengel was the small, wiry, dull-black boy who had sardonically reminded Banjo of his recent high-flying. He was always aggressive of attitude. The fellows said that he was bughouse and he delighted in the name of Bugsy that they gave him.

They were all on the beach, and there were many others besides them—white men, brown men, black men. Finns, Poles, Italians, Slavs, Maltese, Indians, Negroids, African Negroes, West Indian Negroes—deportées from America for violation of the United States immigration laws—afraid and ashamed to go back to their own lands, all dumped down in the great Provençal port, bumming a day's work, a meal, a drink, existing from hand to mouth, anyhow any way, between box car, tramp ship, bistro, and bordel.

"But you ain't broke, man," Malty said, pointing to the banjo, "when you got that theah bit a business. Ain't a one of us here that totes around anything that can bring a little money outa this burg a peddlers."

Banjo caressed his instrument. "I nevah part with this, buddy. It is moh than a gal, moh than a pal; it's mahself."

"You don't have to go hungry round here, either, ef you c'n play a li'l' bit," drawled Ginger. "You c'n pick up enough change foh you'self even as much to buy us all a li'l' red wine to wet our whistle when the stuff is scarce down the docks—jest by playing around in them bars in Joliette and uptown around the Bum Square."

"We'll see what this burg can stand," said Banjo. "It ain't one or two times, but plenty, that mah steady here did make me a raise when I was right down and out. Oncet away back in Montreal, after I done lost every cent to mah name on the racetracks, I went into one swell spohting-place and cleaned up twenty-five dollars playing. But the best of all was the bird uvva time I had in San Francisco with three buddies who hed a guitar and a ukulele and a tambourine between them. My stars! I was living in clovah for six months."

"You'll make yours here, too," said Malty. "Although this heah burg is lousy with pifformers, doing their stuff in the cafés, it ain't often you come across one that can turn out a note to tickle a chord in you' apparatus. Play us a piece. Let us hear how you sound."

"Not now," said Banjo. "Better tonight in some café. Maybe they won't like it here."

"Sure they will. You c'n do any ole thing at any ole time in this country."

"That ain't a damn sight true," Bugsy jumped sharply in. "But you can play all the time," he said to Banjo. "People will sure come and listen and the boss will get rid a some moh of his rotten wine."

"This wine ain't so bad——" Ginger began.

"It sure is," insisted Bugsy, whose palate had never grown agreeable to *vin rouge ordinaire*. He drank with the boys, as drinking played a big part in their group life, but he preferred syrups to wine, and he was the soberest among them.

"The wine outa them barrels we bung out on the docks is much better," he declared.

"Why, sure it's better, you black blubberhead," exclaimed Ginger. "Tha's the real best stuff we make down there. Pure and strong, with no water in it. That's why we get soft on it quicker than when we drink in a café. In all them little cafés the stuff is doctored. That's the profit way."

Banjo played "Yes, sir, that's my baby." He said

it was one of the pieces that were going wild in the States. The boys began humming and swaying. What Bugsy predicted happened. Some dockers who were not working were drawn to the bistro. They seated themselves at a rough long table, across from the boys' by the other side of the door, listened approvingly to the music, drank wine, and spat pools.

Malty ordered more wine. Ginger and Bugsy stood up to each other and performed a strenuous movement of the "Black Bottom," as they had learned it from Negro seamen of the American Export Line. The *patrone* came and stood in the door, very pleased, and exhibited a little English, "Good piece you very well play. . . ."

Banjo played another piece, then suddenly stopped, stood up and stretched his arms.

"You finish' already?" demanded Malty.

"Sure; it was just a little exhibition of my accomplishment foh your particular benefit."

"Youse as good a musician as a real artist."

"I *is* an artist."

The workmen regarded Banjo admiringly, drained their glasses, and sauntered off.

"Imagine those cheap skates coming here jest to listen to mah playing and not even offering a man a drink," Banjo sneered. "Why, ef I was in Hamburg or Genoa they woulda sure drownded me in liquor."

"The Froggies am all tight that way," said Malty. "They're a funny people. If you'd a taken up a collection every jack man a them woulda gived you a copper, thinking that you make you' living that way——"

"Hell with their coppers," said Banjo. "I expected them to stand a round just for expreciation only of a good thing."

"As for that, they ain't the treating kind a good fellahs

that you and I am used to on the other side," said Malty. . . .

From the bistro on the breakwater, the boys rocked slowly along up to Joliette. Ginger had a favorite drinking-place on the Rue Forbin, a dingy tramps' den. They stopped there, drinking until twilight. Ginger and Dengel became so staggeringly soft that they decided to go back to the box car and sleep.

Malty said to Banjo and Bugsy, "Let's take our tail up to the Bum Square."

The Place Victor Gelu of the Vieux Port was called by the boys on the beach the "Bum Square" because it was there they gathered at night to bum or panhandle seamen and voyagers who passed through to visit the Quartier Réservé. The Quartier Réservé they called "the Ditch" with the same rough affection with which they likened their ship to an easy woman by calling it the "broad."

Avoiding the populous Rue de la République, Malty, Banjo, and Bugsy followed the little-frequented Boulevard de la Major, passing by the shadow of the big cathedral and the gate of the Central Police Building, to reach the Bum Square. They took two more rounds of red wine on the way, the last in a little café in the Place de Lenche before they descended to the Ditch.

Malty had a dinner engagement with a mulatto seaman from a boat of the American Export Line, whom he was to meet in the Bum Square. The wine had worked so hard on their appetites that all three were hungry again. Malty looked in all the cafés of the square, but did not find his man. A big blond fellow, his clothes starched with dirt, was standing in the shadow of a palm, looking sharply out for customers. Malty asked him if he had seen his mulatto.

"He went up that way with a tart," replied the blond, pointing toward the Canebière.

"Let's go and eat, anyway," Malty said to Banjo and Bugsy. "I got some money yet."

"Latnah musta gived you an extry raise; she is always handing you something," said Bugsy.

"I ain't seen her for ovah three days," replied Malty.

"Oh, you got a sweet mamma helping you on the side?" Banjo asked, laughing.

"Not mine, boh," replied Malty. "Is jest a li'l' woman bumming like us on the beach. I don't know whether she is Arabian or Persian or Indian. She knows all landwidges. I stopped a p-i from treating her rough one day, and evah since she pals out with our gang, nevah passing us without speaking, no matter ef she even got a officer on the string, and always giving us English and American cigarettes and a little change when she got 'em. It's easy for her, you see, to penetrate any place on a ship, when we can't, 'cause she's a skirt with some legs all right, and her face ain't nothing that would scare you."

"And none a you fellahs can't make her?" cried Banjo. "Why you-all ain't the goods?"

"It ain't that, you strutting cock, but she treats us all like pals and don't leave no ways open for that. Ain't it better to have her as a pal than to lose out ovah a li'l' crazy craving that a few sous can settle up here?"

They went up one of the humid, somber alleys, thick with little eating-dens of all the Mediterranean peoples, Greek, Jugo-Slav, Neapolitan, Arab, Corsican, and Armenian, Czech and Russian.

When they had finished eating, Malty suggested that they might go up to the gayer part of the Ditch. Bugsy said he would go to the cinema to see Hoot Gibson in a Wild West picture. But Banjo accepted the invitation with alacrity. Every chord in him responded to the loose, bistro-love-life of the Ditch.

Banjo was a great vagabond of lowly life. He was a child of the Cotton Belt, but he had wandered all over America. His life was a dream of vagabondage that he was perpetually pursuing and realizing in odd ways, always incomplete but never unsatisfactory. He had worked at all the easily-picked-up jobs—longshoreman, porter, factory worker, farm hand, seaman.

He was in Canada when the Great War began and he enlisted in the Canadian army. That gave him a glimpse of London and Paris. He had seen a little of Europe before, having touched some of the big commercial ports when he was a husky fireman. But he had never arrived at the sailor's great port, Marseilles. Twice he had been to Genoa and once to Barcelona. Only those who know the high place that Marseilles holds in the imagination of seamen can get the feeling of his disappointment. All through his seafaring days Banjo had dreamed dreams of the seaman's dream port. And at last, because the opportunity that he had long hoped for did not come to take him there, he made it.

Banjo had been returned to Canada after the general demobilization. From there he crossed to the States, where he worked at several jobs. Seized by the old restlessness for a sea change while he was working in an industrial plant, he hit upon the unique plan of getting himself deported.

Some of his fellow workmen who had entered the United States illegally had been held for deportation, and they were all lamenting that fact. Banjo, with his unquenchable desire to be always going, must have thought them very poor snivelers. They had all been thunderstruck when he calmly announced that he was not an American. Everything about him—accent, attitude, and movement—shouted Dixie. But Banjo had insisted that his parentage was really foreign. He had served in the Canadian army. . . . His declaration had to be accepted by his bosses.

Banjo was a personality among the immigration officers. They liked his presence, his voice, his language of rich Aframericanisms. They admired, too, the way he had chosen to go off wandering again. (It was nothing less than a deliberate joke to them, for Banjo could never convince any American, especially a Southern-knowing one, that he was not Aframerican.) It was singular enough to stir their imagination, so long insensible to the old ways of ship desertion and stowing away. The officials teased Banjo, asking him what he would ever do in Europe when he spoke no other language than straight Yankee. However, their manner betrayed their feeling of confidence that Banjo would make his way anywhere. He was given a chance to earn some money across and they saw him go regretfully and hopefully, when he signed up on the tramp that would eventually land him at Marseilles.

Banjo's tramp was a casual one. So much so that it was four months and nineteen days after sailing down through the Panama Canal to New Zealand and Australia, cruising cargo around the island continent and up along the coast of Africa, before his dirty overworked "broad" reached the port of Marseilles.

Banjo had no plan, no set purpose, no single object in coming to Marseilles. It was the port that seamen talked about—the marvelous, dangerous, attractive, big, wide-open port. And he wanted only to get there.

Banjo was paid off in francs, and after changing a deck of dollars that he had saved in America, he possessed twelve thousand five hundred and twenty-five francs and some sous. He was spotted and beset by touting guides, white, brown, black, all of them ready to show and sell him everything for a trifle. He got rid of them all.

Banjo bought a new suit of clothes, fancy shoes, and a vivid *cache-col.* He had good American clothes, but he wanted to strut in Provençal style.

Instinctively he drifted to the Ditch, and as naturally he found a girl there. She found a room for both of them. Banjo's soul thrilled to the place—the whole life of it that milled around the ponderous, somber building of the Mairie, standing on the Quai du Port, where fish and vegetables and girls and youthful touts, cats, mongrels, and a thousand second-hand things were all mingled together in a churning agglomeration of stench and sliminess.

His wonderful Marseilles! Even more wonderful to him than he had been told. Unstintingly Banjo gave of himself and his means to his girl and the life around him. And when he was all spent she left him.

Now he was very light of everything: light of pocket, light of clothing (having relieved himself at the hock shop), light of head, feeling and seeing everything lightly.

It was Banjo's way to take every new place and every new thing for the first time in a hot crazy-drunk manner. He was a type that was never sober, even when he was not drinking. And now the first delirious fever days of Marseilles were rehearsing themselves, wheeling round and round in his head. The crooked streets of dim lights, the gray damp houses bunched together and their rowdy signs of many colors. The mongrel-faced guides of shiny, beady eyes, patiently persuasive; the old hags at the portals, like skeletons presiding over an orgy, with skeleton smile and skeleton charm inviting in quavering accents those who hesitated to enter. Oh, his head was a circus where everything went circling round and round.

Banjo had never before been to that bistro where Malty was taking him. It had a player-piano and a place in the rear for dancing. It was a rendezvous for most of the English-speaking beach boys. If they were spending a night in the Vieux Port, they went there (after panhandling the Bum Square) for sausage sandwiches and red wine. And when all their appetites were appeased, they flopped together in a room upstairs.

The mulatto cook from the Export Line boat was there, sitting between a girl and an indefinite Negroid type of fellow. There were two bottles of wine and a bottle of beer before them. The cook called Malty and Banjo to his table and ordered more wine. There were many girls from the Ditch and young touts dancing. One of the girls asked Banjo to play. Another made the mulatto dance with her. Banjo played "Yes, sir, that's my baby." But as soon as he paused, a girl started the player-piano. The banjo was not loud enough for that close, noisy little market. Everybody was dancing.

Banjo put the instrument aside. It wasn't adequate for the occasion. It would need an orchestry to fix them right, he thought, good-humoredly. I wouldn't mind starting one going in this burg. Gee! That's the idea. Tha's jest what Ise gwine to do. The American darky is the performing fool of the world today. He's demanded everywhere. If I c'n only git some a these heah panhandling fellahs together, we'll show them some real nigger music. Then I'd be setting pretty in this heah sweet dump without worrying ovah mah wants. That's the stuff for a live nigger like me to put ovah, and no cheap playing from café to café and a handing out mah hat for a lousy sou.

He was so exhilarated with the thought of what he would do that he felt like dancing. At that moment the girl of his first Marseilles days came in with a young runt of a tout. Banjo looked up at her, smiling expectantly. She was still going round in his head with the rest of the Ditch. She had left him, of course, but he had accepted that as inevitable when he could no longer afford her. Yet, he had mused, she might have been a little extravagant and bestowed on him one spontaneous caress over all that was bought. She had not. Because she only knew one way—the way of the Ditch. She did not know the way of a brown girl back home who could say with sweet exaggeration: "Daddy, we two will go home and spread joy and not wake up till next week sometime and want nothing but loving."

Ah no! Nothing so fancifully real. Nevertheless, she was the first playmate of his dream port.

The girl, seeing Banjo, turned her eyes casually away and went to sit where she could concentrate her charms on the mulatto. Banjo had no further interest for her. He had spent all his money and, like all the beach boys, would never have more for a wild fling as long as he remained in port. It was the mulatto that had brought her there. For as soon as a new arrival enters any of the dens of the Ditch, the girls are made aware of it by the touts, who are always on the lookout. Banjo was vexed. Hell! She might have been more cordial, he thought. The player-piano was rattling out "Fleur d'Amour." He would ask her to dance. Maybe her attitude was only an insolent little exhibition of cattishness. He went over to her and asked, "Danser?"

"No," she said, disdainfully, and turned away. He touched her shoulder playfully.

"Laissez-moi tranquil, imbecile." She spat nastily on the floor.

A rush of anger seized Banjo. "You pink sow!" he cried. His eyes caught the glint of the gold watch he had given to her, and wrenching it from her wrist, he smashed it on the red-tiled floor and stamped his heel upon it in a rage. The girl screamed agonizingly, wringing her hands, her wide eyes staring tragically at the remains of her watch. The little tout who had come in with her leaped over at Banjo. "What is it? What is it?" he cried, and hunching up his body and thrusting his head up and out like a comic actor, he began working his open hands up and down in Banjo's face, without touching him. Banjo looked down upon the boy contemptuously and seized his left wrist, intending to twist it and push him outside, for he could not think of fighting with such an undersized antagonist. But in a flash the boy drew a knife across his wrist and, released, dashed through the door.

Banjo wrapped the cut in his handkerchief, but it was soon soaked with blood. It was late. The pharmacies were closed. The *patrone* of the bistro said that there were pharmacies open all night. Malty took Banjo to hunt for one.

As they were passing through the Bum Square a woman's voice called Malty. They stopped and she came up to them. She was a little olive-toned woman of an indefinable age, clean-faced, not young and far from old, with an amorous charm round her mouth. It was Latnah.

"Ain't gone to bed yet?" Malty said to her. "Ise got a case here." He exhibited Banjo's hand.

"It plenty bleed," she said. She looked at Banjo and said, "I see you before around here."

Banjo grinned. "Maybe I seen you, too."

"I no think. Pharmacie no open now," she answered Malty's question. Then she said to Banjo: "Come with me. I see your hand. Tomorrow see you, Malty. Good night." She took Banjo away, while Malty's eyes followed them in a wistful, bewildered gaze.

She took Banjo back in the direction from which he had come, but by way of the Quai du Port. After a few minutes' walk they turned into one of the somber side streets. They went into a house a little southwest of the Ditch. Her room was on the top floor, a quaint, tiny thing, the only one up there, and opened right on the stairs. There was a little shutter-window, the size of a *Saturday Evening Post,* that gave a view of the Vieux Port, where the lights of the boats were twinkling. A bright, inexpensive Oriental shawl covered the cot-bed. On the table was a washbowl, two little jars of cosmetics, and packets of different brands of cigarettes.

There was no water in the room, and Latnah went down two flights of stairs to get a jugful. When she returned she washed Banjo's wound, then, getting a bottle of liquid from a basket against the foot of the cot, she anointed and bandaged it.

Banjo liked the woman's gentle fussing over him. He thanked her when she had finished. *"Rien du tout,"* she replied. There was a little silence between them, slightly embarrassing but piquant.

Then Banjo said: "I wonder whereat I can find Malty now? I didn't have a room yet for tonight."

"You sleep here," she said, simply.

He undressed while she found something to do—empty the washbowl, wipe the table, and when at last he caught a glimpse of her between her deshabille and the covers he murmured softly to himself: "Don't care how I falls, may be evah so long a drop, but it's always on mah feets."

II. The Breakwater

THE quarter of the old port exuded a nauseating odor of mass life congested, confused, moving round and round in a miserable suffocating circle. Yet everything there seemed to belong and fit naturally in place. Bistros and love shops and girls and touts and vagabonds and the troops of dogs and cats—all seemed to contribute so essentially and colorfully to that vague thing called atmosphere. No other setting could be more appropriate for the men on the beach. It was as if all the derelicts of all the seas had drifted up here to sprawl out the days in the sun.

The men on the beach spent the day between the breakwater and the docks, and the night between the Bum Square and the Ditch. Most of the whites, especially the blond ones of northern countries, seemed to have gone down hopelessly under the strength of hard liquor, as if nothing mattered for them now but that. They were stinking-dirty, and lousy, without any apparent desire to clean themselves. With the black boys it was different. It was as if they were just taking a holiday. They were always in holiday spirit, and if they did not appear to be specially created for that circle, they did not spoil the picture, but rather brought to it a rich and careless tone that increased its interest. They drank wine to make them lively and not sodden, washed their bodies and their clothes on the breakwater, and sometimes spent a panhandled ten-franc note to buy a second-hand pair of pants.

Banjo had become a permanent lodger at Latnah's. His wound was not serious, but it was painful and had given him a light fever. Latnah told him that when his wrist was well enough for him to play, she would go with him to perform in some of the bars of the quarter and take up a collection.

In the daytime Latnah went off by herself to her business, and sometimes the nature of it detained her overnight and she did not get back to her room. Banjo spent most of his time with Malty's gang. He was not altogether one of them, but rather a kind of honorary member, having inspired respect by his sudden conquest of Latnah and by being an American.

An American seaman (white or black) on the beach is always treated with a subtle difference by his beach fellows. He has a higher face value than the rest. His passport is worth a good price and is eagerly sought for by passport fabricators. And he has the assurance that, when he gets tired of beaching, his consulate will help him back to the fabulous land of wealth and opportunity.

Banjo dreamed constantly of forming an orchestra, and the boys listened incredulously when he talked about it. He had many ideas of beginning. If he could get two others besides himself he could arrange with the proprietor of some café to let them play at his place. That might bring in enough extra trade to pay them something. Or he might make one of the love shops of the Ditch unique and famous with a black orchestra.

One day he became very expansive about his schemes under the influence of wine-drinking on the docks. This was the great sport of the boys. They would steal a march on the watchmen or police, bung out one of the big casks, and suck up the wine through rubber tubes until they were sweetly soft.

Besides Banjo there were Malty, Ginger, and Bugsy. After they had finished with the wine, they raided a huge heap of peanuts, filled up their pockets, and straggled across the suspension bridge to lie in the sun on the breakwater.

"I could sure make one a them dumps look like a real spohting-place," said Banjo, "with a few of us niggers pifforming in theah. Lawdy! but the chances there is in a wide-open cat town like this! But everybody is so hoggish after the sous they ain't got no imagination left to see big money in a big thing——"

"It wasn't a big thing that dat was put ovah on you, eh?" sniggered Bugsy.

"Big you' crack," retorted Banjo. "That theah wasn't nothing at all. Ain't nobody don't put anything ovah on me that I didn't want in a bad way to put ovah mahself. I like the looks of a chicken-house, and I ain't nevah had no time foh the business end ovit. But when I see how these heah poah ole disabled hens am making a hash of a good thing with a gang a cheap no-'count p-i's, I just imagine what a high-yaller queen of a place could do ovah heah turned loose in this sweet clovah. Oh, boy, with a bunch a pinks and yallers and chocolates in between, what a show she could showem!"

"It's a tall lot easier talking than doing," said Bugsy. "Theyse some things jest right as they is and ain't nevah was made foh making better or worser. Now supposing you was given a present of it, what would you make outa one a them joints in Boody Lane?"

Boody Lane was the beach boys' name for the Rue de la Bouterie, the gut of the Ditch.

"Well, that's a forthrightly question and downrightly hard to answer," said Banjo. "For I wasn't inclosing them in mah catalogory, becausen they ain't real places, brother; them's just stick-in-the-mud holes. Anyway, if one was gived to me I'd try everything doing excep'n' lighting it afire."

At this they all laughed. "Don't light it afire" was the new catch phrase among the beach boys and they passed it on to every new seaman that was introduced to the Ditch. When the new man, curious, asked the meaning, they replied, laughing mysteriously, "Because it is six months."

The phrase was the key to the story of an American brown boy who went on shore leave and would not keep company with any of his comrades. At the Vieux Port he was besieged by the black beach boys, but he refused to give them anything and told them that they ought to be ashamed to let down their race by scavengering on the beach. When he started to go up into the Ditch the boys warned him that it was dangerous to go alone. He went alone, replying that he did not want the advice or company of bums.

He went proud and straight into one of the stick-in-the-mud places of Boody Lane. And before he could get out, his pocketbook with his roll of dollars was missing. He accused the girl by signs. She replied by signs and insults that he had not brought the pocketbook there. She mentioned "police" and left the box. He thought she had gone to get the police to help him find his money. But he waited and waited, and when she did not return, realizing that he had been tricked, he struck a match and set the bed on fire. That not only brought him the police, but also the fire brigade and six months in prison, where he was now cooling himself.

Ginger said: "I ain't no innovation sort of a fellah. When I make a new beach all I want is to make mah way and not make no changes. Just make mah way somehow while everything is going on without me studying them or them studying me."

He was lying flat on his back on one of the huge stone blocks of the breakwater. The waves were lapping softly around it. He had no shirt on and, unfastening the pin at the collar of his old blue coat, he flung it back and exposed his brown belly to the sun. His trousers waist was pulled down below his navel. "Oh, Gawd, the sun is sweet!" he yawned and, pulling his cap over his eyes, went to sleep. The others also stretched themselves and slept.

Along the great length of the breakwater other careless vagabonds were basking on the blocks. The day was cooling off and the sun shed down a warm, shimmering glow where the light fell full on the water. Over by l'Estaque, where they were extending the port, a P. L. M. coal ship stood black upon the blue surface. The factories loomed on the long slope like a rusty-black mass of shapes strung together, and over them the bluish-gray hills were bathed in a fine, delicate mist, and further beyond an immense phalanx of gray rocks, the inexhaustible source of the cement industry, ran sharply down into the sea.

Sundown found the boys in the Place de la Joliette. In one of the cafés they found a seaman from Zanzibar among some Maltese, from whom they took him away.

"Wese just in time for you," Malty declared. "What youse looking for is us. Fellahs who speak the same as you speak and not them as you kain't trust who mix up the speech with a mess of Arabese. Them's a sort of bastard Arabs, them Maltese, and none of us likes them, much less trusts them."

The new man was very pleased to fall in with fellows as friendly as Banjo and Malty. He was on a coal boat from South Shields and had a few pounds on him. He was generous and stood drinks in several cafés. From the Place de la Joliette, they took the quiet way of the Boulevard de la Major to reach the Ditch. It was the best way for the beach boys. Some of them had not the proper papers to get by the police and tried to evade them always. By way of the main Rue de la République they were more likely to be stopped, questioned, searched, and taken to the police station. Sometimes they were told that their papers were not in order, but they were only locked up for a night and let out the next morning. Some of them complained of being beaten by the police. Ginger thought the police were getting more brutal and strict, quite different from what they were like when he first landed on the beach. Then they could bung out a cask of wine in any daring old way and drink without being bothered. Now it was different. It was not very long since two fellows from the group had got two months each for wine-stealing. Happily for them, Malty, Ginger, and Bugsy all had passable papers.

On the way to the Ditch they stopped in different bistros to empty in each a bottle of red wine. These fellows, who were used to rum in the West Indies, gin and corn liquor in the States, and whisky in England, took to the red wine of France like ducks to water. They never had that terribly vicious gin or whisky drunk. They seemed to have lost all desire for hard liquor. When they were drunk it was always a sweetly-soft good-natured wine drunk.

They had a big feed in one of the Chinese restaurants of the Rue Torte. The new man insisted on paying for it all. After dinner they went to a little café on the Quai du Port for coffee-and-rum. The newcomer took a mouth organ from his pocket and began playing. This stimulated Banjo, who said, "I guess mah hand c'n do its stuff again," and so he went up to Latnah's room and got his banjo.

They went playing from little bistro to bistro in the small streets between the fish market and the Bum Square. They were joined by others—a couple of Senegalese and some British West Africans and soon the company was more than a dozen. They were picturesquely conspicuous as they loitered along, talking in a confused lingo of English, French, and native African. And in the cafés the bottles of beer and wine that they ordered and drank indiscriminately increased as their number increased. Customers were attracted by the music, and the girls, too, who were envious and used all their wiles to get away the newly arrived seaman from the beach boys. . . .

"Hot damn!" cried Banjo. "What a town this heah is to spread joy in!"

"And you sure did spread yours all at once," retorted Bugsy. "Burn it up in one throw and finish, you did."

"Muzzle you' mouf, nigger," replied Banjo. "The joy stuff a life ain't nevah finished for this heah strutter. When I turn mahself loose for a big wild joyful jazz a life, you can bet you' sweet life I ain't gwine nevah regretting it. Ise got moh joy stuff in mah whistle than you're got in you' whole meager-dawg body."

"And I wouldn't want to know," said Bugsy.

At midnight they were playing in one of the cafés of the Bum Square, when an oldish man came in wearing faded green trousers, a yellowy black-bordered jacket, with a wreath of flowers around his neck and began to dance. He manipulated a stick with such dexterity that it seemed as if his wrist was moving round like a wheel, and he jigged and hopped from side to side with amazing agility while Banjo and the seaman played.

When they stopped, the garlanded dancer said he would bet anybody a bottle of *vin blanc supérieur* that he could stand on his head on a table. A youngster in proletarian blue made a sign against his head and said of the old fellow, *"Il est fada."* And the old man did indeed look a little mad in his strange costume and graying hair, and it seemed unlikely that his bones could support him in the feat that he proclaimed he could perform. But nobody took up the bet.

Somebody translated what was what to the new seaman, who said, carelessly, "May as well bet and have a little fun outa him."

"Très bien," said the old man. He made several attempts at getting headdown upon the table and failed funnily, like professional acrobats in their first trials on the stage, and the café resounded with peals of laughter and quickly filled up. Suddenly the old fellow cried: *"Ca y est!"* and spread his hands out, balancing himself straight up on his head on the table. In a moment he jumped down and, twisting his stick and executing some steps, went round with his hat and took up a collection before the crowd diminished. The beach boys threw in their share of sous and the seaman promptly paid for the bottle of white wine. The old man took it and left the café, followed by a woman.

Latnah, passing through the Bum Square and seeing Banjo playing, had entered the café just when the old man stopped dancing and asked who would take up his bet. The good collection he took up and the bottle of wine in addition awakened all her instincts of acquisitiveness and envious rivalry. She turned on Banjo.

"All that money man take and gone is you' money. You play and he take money. You too proud to ask money and you no have nothing. You feel rich, maybe."

"Leave me be, woman," said Banjo.

"And you make friend pay wine for man. Man make

nothing but bluff. You colored make the white fool you all time ——"

"I didn't tell him to bet nothing. But even then, what is a little lousy bet? Gawd bless mah soul! The money I done bet in *my* life and all foh big stakes on them race tracks in Montreal. What do you-all know about life and big stakes?" Banjo waved his hand in a tipsy sweep as if he saw the old world of race-track bettors before him.

"This no Montreal; this Marseilles," replied Latnah, "and you very fool to play for nothing. You need money, you bitch-commer ——"

"Now quit you' noise. Ise going with you, but I ain't gwine let you ride me. Get me? No woman nevah ride me yet and you ain't gwine to ride me, neither."

He stood up, resting the banjo on a table.

"And it not me doing the riding, I'm sure," said Latnah.

"Come on, fellahs; let's get outa this. Let's take our hump away from here," said Banjo.

III. Malty Turned Down

BANJO had taken Latnah as she came, easily. It seemed the natural thing to him to fall on his feet, that Latnah should take the place of the other girl to help him now that he needed help. Whatever happened, happened. Life for him was just one different thing of a sort following the other.

Malty was more emotional and amorously gentle than Banjo. He was big, strong, and jolly-natured, and everybody pronounced him a good fellow. He had made it easy for the gang to accept Latnah, when she came to them different from the girls of the Ditch. But there was just the shadow of a change in the manner of the gang toward her since she had taken up steadily with Banjo.

"Some of us nevah know when wese got a good thing," said Malty to Banjo as they sat up on the breakwater, waiting to be signaled to lunch on a ship. "I think youse the kind a man that don't appreciate a fust-rate thing because he done got it too easy."

"Ise a gone-fool nigger with any honey-sweet mamma," replied Banjo, "but I ain't gwina bury mah head under no woman's skirt and let her cackle ovah me."

"All that bellyaching about a skirt," retorted Malty. "We was all made and bohn under it."

Banjo laughed and said: "Easy come, easy go. Tha's the life-living way. We got met up easy and she's taking it easy, and Ise taking it easy, too."

A black seaman came on deck and signaled them. They hurried down from the breakwater and up the gangway.

Latnah was the first woman that Malty and his pals had ever met actually on the beach. Malty first became aware of her one day on the deck of a ship from which he and Bugsy and Ginger had been driven by a Negro steward.

"G'way from here, you lazy no-'count bums," the steward had said. "I wouldn't even give you-all a bone to chew on. Instead a gwine along back to work, you lay down on the beach a bumming mens who am trying to make a raspactable living. You think if you-all lay down sweet and lazy in you' skin while we others am wrastling with salt water, wese gwine to fatten you moh in you' laziness? G'way from this heah white man's broad nigger bums."

The boys were very hungry. For some days they had been eating off a coal boat with a very friendly crew. But it had left the moorings and anchored out in the bay, and now they could not get to it. Irritated, but rather amused by the steward's onslaught, they shuffled off from the ship a little down the quay. But Malty happened to look behind him and see Latnah waving. He went back with his pals and they found a mess of good food waiting for them. Latnah had spoken in their behalf, and one of the mates had told the chief steward to feed them.

The boys saw her often after that. They met her at irregular intervals in the Bum Square and down the docks. One day on the docks she got into a row with one of the women who sold fancy goods on the boats. The woman was trying to tempt one of the mates into buying a fine piece of Chinese silk, but the mate was more tempted by Latnah.

"Go away from me," the mate said. "I don't want a bloody thing you've got."

The woman was angry, but such rebuffs were not strange to her. To carry on her business successfully she had to put up with them. She had seen at once that the officer was interested in Latnah, and in passing she swung her valise against Latnah's side.

"Oh, you stupid woman!" cried Latnah, holding her side.

"You dirty black whore," returned the woman.

"You bigger white whore," retorted Latnah. "I know you sell everything you've got. I see you on ship." And Latnah pulled open her eye at the woman and made a face.

Later, when Latnah left the ship, she again met the woman with her man on the dock. The man was a slim tout-like type, and he tried to rough-handle Latnah. But Malty happened along then and bounced the fellow with his elbow and said, "Now what you trying to do with this woman?" The man muttered something in a language unfamiliar to Malty and slunk off with his woman. He hadn't understood what Malty had said, either, but his bounce and menacing tone had been clear enough.

"I glad you come," said Latnah to Malty. "I thank you plenty, plenty, for if you no come I would been in big risk. I would stick him."

She slipped from her bosom a tiny argent-headed dagger, exquisitely sharp-pointed, and showed it to Malty. He recoiled with fear and Latnah laughed. A razor or a knife would not have touched him strangely. But a dagger! It was as if Latnah had produced a serpent from her bosom. It was not an instrument familiar to his world, his people, his life. It reminded him of the strange, fierce, fascinating tales he had heard of Oriental strife and daggers dealing swift death.

Suddenly another side of Latnah was revealed to him and she stood out more clearly, different from the strange creature of quick gestures and nimble body who panhandled the boats and brought them gifts of costly cigarettes. She was different from the women of his race. She laughed differently, quietly, subtly. The women of his race could throw laughter like a clap of thunder. And their style, the movement of their hips, was like that of fine, vigorous, four-footed animals. Latnah's was gliding like a serpent. But she stirred up a powerfully sweet and strange desire in him.

She made him remember the Indian coolies that he had known in his West Indian Island when he was a boy. They were imported indentured laborers and worked on the big sugar plantation that bordered on his seaside village. The novelty of their strangeness never palled on the village. The men with their turbans and the loin-cloths that the villagers called coolie-wrapper. The women weighted down with heavy silver bracelets on arms, neck and ankles, their long glossy hair half hidden by the cloth that the natives called coolie-red. Perhaps they had unconsciously influenced the Negroes to retain their taste for bright color and ornaments that the Protestant missionaries were trying to destroy.

Every 1st of August, the great native holiday, anniversary of the emancipation of the British West Indian slaves in 1834, the Negroes were joined by some Indians in their sports on the playground. The Indians did athletic stunts and sleight-of-hand tricks, such as unwinding yards of ribbon out of their mouths, cleverly making coins disappear and finding them in the pockets of the natives, and fire-eating.

Some of the Indians were regarded as great workers

in magic. The Negroes believed that Indian magic was more powerful than their Obeah. Certain Indians had given up the laborious hoeing and digging of plantation work to practice the black art among the natives. And they were much more influential and prosperous than the Negro doctors of Obeah.

The two peoples did not mix in spite of the friendly contact. There were, however, rare instances of Indians who detached themselves from their people and became of the native community by marrying Negro women. But the Indian women remained more conservative. Malty remembered one striking exception of a beautiful Indian girl. She went to the Sunday-evening class that was conducted by the wife of the Scotch missionary. And she became a convert to Christianity and was married to the Negro schoolmaster.

He also remembered a little Indian girl who was for some time in his class at grade school. Her skin was velvet, smooth and dark like mahogany. She was the cleverest child in the class, but always silent, unsmiling, and mysterious. He had never forgotten her.

Malty's boyhood memories undoubtedly played a part in his conduct toward Latnah. He could not think of her as he did about the women of the Ditch. He felt as if he had long lost sight of his exotic, almost forgotten schoolmate, to find her become a woman on the cosmopolitan shore of Marseilles.

After her encounter with the peddling woman, Latnah attached herself more closely to the beach boys. Maybe (not being a woman of the Ditch, with a tout to fight for her) she felt insecure and wanted to belong to a group or maybe it was just her woman's instinct to be under the protection of man. She was accepted. With their wide experience and passive philosophy of life, beach boys are adepts at meeting, understanding, and accepting everything.

Latnah was following precisely the same line of living as they. She came as a pal. She was made one of them. Whatever personal art she might use as a woman to increase her chances was her own affair. Their luck also depended primarily on personality. Often they traveled devious and separate routes in pursuit of a "handout," and sometimes had to wander into strange culs-de-sac to obtain it. It did not matter if Latnah was not inclined to be amorous with any of them. Perhaps it was better so. She was more useful to them as a pal. Love was cheap in the Ditch. It cost only the price of a bottle of red wine among the "leetah" girls, as the beach boys called the girls of Boody Lane, because their short-time value was fixed at about the price of a liter of cheap red wine.

Malty had wanted Latnah for himself. But she had never given him any chance. She remained just one of the gang.

The boys were rather flattered that she stayed with them and shunned the Arab-speaking men, with whom she was identified by language and features. When Banjo arrived at Marseilles, Latnah's place on her own terms among the boys was a settled thing. But when, falling in love with Banjo at first sight, she took him as her lover, they were all surprised and a little piqued. And the latent desire in Malty was stirred afresh.

After their lunch, Banjo and Malty went across the suspension bridge to the docks on the other side. They were joined by Dengel, who approached them rocking rhythmically, now pausing a moment to balance himself in his tracks. He was much blacker than Malty, a shining anthracite. And his face was moist and his large eyes soft with liquor.

Dengel was always in a state of heavenly inebriety; sauntering along in a soft mist of liquor. He was never worried about food. The joy of his being was the wine of the docks. He always knew of some barrel conveniently placed that could be raided without trouble.

"Come drink wine," he said, "if you like sweet wine. We find one barrel, good, good, very sweet."

Banjo and Malty followed him. In a rather obscure position against a freight car they found Ginger and Bugsy and three Senegalese armed with rubber tubes and swilling and swaying over a barrel of sweet wine. Malty got his tube out of the knapsack that he always toted with him, and Ginger handed Banjo his. Banjo bent over the barrel, spreading his feet away the better to imbibe. He was a long time sucking up the stuff. And when he removed his mouth from the tube, he brought up a long rich and ripe sound from belly to throat, smacked his lips, and droned, "Gawd in glory, ef this baby ain't some sweet boozing!"

"Tell it to Uncle Sam," said Bugsy.

"Tell it and shout nevah no moh," added Ginger.

"Nevah no moh is indeed mah middle name," said Banjo, "but brown me ef I'm a telling-it-too-much kind a darky. I ain't got no head for remembering too much back, nor no tongue for long-suffering delivery. I'm just a right-there, right-here baby, yestiday and today and tomorraw and forevah. All right-there right-here for me now."

"Hallelujah! Lemme crown you. You done said a mou'ful a nigger stuff," said Ginger.

After they had quenched their craving they returned to the far, little-frequented end of the breakwater and lay lazily in the sun. There Latnah, her morning's hustling finished, found them. Her yellow blouse was soiled and she slipped it off and began washing it. That was a sign for the boys to clean up. All except Dengel, the only Senegalese that had crossed over to the breakwater; he was feeling too sweet in his skin for any exertion. The boys stripped to the waist and began to wash their shirts. Bugsy went down between two cement blocks and brought up a can he had secreted there with a hunk of white soap. Finished washing, they spread the clothes on the blocks. Soon the vertical burning rays of the sun would suck them dry.

Malty suggested that they should swim. The beach boys often bathed down the docks, making bathing-suits of their drawers. And sometimes, when they had the extreme end of the breakwater to themselves, they went in naked. They did this time, cautioning Dengel to keep watch for them.

Latnah went in too. Malty was the best swimmer. He made strong crawl strokes. He was also an excellent diver. When he was a boy in the West Indies, he used to dive from the high deck railings for the coins that the tourists threw into the water. When he got going about wharf life in the West Indian ports of Kingston, Santiago, Port of Spain, he told stories of winning dollar bills in competition with other boys diving for coins from the bridges of ships. Of how he would struggle under water against another boy while the coin was whirling down away from them. How the cleverest boy would get it or both lose it when they could not stay down under any longer and came up breathless, blowing a multitude of bubbles.

Latnah was a beautiful diver and shot graceful like a serpent through the water. A thrill shivered through Malty's blood. He had never dreamed that her body was so lovely, limber, and sinewy. He dived down under her and playfully caught at her feet. She kicked him in the mouth, and it was like the shock of a kiss wrestled for and stolen, flooding his being with a rush of sweetly-warm sensation.

Latnah swam away and, hoisting herself upon a block, she gamboled about like a gazelle. Malty and Banjo started to swim round to her, bantering and beating up heaps of water, with Malty leading, when Dengel called: "Attention! Police!" His sharp native eye had discerned two policemen far away up the eastern side of the breakwater, cycling toward them. The swimmers dashed for their clothes.

In a few moments the policemen rode down and, throwing a perfunctory glance at the half-dressed bathers, they circled round and went off again. *"Salauds!"* Dengel said. "Always after *us,* but scared of the real criminals."

For the rest of the afternoon they basked in the sun on the breakwater. With its cooling they returned to the Place de la Joliette, where the group broke up to forage separately for food.

They came together again in the evening in a rendezvous bar of a somber alley, just a little bit out of the heart of the Ditch. Banjo had his instrument and was playing a little saccharine tune that he had brought over from America:

"I wanna go where you go, do what you do,
Love when you love, then I'll be happy. . . ."

The souvenir of Latnah's foot in his mouth was a warm fever in Malty's flesh. And the red wine that he was drinking turned the fever sweet. It was a big night. The barkeeper, a thin Spanish woman, was busy setting up quart bottles of wine on the tables. Only black drinkers filled the little bar, and their wide-open, humorous, frank white eyes lighted up the place more glowingly than the dirty dim electric flare.

Senegalese, Sudanese, Somalese, Nigerians, West Indians, Americans, blacks from everywhere, crowded together, talking strange dialects, but, brought together, understanding one another by the language of wine.

"I'll follow you, sweetheart, and share your little love-nest.
I wanna go where you go . . ."

Malty had managed to get next to Latnah, and put his arm round her waist so quietly that it was some moments before she became aware of it. Then she tried to remove his arm and ease away, but he pressed against her thigh.

"Don't," she said. "I no like."

"What's the matter?" murmured Malty, thickly. "Kaint you like a fellah a li'l' bit?"

He pressed closer against her and said, "Gimmie a kiss."

She felt his strong desire. *"Cochon,* no. Go away from me." She dug him sharply in the side with her elbow.

"You' mout' it stink. I wouldn't kiss a slut like you," said Malty, and he got up and gave Latnah a hard push.

She fell off the bench and picked herself up, crying. She was not hurt by the fall, but by Malty's sudden change of attitude. Malty glowered at her boozily. Banjo stopped playing, went up to him, and shook his fist in his face.

"Wha's matter you messing around mah woman?"

"Go chase you'self. I knowed her long before you did, when she was running after me."

"You're a dawggone liar!"

"And youse another!"

"Ef it's a fight youse looking for, come on outside."

Banjo and Malty staggered off. At the door, Malty stumbled and nearly fell, and Banjo caught his arm and helped him into the street. All the boys crowded to the door and flowed out into the alley, to watch. The antagonists sparred. Malty hiccoughed ominously, swayed forward, and, falling into Banjo's arms, they both went down heavily, in a helpless embrace, on the paving-stones.

IV. Hard Feeding

THE boys had a canny ear for the sounds of "good" ships. They knew them by the note of the horns. They might be bunging out a barrel of wine, or picking up peanuts, or lying on the breakwater when one of the good ships (ships whose crews were friendly and gave the beach boys food) signaled its coming in. One would shout, tossing his cap into the air, "Oh, boy! That theah's a regular broad coming in!" And it would surely be one of their ships.

Sometimes it would be a ship that one of them saw last in Pernambuco, or the ship that another had allowed to leave him in Casablanca. Three months, six months, a year, two years since any of the crew had met this beach boy. Indescribably happy surprise reunions, and stories reminiscent of how they got messed up with wine, girls, and police and missed their ships.

Ginger's little story was brought out by one of these meetings. And for a while it made him "Lights-out" Ginger and the butt of the boys until another incident superseded it. Ginger had often mentioned that he had lost quite a bit of money in Marseilles in one night, but nobody knew just how. Then he met the pal who had been with him on the boat he had left and it all came out. In a bistro by the breakwater, over a table loaded with red wine, the story was told of Ginger's going into one of the little houses of amusement in the Ditch. He was boozy and very happy, singing and swaying. He sang, "Money is no object. I'll pay for anything in the place." And he paid. He did it with great gusto, was really amusing, and all the girls and touts and the other customers were delighted.

There was a little mangy-faced white there who could make himself intelligible in English. And he said to Ginger, "The whole house is yours."

"I know it," Ginger grinned back, "and I'll show it. I'll give this here money to the boss ef she puts the lights out for five minutes." And he waved a thousand-franc note. The *patrone's* eyes popped fire.

"Why, you big stiff," said the boy who told the story and who had been with Ginger, "that's a whole lot a money and tha's all youse got."

"Don't I know what Ise doing?" cried Ginger. "Ise one commanding nigger who'll always pay for a show."

"You can have you' show, but Ise sure gwine away from here, leaving you." And he left.

Ginger paid for his five-minute show and got all of it. Nor did he rejoin his pal, but remained on the beach to become a bum and a philosopher. Bantered as a scholar by the boys, Ginger always had a special opinion, a little ponderous, to give on topics arising among them. And whenever they were up against any trouble, he always advised taking the line of least resistance.

Ginger laughed with the rest when his story was told, and said: "There ain't a jack man of us that ain't got a history to him as good as any that evah was printed. And Ise one that ain't got no case against life."

Ginger's former pal was now again in Marseilles, for the third time since Ginger had fallen for the beach. And the beach boys were invited to his ship to lunch. The galley of that ship was Negro and it was one of the best of "good" ships.

Banjo went along with Malty and company. He

was not a regular panhandler like the other boys. He could not make a happy business of it like them. Because sometimes they were savagely turned down and insulted and he was not the type to stand that. He would have gone to work on the docks, as he had intended at first when he went broke, if his personality and his banjo had not fixed him in a situation more favorable than that of his mates. There was always a pillow for his head at Latnah's, and when he played in any of the bistros of the quarter and she was there, she always took up a collection. Indeed, she collected every time Banjo finished a set of tunes. That was the way the white itinerants did it, she said. *They* never played for fun as Banjo was prone to do. They played in a hard, unsmiling, funereal way and only for sous. Which was doubtless why their playing in general was so execrable. When Banjo turned himself loose and wild playing, he never remembered sous. Perhaps he could afford to forget, however, with Latnah looking out for him and always ready with a ten-franc note whenever his palm was itching for small change.

The ship of Ginger's pal had such a beach-known reputation for handing out the eats that, besides Malty and company, other men of the beach, white and colored, had assembled down by it to feed. Some dozen of them.

When the officers and men had finished eating, Ginger's old friend brought out what was left to the hungry group waiting on the deck. Good food and plenty of it in two pans. Thick, long slices of boiled beef, immense whole boiled potatoes, pork and beans, and lettuce.

All the men rushed the food like swine, each roughly elbowing and snapping at the other to get his hand in first. While they were stuffing themselves, smacking, grunting, and blowing with the disgusting noises of brutes, the food all over their faces, a mess boy brought out a large broad pan half filled with sweet porridge and set it down on the deck. Immediately the porridge was stormed. A huge blond Nordic, who looked like a polar bear that had been rolling in mud, was tripped up by an Armenian and fell sprawling, his lousy white head flopping in the pan of porridge. The blond picked himself up and, burying his greasy-black hand in the porridge, he brought up a palmful and dashed it in the face of the Armenian. That started a free fight in which the pan of porridge was kicked over, whole boiled potatoes went flying across the deck, and Bugsy seized the moment to slap in the face with a slice of beef a boy from Benin whom he hated.

"Goodoh Bugsy!" cried Malty. "Tha's sho some moh feeding his face."

Banjo was standing a little way off, watching the *mêlée* in anger and contempt. A lanky, prematurely-wrinkle-faced officer passed by with a sneering glance at the beach fellows and went to the galley. The cook, a well-fleshed broad-chested brown Negro, came out on the deck.

"You fellahs am sure a bum lot," he said. "The victuals I done give you is too good foh you-all. The garbage even is too good. You ain't no good foh nothing at all."

But the boys were again eating, picking up potatoes and scraps of meat from the deck and scooping up what was left of the porridge.

Banjo had started for the gangway, and Bugsy called to him, "Hi, nigger, ain't you gwine put away some a this heah stuff under you' shirt?"

"The mess you jest fight and trample ovah?" retorted Banjo. "You c'n stuff you' guts tell youse all winded, but *my* belly kain't accommodate none a that theah stuff, for that is too hard feeding for mine."

Having finished eating, the men came off the deck, all friendly vagabonds again. Squabbling and scuffling came natural to them, like eating and drinking, dancing and bawdying, and did not have any bad effect upon the general spirit of their comradeship.

Malty's group picked up Banjo on the dock and separated from the others. Their next objective was to find some conveniently situated barrel of wine that they could bung out and guzzle without trouble.

"It's all the same in the life of the beach," Malty said to Banjo. "Once you get used to it, you kain't feel you'self too good for anything!"

"Theah's some things that this heah boy won't evah get used to," said Banjo. "I heah that officer call you all 'a damned lot a disgusting niggers,' and I don't want no gitting used to that. You fellahs know what the white man think about niggers and you-all ought to do better than you done when he 'low you on his ship to eat that dawggone grub. I take life easy like you-all, but I ain't nevah gwine to lay mahself wide open to any insulting cracker of a white man. For I'll let a white man mobilize mah black moon for a whupping, ef he can, foh calling me a nigger."

"Nix on the insults when a man is on the beach," said Malty. "Gimme a bellyful a good grub and some wine to wash it down is all I ask for."

"You ain't got no self-respecting in you, then," said Banjo. "Youse just a bum and no moh. I ain't a big-headed nigger, but a white man has got to respect me, for when I address myself to him the vibration of brain magic that I turn loose on him is like an electric shock on the spring of his cranium."

"Attaboy!" applauded Ginger, who loved big words

with a philosophical flavor. "You done deliver a declaration of principle, but a declaration of principle is a dependant usynimous with the decision of the destiny of the individual in the general."

" 'Gawd is the first principle,' I done heard that said," declared Malty.

Bugsy grinned, saying, "And Gawd is in Boody Lane."

"Youse a nut!" said Malty. "Don't be calling up Gawd's name as if he was a nigger."

"I seen him there, I tell you," laughed Bugsy, "the day of the big church *fête*. I seen that there blond broad burning her candle before his image."

"It was nothing," said Ginger, "but the eternal visible of imagination."

No barrel was found in a position favorable for a raid, and so the boys filled their pockets with peanuts and walked across the suspension bridge toward the breakwater. Banjo was in a discontented mood and did not join in the jests. At the end of the breakwater a small boat was letting off passengers. Banjo went up to it and said, *"Bonjour"* to the *patron,* who greeted him with a smile.

Banjo stepped into the boat and, waving his hand airily at his pals, said: "Good by!" The *patron* started the motor and the boat went sheering off against the breakwater toward the direction of the Vieux Port.

The boys gazed after him pop-eyed and gaping. What a fellow Banjo was to put himself over! None of them knew that when Banjo's pockets were bulging with real money that very boat had taken him and his girl on two excursions, one to the Château d'If and another to the Canal du Rove at l'Estaque. The boat was just then returning from a trip to the canal, and had stopped to let off passengers who wanted to see the breakwater.

Banjo had merely struck, accidentally, a pretty thing again, but it seemed very wonderful to his pals, as if a special pilot had appeared for him and he had walked away from them into a boat that was conveying him to some perfect paradise.

V. "Jelly Roll"

SHAKE That Thing. The opening of the Café African by a Senegalese had brought all the joy-lovers of darkest color together to shake that thing. Never was there such a big black-throated guzzling of red wine, white wine, and close, indiscriminate jazzing of all the Negroes of Marseilles.

For the Negro-Negroid population of the town divides sharply into groups. The Martiniquans and Guadeloupans, regarding themselves as constituting the dark flower of all Marianne's blacks, make a little aristocracy of themselves. The Madagascans with their cousins from the little dots of islands around their big island and the North African Negroes, whom the pure Arabs despise, fall somewhere between the Martiniquans and the Senegalese, who are the savages. Senegalese is the geographically inaccurate term generally used to designate all the Negroes from the different parts of French West Africa.

The magic thing had brought all shades and grades of Negroes together. Money. A Senegalese had emigrated to the United States, and after some years had returned with a few thousand dollars. And he had bought a café on the quay. It was a big café, the first that any Negro in the town ever owned.

The tiny group of handsomely-clothed Senegalese were politely proud of the bar, and all the blue overall boys of the docks and the ships were boisterously glad of a spacious place to spread joy in.

All shades of Negroes came together there. Even the mulattoes took a step down from their perch to mix in. For, as in the British West Indies and South Africa, the mulattoes of the French colonies do not usually intermingle with the blacks.

But the magic had brought them all together to shake that thing and drink red wine, white wine, sweet wine. All the British West African blacks, Portuguese blacks, American blacks, all who had drifted into this port that the world goes through.

A great event! And to Banjo it had brought a unique feeling of satisfaction. He did not miss it, as he never missed anything rich that came within his line of living. There was music at the bar and Banjo made much of it. He got a little acquainted with the *patron,* who often chatted with him. The *patron* was proud of his English and liked to display it when there was any distinguished-appearing person at the café.

"Shake That Thing!" That was the version of the "Jelly-Roll Blues" that Banjo loved and always played. And the Senegalese boys loved to shake to it. Banjo was treated to plenty of red wine and white wine when he played that tune. And he would not think of collecting sous. Latnah had gone about once and collected sous in her tiny jade tray. But she never went again. She loved Banjo, but she could not enter into the spirit of that all-Negro-atmosphere of the bar. Banjo was glad she stayed away. He did not want to collect sous from a crowd of fellows just like himself. He preferred to play for them and be treated to wine. Sous! How could he respect sous? He who had burnt up dollars. Why should he care, with a free bed, free love, and wine?

His plan of an orchestra filled his imagination now. Maybe he could use the Café African as a base to get some fellows together. Malty could play the guitar right splendid, but he had no instrument. If that Senegalese *patron* had a little imagination, he might buy Malty a guitar and they would start a little orchestra that would make the bar unique and popular.

Many big things started in just such a little way. Only give him a chance and he would make this dump sit up and take notice—show it how to be sporty and game. How he would love to see a couple of brown chippies from Gawd's own show this Ditch some decent movement—turn themselves jazzing loose in a back-home, brownskin Harlem way. Oh, Banjo's skin was itching to make some romantic thing.

And one afternoon he walked straight into a dream—a cargo boat with a crew of four music-making colored boys, with banjo, ukelele, mandolin, guitar, and horn. That evening Banjo and Malty, mad with enthusiam, literally carried the little band to the Vieux Port. It was the biggest evening ever at the Senegalese bar. They played several lively popular tunes, but the Senegalese boys yelled for "Shake That Thing." Banjo picked it off and the boys from the boat quickly got it. Then Banjo keyed himself up and began playing in his own wonderful wild way.

"Old Uncle Jack, the jelly-roll king,
Just got back from shaking that thing!
He can shake that thing, he can shake that thing
For he's a jelly-roll king. Oh, shake that thing!"

It roused an Arab-black girl from Algeria into a shaking-mad mood. And she jazzed right out into the center of the floor and shook herself in a low-down African shimmying way. The mandolin player, a stocky, cocky lad of brown-paper complexion, the lightest-skinned of the playing boys, had his eyes glued on her. Her hair was cropped and stood up shiny, crinkly like a curiously-wrought bird's nest. She was big-boned and well-fleshed and her full lips were a savage challenge. Oh, shake that thing!

"Cointreau!" The Negroid girl called when, the music ceasing, the paper-brown boy asked her to take a drink.

"That yaller nigger's sure gone on her," Malty said to Banjo.

"And she knows he's got a roll can reach right up to her figure," said Banjo. "Looka them eyes she shines on him! Oh, boy! it was the same for you and I when we first landed—every kind of eyes in the chippies' world shining for us!"

"Yes, but you ain't got nothing to kick about. The goodest eyes in this burg ain't shining for anybody else but you."

"Hheh-hheh," Banjo giggled. "I'll be dawggone, Malty, ef I don't think sometimes youse getting soft. Takem as they come, easy and jolly, ole boh."

He poured out a glass of red wine, chinked his glass against Malty's, and toasted, "Oh, you Dixieland, here's praying for you' soul salvation."

"And here is joining you," said Malty.

> "Dry land will nevah be my land,
> Gimme a wet wide-open land for mine."

Handsome, happy brutes. The music is on again. The Senegalese boys crowd the floor, dancing with one another. They dance better male with male or individually, than with the girls, putting more power in their feet, dancing more wildly, more natively, more savagely. Senegalese in blue overalls, Madagascan soldiers in khaki, dancing together. A Martiniquan with his mulattress flashing her gold teeth. A Senegalese sergeant goes round with his fair blonde. A Congo boxer struts it with his Marguerite. And Banjo, grinning, singing, white teeth, great mouth, leads the band. . . . Shake that thing.

The banjo dominates the other instruments; the charming, pretty sound of the ukelele, the filigree notes of the mandolin, the sensuous color of the guitar. And Banjo's face shows that he feels that his instrument is first. The Negroes and Spanish Negroids of the evenly-warm, evergreen and ever-flowering Antilles may love the rich chords of the guitar, but the banjo is preëminently the musical instrument of the American Negro. The sharp, noisy notes of the banjo belong to the American Negro's loud music of life—an affirmation of his hardy existence in the midst of the biggest, the most tumultuous civilization of modern life.

Sing, Banjo! Play, Banjo! Here I is, Big Boss, keeping step, sure step, right long with you in some sort a ways. He-ho, Banjo! Play that thing! Shake that thing!

> "Old Brother Mose is sick in bed.
> Doctor says he is almost dead
>   From shaking that thing, shaking that thing.
>   He was a jelly-roll king. Oh, shake that thing!"

A little flock of pinks from the Ditch floated into the bar. Seamen from Senegal. Soldiers from Madagascar. Pimps from Martinique. Pimps from everywhere. Pimps from Africa. Seamen fed up with the sea. Young men weary of the work of the docks, scornful of the meager reward—doing that now. Black youth close to the bush and the roots of jungle trees, trying to live the precarious life of the poisonous orchids of civilization.

Shake That Thing! . . .

The slim, slate-colored Martiniquan dances with a gold-brown Arab girl in a purely sensual way. His dog's mouth shows a tiny, protruding bit of pink tongue. Oh, he jazzes like a lizard with his girl. A dark-brown lizard and a gold-brown lizard. . . .

"Oh, shake that thing,
He's a jelly-roll king."

A coffee-black boy from Cameroon and a chocolate-brown from Dakar stand up to each other to dance a native sex-symbol dance. Bending knee and nodding head, they dance up to each other. As they almost touch, the smaller boy spins suddenly round and dances away. Oh, exquisite movement! Like a ram goat and a ram kid. Hands and feet! Shake that thing!

Black skin itching, black flesh warm with the wine of life, the music of life, the love and deep meaning of life. Strong smell of healthy black bodies in a close atmosphere, generating sweat and waves of heat. Oh, shake that thing!

Suddenly in the thick joy of it there was a roar and a rush and sheering apart as a Senegalese leaped like a leopard bounding through the jazzers, and, gripping an antagonist, butted him clean on the forehead once, twice, and again, and turned him loose to fall heavily on the floor like a felled tree.

The *patron* dashed from behind the bar. A babel of different dialects broke forth. Policemen appeared and the musicians slipped outside, followed by most of the Martiniquans.

"Hheh-hheh," Banjo laughed. "The music so good it put them French fellahs in a fighting mood."

"Niggers is niggers all ovah the wul'," said the tall, long-faced chocolate who played the guitar. "Always spoil a good thing. Always the same no matter what color their hide is or what langwidge they talk."

"And I was fixing for that fair brown. I wonder where at she is?" said the mandolin-player.

"Don't worry," said Banjo. "Theah's always some'n' better or as good as what you miss. You should do like me whenevah you hit a new port. Always try to make something as different from what you know as a Leghorn is from a Plymouth Rock."

"Hi-ee! But youse one chicken-knowing fool," said Malty.

Banjo did a little strut-jig. "You got mah number all right, boh. And what wese gwine to do now? The night ain't begin yet at all foh mine. I want to do some moh playing and do some moh wine and what not do?"

A Martinique guide, who had had them under surveillance for a long while, now stepped up and said that he knew of a love shop where they could play music and have some real fun.

"You sure?" asked Banjo. "Don't fool us now, for I lives right down here in this dump and know most a them. And if that joint you know ain't a place that we can lay around in for a while, nothing doing I tell you straight. I'll just take all mah buddies right outa there."

The guide assured the boys that his place was all right. They all went into another bar on the quay and the guitar-player paid for a round of drinks. From there they turned up the Rue de la Mairie and west along the Rue de la Loge to find the Martiniquan's rendezvous.

They went by the Rue de la Reynarde, where a loud jarring cluster of colored lights was shouting its trade. Standing in the slimy litter of a narrow turning, an emaciated, middle-aged, watery-eyed woman was doing a sort of dance and singing in a thin streaky voice. She was advertising the house in whose shadow she danced, and was much like a poorly-feathered hen pecking and clucking on a dunghill.

The boys hesitated a little before the appearance of the drab-fronted building that their escort indicated. Then they entered and were surprised at finding themselves in a showy love shop of methodically assorted things. It was very international. European, African, Asiatic. Contemporary feminine styles competed with old and forgotten. Rose-petal pajamas, knee-length frocks, silken shifts, the nude, the boyish bob contrasted with shimmering princess gowns, country-girl dresses of striking freshness, severe glove-fitting black setting off a demure lady with Italian-rich, thick, long hair, the piquant semi-nude and Spanish-shawled shoulders.

Banjo saw his first flame of the Ditch between two sailors with batik-like kerchiefs curiously knotted on their heads. They were Malay, perhaps. This time he was not aroused. The Martiniquan talked to a strangely attractive girl. She had almond eyes that were painted in a unique manner to emphasize their exotic effect. Evidently she was not pure Mongolian, but perhaps some casual crossing of Occident and Orient, commerce-spanned, dropped on the shore of the wonderful sea of the world.

There were half a dozen touts. One seemed a person of authority in the place. He was this side of forty, above average height, of meager form, Spanish type, with a face rather disgusting, because, although dark, it was sallow and deep-sunken under the cheek bones. He wore a blue suit, white scarf, heavy gold chain, and patent-leather shoes. The other five were youths. Three sported bright suits and fancy shoes of two and three colors, and two were in ordinary proletarian blue.

The proletarian suits among all the striking feminine finery gave a certain elusive tone of distinction to the atmosphere, and one dressed thus was particularly conspicuous, reclining on a red-cushioned seat, under the lavish and intimate caresses of a Negress from the Antilles. Her face was like that of a Pekinese. She wore a bit of orange chiffon and had a green fan, which she opened at intervals against her mouth as she grinned deliciously.

Sitting like a queen in prim fatness, quite high up against a desk near the staircase that led to the regions above, a lady ruled over the scene with smiling business efficiency. When the Martiniquan spoke to her, introducing his evening's catch by a wave of the hand toward where the boys had seated themselves, and explaining that they wanted to play their own music, she smiled a gay acquiescence.

> "Oh, shake, shake, shake that thing!"
> He's a jelly-roll king. . . ."

When Banjo and his fellows entered, many eyes had followed them. And now as they played and hummed and swayed, all eyes were fixed on them, and soon the whole shop was right out on the floor, shaking that thing. Oh, shake that thing!

The little black girl was all in a wild heat of movement as she went rearing up and down with her young Provençal. But he seemed unequal to catch and keep up with her motion, so she exchanged him for the Martiniquan, who went prancing into it. And round and round they went, bounding in and out among the jazzers, rearing and riding together with the speed and freedom of two wild goats. Oh, shake that wonderful thing!

The players paused and some girls tried to order

champagne on them, but the Martiniquan intervened and demanded wine and spirits.

"He knows his business," the mandolin-player said to Banjo.

"He's gotta," Banjo replied, "because he's got himself to look out for and me to reckin with."

Suddenly the air was full of a terrible tenseness and gravity as an altercation between the lady at the desk and the meager, sallow-faced man seemed at the point of developing into a fateful affair. The man was leaning against the desk, looking into the woman's face with cold, ghastly earnestness, his hand resting a little in his hip pocket. The woman's face fell flat like paste and all the girls stood tiptoe in silence and trembling excitement. Abruptly, without a word, the man turned and left the room with murder in his stride.

"That must be the boss-man," the mandolin-player said.

"And he looks like a mean mastiff," said the guitar-player.

"Sure seems lak he's just that thing," agreed Banjo.

Tem, tem, ti-tum, tim ti-tim, tum, tem. Banjo and the boys were chording up. Back . . . thing . . . bed . . . black . . . dead. . . . Oh, shake that thing. . . . Jelly-r-o-o-o-o-oll! Again all the shop was out on the floor. No graceful sliding and gliding, but strutting, jigging, shimmying, shuffling, humping, standing-swaying, dogging, doing, shaking that thing. The girls were now tiptoeing to another kind of excitement. Blood had crept back up into the face of the woman at the desk. . . .

The sallow-faced man appeared in the entrance and strode through the midst of it to the desk. Bomb! The fearful report snuffed out the revel and the dame tumbled fatly to the floor. The murderer gloated over the sad mess of flesh for an instant, then with a wild leap he lanced himself like a rat through the paralyzed revelers and disappeared.

The bewildered music-makers halted hesitantly at the foot of the alley.

"Let's all go in here and take a stiff drink." Banjo indicated a little bistro at the corner.

"Better let's leg it a li'l' ways longer," said the ukelele-player, "so the police won't come fooling around us now that wese good and well away outa there. I don't wanta have no truck with the police."

"And they ain't gwineta mess around us, pardner," said Malty. "We don't speak that there lingo a theirn and they ain't studying us. Ise been in on a dozen shooting-ups in this here Ditch, ef Ise been in on one, with the bullets them jest burning pass mah black buttum, and Ise nevah been asked by the police, 'What did you miss?' nor 'What did you see?'"

"Did you say a dozen?" cried the ukelele-player.

"Just that I did, boh, which was what I was pussonally attached to. But that ain't nothing at all, for theah's a shooting-up or a cutting-up—and sometimes moh—every day in this here burg."

"Malty," said Banjo, "youse sure one eggsigirating spade."

"Doughnuts on that there eggsigirating. It's the same crap to me whether there was a dozen or a thousand. They ain't nevah made a hole in me, for Ise got magic in mah skin foh protection, when you done got you souvenir there on you' wrist, Banjo boy."

"Gawd! But it was a bloody affair, all right," said the guitar-player. "I was so frightened I didn't really know what was happening. Bam! Biff! And the big boss-lady was undertaker's business before you could squint."

"Jest spoiled the whole sport," said the ukelele-player. "I kinda liked the nifty dump. It was the goods, all right."

"You said it, boh," the mandolin-player grinned, scratching his person. "It was some moh collection. All the same, I gotta plug."

"With you, buddy," cried Banjo. "Right there with you I sure indeed is."

"Let's go back to the African Bar," suggested the mandolin-player. The picture of the North African girl shaking that jelly-roll thing was still warmly working in his blood.

They found the African Bar closed. Again they left the quay, and Banjo took them up one of the somber, rubbish-strewn alleys of the Ditch. On both sides of the alley were the dingy cubicles whose only lights were the occupants who filled the fronts, gesturing and calling in ludicrous tones: "Viens ici, viens ici," and repeating pridefully the raw expressions of the low love shops that they had learned from English-speaking seamen.

Out of a drinking hole-in-the-wall came the creaky jangling notes of a small, upright and ancient pianola. The place was chock-full of a mixed crowd of girls, seamen, and dockers, with two man-of-war sailors and three soldiers among them.

"What about this here dump?" asked Banjo.

The mandolin-player looked lustfully up and down the alley and into the bistro, where wreaths of smoke settled heavily upon the frowsy air. "Suits me all right," he drawled. "What about you fellows?"

"Well, I hope it won't turn into another bloody mess of a riot this time," said the ukelele-player.

"Here youse just like you would be at home. This is *my* street," said Banjo. A girl came up and, patting him on the shoulder with a familiar phrase, she pushed him into the bistro.

As they entered a Senegalese who had been dancing to their voluptuous playing at the African Bar, exclaimed: "Here they are! Now we're going to hear some real music—something ravishing." And he begged Banjo to play the "Jelly-Roll."

One of the soldiers was evidently "slumming." There was a neat elegance about his uniform and shoes that set him apart from the ambiguous dandies of military service, the *habituées* of shady places. His features and his manner betrayed class distinction. He offered Banjo and his companions a round of drinks, saying in slow English: "Please play. You American? I like much *les Negres* play the jazz American. I hear them in Paris. *Epatant!*"

Banjo grinned and tossed off his Cap Corse. "All right, fellows. Let's play them that thing first."

"And then the once-over," said the mandolin-player.

Shake That Thing! That jelly-roll Thing!

Shake to the loud music of life playing to the primeval round of life. Rough rhythm of darkly-carnal life. Strong surging flux of profound currents forced into shallow channels. Play that thing! One movement of the thousand movements of the eternal life-flow. Shake that thing! In the face of the shadow of Death. Treacherous hand of murderous Death, lurking in sinister alleys, where the shadows of life dance, nevertheless, to their music of life. Death over there! Life over here! Shake down Death and forget his commerce, his purpose, his haunting presence in a great shaking orgy. Dance down the Death of these days, the Death of these ways in shaking that thing. Jungle jazzing, Orient wriggling, civilized stepping. Shake that thing! Sweet dancing thing of primitive joy, perverse pleasure, prostitute ways, many-colored variations of the rhythm, savage, barbaric, refined—eternal rhythm of the mysterious, magical, magnificent—the dance divine of life. . . . Oh, Shake That Thing!

SECOND PART

VI. Meeting-up

BANJO'S place at Latnah's was empty for many days, for he was deep down in the Ditch again. He was even scarce with Malty and the other boys, and they did not know where he was lying low. Malty, Bugsy, and Ginger had the run of a ship, where they ate, did a little galley work, and could even sleep when they wanted to, and Banjo was supposed to eat there, too. But only once had he honored the beach boys' new mess with his presence. He did, however, send down some dozen white and colored fellows to bum off Malty. For on that ship there was always enough left-over food to feed a regiment of men.

Banjo did not go to the boat to feed because he was having a jolly fat time of it. While his pals had felt quite satisfied with the big treat of eats and drinks and a few francs in coins from the musical seamen, Banjo's infectious spirit had touched his fellow artistes for over two hundred francs, which they considered nothing at all for the time and freedom of the Ditch that he had so generously given to them.

Latnah was not fretful about his absence. He would come again when he wanted to, just as casually as when they had first met. She had no jealous feeling of possession about him. She was Oriental and her mind was not alien to the idea of man's insistence on freedom of desire for himself. Perhaps she liked Banjo more because he was vagabond.

Banjo arose from his close corner in the Ditch, yawned, stretched, and proceeded with the necessity of toilet. This was always an irksome affair to him when he was not dressing to strut. And he had nothing now worth showing off except an American silk shirt with blue and mauve stripes, and, jauntily over his ear, a fine bluish felt that the mandolin-player had forced on him.

He was bidding good-by to the heart of the Ditch for the present, because he had only ten negotiable francs for the moment. He was going to feed himself and he felt that he could feed heavily, for the final exhaustion of his long spell of voluptuous excitement had left him with a feeling of intense natural thirst and hunger. In America, after such a prolonged, exquisite excess, he always experienced a particular craving for swine—pig's tail, pig's snout, pig's ears, pig's feet, and chittlings.

Banjo smacked his lips recalling and anticipating the delicious taste of pig stuff. He had a special fancy for *gras double* and *pieds paquet Marseillaise.* Banjo nosed through the dirty alleys of wine shops and cook shops, hunting for a chittlings joint. He did not want to go through the embarrassing business of entering and sitting down in an eating-place and then having to leave because what he wanted was not there. At last he stood before a long, low, oblong box, the only window of which was packed with a multitude of pink pigs' feet, while over them stretched an enormous maw of the color of sea-weed. In the center of the low ceiling an electric bulb shed a soiled light. On a slate was chalked: *Repas, prix fixe: fs. 4 vin compris.*

The place was full. Banjo found an end seat not far from the window. A big slovenly woman brought him knife, fork, spoon, a half-pint of red wine, a length of bread, and a plate of soup. Following the soup he had a large plate of chittlings with a good mess of potatoes.

Lastly a tiny triangular cut of Holland cheese. It was a remarkably good meal indeed for the price charged, and quite sufficient for an ordinary stomach. But Banjo's stomach was not in an ordinary state. So he set his bit of cheese aside and asked for a second helping of chittlings and another pint bottle of red wine.

By the time he had finished his supplementary portion the place was three-quarters empty and he was the only person left at his table. Banjo patted his belly and a contented, drowsy noise way down from it escaped from his mouth. He took the folded ten-franc note from his breast pocket, opened it out, and laid it on the table. The woman, instead of picking it up, presented a dirty scrap of bill for fs. 12.50.

"Dawg bite me!" Banjo threw up his hands. He had been expecting change out of which he could get his *café-au-rhum*. How could an extra plate play him such a dirty trick? He turned out his pockets and said: "No more money, nix money, no plus billet."

The woman thrust the bill under his nose, gesticulated like a true Provençale and cried with all the trumpets of her body: *"Payez! Payez! Il faut payer."* Banjo's tongue turned loose a rich assortment of Yankee swear words. . . . "God-damned frog robbers. I eat *prix fixe*. I pay moh'n enough. *Moi paye rien plus*. Hey! Ain't nobody in this tripe-stinking dump can help a man with this heah dawggone lingo?"

A black young man who had been sitting quietly in the back went over to Banjo and asked what he could help about.

"Can you get a meaning, boh, out a this musical racket?" Banjo asked.

"I guess I can."

"Well, you jest tell this jabberway lady for me to go right clear where she get off at and come back treating me square. I done eat *prix fixe* as I often does, and jest because I had a li'l moh place in mah stimach I could fill up and ask for an extry plate, she come asking for as much money as I could eat swell on in Paree itself."

The intermediary turned to argue with the woman. She said Banjo had not asked for the *table d'hôte* meal. But it was pointed out to her that she had not served him *à la carte*. However, there was a slate over the decrepit desk scrawled with *à la carte* prices, and according to it, and by the most liberal calculation, she seemed to have made the mistake of overcharging Banjo. The woman had been hiding her discomfiture behind a barrage of noise and gesticulation, but suddenly she said, *"Voilà,"* and threw down a two-franc piece on the table.

Banjo picked it up and said: "Dawgs mah tail! You done talk her into handing me back change? I be fiddled if you don't handle this lingo same as I does American."

As they departed the woman vehemently bade them good-by, *à la* Provençale, with a swishing stream of saliva sent sharply after them, crying, *"Je suis français, moi."*

Je suis français. . . . Ray (it was he who had intervened) smiled. No doubt the woman thought there could be no more stinging insult than making them sensible of being *étrangers*. Thought, too, perhaps, that that gave her a moral right to cheat them.

"Le's blow this heah two francs to good friendship beginning," said Banjo. "My twinkling stars, but this Marcelles is a most wonderful place foh meeting-up."

Ray laughed. Banjo's rich Dixie accent went to his head like old wine and reminded him happily of Jake. He had seen Banjo before with Malty and company on the breakwater, but had not yet made contact with any of them.

Since he had turned his back on Harlem he had done much voyaging sometimes making a prolonged stay in a port whose aspect had taken his imagination. He had not renounced his dream of self-expression. And sometimes when he was down and out of money, desperate in the dumps of deep problematic thinking, unable to find a shore job, he would be cheered up by a little cheque from America for a slight sketch or by a letter of encouragement with a banknote from a friend.

He was up against the fact that a Negro in Europe could not pick up casual work as he could in America. The long-well-tilled, overworked Old World lacked the background that rough young America offered to a romantic black youth to indulge his froward instincts. In America he had lived like a vagabond poet, erect in the racket and rush and terror of that stupendous young creation of cement and steel, determined, courageous, and proud in his swarthy skin, quitting jobs when he wanted to go on a dream wish or a love drunk, without being beholden to anybody.

Now he was always beholden. If he was not bold enough, when he was broke and famishing, to be a bum like Malty in the square, he was always writing panhandling letters to his friends, and naturally he began to feel himself lacking in the free splendid spirit of his American days. More and more the urge to write was holding him with an enslaving grip and he was beginning to feel that any means of achieving self-expression was justifiable. Not without compunction. For Tolstoy was his ideal of the artist as a man and remained for him the most wonderful example of one who balanced his creative work by a life lived out to its full illogical end.

It was strange to Ray himself that he should be so powerfully pulled toward Tolstoy when his nature, his outlook, his attitude to life, were entirely turned away from the ideals of the great Russian. Strange that he who was so heathen and carnal, should feel and be responsive to the intellectual superiority of a fanatic moralist.

But it was not by Tolstoy's doctrines that he was touched. It was depressing to him that the energy of so many great intellects of the modern world had been, like Tolstoy's, vitiated in futile endeavor to make the mysticism of Jesus serve the spiritual needs of a world-conquering and leveling machine civilization.

What lifted him up and carried him away, after Tolstoy's mighty art was his equally mighty life of restless searching within and without, and energetic living to find himself until the very end. Rimbaud moved him with the same sympathy, but Tolstoy's appeal was stronger, because he lived longer and was the greater creator.

Drifting by chance into the harbor of Marseilles, Ray had fallen for its strange enticement just as the beach boys had. He had struck the town in one of those violent periods of agitation when he had worked himself up to the pitch of feeling that if he could not give vent to his thoughts he would break up into a thousand articulate bits. And the Vieux Port had offered him a haven in its frowsy, thickly-peopled heart where he could exist *en pension* proletarian of a sort and try to create around him the necessary solitude to work with pencil and scraps of paper.

He too was touched by the magic of the Mediterranean, sprayed by its foamy fascination. Of all the seas he had crossed there was none like it. He was ever reminiscent of his own Caribbean, the first salty water he had dipped his swarthy boy's body in, but its dreamy, trade-wind, cooling charm could not be compared with this gorgeous bowl of blue water unrestingly agitated by the great commerce of all the continents. He loved the docks. If the aspect of the town itself was harsh and forbidding, the docks were of inexhaustible interest. There any day he might meet with picturesque proletarians from far waters whose names were warm with romance: the Caribbean, the Gulf of Guinea, the Persian Gulf, the Bay of Bengal, the China Seas, the Indian Archipelago. And, oh, the earthy mingled smells of the docks! Grain from Canada, rice from India, rubber from the Congo, tea from China, brown sugar from Cuba, bananas from Guinea, lumber from the Soudan, coffee from Brazil, skins from the Argentine, palm-oil from Nigeria, pimento from Jamaica, wool from Australia, oranges from Spain and oranges from Jerusalem. In piled-up boxes, bags, and barrels, some broken, dropping their stuff on the docks, reposing in the warm odor of their rich perfumes—the fine harvest of all the lands of the earth.

Barrels, bags, boxes, bearing from land to land the primitive garner of man's hands. Sweat-dripping bodies of black men naked under the equatorial sun, threading a caravan way through the time-old jungles, carrying loads steadied and unsupported on kink-thick heads hardened and trained to bear their burdens. Brown men half-clothed, with baskets on their backs, bending low down to the ancient tilled fields under the tropical sun. Eternal creatures of the warm soil, digging, plucking for the Occident world its exotic nourishment of life, under the whip, under the terror. Barrels . . . bags . . . boxes. . . . Full of the wonderful things of life.

Ray loved the life of the docks more than the life of the sea. He had never learned to love the deep sea. Out there on a boat he always felt like a reluctant prisoner among prisoners cast out upon a menacing dreariness of deep water. He had never known a seaman who really loved the deep sea. . . . He knew of fellows who could love an old freighter as a man might love a woman. Nearly all the colored seamen he knew affectionately called their ship the old "broad." The real lure of the sea was beyond in the port of call. And of all the great ports there was none so appealing to seamen as Marseilles in its cruel beauty.

The port was a fine big wide-open hole and the docks were wide open too. Ray loved the piquant variety of the things of the docks as much as he loved their colorful human interest. And the highest to him was the Negroes of the port. In no other port had he ever seen congregated such a picturesque variety of Negroes. Negroes speaking the civilized tongues, Negroes speaking all the African dialects, black Negroes, brown Negroes, yellow Negroes. It was as if every country of the world where Negroes lived had sent representatives drifting in to Marseilles. A great vagabond host of jungle-like Negroes trying to scrape a temporary existence from the macadamized surface of this great Provençal port.

Here for Ray was the veritable romance of Europe. This Europe that he had felt through the splendid glamour of history. When at last he did touch it, its effect on him had been a negative reaction. He had to go to books and museums and sacredly-preserved sites to find the romance of it. Often in conversation he had politely pretended to a romance that he felt not. For it was America that was for him the living, hot-breathing land of romance. Its mighty business palaces, vast *depots* receiving and discharging hurrying hordes of humanity, immense cathedrals of pleasure, far-flung spans of steel roads and tumultuous traffic—the terrible buffalo-tramping crush of life, the raucous vaudeville mob-shouting of a newly-arrived nation of white throats, the clamor and clash of races and the grim-grubbing position of his race among them—all was a great fever in his brain, a rhythm of a pattern with the time-beat of his life, a burning, throbbing romance in his blood.

There was a barbarous international romance in the ways of Marseilles that was vividly significant of the great modern movement of life. Small, with a population apparently too great for it, Europe's best back door, discharging and receiving its traffic to the Orient and Africa, favorite port of seamen on French leave, infested with the ratty beings of the Mediterranean countries, overrun with guides, cocottes, procurers, repelling and attracting in its white-fanged vileness under its picturesqueness, the town seemed to proclaim to the world that the grandest thing about modern life was that it was bawdy.

Banjo wanted to see what Ray's work was like and Ray took him up to his place, which was a little up beyond the Bum Square. Banjo had been interested in Ray's talking about his work, but when he saw the sheets of ordinary composition paper, a little soiled, and the shabby collection of books, he quickly lost interest and changed the conversation to the hazards of the vagabond panhandling life.

Ray suggested taking a turn along the Corniche. Banjo had never been on the Corniche. Ray said it was one of the three interesting things of the town from a pictorial point of view—the Ditch, the Breakwater and the Corniche. He liked the Corniche in a special way, when he was in one of those oft-recurring solitary, idly-brooding moods. Then he would watch the ships coming in from the east, coming in from the west, and speculate about making a move to some other place.

They went by the Quai de Rive Neuve toward Catalan.

At a unique point beyond the baths of that name Ray waved back toward the breakwater.

"Hot damn! What a mahvelous sight!" exclaimed Banjo. "I been in Marcelles all this time and ain't never come this heah side."

Two ships were going down the Mediterranean out to the East, and another by the side of l'Estaque out to the Atlantic. A big Peninsular and Orient liner with three yellow-and-black funnels was coming in. The fishing-boats were little colored dots sailing into the long veil of the marge. A swarm of sea gulls gathered where one of the ships had passed, dipping suddenly down, shooting up and circling around joyously as if some prize had been thrown there to them. In the basin of Joliette the ships' funnels were vivid little splashes of many colors bunched together, and, close to them in perspective, an aggregate of gray factory chimneys spouted from their black mouths great columns of red-brown smoke into the indigo skies. Abruptly, as if it rose out of the heart of the town, a range of hills ran out in a gradual slope like a strong argent arm protecting the harbor, and merged its point in the far-away churning mist of sea and sky.

"It's an eyeful all right," said Banjo.

Ray said nothing. He was so happily moved. A delicious symphony was playing on the tendrils that linked his inner being to the world without, and he was afraid to break the spell. They walked the whole length of the Corniche down to the big park by the sea. They leaped over a wall and a murky stream, crossed the race track, and came to rest and doze in the shade of a magnolia.

It was nightfall when they got back to town, returning by the splendid avenue called the Prado. The Bum Square was full of animation. All the life of the dark alleys around it—clients of little hotels and restaurants, bistros, cabarets, love shops, fish shops, meat shops—poured into the square to take the early evening air. A few fishermen were gathered round a table on a café terrace, and fisher-girls promenaded arm in arm, their wooden shoes sounding heavily in the square. The Arab-black girl who had danced so amorously at the Senegalese café was parading with a white girl companion. Five touts, one of whom was a mulatto, stood conversing with a sniffing, expectant air near the urinal. The dogs at their old tricks gamboled about in groups among the playing children. A band of Senegalese, nearly all wearing proletarian blue, were hanging round the entrance of a little café in striking, insouciant ease, talking noisily and laughing in their rich-sounding language. A stumpy fat cocotte and a tall one entered the Monkey Bar, and the loud voice of the pianola kicking out a popular trot rushed across the square.

Suddenly the square emptied before an onrushing company of white laborers, led by a stout, bull-bodied man, heading for the little group of Senegalese. The group of Senegalese broke up and scattered, leaving two of their number knocked down, and one of the white attackers who had caught a clout in the head. At that moment, Bugsy and Dengel, coming from the docks, appeared at the southwest corner of the square, just as one of the blacks was felled.

"He—ey! You see that theah! You see that!" Bugsy cried, and to his amazement the big white man, followed by his gang, came charging toward him. Militant by nature and always ready to defend himself, Bugsy exclaimed: "Hey—hey! Now what they coming to mess with me for?" And he stood his ground, on guard. But when he saw the whole gang coming unswervingly down upon him, he wavered, backed a few steps, then turned and ran nimbly like a rat up one of the dark alleys.

Dengel was soft with the wine of the docks and, comprehending nothing of what was in the air, stood swaying in his tracks where he was struck a vicious blow in the face that felled him.

As suddenly as it had commenced, the onslaught was ended. Bugsy and Dengel went to the African café where some of the Senegalese had gathered. Banjo and Ray also went there. They had seen the eruption from a café in the square.

Dengel's nose was bleeding badly.

"It's sure counta you always getting in a fight that Dengel he got hit," said Banjo to Bugsy.

"Me! It wasn't no fault a mine. What was I to do, pardner?"

"Jest keep you' mouth shut and do what you done did at the critical moment—run! What else was there to do when the whole damn ditch a white mens is after one nigger?"

"If them Senegalese had done stand up to it——" Bugsy began.

"They tried to, but what could five men do against an army?"

"But Gawd in heab'n!" exclaimed Bugsy. "I almost got like feeling I was in Dixie with the fire under mah tail."

"H'm. If it was in Dixie, you wouldn't be sitting there now, blowing a whole lot a nonsense off'n you' liver lips."

Ray was talking to the proprietor of the bar and a Senegalese, who was explaining that the trouble arose out of differences between the Italian dock workers and the Senegalese. There was much jealousy between the rival groups and the Senegalese aggressively reminded the Italians that they were French and possessed the rights of citizens.

"There is no difference between Italians and Frenchmen," said the barkeeper. "They are all the same white and prejudiced against black skin."

"C'est pas vrai, pas vrai," a tall Senegalese seaman jumped to his feet. *"Ça n'existe pas en France."*

"It exists, it exists all right," insisted the *patron.* He was small and eager and wore glasses and a melancholy aspect. "France is no better than America. In fact, America is better every time for a colored man."

Upon that a clamorous dispute broke out in Senegalese and French, interspersed with scraps of English. Ray sat back, swallowing all of it that he could understand. The proprietor was a fervid apostle of Americanism and he warmed up to defend his position. He praised American industry, business, houses, theaters, popular music, and progress and opportunity for everybody—even Negroes. He said the Negroes knew how they stood among the Americans, but the French were hypocrites. They had a whole lot of say, which had nothing to do with reality.

At this the Senegalese seaman bellowed another protest, punctuated with swearing *merde* on the Anglo-Saxons and all those who liked their civilization, and the proprietor invited him to leave his café if he could not be polite to *him.* The seaman told the proprietor that even though he had been to the United States and made money enough to return to Marseilles and buy a bar, he should not forget that he was only a common blackamoor of the Dakar streets, while he (the seaman) was a *fils des nobles,* belonging to an old aristocratic Senegambian family. The proprietor retorted that there was nothing left to the African nobility but "bull." Ask Europe about that, especially France, which was the biggest white hog in Africa.

The Senegalese started again, as if he had been pinched behind, to the defense of the protectress of his country. But the proprietor brought down *La Race Negre* on him. This was a journal for the "Defense de la race Negre" published by a group of French West Africans in Paris. The journal was displayed conspicuously for sale in the café, although some colored visitors had told the proprietor they did not think it was good for his business to sell it there.

But the proprietor had a willful way. He was rather piqued that the café was not doing so well since the first opening days. Before he bought it the clients were all white, and now no whites went there except the broken-down girls of the Ditch. He remarked white people peeping in at the door and not entering when they saw the black boys. The handful of well-dressed Senegalese who went there said they were sure the whites did not enter not because of prejudice, but because the black boys lounging all over the café were dirty, ragged, and smelly. The proprietor stressed his feeling that it was all a matter of prejudice. White people, no matter of what nation, did not want to see colored people prosper.

Also, the proprietor was intransigant about *La Race Negre* because he had been rebuked for selling it by a flabby bulk of a man who had once been an official out in one of the colonies, and who now had something to do with the welfare of the *indigenes* in Marseilles. The white gentleman had told the proprietor that the Negroes who published *La Race Negre* were working against France and such a journal should be suppressed and its editors trapped and thrown into jail as criminals. The proprietor of the bar replied that he was not in West Africa, where he had heard the local authorities had forbidden the circulation of the *Negro World,* but in Marseilles, where he hoped to remain master in his own café. As the proprietor said that the gentleman from the colonies left the café brusquely and unceremoniously without saying good-by. The patron exploded: "He thought he was in Africa. He wanted to know everything about me. Wanted to see my papers. Like a policeman. If it wasn't on account of my business I would have shown him my black block. Even wanted to know how I made my money in America. I told him I would never have made it in France.

"That was like a cracker now," he continued. "I never had a white man nosing into my business like that in America. But these French people are just like detectives. They want to know everything about you, especially if you're a black. I'm going to let them see I'm not a fool."

Some time later the barkeeper learned from an *indigene* employed by his gentleman visitor that that personage had been very offended by the barkeeper's use of the word "master," that he had not remained uncovered when talking to him, and that the Senegalese lounging in the café had not saluted when he entered.

The barkeeper spread out the copy of *La Race Negre* and began reading, while the Senegalese crowded around him with murmurs of approval and that attitude of credulity held by ignorant people toward the printed word.

He read a list of items:

Of forced conscription and young Negroes running away from their homes to escape into British African territory.

Of native officials paid less than whites for the same work.

Of forced native labor, because the natives preferred to live lazily their own lives, rather than labor for the miserable pittance of daily wages.
Of native women insulted and their husbands humiliated before them.
Of flagellation.
Of youths castrated for theft.
Of native chiefs punished by mutilation.
Of the scourge of depopulation. . . .

"That's how the Europeans treat Negroes in the colonies," said the barkeeper. The protesting seaman appeared crushed under the printed accounts. The barkeeper launched a discourse about Africa for the Africans and the rights of Negroes, from which he suddenly shot off into a panegyric of American culture. He had returned from America inspired by two strangely juxtaposed ideals: the Marcus Garvey Back-to-Africa movement and the grandeur of American progress. He finished up in English, turning toward the English-speaking boys:

"Negroes in America have a chance to do things. That's what Marcus Garvey was trying to drive into their heads, but they wouldn't support him——"

"Ain't no such thing!" exclaimed Banjo. "Marcus Garvey was one nigger who had a chance to make his and hulp other folks make, and he took it and landed himself in prison. That theah Garvey had a white man's chance and he done nigger it away. The white man gived him plenty a rope to live, and all he done do with it was to make a noose to hang himse'f. When a ofay give another ofay the run of a place he sure means him to make good like a Governor or a President, and when a darky gets a chance—— I tell you, boss, Garvey wasn't worth no more than the good boot in his bahind that he done got."

"Garvey was good for all Negroes," the barkeeper turned upon Banjo,—"Negroes in America and in Europe and in Africa. You don't know what you're talking about. Why, the French and the British were keeping the *Negro World,* Garvey's newspaper, out of Africa. It was because Garvey was getting too big that they got him."

"There was nothing big left to him, if you ask me," said Banjo. "I guess he thought like you, that he was Moses or Napoleon or Frederick Douglass, but he was nothing but a fool, big-mouf nigger."

"It's fellahs like you that make it so hard for the race," replied the barkeeper. "You have no respect for those who're trying to do something to lift the race higher. American Negroes have the biggest chance that black people ever had in the world, but most of them don't grab hold of it, but are just trifling and no-'count like you."

Banjo made a kissing noise with his lips and looked cross-eyed at the barkeeper. "Come on, pard, let's beat it," he said to Ray. Outside he remarked: "He grabbed his, all right, and growed thin like a mosquito doing it. Look how his cheeks am sunkin'! I guess he's even too cheap to pay the price of a li'l' pot a honey. Why didn't you say some'n', Ray? I guess you got more brains in you' finger nail than in twenty nigger haids like his'n jest rising up outa the bush of Africa."

"I always prefer to listen," replied Ray. "You know when he was reading that paper it was just as if I was hearing about Texas and Georgia in French."

"But, oh, you kink-no-more!" laughed Bugsy. "Did you notice his hair? It's all nice and straightened out."

"You don't have to look two time to decipher an African nigger in him, all the same," said Banjo, contemptuously. "A really and truly down-there Bungo-Congo."

"Get out!" said Ray. "You're a mean hater, Banjo. He's just like other Negroes from the States and the West Indies."

"Not from the States, pard. Maybe the monkeys them ——"

"Monkey you' grandmother's blue yaller outa the red a you' charcoal-black split coon of a baboon moon!" cried Bugsy, shaking off his rag of a coat. "I'll fight any nigger foh monkeying me."

" 'Scuse me, buddy, I thought you said you was American. I didn't know you come from them Wesht Indies country. Put you' coat on. You and me and Ginger and Malty am just like we come from the same home town. We ain't nevah agwine to fight against one another."

"But you' friend there, he's West Indian, too." The little wiry belligerent Bugsy was cooling down as quickly as he had warmed up.

Banjo waved his hand deprecatingly: "He ain't in that class. *You* know that."

In the Bum Square they met Latnah and Malty. From the Indian steward of a ship from Bombay, Latnah had gotten a little bag of curry powder and a great choice chunk of mutton, and she was preparing to make a feast.

"Hi, but everything is setting jest as pretty as pretty could be!" cried Banjo. "I been thinking about you, Latnah."

"Me too think," said Latnah. "Long time you no come."

"The fellahs them, you know how it is when we get tight. All night boozing and swapping stories."

"Stray cock done chased off a neighbor's lot going strutting back home to his roost," added Malty.

Banjo kicked him on the heel.

Ray was going off to a little alley restaurant, but Banjo would not hear of that. Latnah supported him.

"Sure, you-all come my place," she said.

She cooked the food on the step just outside the door. The wood coal that she took from a bright-covered box and lit with a wad of paper, crackled tinnily in the stove, which was the bottom part of some throw-away preserve can, such as tramps use to warm themselves in winter.

The cooking touched pungently the boys' nostrils and made Ray remember the Indian restaurant in New York where sometimes he used to go for curry food.

"Oh, the wine!" cried Latnah. "Who got money?"

Banjo shrugged, Malty grinned, and Ray said, "I got a couple a francs."

"No, no you, *camarade,*" she christened Ray.

"Who's to have money ef you no got?" Bugsy asked her. She fussed for a while about her waist and extracted a note, which she handed to Banjo. She made Ray shift his position where he was sitting on the box from which she had taken the coal, and got out two quart bottles.

"You get one extra bottle *vin blanc,*" she said.

"What for *vin blanc?*" demanded Banjo. "It's dearer."

"Mebbe you' friend ——"

"No, I always prefer red," said Ray.

"All right, get three bottles *vin rouge,*" said Latnah, counting over her guests with a quick birdlike nodding.

"No forget change," she called after Banjo, tramping heavily down the stairs.

"Not much change coming outa ten francs," he flung back.

"It's no ten; it's twenty," she said. "Don't let the whites rob you."

"Sweet nuts, ef it ain't!" exclaimed Banjo. "All right, mamma. I got you."

When Banjo returned with the wine he forgot to hand over the change. Latnah drew the cot into the middle of the little room and, spreading newspapers, she served the feast on it. The boys ranged themselves on each side of the cot, Latnah sitting where she could lean a little against Banjo. Ginger came in when they were in the middle of the feast.

"Whar you been? We been looking for you all over," said Malty.

"I was cruising around," said Ginger, "but Ise right here with you, all right. What it takes to find you when there's a high feeding going on Ise got right here." He pointed to his nose.

"Sure, youse got a combination of color there," said Banjo, "that oughta smell out lots a things in this heah white man's wul'."

"Chuts, combination!" said Bugsy. "You got to show me that there's any more to it than there is to naturalization, that you and me and Malty is. Ginger here ain't nothing from combination but a mistake."

"What's that, you Bugsyboo?" said Ginger.

"You heared me, Lights-out," replied Bugsy.

Latnah rolled up the newspapers in a bundle and put them in a corner. They smoked cigarettes. Banjo fell into a talking mood and gave a highly extravagant account of how he met Ray. The proprietress of the restaurant became a terrifying virago who would have him arrested by the police, if Ray had not intervened. And when *he* threatened to call in the police against her, she begged him not to and handed over the change in tears.

"I got something for you," Latnah said to Banjo. "Bet you no guess."

"American cigarettes—or English?" asked Banjo.

"No."

"Oh, I can't guess. What is it?"

Latnah took a paper packet out of a cardboard suit box and gave it to Banjo. It contained a pair of pyjamas all bright yellow and blue and black.

"Oh, Lawdy! Lemme see you in them, Banjo!" cried Malty, who jumped up and made a few fairy motions.

"What you want waste money on these heah things for?" demanded Banjo.

"A man had plenty of them selling cheap," said Latnah. "Ten francs. I think he steal them. They good for you."

"You evah hear a seaman fooling with pyjamas?" said Banjo.

"Sure," said Ginger. "I used to wear pyjamas mahself one time. It's good for a change. You' hide will feel better in them tonight."

Latnah tried to hide her coy little smile behind her hand.

"Plugging home, plugging home," chanted Malty to the air of the "West Indies Blues."

They were short of cigarettes and Banjo went off to get some. Banjo remained so long Bugsy and Ginger left to look for him. Ginger returned after a while, stuck his head through the door, and tossed a packet of yellow French cigarettes at Latnah. "Can't find that nigger Banjo anywheres," he said. "He done vanish like a spook."

"Like a rat into one a them holes, you mean," said Malty.

Latnah became fidgety and melancholy. She tossed a cigarette at Ray. "Banjo is one big dirty man," she said.

"Oh, he'll come all right," said Malty. "He's broke."

"He no broke," said Latnah. "He got change of the twenty francs."

"Oh!" exclaimed Malty. And he slightly shifted his position where he was squatting on an old cushion, so that his feet could touch Latnah's. "Gee! Latnah, you' cooking was so mahvelous it makes me feel sweet and drowsy all over."

"You good friend, Malty, very good friend." And she did not change her position. "You more appreciate than Banjo."

"Oh, he's all right, though; but you know his way. . . . I ain't got the price of a room to stay up this end tonight, and I feels too good and tired to walk way back to the box car. I wish you'd let me sleep on the floor here."

Latnah gave no reply. Ray slipped out, saying he would see them tomorrow.

VII. The Flute-boy

A POTATO-SKINNED youth posed nonchalantly in the Bum Square, a flute in his hand, his features distinguished by a big beatific grin.

Banjo, passing through with Ray, saw him and remarked, "He's a back-home, sure thing."

"You think so?" replied Ray.

"Sure. Jest look at the pose he's putting on. He's South Carolina so sure as corn pone is Dixie. Watch me pick him up. . . . Hello, Home town!"

"Hello, you there!" The three came together.

"Jes' arrive?" asked Banjo. "Youse sure looking hallelujah happy like a man jest made a fortune."

"Fortune is me in a bad way," said the flute-holder, "I've just gotten rid of all that I had." And he turned his trousers pockets out.

"You mean they just done rid you," laughed Banjo.

The flute-boy told his story. He had fine white teeth and red gums, and contentedly displaying them, he told his story of the "broad" and the Ditch, told it heartily as many other colored boys before him had done.

He began with how he had quit the "broad" after disputing with an officer. The "broad" was something like the one that brought Banjo to Marseilles. One of those rare slow-cruising American tramps that sometimes look in on Marseilles. The galley crew was Negro, with the flute-boy the only "blond" among them. Another of the crew was a West African *deportée* named Taloufa, who, slated to be paid off at a European port, had chosen Marseilles as the least troublesome.

The flute-boy and Taloufa were great chums. They were the most interesting persons of the ship. Taloufa came from a colony of British West Africa, had attended a mission school there, and was intelligent. The flute-boy came from the Cotton Belt country, but his people had moved to New Jersey when he was a kid. He went to school in New Jersey and had finished with a high-school diploma. It was his first trip away from the States. Before he had sailed only coastwise, between New York and New England and New York and the South.

In high school he had learned a little composition French. He was enchanted to reach Marseilles, having heard about its marvels from older seamen. He wished to have a good spell of the town, but his ship was staying just three days. He was serving in the officers' mess and he maneuvered himself into getting a reprimand from one of the officers.

"I told him off," the flute-boy said. "He called me a damned yaller nigger and I gave him a standing invitation to go chase himself."

For this offense the captain had the flute-boy up before the American consulate, but there he was not granted the permission to finish with the boy's services.

"American consul don't want no seamen hanging around this heah sweet wide-open dump," Banjo giggled, voluptuously.

"You bet he don't," agreed the flute-boy. "He told the captain to take me back to the ship and that I should watch my step. I told him I'd rather be paid off. But he said, 'Not on your life, mah boy. You go back home to your sweet 'taters and wat'melon. Gee! I wish I was back home now biting into one mahself.' He spoke that common darky language, kidding me, I guess."

The flute-boy returned with the captain to the ship and was put in the crew's mess. But before he had been given anything to do he was disputing with the donkeyman.

"I'm going to quit this dirty broad," he cried, and the captain was delighted to see the flute-boy go down the gangway with his suitcase. Taloufa was still aboard, waiting to be paid off the next day. The flute-boy had ten dollars, which he changed into francs. He took a room in a hotel in Joliette and went from there straight to the Ditch.

The flute-boy loitered, fascinated, around the marvelous fish market of the place. Red fish and blue, silver, gold, emerald, topaz, amethyst, brown-black, steel-gray, striped fish, scaly fish, big-bellied fish, and curs and cats growling and spitting over the bowels of gutted fish. A great fish town, Marseilles, and here was the big central market which supplies (for nourishment and lotteries and what not) the little markets and sheds and bistros that stink all over the city, the slimy, scaly, cold-blooded things.

Fresh catches from the bay and fish transported from other ports. The fishermen tramped in in their long felt boots. The fish-women spread themselves broadly behind their stalls. And in bright frocks and thick mauve socks and wooden shoes, the fish-girls pattered noisily about with charming insouciant ease, two between them bearing a basket, buxom and attractive and beautiful in their environment, like lush water-lilies in a lagoon.

The stuff of the groceries thick around the fish market was exposed on the sidewalk: piles of cheeses, blocks of butter, dried fish, salt herrings, sauerkraut, ham, sausages, salt pork, rice, meal, beans, garlic. Stray dogs nosing by stopped near the boxes. Cats prowled around. A sleek black one leaped upon a keg of green olives, sniffing and humping up his back. A laughing boy grabbing at its tail; the cat leaped down, shooting into a dark doorway. A pregnant woman passing popped one of the olives into her mouth, smacked her lips with fine relish, and called the grocery boy to give her one hecto.

The flute-boy wandered among the mixed conglomeration of people, domestic beasts, and things. He had an air about him that, even amid that humid bustle, invited attention enough.

A roving-eyed fish youth, wearing proletarian blue, spotted him. He had an odd little stock of English words, just enough to serve the purpose of soliciting, but the flute-boy responded in French, happily proud to try out his high-school acquirement.

"*Tu parle français tres bien,*" said the fish boy.

"*Vraiment?*"

"*Mais oui. Tu a un bon accent, camarade.*"

The flute-boy was overwhelmed with a peacock feeling. They were just a step from Boody Lane, which led inevitably into the fish market. A painted old girl, a fish in her hand, elbowed them purposely and went shaking herself mournfully into the alley.

"*Ici on nique-nique beaucoup,*" said the fishy white with a nasty smirk, bringing palm and fist together in a disgusting manner to emphasize his words. And he showed his find into Boody Lane.

It was a few yards of alleyway with a couple of drinking-dens, a butcher shop, and hole-in-the-wall rooms where the used-up carnivora of the city find their final shelter. Dismal, humid rooming-houses inhabitated by youthful scavengers of proletarian life—Provençales, Greeks, Arabs, Italians, Maltese, Spaniards, and Corsicans.

A slimy garbage-strewn little space of hopeless hags, hussies, touts, and cats and dogs forever chasing one another about in nasty imitation of the residents. The hub of low-down proletarian love, stinking, hard, cruel. A ditch abandoned by the city to pernicious manure, harmless-appearing on the surface. Yet ignorant seamen tumbling into it had been relieved of hundreds and thousands of francs, and many of the stupid, cold-blooded murders of the quarter might be traced there. The little trick of hat-snatching was practiced there and the uninitiate, fancying a bawdy joke, might follow that gesture to the loss of his money or his life.

The white boy conducted the yellow toward one of the drinking-places where a pianola was rapidly hammering out a popular song. Near by were two policemen. One stood on the corner and the other paced slowly along the alley, eating peanuts. A young male, wearing rosy pyjamas and painted like a scarecrow, came smirking out of the bar and minced along beside the policeman.

"Ou tu vas?" asked a sloven woman, standing broadly in the door of the bar.

"Coucher," the policeman flung back at her.

The woman cackled with the full volume of her raucous voice digging her hands into her flabby sides and agitating her clothes so that she displayed all of her naked discolored pillars of legs. *"Peut-être, peut-être. . . . On ne sait jamais."* And she cackled again.

When the flute-boy entered the bar he ordered beer for himself and beer for his guide. The woman who served wanted a small bottle of lemonade-like drink for herself, and all the old girls of the place, crowding around the flute-boy, took the same drink. The flute-boy thought the stuff was cheaper than beer and said, with a grin, "Go ahead."

But when he was ready to leave he received a bill for four hundred and seventy-five francs. He cried out that he would not pay. It was too much. The *patrone* showed him her price list. Forty francs a bottle for the lemonade-like drink. The flute-boy said he could not pay. They tried to take his purse. He hugged the pocket. They called the police. The two policemen that he had seen outside the place came in and told him he had to pay. They told him that if he was not satisfied he could lodge a complaint at the police station—afterward. The flute-boy showed his pocketbook. It contained three hundred and fifty francs only. The *patrone* took that and told him to return with the balance when he got more money. The policemen turned him loose, one of them exchanging a sly wink with the *patrone* as they walked away.

While the flute-boy was telling his story to Banjo and Ray, Bugsy and Dengel came surreptitiously up behind them in the shadow of the little palm tree. Bugsy made a sharp noise with his mouth and snapped his fingers, and the flute-boy started apprehensively.

"Hi, but you sure is goosey," laughed Banjo. And right there and thenceforth the flute-boy was dubbed "Goosey."

"I wish the fire that was lit by that fellow that got six months for it had burned the damned Ditch down," said Ray.

"Why, whatsmat pardner?" said Banjo. "The Ditch is all right. Nobody don't have to go rooting in Boody Lane unless you want to. Let everything take its chance, says I."

"Chance! What good is it, then, Banjo, when the

people who should get some fun out of it—the seamen—are always the victims? Think of the police making this boy pay. It's a crime and graft all round."

"All the policemen in this Ditch are in league with the women and the *maquereaux,"* said Dengel. "Some of the police have women in the boxons."

"Not possible!" exclaimed Ray.

"What will you?" responded Dengel. "The police are just like everybody else, except that they are perhaps the bigger hogs. Their pay is twenty-five francs a day. What will you?"

"We should worry, pardner," said Banjo. "Look at Goosey. He's happy about it."

Goosey's grin gave an ineffable expression to his features.

"D'you blow the flute?" Banjo asked.

"I sure think that I do."

"If you blow it real good I can use you."

"In what way?"

"It's like this."

Banjo explained his intention to form an orchestra. There was one thing that he was sure of about this town, and that was that the people loved music. All over the Ditch you never heard anything but bad music. If we could get a set of fellows together to turn out some good music we would sure make a success of the thing. But it was a hard job getting them. The fellows with instruments never stay long in port. Malty could play the guitar, but he had no instrument.

"He would put it in hock if he had one," said Bugsy.

"If I get him one I'd sure see that he didn't, though," returned Banjo.

Goosey said that his friend Taloufa had a fine guitar.

"Oh, does he do? Jest lead me along to that darky. Where is he burying his head now?"

"He's still on the ship," Goosey replied, "going to be paid off tomorrow. He'll fix me up so I don't have to worry."

"He's a sucker, eh?" said Bugsy. "That's why you done dumped all you hed in Boody Lane."

"Lay off the kid, Bugsy," said Banjo. "You got too much lip."

"As much as a baboon," added Goosey, laughing. "But where you get that 'kid' from?" he asked Banjo. "I don't see my daddy in you."

"Nevah mind, but youse a green kid, all the same," replied Banjo. "Anyway, I think we c'n do some business together, you and the flute, you' friend and the guitar ——"

"He's got a little horn, too," said Goosey.

"Sure enough? That's the ticket and me and mah banjo."

"Banjo! That's what you play?" exclaimed Goosey.

"Sure that's what I play," replied Banjo. "Don't you like it?"

"No. Banjo is bondage. It's the instrument of slavery. Banjo is Dixie. The Dixie of the land of cotton and massa and missus and black mammy. We colored folks have got to get away from all that in these enlightened progressive days. Let us play piano and violin, harp and flute. Let the white folks play the banjo if they want to keep on remembering all the Black Joes singing and the hell they made them live in."

"That ain't got nothing to do with me, nigger," replied Banjo. "I play that theah instrument becaz I likes it. I don't play no Black Joe hymns. I play lively tunes. All that you talking about slavery and bondage ain't got nothing to do with our starting up a li'l' orchestry."

"It sure has, though, if you want me and my friend

Taloufa in with you. We aren't going to do any of that black-face coon stuff."

"Nuts on that black-face. Tha's time-past stuff. But wha' you call coon stuff is the money stuff today. That saxophone-jazzing is sure coon stuff and the American darky sure knows how to makem wheedle-whine them 'blues.' He's sure-enough the one go-getting musical fool today, yaller, and demanded all ovah the wul'."

"Hm." Goosey reflected a little. "I'm a race man and Taloufa is race crazy. Pity he isn't more educated. It's a new day for the colored race. Up the new race man and finish the good nigger. I as much as told that captain that when he tried to monkey with me. I told him I was in France and not in the United States."

"You were very foolish," said Ray. "That wasn't helping your race any."

"That's what you think, but I know I was right. France isn't like the United States nor Africa ——"

"And what's wrong with Africa?" demanded Dengel.

"Africa is benighted. My mother always advised me when I was a kid to get away as far as farthest from Africa. 'Africa is jungleland,' she used to say; 'there's nothing to learn from it but dark and dirty doings.' That's where I don't go with my friend Taloufa. He's gone Back-to-Africa. He thinks colored people scattered all over the world should come together and go Back-to-Africa. He bought a hundred dollars of Black Star Line shares."

"He did!" exclaimed Banjo. "And what does he think now they got the fat block a that black swindler in the jail-house?"

"Taloufa thinks better of him," said Goosey. "Garvey is a bigger man among colored people since they jailed him. Taloufa was at Liberty Hall for the big manifestation. And all the speakers said that the British were back of Garvey catching jail. They were scared of him in Africa and wouldn't let the *Negro World* through the mails. Taloufa can tell you all about it tomorrow. I don't know much. I am no Back-to-Africa business. That's a big-fool idea. But I'm a race man."

"If you think about you' race as much as you do about Boody Lane you'd be better off, maybe," said Bugsy.

They all laughed heartily.

"Chuts! All that race talking," continued Bugsy, "is jest a mess a nothing. That saloon-keeper is race talking all the time, and he is robbing his countrymen them, too, giving them more rotten stuff to drink than the white man. He's wearing gold spectacles with a gold chain, and looking so like he can't see natural; but mark me, when the white man done get through with him, he'll sure enough find his own eyesight and be walking around here like any other nigger."

More laughter, and Banjo asked: "Where do we go from here? The Ditch is getting ready to eat, and I feel like heavy loading. Whose the money guy tonight?"

"I got a little money today," Ray said. "You can all come up to my dump."

"Tha's the ticket!" Banjo applauded. "There's mah pardner for you, Goosey. Guess he could clean you up on that race stuff. Yet he ain't nevah hunting down no coon nor bellyaching race on me."

"But you're interested in race—I mean race advancement, aren't you?" Goosey asked Ray.

"Sure, but right now there's nothing in the world so interesting to me as Banjo and his orchestra."

VIII. A Carved Carrot

BANJO had the freedom of the Ditch and, as his pal, Ray shared some of it and was introduced to the real depths of the greater Ditch beyond his alley at the extreme end. Banjo had the right of way through Boody Lane and Ray could go through it now without his hat being snatched, as Banjo had a speaking acquaintance with all the occupants of the boxes.

One afternoon Banjo and Ray were playing checkers in a little café of the quarter, with a bottle of wine between them. A demi-crone of the hole came in with a ready-made gladness which seemed as if it might change at any moment into something poisonous. She asked Ray to pay for a drink, calling the *patrone* of the bistro, who was in the kitchen. Ray agreed and she took a camouflage absinthe. After drinking it, she leaned over Ray's chair, caressing him. Her touch imparted to him an unbearable sensation as of a loathsome white worm wriggling down his spine. And mingled with that was the smell of the absinthe on her breath. He detested the nauseating sweet-garlicky odor of absinthe. In the thing bending over him he felt an obscene bird, like the pink-headed white buzzard of the Caribbean lands that also exuded an odor like absinthe-and-garlic.

Abruptly Ray shifted away from the creature, who fell awkwardly over the back of the chair.

"I pay you a drink, but I don't want you to touch me."

"*Merde alors!* Why? I am not rotten."

"I didn't say you were. Maybe I am. All the same, it is finished. We won't talk about it any more."

"Gee, pardner, why you so hard on the old thing?" demanded Banjo.

"To protect myself, Banjo. You've got your way with the Ditch and I've got mine."

Banjo laughed. "Youse right, pardner. Gotta meet them as they come—rough. Talk rough, handle them rough, everything make rough. For way down heah is rough-house way and there ain't no other way getting by."

"I don't mind the roughness at all," replied Ray. "I like it. I prefer it to the nice pretensions of the upstage places. What gets me down here is the sliminess and rattiness. The only thing rough and real down here is the seamen and the Senegalese."

"And the onliest thing is the one thing, pardner, that we know."

"I wouldn't know if *that's* the whole truth."

" 'Cause youse tight-wad business. You know that Algerian brown gal got a scrunch on you?"

"I know it, but I'm scared of her."

"Why is you?"

"Because of her mouth. What a marvelous piece of business it is. But she'd just make tiger's feed of me. Anyhow, I am safe. She thinks I have the change to take her on because I have one good suit of clothes and keep clean. As I haven't, there's nothing doing. She isn't like Latnah."

"Latnah is all right, eh?" Banjo said, carelessly.

"Sure. *She's* the *only* thing down here I can see," said Ray.

"Oh, *you* done fall for her, too?" Banjo chuckled.

It was dinner time. They went to a Chinese restaurant in the Rue Torte to feed for four francs each.

After dinner the boys came together in a café that they called Banjo's hang-out. Dengel, Goosey, Taloufa, Bugsy, Ginger, and Latnah, with Malty fooling near her, quite funny, grinning and gesturing like an overgrown pickaninny in amorous play.

Ray and Banjo came in and, relishing the situation, Banjo smacked his lips aloud and grinned so contagiously that all the beach boys, following his lead, imitated him. Malty became a little embarrassed, and Banjo said: "Go right on with you, buddy. Git that theah honey while the honeycomb is sweet foh you."

Vexed momentarily, Latnah turned away, humping up her back like a little brown cat against Malty. Although under the reaction of resentment she had loaned those fancy pyjamas to decorate Malty's limbs first, it had been no real conquest for Malty at all, for when Banjo did at last decide to take a turn in the pretty things, she felt the second-hand wear incomparably better than the first, and realized that for her Malty would never be able to hold a candle to the intractable Banjo.

The *patrone* of the café was quite taken by Banjo and his hearty-drinking friends, and she had given them a free option on the comfortable space at the rear for the use of their orchestra.

Taloufa had taught them a rollicking West African song, whose music was altogether more insinuating than that of "Shake That Thing."

"Stay, Carolina, stay,
Oh, stay, Carolina, stay!"

That was the refrain, and all the verses were a repetition, with very slight variations, of the first verse.

Taloufa had a voluptuous voice, richly colored like the sound of water lapping against a bank. And he chanted as he strummed the guitar:

"Stay, Carolina, stay. . . ."

The whole song—the words of it, the lilt, the pattern, the color of it—seemed to be built up from that one word, Stay! When Taloufa sang, "Stay," his eyes grew bigger and whiter in his charmingly carnal countenance, the sound came from his mouth like a caressing, appealing command and reminded one of a beautiful, rearing young filly of the pasture that a trainer is breaking in. Stay!

"Stay, Carolina, stay. . . ."

"There isn't much to it," said Goosey: "it's so easy and the tune is so slight, just one bar repeating itself."

"Why, it's splendid, you boob!" said Ray. "It's got more real stuff in it than a music-hall full of American songs. The words are so wonderful."

"I took her on a swim and she swim more than me,
I took her on a swim and she swim more than me,
I took her on a swim and she swim more than me,
Stay, Carolina, stay,
Stay, Carolina, stay. . . ."

"Don't blow on the flute so hard; you kinder kill the sound a the banjo," said Banjo to Goosey.

"I can't do it any other way. A flute is a flute. It mounts high every time above everything else."

"I tell you what, Banjo," said Ray. "Let Goosey play solo on the flute, and you fellows join in the chorus. The chorus is the big thing, anyway."

"Tha's the ticket," agreed Malty, who was blowing the tiny tin horn and looked very comical at it, as he was the heftiest of the bunch.

So Goosey played the solo. And when Banjo, Taloufa, and Malty took up the refrain, Bugsy, stepping with Dengel, led the boys dancing. Bugsy was wiry and long-handed. Dengel, wiry, long-handed, and long-legged. And they made a striking pair as abruptly Dengel turned his back on Bugsy and started round the room in a bird-hopping step, nodding his head and working his hands held against his sides, fists doubled, as if he were holding a guard. Bugsy and all the boys imitated him, forming a unique ring, doing the same simple thing, startlingly fresh in that atmosphere, with clacking of heels on the floor.

It was, perhaps, the nearest that Banjo, quite unconscious of it, ever came to an æsthetic realization of his orchestra. If it had been possible to transfer him and his playing pals and dancing boys just as they were to some Metropolitan stage, he might have made a bigger thing than any of his dreams.

"I took her on a ride and she rode more than me,
I took her on a ride and she rode more than me,
Oh, I took her on a ride and she rode more than me,
Stay, Carolina, stay,
Stay, Carolina, stay. . . ."

Five men finishing a round of drinks at the bar went and sat at a table among the beach boys. They wore Basque caps. They applauded the playing. One of them was fat and round with a kind of rump roundness all over, but it was the compact fatness of muscle and blood and not of some pulpy fruit. He bought wine for the players and asked Banjo to play more. Glasses chinked. Goosey shook his flute, wiped the mouth of it, and started.

A troop of girls filed in from the boxes, led by Ray's absinthe lady. They broke in among the boys and began dancing with them in their loud self-conscious way.

But as soon as the music stopped they turned to the newcomers. Like sea gulls following a ship, the girls were always after the beach boys, whenever the boys had some paying business in hand. Between the sorority and the fraternity down there in the Ditch the competition was keen. The girls amused themselves with the beach boys when the beach boys had paying guests that they wanted to get at, but when the beach boys, having no money nor any potential catch, attempted, with masculine vanity, to make jolly with the girls, they were ruthlessly given a very contemptuous shoulder—especially if there were any possibility of a "prize" in sight—some white thing prejudiced against the proximity of black beach boys and envious of their joy.

The girls obtained drinks from the white seamen—enough to warm them up to work for more substantial favors. But on this occasion the seamen were limiting themselves to wine and song. However, after a little well-managed, persistent persuasion, one of them, a swarthy, thin-faced, middling type, was carried off.

His remaining companions called for more wine for Banjo and his boys. The girls, all but one, gave them their backs and went off shaking themselves disdainfully. The one who remained was the absinthe lady. Guzzling down his wine, Goosey fondled his flute again.

"I took her on a jig and she jigged more than me,
I took her on a jig and she jigged more than me,
Oh, I took her on a jig and she jigged more than me!
Stay, Carolina, stay. . . ."

The playing was so good that it stirred the very round sailor to get a little nearer to the musicians. And when the music stopped he put a fraternal arm round Goosey's shoulder. Banjo grinned at them comically and drawled in rough-ripe accents: "I'm a rooting hog!"

"And I'm a dog," said Goosey in a giggling fit, and he chanted the little fairy song:

> "List to me while I sing to you
> Of the Spaniard that ruined my life. . . ."

"Come on, git on to that theah flute," said Banjo, affecting a rough manner with him.

"What about the 'West Indies Blues'?" suggested Goosey.

"Why no play 'Shake That Thing'?" said Dengel.

"'Carolina' once again," decided Banjo. "We'll do the whole show from start to finish and Ray'll tell us how it was. Eh, pardner?"

Goosey took up his flute and the round sailor sat down with his forefinger posed on his lip. The tout of the absinthe girl, an undersized, mangy-faced man of dead glassy eyes, and wearing proletarian blue, looked in at the bistro and beckoned to her. She went to the entrance and he handed her something and slunk off. It was an enormous carrot, out of the fertile peasant soil of Provence, crudely carved.

The girl went back to the rear and thrust the carrot under the nose of the tight-round sailor. He reddened and, crying, "Slut!" cuffed the girl full in the face, and as she fell he drove a kick at her. The girl shrieked.

The *patrone* rushed quickly to the door and locked out the crowd that was gathering. In a moment the girl picked herself up and the *patrone's* man, a docker who had come in during the evening, let her out and closed the door again. The crowd dispersed.

> "Stay, Carolina, stay. . . ."

The sailor who had slapped the girl stood the beach boys some more wine.

"It's a rough life, pardner," Banjo said to Ray. "Got to treat 'em rough, all right, or they'll walk all ovah you."

"I woulda choked her to death with these black hands of mine," said Ray.

The swarthy sailor who had gone out returned with his girl and bought her a liqueur—a *cointreau.* Soon after the five men left. They had gone a few paces only up the alley when two shots barked out, precipitating the beach boys to the door of the bistro. The plump round sailor came running back.

"They have killed my comrade! They have killed my comrade!" he cried. Two bicycle policemen came sprinting from the waterfront. From out of the sinister houses and bistros the same curious crowd was gathering again, but there was not a witness who had seen the murderer nor could tell whence the shots came. The four sailors stood over their prostrate comrade, the swarthy one who had bought the girl the *cointreau.* The bullets, really intended for the round one, had clean finished him.

IX. Taloufa's Shirt-tail

TALOUFA came from the Nigerian bush. He had attended a mission school where he learned reading, arithmetic, and writing. He was taken to Lagos by a minor British official. And when the Englishman was returning to England he took Taloufa along as a "boy." Taloufa was thirteen years old at that time. For nearly three years he served his master in a Midland town. Then he got tired of it, full fed up of seeing white faces only. He ran away to Cardiff, where he found more contentment among the hundreds of colored seamen who live in that port. And young, fresh, and naïve, he became a great favorite among the port girls. He shipped to sea as a "boy," making Cardiff his home. He was there during the riots of 1919 between colored and whites, and he got a brick wound in the head.

He went to America after the riots and jumped his ship there. He lived in the United States until after the passing of the new quota immigration laws, when, the fact of his entering the country illegally getting known, he was arrested and deported. In America he had joined the Back-to-Africa crusade and was a faithful believer in the Black Star Line bubble, the great dream of commerce that was to link Negroes of the New World with those of Africa. He bought shares in it and, although the bubble burst with the conviction and imprisonment of the leader for fraudulent dealings, Taloufa still believed in him and his ideas of Back-to-Africa.

Taloufa maintained that the Back-to-Africa propaganda had worked wonders among the African natives. He told Ray that all throughout West Africa the natives were meeting to discuss their future, and in the ports they were no longer docile, but restive, forming groups, and waiting for the Black Deliverer, so that, becoming aroused, the colonial governments had acted to keep out all propaganda, especially the *Negro World,* the chief organ of the Back-to-Africa movement.

"The Black Deliverer has delivered himself to the ofays' jail-house," said Ray.

"It's the damned English that got him there," said Taloufa.

Taloufa firmly believed the rumor, current among Negroes, that representatives of the British Intelligence Service had instigated the prosecution and conviction of Marcus Garvey in the United States.

However, Taloufa had no immediate intention of returning to West Africa. It was his first trip to this great Provençal port of which he also had heard and dreamed much. And after tasting it for a while he expected to go on to England.

He had at once fallen in with the idea of Banjo's orchestra. Unlike Goosey, he was not squeamish about the choice of music. He loved all music with a lilt, and especially music that was heady with sensuousness. Banjo found it easy to work along with him. If Taloufa had a little word to say about Back-to-Africa, Banjo would listen deferentially, and for his answer refer him to Ray.

"I ain't edjucated, buddy. Ask mah pardner, Ray."

The day following their big musical night, Banjo took Taloufa down to look the breakwater over. Returning from Joliette to the Vieux Port in the afternoon, they stopped in a bistro of the Place de Lenche for a cool guzzle of wine. The Place de Lenche is midway between Joliette and the Bum Square. The Quartier Réservé slopes up a somber crisscross of alleys to its edge, where it ends.

Finishing their bottle, the boys started down one of the alleys into the Ditch, when they were attracted by a striking girl framed in front of a bistro. She was straight, boyish, and carrot-headed. And she stood right-arm akimbo and the left up against the jamb of the door, between her fingers a cigarette at which she whiffed with an infinitely bored mechanical manner. A young Chinese, leaning against a lamppost a little farther down on the opposite side of the alley, was beckoning to her. Lizard-like, excessively slim and hipless, his smooth buff-yellow countenance was rigidly immobile, but the balls of his eyes behind the curious little slits were burning with rage.

"Gawd on his golden moon! What a saucy-looking doll that one is!" Banjo exclaimed.

"I ain't studying any kelts," replied Taloufa.

"Watch her and that sweet chink. She's scared a him."

Not a muscle of the Chinese youth's face twitched as the girl went slowly, reluctantly toward him. He stood fixed in his tracks until she came to him, her toes up to his toes, her face almost touching his face. Then he said something to her, his lips barely moving, and as she opened her mouth to reply he lifted his knee and drove a terrific kick into her belly. The girl fell backward with a shriek on the cobblestones.

A policeman then coming down from the Place de Lenche, bicycle in hand, rushed over, and apprehended the Chinese. Immediately the girl picked herself up and grabbed the arm of the youth, crying to the policeman: "Leave him alone! Leave him alone!" The policeman left them a little shamefacedly as the gang of spectators that had quickly gathered laughed derisively.

"Sale vache au roulette," said the Chinese boy, and putting the girl before him he said, "Go on," and began kicking her all the way down into the Ditch. And subdued, without a whine, she went. A little knot of pasty-faced kids frisked about and, laughing, cried: *"Chinois! Chinois!"*

"She honors and obeys her boss all right," Taloufa remarked, dryly.

"They're the only real sweetbacks in this Ditch, them Chinese," said Banjo. "The only ones kain bring you a decent change a suit and strut the stuff like a fellow back home."

Taloufa went to the Antilles Restaurant for dinner. Banjo had taken a dislike for that restaurant and would not go there. Taloufa promised to meet him after dinner at the beach boys' café on the other side of the Bum Square, where they would play.

Taloufa had not gone Back-to-Africa in ideas only, but also in principle . . . and nature. He put up at the Antilles because it was a hotel primarily for Negroes (although it did not at all exclude the little pinks of the Ditch who went there for chocolate trade and brought in business), owned by a Negro couple.

The Antilles Restaurant was right off the Bum Square. It was situated in one of the narrowest, dampest, and most rubbishy of the alleys, but as you entered it you were stirred by the warm cheerfulness of the little oblong place. With its high narrow benches and painted walls it had something of the aspect of a Greenwich Village den. And, if you knew anything of the cooking of the West Indies with its rice-and-Congo-peas dishes, fish fried in cocoanut oil and annatto-colored sauces, you would be charmed by the pepper-pot flavor of the place. . . .

The customers were colored seamen, soldiers from Martinique and Guadeloupe, a few from Madagascar, and three brown girls. During the dinner a brown, jolly-faced soldier played an accordion while a Martinique guide and sweetman, who was sweet in the Ditch for every purchasable thing, was shaking a steel pipe, about the size of a rolling-pin, containing something like beans or sand grains. The curious thing went beautifully with the accordion.

They played the "beguin," which was just a Martinique variant of the "jelly-roll" or the Jamaican "burru" or the Senegalese "bombé." The tall, big-boned *patrone* started the dancing. She radiated energy like a boiler giving off steam. She danced with a whopping sergeant, talking all the time the Martinique dialect in a deep voice of the color and flavor of unrefined cane sugar. She was easily the central figure, making the girls look like dancing attendants. It was an eye-filling ensemble of delicious jazzing, and the rhythm of it went tickling through the warm blood of Taloufa, who was still smacking his lips over his sausage-and-rice, tempered with a bottle of old Bordeaux.

"Beguin," "jelly-roll," "burru," "bombé," no matter what the name may be, Negroes are never so beautiful and magical as when they do that gorgeous sublimation of the primitive African sex feeling. In its thousand varied patterns, depending so much on individual rhythm, so little on formal movement, this dance is the key to the African rhythm of life. . . .

In company with a pretty Provençale, the Arab-black girl came in. Her hair stood up stiff, thick and exciting. Her mouth was like a full-blown bluebell with a bee on its rim, and her eyes were everywhere at once, roving round as only Arab eyes can. She had disappeared since the night of her glorious performance at the "Shake-That-Thing" festival and was just this day returned to Marseilles again.

Taloufa saw her for the first time and fell for her. Their eyes met, his a question, hers a swift affirmative, and he went to dance with her. There was no common language between them, but what did that matter? Taloufa's swelling emotion was eloquent enough. And mingled with that emotion was the patriotic feeling of kinship with his pick-up that made him do the "beguin" with a royal African strut.

After that dance they sat together, the girl choosing a bottle of *mousseux* for the treat. . . . Taloufa was filling the glasses from a second bottle when Banjo entered in search of him.

"For the love of a li'l' piece!" Banjo cried. "Ain't you coming to play noneatall tonight, buddy?"

Not understanding, but guessing that Banjo wanted to get Taloufa away, the girl looked at him in a hostile manner. She knew, of course, that Banjo was on the beach.

"You gotta carry on without me tonight," Taloufa said in a thick, ripe-brown voice, slowly, pointlessly fingering his guitar.

"Get outa that," said Banjo. "You ain'ta gwine to drop a fellah flat like that. Come and give us a hand. You got all the balance a the night foh sweet flopping. Ray's got two ofays with him and I wanta turn loose some'n' splendacious foh them. Them's English and might hulp us some. A fellah nevah know his luck. Theyse done some moh running around the wul' jest lak you and me and Malty, and they knows every knowingest place in this white man's Europe."

"But I've got this sweet business with me," objected Taloufa.

"Man, tell her you'll see it later. I'll fix it up with her. This is Marcelles. Everything wait on you down to Time himse'f when youse gotta roll on you."

It was not so easy to get Taloufa away from the girl, but Banjo managed it, making eloquent promises of returning him to the Antilles.

"You come back without fail," said the girl as Banjo opened the door.

"Youse clean gone on her, eh?" remarked Banjo as they went along the Bum Square.

"She's a bird of a brown," was Taloufa's response.

"Watch out! Our own color is the most expensive business in this sweet burg. Ise one spade can live without prunes when I ain't in chocolate country. You see Latnah. I got her all going mah own way becazen Ise one independent strutter."

"I've noticed all right you aren't foolish about her," agreed Taloufa. "Malty's more that way. But I'm different from you. I haven't got any appreciation at all for the kelts."

"You're joking," exclaimed Banjo, laughing. "You ain't telling me that you done gone all the way back home to Africa even by that most narrow and straitest road that a human mortal was nevah made to trod?"

"I'm not kidding at all," responded Taloufa. "I'm foursquare one hundred per cent African."

At the hangout Bugsy, Goosey, Ginger, Dengel, Malty, and Ray with his two guests were waiting. They were two Britishers who lived uptown, but were frequently down in the Ditch. Ray had met them by one of the tourist bureaus of the Cannebière. Like himself, they were always traveling. But they had been staying for some length of time in Marseilles. Ray knew nothing about them yet—what hobby they pursued and what they were doing in Marseilles. They spoke cultivated English and the taller of the two had a colonial accent that Ray could not place. At the hangout they treated the beach boys, and the girls that their presence attracted there, to the best liqueurs and *fines* in the place.

"He was just falling down for a wonderful brown," cried Banjo as he entered with Taloufa, "but I carried him right off away from it."

The old bistro shook with everybody's laughter.

"Which one a them was it?" demanded Malty.

"That saucy-lipped, shakem-shimmying sweet mam-ma."

"The dawggonest, hardest, and dearest piece a brownness in this bum hussy," said Bugsy.

"Now Ise got mah man, we'll play 'Carolina' for yo-all," Banjo announced.

> "I took her on a jig and she jigged more than me. . . ."

Lustily Goosey fluted it and the boys charged mightily into the chorus.

> "Stay, Carolina, stay. . . ."

The Britishers demanded champagne for the boys. The bistro-keeper had only *vins mousseux,* Clairette, and Royal Provence. They made her send her husband out for champagne. He returned with four bottles of white-label Mercier.

"That's better," said the taller white. "I hate the vile taste of those sickly-sweetish *mousseux* wines."

Between intervals of champagne-swilling the boys played and danced. "Carolina," "Mammy-Daddy," "That's My Baby," "Shake That Thing," "The Garvey Blues," and all the "blues" that Banjo's memory could rake up.

When the Britishers left the bistro there was still champagne in the bottles, and by the time the boys were finished, they were all posing in attitudes of soft ecstasy.

In the Bum Square, Latnah appeared and hung on to Banjo. The group began to break up, every man to his own dream! Taloufa was all in a haze of intoxication, but he remembered his rendezvous with the girl at the Antilles bar. Latnah and Banjo went along with him, but when they got there the Antilles was closed.

Returning to the Bum Square, they found Malty, Bugsy, and Ginger, undecided about their aims, swaying softly in their tracks.

"Let's all have a chaser of some'n'," suggested Banjo.

"No, no," protested Latnah. "It too late and you-all saoul."

"Shut up," said Banjo. "This is a man's show."

They walked a little along the quay and into a café. And there was Taloufa's girl disdainfully drinking beer with a white corporal, who seemed broke and quite fed up with the business of life, because a common soldier could not enjoy its pleasures when he was far away from pay day.

The girl brightened up with a smile and brusquely left the soldier to take charge of Taloufa, whose legs were like reeds under him. She had been much put out that he had not returned to the Antilles. She had even changed for the occasion and was wearing a wine-colored frock, all soft and gleaming. Her crinkly hair was done up in the shape of a bowl, and in her buxom beauty and the magnetic aura of fascination around her she looked like some perfect marvel of mating between amber-skinned Egypt and black Sudan.

Malty took Taloufa's guitar. "I wanta play some moh," he droned in a singsong. "I ain't noways sleepy."

The girl went off with Taloufa.

Outside, Latnah said to Banjo: "She no good girl for your friend. I know her. She very wicked."

"Oh . . . she can't kill him," he replied. "Let's *allez* to turn the spread back."

Malty had reached that delightful attitude of inebriation when a man feels like staying the night through, tippling and fooling with boon companions. Bugsy, who had contrived to pass many of his glasses over to the other boys, was quite aware of what was happening, but Ginger was all enveloped in a brown fog.

"Let's carry on, fellahs," said Malty, "till the stars them fade out."

He had some money and they went into a little open-all-night café. Malty strummed softly on the guitar and hummed snatches of West Indian "shay-shay" and "jamma."

"When you feel a funny feel,
When you feel a funny feel,
When you feel a funny feel,
Get in the middle of the wheel. . . ."

"The daughter of Cordelia is going round the town—
Sailor men in George's Lane after the sun gone down,
Going round, going round Cordelia Brown. . . ."

"I love her oh, oh, oh. . . .
I love her so, so, so. . . .
I love the little-brown soul of her,
I love the classy-town stroll of her.
And every move she makes is like a picture to me,
I love her to mah haht and I love her on mah knee."

They had finished four bottles of white wine tempered with lemonade when Taloufa came rushing in in shirt sleeves, his shirt-tail flying.

"She gypped me! She gypped me!" he cried. "Took every cent I had and beat it."

"All you' money? Banjo said you had about three thousand francs!" cried Malty.

"How you mean rob you?" from Bugsy.

"Rob you—rob you . . ." Ginger singsonged.

All three of them spoke together.

"Cleaned you outa all that money?" Malty questioned.

Taloufa explained that he had been long-headed enough to leave two thousand five hundred francs at his hotel, but the girl had got away with all he had—over three hundred francs. Bugsy, scornful of his incompetence, interrupted him while he was talking:

"Git you' shirt in you' pants, mon, git it in. You ain't in the African jungle with the monkeys in the trees now. Youse on the sidewalk of the white man's big city. Git it in, I say."

Taloufa was too agitated to pay any attention. Ginger reached over and arranged his clothes for him.

"I was so boozy and all in I fell asleep," Taloufa said, "and when I woke up she was gone. I thought of my pocketbook right away, and looked in my coat pocket, but every nickel was clean gone."

"So you done got rooked foh nothing at all!" exclaimed Bugsy. "My Gawd! The baboons them in the bush where you come from has got moh sense than you. And what youse gwine do about it?"

"I don't know," replied Taloufa.

"Don't know?" repeated Bugsy. "Why, lock her up, man! Lock her up! You ain't gwine a let that black slut pass all that buck to her white p-i, when we fellahs am hungry on the beach. Lock her up, I say."

Taloufa hesitated about the police. Malty was indifferent, but Ginger was flatly for letting the matter rest.

"You shoulda leave the money with us. Now she done

had it I wouldn't mess with no police. Just as cheap be magnamisuch."

"Crap on that magnamisuch!" retorted Bugsy. " 'Causen you done make the same fool a you'self, you think everybody is a sucker like you."

"I don't want to arrest a girl of my own race," said Taloufa.

"In the can with race!" cried Bugsy. "A slut is a slut, whether she is pink or blue. You don't have to arrest her nohow. Jest get a policeman to get back that good money and let him turn her loose after you get it."

But Ginger, who was the only one who could make himself intelligible in French, refused to budge in search of a policeman.

"Let the blighting thing be," he said. "It'll soon turn sewer stuff. When the *maquereaux* in the Ditch finish with it, they pass it to them cousins in the sea."

Bugsy induced Taloufa to go with him to find a policeman. "You don't have to lock her up. Jest get you' money back."

They found a policeman and brought him back for Ginger to explain. Ginger explained, but he and Malty refused to go along to search out the girl.

"You scared a them lousy *maquereaux,"* Bugsy taunted.

"Not a damn sight," declared Malty. "I ain't studying them babies. I was thinking personally of the principle of this heah algebra."

"That's some'n' sure said," Ginger applauded. "The principle of the thing is the supposition of its circumference. Now you, Bugsy, ef you was in that gal's place ——"

"You fiddling, low-down, wut'less yaller nigger!" swore Bugsy. "What you think I is to put *myself* in her place? You think Ise gwine be everything like you because Ise on the beach? Not on you' crack!"

He went off with Taloufa and the policeman. He knew the house where the Algerian girl lived in an alley above the Bum Square. They routed her out of bed. They searched her room thoroughly. They found nothing. She pretended to vexed amazement that they should molest her. She had left Taloufa, she said, simply because he had gone to sleep! Bugsy urged Taloufa to jail the girl, but Taloufa refused and told the policeman to turn her loose.

When they returned empty-handed to Ginger and Malty on the quay, Ginger sat right down on the pavement and gurgled.

"I knowed you wouldn't find a dimmity dime," he droned. "When one a them gals make a getaway she pass that dough tutswit to her p-i, and he transfer it to a safe spot."

"I'm going back to the hotel," said Taloufa. "I am tired."

Dawn was just lifting the shroud of night from the face of the Ditch, turning silver-blue the shadows, lighting the somber fronts of love shops and bistros, the gray granite of the Mairie, the fish market, the fishing-boats, and the excursion boats in faint motion. Toward the Catalan baths the horizon was suffused by a russet flush. A soft breeze floated gracefully like a sloping wave of sea gulls into the walled squareness of the calm Vieux Port.

"Let's go down to the breakwater and sleep," Ginger yawned.

X. Story-telling

THE beach boys were at the Senegalese café. It was afternoon of a rainy day. Ray was trying to get some of the Senegalese to tell stories like the Brer Rabbit kind or the African animal fables of the West Indies. But the Senegalese were not willing to talk. Banjo had said openly that Ray was a writing black, for Banjo felt proud of that. The Senegalese got the information from Dengel and became a little suspicious of Ray, imagining, perhaps, that he would write something funny or caustic of their life that would make them appear "uncivilized" or inferior to American Negroes.

Ray himself hadn't the habit of exhibiting his unprofitable literary talent in the workaday world that he loved to breathe in, for experience had taught him that many common people, like many uncommon people, fearing or hoping to be used in a story, are always unnatural and apt to pose in the presence of a writer. And, apart from modesty, he enjoyed life better without wearing the badge. That the badge, indeed, might be useful he was too often made aware, in a world of impressive appearances. But that was another matter. If, when alone, writing, he lived in an unconsciously happy state, he was also inexpressibly happy when he was just one of the boys cruising the docks or in a drinking revel.

Banjo had thought that the boys would take Ray's writing as naturally as he took it and everything else. But Goosey, for one, didn't.

"You mean to say you'd write about how these race boys live in the Ditch here and publish it?" he asked Ray. In speaking of Negro people Goosey always avoided the word "Negro" and "black" and used, instead, "race men," "race women," or "race."

"Sure I would," answered Ray. "How the black boys live is the most interesting thing in the Ditch."

"But the crackers will use what you write against the race!"

"Let the crackers go fiddle themselves, and you, too. I think about my race as much as you. I hate to see it kicked around and spat on by the whites, because it is a good earth-loving race. I'll fight with it if there's a fight on, but if I am writing a story—well, it's like all of us in this place here, black and brown and white, and I telling a story for the love of it. Some of you will listen, and some won't. If I am a real story-teller, I won't worry about the differences in complexion of those who listen and those who don't, I'll just identify myself with those who are really listening and tell my story. You see, Goosey, a good story, in spite of those who tell it and those who hear it, is like good ore that you might find in any soil—Europe, Asia, Africa, America. The world wants the ore and gets it by a thousand men scrambling and fighting, digging and dying for it. The world gets its story the same way."

"That's all right. But what do you find good in the Ditch to write about?"

"Plenty. I'm here, and mean to make a practical thing of the white proverb, 'Let down your bucket where you are.' "

"You might bring up a lot of dirt." Goosey turned up his nose in a tickling, funny, disdainful way.

"Many fine things come out of dirt—steel and gold,

pearls and all the rare stones that your nice women must have to be happy."

"Why don't you write about the race men and women who are making good in Paris?"

"I'm not a reporter for the Negro press. Besides, I can't afford to keep up with the Negroes of Paris. And as they are society folk, they might prefer to have a society writer do them, like Monsieur Paul Morand, perhaps."

"You don't have to sneer at race society because you are out of it. It's a good thing. Our society folks are setting a fine example of a high standard of living for the race."

"I can't see that. They say you find the best Negro society in Washington. When I was there the government clerks and school-teachers and the wives of the few professional men formed a group and called themselves the 'upper classes.' They were nearly all between your complexion and near-white. The women wore rich clothes and I don't know whether it was that or their complexions or their teaching or clerking ability that put them in the 'upper class.' In my home we had an upper class of Negroes, but it had big money and property and power. It wasn't just a moving-picture imitation. School-teachers and clerks didn't make any ridiculous pretenses of belonging to it. . . . I could write about the society of Negroes you mean if I wrote a farce.

"Gee! I remember when I was in college in America how those Negroes getting an education could make me tired talking class and class all the time. It was funny and it was sad. There was hardly one of them with the upper-class bug on the brain who didn't have a near relative—a brother or sister who was an ignorant chauffeur, butler, or maid, or a mother paying their way through college with her washtub.

"If you think it's fine for the society Negroes to fool themselves on the cheapest of imitations, I don't. I am fed up with class. The white world is stinking rotten and going to hell on it."

"But since you're a Negro, wouldn't it be a good thing for the race if the best Negroes appreciate what you write?"

"The best Negroes are *not* the society Negroes. I am not writing for them, nor the poke-chop-abstaining Negroes, nor the Puritan Friends of Color, nor the Negrophobes nor the Negrophiles. I am writing for people who can stand a real story no matter where it comes from."

"I don't care what you do, brother," said Goosey. "I was talking for the race and not for myself, for I am never going back to those United Snakes."

"What's that you call 'em?" Banjo filled the bar with a roar of rich laughter.

"You heard me." Goosey was grinning and shaking all over at his witty turn.

"Why, Goosey, you're all right!" cried Ray. "Where did you hear that? You didn't invent it, did you?"

"Sure I made it up myself," Goosey replied, proudly.

United Snakes. The simile struck Ray's imagination, giving him a terrible vision of the stripes of Old Glory transformed into wriggling snakes and the stars poisonous heads lifted to strike at an agonized black man writhing in the midst of them.

"Now that one theah is a new exploitation in geography that will sure stand remembering," commented Ginger.

"What about this story business?" demanded Banjo. "Ain't noneathem cannibals gwine tell anything?"

Ray kicked his shins and whispered: "Watch out the *patron* doesn't hear you. It'll start a roughhouse and spoil everything and you know he hasn't much time for you."

Banjo growled a low-down defiance. "Well, I don't care a raw damn who don't want to tell anything, pardner. I gotta personal piece to tell without any trimmings atall and I don't care ef you publish it in the Book of Life itself and hand it to Big Massa as a prayer."

"You ain't got any shame, not to mention race pride, for you don't understand that," said Goosey.

A discharged Senegalese sergeant told a weird tale of his shooting up a barracks in Syria, killing a white private and an adjutant and escaping on an officer's mount into Turkey. From there he negotiated with his captain, who permitted him to return without standing trial or punishment.

A smiling scepticism greeting him blandly from all faces, he glanced round humorously, remarking: "You don't believe me, eh? You don't believe." And he burst into laughter.

"I'll tell one of the African folk tales we know at home," said Ray. . . .

"Once upon a time there was a woman who lived in a pretty house in the midst of a blooming garden. It was the prettiest house and the best garden in the land. The woman was very old, unmarried, but she was stout and fresh. She had a stunted little girl in the house waiting on her. People said the girl was her grandniece. They said the grandaunt had bewitched the girl and taken her growth and youth for herself.

"The little girl's mother had died when she was a child and left her to her grandaunt to bring up. The girl had had a tiny, tiny red mole on her throat, which her mother had tattooed on it as a charm. The mole was made of blood that came from the heart of a crocodile, and so long as it was on the girl's throat she would be happy and young and beautiful and never want for anything. But when the girl's mother died the grandaunt hoodooed the mole away and fixed it on her own throat.

"Before the girl's mother died she had pledged her to be married to the son of a chief in another land. And when the son reached marrying age, the dead mother appeared to him in a dream and told him what the grandaunt had done.

"The great Witch God gave back to the spirit of the dead mother the power that she had had on earth. And she transformed the young chief into a beautiful bird of many colors, and he flew to the pretty house in the blooming garden. He flew three times around the house and pecked on the door, and, the little girl opening it, he flew into the room where the old aunt was sleeping, and pecked the red mole from her throat and flew right out.

"And when the grandaunt woke she was frightened to see herself all shriveled up, wrinkled, and gray-haired. She looked at her throat and the mole was gone. She accused the little girl of taking it. The girl said she had not touched the mole.

"The grandaunt said she would put her through the trial by water. And she took the girl down to the Dry River. She put the girl in the middle of the river bed while she stood on the bank and worked her magic.

"And the girl sang, wailing:

"'Aunty I didn't do it,
Aunty I didn't do it,
Aunty I didn't do it oh. . . .
Water, stay, oh!'

"The grandaunt replied:

"'My pickney, I never say't was you,
My pickney, I never say't was you,
My pickney I never say't was you oh. . . .
Water, come, oh!'

"The river rose to the girl's ankles. She sang again and her aunt replied. The water rose to her knees. The singing continued. The water rose to her waist. The girl's singing grew weaker. The grandaunt's reply grew stronger. The water was at the girl's breast. She sang faintly:

"'Aunty I didn't do it. . . .
Water, stay, oh!'

"The grandaunt replied fiercely:

"'Water, come, oh!'

"Now the water was at the girl's throat and the grandaunt shrieked aloud, writhing her shriveled body like a black serpent:

"'Water, come, oh!'

"And the river roared, flooding over the girl and sweeping her away. Far down its course the grandaunt saw a crocodile slip from the bank and gobble up the girl. And the grandaunt's bones rattled with her thin witch laughter of joy.

"'She stole the crocodile's blood and the crocodile swallowed her up.'

"But when the grandaunt returned to her home, the house and the garden had disappeared and the people called her a bad witch and drove her from the land. She went wandering far away. And one beautiful sky-blue day the old withered thing came into a new country, and suddenly she found herself before the old garden with the pretty house. And standing at the gate was her grandniece, now a beautiful black princess, with the young chief, her husband, beside her.

"Hardly could the grandaunt recognize the stunted girl in the woman before her. But the princess said:

'Aunt, you thought I was dead, but the crocodile was my husband.'

"The old thing fell on her knees and cried: 'Give me to the leopards, my child, for I was a bad relative to you.'

"The princess replied: 'No, aunt, we're flesh and blood of the same family and you will come and live in this house and garden all the rest of your days.' "

When Ray had finished, nearly all the Senegalese wanted to tell a native story.

"We have the same kind of stories," said the sergeant. "We have the trial by water and fire. . . . Let me tell a story."

The sergeant said:

"Leopard was a terror all over the land. He was always setting traps for the other animals and getting the best of them. And the other animals were so afraid of him, they couldn't move about with any freedom. They called secret meetings to make plans to get rid of leopard, but they were no match for him.

"One day leopard was trotting proudly along over the country when, passing under a tree, he heard a sweet musical sound above. Leopard stopped and looked up. He scrambled up the tree and found a hole out in the main limb from which the sound was coming. He put his hand in the hole and something grabbed it.

" 'Who's holding me?' leopard cried.

" 'Me, spinner,' a voice replied from the hole.

" 'All right, spin let me see.'

"And suddenly leopard felt himself going round and round, round and round, until he was almost out of breath when he was let go hurtling through the air, to fall yards away in a clump of bushes. There leopard lay stunned for some time. When he was revived he carefully marked the exact spot where he had fallen. Then he went off to a blacksmith and ordered six steel prongs, stout and sharp.

"Leopard returned to the place to which he had been hurled and set up the steel prongs there. He went back under the tree and waited for the animals that passed by singly. First came bear. Leopard told bear that there was sweet stuff up there in the tree, and sent him up after it. When bear's hand got caught, leopard told him to say just what he had said. And bear was spun round and round and sent whirling through the air to drop bellyways upon the steel prongs, and was instantly killed. Leopard ran to pick up the carcass and hide it away in the bushes.

"Cow passed by and also met his doom. Dog, pig, goat, rabbit, donkey, cat, gazelle—a troop of animals—all went the way of bear and cow. Then monkey came strutting along. Monkey had watched the whole affair from his perch in a treetop, and monkey was known as the one animal that could outwit leopard.

"When he came up to leopard he greeted him casually and was going by. But leopard stopped him.

" 'Hi, monkey, there's sweet stuff up there!'

" 'Where?' monkey asked.

" 'Up there in the tree. Don't you hear the music? Go on up and see. There's a hole full of sweet stuff. I tasted it.'

"Monkey ran nimbly up the tree and, leaping from branch to branch and looking round him, he declared he could not find any hole. Impatiently leopard climbed the tree and pointed to the hole. 'It is there!'

"Monkey turned backsideway and curled up his tail against the hole. 'I don't see it.'

"Leopard leaped over by monkey, shoved him aside, and pointing in the hole said, 'There it is!'

"Monkey gave leopard a hard push. Leopard's hand went way down deep in the hole and was grabbed. Monkey ran cackling down the tree, his tail high in the air.

" 'Oh, my good monkey,' leopard wailed, 'something got me.'

" 'What thing?' monkey demanded.

" 'Oh, I don't know. Some terrible thing. Some evil thing.'

" 'What is the name of the thing?'

" 'I don't know.'

"The conversation stopped and monkey frisked around the tree, striking his face with his hand in mimic mood. At last leopard spoke again:

" 'Oh, good monkey, out yonder in that clump of bush there are some prongs set up. Won't you go out there and pull them up for me?'

"Monkey went and fixed the prongs more securely in their place. Leopard saw them gleaming sharply out there in the sun and he groaned.

"At last monkey ran up the tree and bawled, 'Who's holding me?'

"Leopard began to howl.

" 'Me, spinner,' replied the voice from the hole.

" 'Spin let me see!' monkey bawled.

"And leopard was whirled round and round and sent flying through the air to land on the steel prongs. Monkey uncovered the pile of dead victims and called all the other animals for a big feast. Leopard they skinned, and kept the hide as a trophy. And all the animals made monkey king over them and the land was happy again."

"Now lemme tell you-all one story," said Bugsy.

"One time down home in Alabam' there was a white

man's nigger whose name was Sam. He was a house darky and he was right there on the right side a the boss and the missus. But Sam wasn't noneatall satisfied to be the bestest darky foh the boss folks. He aimed to be the biggest darky ovah all the rest a darkies. So Sam started in to profitsy and done claimed he could throw the fust light on anything that was going to happen.

"Sam had some sort of a way-back befoh-slavery connection with thunder and lightning and he could predick when it was gwine to rain. But all the same he couldn't put himself ovah the field niggers, 'causen there was a confidential fellah among them who was doing a wonderful business in hoodoo stuff. That other conjure man had Sam going something crazy.

"And so, to make the biggest impression on the boss folks and the plantation folks Sam started in hiding things all ovah the place and then challenge the other conjure man to find them. And when the other fellah couldn't find the things Sam would predick where they was.

"He found the guinea pig in the baby's cradle. He found the buck rabbit eating cheese in the pantry. The cock was missing from the hencoop and he found him scratching with the cat in the barn. Ole Mammy Joan lost her bandanna and Sam found it in the buggy house under the coachman's seat. She couldn't noneatall sleep a nights, and he found a big rat done made a nest in her rush baid.

"Sam's fohsightedness made him the biggest darky evah with the boss folks and the black folks, and the news about him spread all ovah the country. And one day a big boss of another plantation comed to visit the boss. And the boss bet the other a bale of cotton that his nigger Sam could find anything that he hid away.

"The other boss took up the bet and had Sam blindfolded and shut up in one a the outhouses, and he made the darkies bring out one a them great big ole-time plantation pot. And he caught a coon and put it under the pot. And then they let Sam out and the boss asks him to tell what was under the pot.

" 'I feel a presumonition nòt to predick today, boss,' Sam said.

" 'But you gotta,' the boss said. 'I done put a bet on you and I know you can tell anything.'

Sam shook his head and, looking at the pot, said, 'This coon is caught today.'

" 'Hurrah!' the boss cried. 'I knowed mah nigger could tell anything.' And he let the coon out from under the pot.

"At first Sam was kinder downhearted and scared. But soon as he saw the coon he got his head up and chested himself and started to strut off just so big and just that proud.

"And from that time the American darky started in playing coon and the white man is paying him for it."

"And who is paying the Wesht Indian foh playing monkey-chaser?" Banjo asked.

"Hi, nigger, what you come picking me up for? I thought you said you was *français!*"

"That's a white man's story," was Goosey's comment.

"I don't care a black damn whose it is, It's a fine story," said Ray.

"I'll tell you a real man story, pardner," said Banjo, "that ain't no monkey-coon affair."

"Shoot," said Ray.

Banjo said: "It's about a cracker that I runned into in Paree when I was in the Kenadian army and I was there on leave. He runned into me in a café on the Grands Boulevards. He looked mah uniform ovah, and although he seed what it was he asked me what I was, and I said, 'Kenadian soldier.'

"He ups and asks me ef I would have a drink and I did. And then he invited me ef I didn't feel any personal objection to take a turn round gay Paree with him. I told that cracker that I was nevah yet objectionable to a good thing. Man, he was a money cracker as sure as gold ain't no darky's color, and he was no emancipated Yankee but a way-back-down-home-in-Dixie peck. That baby took me into the swellest cafés in Paree and wouldn't order nothing but the dearest drinks. And when we had drink and drunk and was one sure-enough pair a drinking fools, he said to me says he: 'Bud, we'll stick the whole day and night out together and if we c'n find any place in this damn city of the frogs that won't serve you-all, we'll wreck it together and I'll pay the damages and give you a thousand-franc note.'"

"The ole bugger! He said that?" cried Goosey.

"He said nothing else, believe me."

Banjo continued: "That young cracker was jest lousy with money. When he started to pay the first drinks he pulled out on me a wad of dollars as thick as a deck a cards. He shoved it back in his pocket as if he had done made a mistake and pulled out a pocketful a French bills. All high ones:—fifty, hundred, five hundred, thousand. Well, fellahs, we went to the swellest part a Paree to eat, a place called Chaunsly. And we went into a restaurant where only dooks and lawds and high sasiety guys ate. There was a man let us in all dressed up like the Prince of Wales on parade——"

"You nevah saw no Prince a Wales, nigger," Bugsy cut in.

"Yes, I did, too. He reviewed our regiment two times. All the soldiers them was crazy about him."

"And what does he look like?" asked Bugsy.

"Looks like—the Prince of Wales—why, he's A number one—a sweet potato in the skin."

"Ise traveled as much as you, Banjo, but you done seen a tall lot a high life that I only know in pictures," said Malty in a tone of admiration.

Banjo carried on: "We had six mens all dressed up in mourning like white gen'men going to a ball to wait on us. Man! I ain't nevah seen no feed spread like that 'cep'n' when I was working on a millionare yacht. And after we ate we jumped into an atmobile for Montmartre. And we sure did do Montmartre some:—Paradese, Tabarin, Cha'noir, Mohlang Rouge. And in every one a them there was darkies with ofays. But that cracker was game. In every bar we went in he treated every darky that would have a drink on him.

"We finished up the night in one a the swellest pulluluxe joints in Paree. Man! I had everything befoh and ovah me. It was just like it had been in all them other places. They was all foh me. And that young cracker wouldn't miss a thing——"

"No!" Bugsy was pop-eyed.

"Not a thing, I tell you."

Banjo went on: "He was one thoroughmost-going baby, and jest so nice and nacheral about it as you makem. I tell you straight that if the Mason and Dixie line and that pale skin didn't deevide us, I wouldn't want a better pal to travel around with. I tell you again he didn't miss anything that was paid for and there wasn't anybody else paying but him for everything that was had. Yessah, we-all flopped together, I ain't telling you no lie, either, and imagine what you want to, but there wasn't no moh than one baid, neither. And befoh he left the next morning he hand me a thousand-franc note and he asted me who I think was the greatest people in the wul'. And I answered back I think it was the French. And he said no they wasn't, that niggers was the greatest people ——"

"Did he say *niggers?*" cried Goosey.

"I should *say* not. He said 'colored people.' "

"Well, I wish you would all learn to say 'colored' and 'Negroes' and drop 'darky' and 'niggers,' " said Goosey. "If we don't respect ourselves as a race we can't expect white people to respect us."

"It's all right among ourselves," said Banjo.

"No, it isn't. We got to drop those slavery names among ourselves, too."

Banjo began whistling "Shake That Thing." Abruptly he stopped and turned to Ray. "What do you say about *my* story for a big write-up, pardner?"

"First-rate."

"All right, then. Go to it and usem all you want."

"I've got a personal-experience one, too," said Ray, "not nearly as rich as yours, but I'll tell it if you fellows want to hear." They did.

Ray said: "I was in Paris myself about three or four years after Banjo's time, I guess. And it was just the same kind of hand-to-mouth business living there as here. I used to hang around the bohemian quarter where there were many English and American joy-birds and bohemian high-brows talking art and books.

"My own inclination was for the less cosmopolitan parts of the city. But I was broke. And Americans are the most generous people in the world when they are out on a tipsy holiday. All you fellows know that and that some of them will do things for you abroad that they could dare not do at home."

"That's the truth said," said Banjo. "A nigger can often bum a raise out of a pierson from Dixie because he'd be ashame' for a nigger to think he ain't got nothing."

"Well," continued Ray, "I picked up a little change among the Americans and got invited to some swell feeding. But that didn't happen every day. Sometimes my temper turned suddenly bilious and I wouldn't accept an invitation to eat, because I couldn't enjoy the food with the party that was paying for it. I remember one day I forced myself against my feelings and nearly puked in a high-class eating-joint. Then sometimes I would put in a half a day boozing with a jolly gang of good fellows and expecting to be asked for a feed. And they'd all ease off at the end and ignore me. Some bohemians are like that, you know. But you all know it, too. They'll drink up a fortune with you, but they won't buy you a meal, and if you ask them for one they'll turn you down as a panhandler, no good for bohemian company.

"With all a that and my kind of temperament, I knew that Paris was no business for me unless I could find a job. One of the Latin-American artists was my friend and he got me a job to pose. It wasn't so easy to find black bodies for that in Paris. I was to pose at a school where there were many English and American students, mostly females. I had to pose in a very interesting tableau—standing naked on a little platform with a stout long staff in my hand and a pretty Parisienne in the nude crouched at the base.

"The woman who owned the studio was a Nordic of Scandinavia. The artist by whom I was recommended said that she was worried about engaging me, because there were many *Américaines* in the class. They were the best-paying students, and, as I belonged to a savage race, she didn't know if I could behave.

"My artist vouched for me. And so I went to work, putting myself rigidly on good behaviour. Everything went along as nice as pie. Personally I felt no temptation to prevent me from being the best-behaving person in the studio. All the students, strong and fair, came and measured me all over to get the right perspective, not hesitating to touch me when they wanted to place me in a better light or position.

"The posing went along famously. Soon the students began making polite conversation with me. They were all fierce moderns. Some of them asked if I had seen the African Negro sculptures. I said yes and that I liked them. They wanted to know what quality I liked in them. I told them that what moved me most about the African sculpture was the feeling of perfect self-mastery and quiet self-assurance that they gave. They seemed interested in what I had to say and talked a lot about primitive simplicity and color and 'significant form' from Cezanne to Picasso. Their naked savage was quickly getting on to civilized things. . . . I got extra appointments for private posing, which paid better than the school. . . .

"Then one beautiful day I forgot students and art and all in the middle of my pose, and was lost away back in Harlem, right there at the Sheba Palace, in a sea of forms of such warmth and color that never was seen in any Paris studio. And—good night! My staff went clattering to the floor and it was refuge for me."

"What happened?" demanded Banjo.

"Nothing. . . . But I decided that only the other sex was qualified for posing in the nude."

While Ray was talking, two white beach fellows entered the café.

"Hello, there!" cried Ginger. "Which one a the bum broad youse running away from now?"

"None a them this time, me man," replied the smaller of the two, going to shake hands with Ginger. He was a young fellow with a mischievous boyish face and a bush of black hair all tousled. He had on an old and well-frayed seaweed-green jersey and a pair of once-black pants, now burned red by the sun, eaten up in the bottom and creased a thousand ways. He was of the breed of white vagabonds that prefer the company of black men and are apt to go native in tropical lands. He had a frank, free manner of approach that made the black boys accept him without any reserve. He had chummed with Ginger the summer before on the beach, and had disappeared sometime during the winter.

"Then where was you all this time? In jail?" Ginger asked.

"You guessed it first shot," said the white, "only it wasn't in this damned frog hole. Was over there," he jerked his thumb toward the boy, "in Africa—Algeria."

"In the A-rabs country?" said Ginger. "How did you likem?"

"Not me," the Irish fellow brought his palms up as a sign of disapproval. "Them babies over there ain't noways like you-all. Be Christ, they ain't got no religion and won't ever have any, it seems to me, so long as they believe that Mohammed is the law and that Jesus ain't born yet, and that some day he's going to be born, if ever he is, of a white man. Oh, Lord! if I didn't have a hell of a time in that country. I stowed away over there, thinking I'd meet up with fellows like you-all, and I found there nothing but red ones that wasn't human at all. And then I landed in prison and the white ones was worse. They wouldn't even give me water to drink. I was burning up all inside and I felt like I'd catch fire and blaze, for I'd been drinking hard. For two days I never had a drop of water. I cried and begged to see the chief warden, and when he did come at last and I begged him for water, he spit in my face."

"Good God!" exclaimed Ray.

"Yes, be Christ he did!" said the Irish boy, "and he

wasn't no A-rab, neither; he was a white man. I'll never make another beach in any of the frogs' country again."

"French or English, they are all the same under this system," said the other white. He was English. His clothes were good. He was returning from Piræus, where he had been paid off from a Greek ship and was now being repatriated home. His home-going thoughts were not happy. He had been an out-of-work before joining the foreign ship and was probably returning to join that army. He was for the left in politics and had been in jail for extremist agitation.

"I was beaten up in the fice at Pentonville Prison," he said. "There's little difference anywhere under the system."

"I could better stand up to the Englishman's fist in me face than the Frenchman's spit in me face," said the Irish lad. "It's better to taste me own blood in me mouth than another man's spit."

XI. Everybody Doing It

RAY had put on his carefully-tended suit for special occasions to go to an agency on the Canebière, the great Main Street of Marseilles. The broad short stretch of thoroughfare was in gala dress, just as crazy as could be.

A Dollar Line boat, and a British ship from the Far East, had come into port that morning and their passengers had swelled the human stream of the ever-overflowing Canebière. Conspicuous on the pavement before a tourist agency of international fame, a bloated, livid-skinned Egyptian solicited all the male tourists that passed by.

"Gu-ide, gentlemen? Will you have a gu-ide?" he insinuated in a tone of the color of mustard and the smell of Camembert. "Show you all the sights of Marseilles. Hot stuff in the quarter. Tableaux vivants and blue cinema."

Other guides were working the crowd, Spanish, French, Italian, Greek—an international gang of them, but none so outstanding as this oleaginous mass out of Egypt with his heavy, eunuch-like face with its drooping fish eyes that seemed unable to look up straight at anything.

There were a number of touring cars filled with sightseers. Cocottes, gigolos, touts, sailors, soldiers everywhere. The cocottes passed in pairs and singly, attractive in their striking frocks and fancy shoes. The Arab-black girl in orange went by arm in arm with a white girl wearing rose. They smiled at Ray, standing on the corner.

Brazenly the gigolos made their signs for the delectation of the tourists. Such signs as monkeys in the zoo delight in when women, fascinated, are watching them.

Two gentlemen in golf clothes, very English-looking and smoking cigarettes, were spending a long time before a shop window, apparently absorbed in a plaster-of-Paris advertisement of a little dog with its nozzle to a funnel. It was a reproduction of the popular American painting that assails the eye in all the shopping centers of the world; under it was the legend: *La voix de son Maître.* The gentlemen were intent on it. A short distance from them were two sailors with large crimson pommels on their jauntily fixed caps, extra-fine blue capes, and their hands thrust deep in their pockets. Glancing furtively at the gentlemen, who were tongue-licking their lips in a curious, gentlemanly way, one of the sailors approached with a convenient cigarette butt. As they were exchanging lights, two passing cocottes bounced purposely into them and kept going, hip-shimmying and smirking, looking behind. . . . Nothing doing.

A small party of English shouldered Ray against the corner, talking animatedly in that overdone accent they call the Oxford. Ray remarked again, as he often had before, how the pronunciation of some of the words, like "there" "here" and "where," was similar to that of the Southern Negro.

Two policemen were standing near and as the party passed one of them spat and said, "Les sale Anglais." Ray started and, looking from the policeman who had spewed out his salival declaration of contempt to the English group crossing the street, he grinned. Just the evening before (he had read in the morning newspaper) an

Englishwoman and her escort were nearly lynched by a theater crowd. Police intervened to save them. The woman had tried to push her way too hastily through the crowd *while talking English.* Commenting on it, the local paper had said such incidents would not happen if the post-war policy of the Anglo-Saxons were not to treat France as if she were a colony.

In Paris and elsewhere tourists were having a hot time of it. The franc was tobogganing and the Anglo-Saxon nations, according to the French press, were responsible for that as well. The panic in the air had reached even Marseilles, the most international place in the country. Up till yesterday these very journals had been doping the unthinking literate mob with pages of peace talk. Today they were feeding the same hordes with war. And to judge from the excitement in the air the mob was as ready for it as the two white apes of policemen standing on the corner.

Ray grinned again, showing all his teeth, and a girl across the street, thinking it was for her, smiled at him. But he was grinning at the civilized world of nations, all keeping their tiger's claws sharp and strong under the thin cloak of international amity and awaiting the first favorable opportunity to spring. During his passage through Europe it had been an illuminating experience for him to come in contact with the mind of the average white man. A few words would usually take him to the center of a guarded, ancient treasure of national hates.

In conversation he sometimes posed as British, sometimes as American, depending upon his audience. There was no posing necessary with the average Frenchman because he takes it without question that a black man under French civilization is better off than he would be under any other social order in the world. Sometimes, on meeting a French West Indian, Ray would say he was American, and the other, like his white compatriot, could not resist the temptation to be patronizing.

"We will treat you right over here! It's not like America."

Yet often when he was in public with one of these black *élites* who could speak a little English, Ray would be asked to speak English instead of French. Upon demanding why, the answer would invariably be, "Because they will treat us better and not as if we were Senegalese."

Ray had undergone a decided change since he had left America. He enjoyed his rôle of a wandering black without patriotic or family ties. He loved to pose as this or that without really being any definite thing at all. It was amusing. Sometimes the experience of being patronized provided food for thoughtful digestion. Sometimes it was very embarrassing and deprived an emotion of its significance.

Nevertheless, he was not unaware that his position as a black boy looking on the civilized scene was a unique one. He was having a good grinning time of it. Italians against French, French against Anglo-Saxons, English against Germans, the great *Daily Mail* shrieking like a mad virago that there were still Germans left who were able to swill champagne in Italy when deserving English gentlemen could not afford to replenish their cellars. . . . Oh it was a great civilization indeed, too entertaining for any savage ever to have the feeling of boredom.

The evening before, an American acquaintance had remarked to Ray that when he had come to Europe he had cut loose from all the back-home strings and had come wanting to *love* it. But Europe had taught him to be *patriotic;* it had taught him that he was an American.

He was a jolly nice fellow with French blood from his mother's line, and after two years of amusing himself in the European scene he was returning to America to settle down to the business of marriage. Ray could see what he was trying to express, but he could not feel it. First, because he had never yet indulged in any illusions about any species of the civilized mammal, and second, because his was not a nature that would let his appetite for the fruit of life be spoiled by the finding of a worm at the core of one apple or more.

The sentiment of patriotism was not one of Ray's possessions, perhaps because he was a child of deracinated ancestry. To him it was a poisonous seed that had, of course, been planted in his child's mind, but happily, not having any traditional soil to nourish it, it had died out with other weeds of the curricula of education in the light of mature thought.

It seemed a most unnatural thing to him for a man to love a nation—a swarming hive of human beings bartering, competing, exploiting, lying, cheating, battling, suppressing, and killing among themselves; possessing, too, the faculty to organize their villainous rivalries into a monstrous system for plundering weaker peoples.

Man loves individuals. Man loves things. Man loves places. And the vagabond lover of life finds individuals and things to love in many places and not in any one nation. Man loves places and no one place, for the earth, like a beautiful wanton, puts on a new dress to fascinate him wherever he may go. A patriot loves not his nation, but the spiritual meannesses of his life of which he has created a frontier wall to hide the beauty of other horizons.

So . . . Ray had fallen into one of his frequent fits of contemplation there on the corner, alone with his mind and the traffic of life surging around him, when he was tapped on the shoulder and addressed by the smaller Britisher of Taloufa's shirt-tail night.

Ray had learned more about the two friends since that entertaining night. The colonial was a careless, roving sort of fellow, ever ready for anything with a touch of novelty that was suggested to him. Yet he seemed to be devoid of any capacity for real enjoyment or deep distaste. He apparently existed for mere unexciting drifting, a purposeless, live-for-the-moment, negative person.

The initiative of planning for both of them rested with his friend, who was English-born. Both had been in the war. The Englishman had a small face with a tight expression. His lips were remarkably thin and compressed, and they twitched, but so imperceptibly that a casual observer would not notice it. He had not been wounded, but had been a prisoner and the experience had left him a little neurotic, and probably more interesting. He liked jazz music, and he liked to hear Negroes play it.

The pair had told Ray that they were just bums. He would not believe it, thinking that they were well-to-do poseurs plumbing low-down bohemian life. But they soon convinced him that it was true. Quite young, they had been called for service during the last year of the war, and, now that it was over, they either could not find a permanent interest in life or could not bring themselves to settle down. Whatever it was, they were gentlemen panhandlers. They had bummed all over continental Europe—Naples, Genoa, Barcelona, Bordeaux, Antwerp, Hamburg, Berlin, and Paris.

Since the night when Banjo had played for them they

had gone over to Toulon to meet a ship coming from Australia, and had cleaned up twenty pounds panhandling and showing passengers through the bordel quarter of that interesting town of matelots.

Strangely, they preferred the great commercial ports and cities to the popular tourist resorts. They were not interested in crooked games. Like the beach boys, they were honest bums.

Ray admired the Britisher's well-fitting clothes.

"It's the only way to get the jack," he said. "Wear good clothes and speak like a gentleman. They'll give you either a real raise or nothing at all, but they won't treat you like a beggar. The Americans are pretty good. And you can tap an Englishman abroad, if you take him the right way, when you couldn't at home."

At that moment a big beefy Englishman went by and Ray's friend said: "Just a minute. I'm going to get him."

He caught up with the man on the opposite corner. The tourist was visibly embarrassed as his compatriot solicited him, and, rather avoiding looking in his face, he handed out a five-franc note. The proffered money hung suspended in air, the gentleman panhandler, not deigning to take it, coldly pressing his need of a more substantial amount. Something he said made the big man turn all puffy red in the face, and glancing hastily at the younger man from head to foot, he took from his pocketbook a pound note and handed it to him. The young man took it and thanked him in a politely reserved manner.

Rejoining Ray, he vented his scorn: "The big bastard. Tried to give *me* five francs." His funny slit of a lip twitched nervously. "Come and have a drink with me," he said.

They turned down the Canebière. An old tune was ringing in Ray's head.

"Everybody's Doing It. . . ."

It was the song-and-dance that had tickled him so wonderfully that first year he had landed in America. Talk about "Charleston" and "Black Bottom!" They're all right for exercise, but for a jazzing jig, when a black boy and a gal can get right up together and do that rowdy thing, "Charlestons" and "Black Bottoms" are a long way behind the "Turkey Trot." . . .

Great big dancing-hall over the grocery store in the barracks town. Day laborers, porters, black students, black soldiers, brown sporting-girls swaying and reeling so close together, turkey-trotting, bunny-hugging, bear-and-dog walking "That Thing" and the delirious black boys singing and playing:

"Everybody's doing it. . . .
Everybody's doing it now. . . ."

Ray and the Britisher took a table on a café terrace at the corner of the Rue de la République and the Quai du Port. Down the Canebière the traffic bore like a flooded river to pile up against the bar of the immense horseshoe (on which rested the weight of the city) and flow out on either side of it.

The scene was a gay confusion—peddlers with gaudy bagatelles; Greek and Armenian venders of cacahuettes and buns; fishermen crying shell-fish; idling boys in proletarian blue wearing vivid cache-col and caps; long-armed Senegalese soldiers in khaki, some wearing the red fez; zouaves in striking Arab costumes; surreptitious sou gamblers with their dice stands; a strong mutilated man in tights stunting; excursion boats with tinted signs and pennants rocking thick against each other at the moorings—everything massed pell-mell together in a great gorgeous bowl.

A waiter brought them two large cool glasses of orangeade. While they were enjoying it one of the many sidewalk-feature girls stopped by their table with a little word for the Englishman.

"Fiche-moi la paix!" he shot at her.

The girl shrugged and went off, working her hips.

"Bloody wench! Because I was with her last night she tries to get familiar now. She wouldn't dare do it in London."

"Don't say!" said Ray. "Why, back home in America we lift our hats to such as exist."

"That's one reason why I don't like democracies."

"Is that how you feel about them?" Ray chuckled. "I can't go with you. Ordinarily I would like to treat those girls like anybody else, but they won't let you. They are too class-conscious."

After the cocotte came Banjo.

"Hello!" said Ray. "How's the plugging?"

"Fine and dandy, pardner. I got the whole wul' going my way. Look at me!"

"Perfection, kid."

Banjo was in wonderful form in his cocoa-colored Provençal suit, the steel-gray Australian felt hat he had bought in Sydney, the yellow scarf hanging down his front, and full-square up-at-the-heel. Banjo had struck it right again.

The blues had bitten Taloufa badly after his praiseworthy little affair of race conservation had turned out so disastrously and he had left soon after for England. But before he went Banjo had persuaded him to redeem his suit from the Mont de Piété and had "borrowed" a little cash from him until they should meet again—an eventuality that was taken as a matter of course in the beach boys' and seamen's life.

"Sit down and have a drink," said the white.

"Time is in a hurry with me now, chief," replied Banjo. "I'm going down to the Dollar Line pier. Theah's a boat in. What about you, pardner? Going? I been looking foh you. The fellahs am waiting foh me down at Joliette."

"Sure thing I'll go," said Ray. "Want to come?" he asked his white friend.

"No. It's too far. It's the farthest dock down. Have a drink with us, Banjo, before you go. Let's go to the little café in that side street up there. They'll serve us quicker at the bar."

The three of them entered the café hurriedly, talking. They had three glasses of *vin blanc*. The Englishman paid with a five-franc note. When he received his change he told the barwoman that it was not right.

"Comment?" she asked.

"Comment? Because day before yesterday here I paid five sous less for a glass of *vin blanc*. And I know the price hasn't gone up since."

"The pound and the dollar have, though," Ray grinned.

"Maybe, but I'm not going to pay for banditry in high places."

"It's always we who pay heaviest for that," said Ray.

"We?"

"Yes, we the poor, the vagabonds, the bums of life. You said you were one; that's why I say we."

The woman made the change right, saying that she had been mistaken, and the boys left the bar.

"Them's all sou-crazy, these folkses," said Banjo.

"It's a cheap trick," said the Briton. "I didn't care about the few sous, but it was the principle of the thing."

"You English certainly love to play with that word 'principle,'" said Ray.

The white laughed slightly, reddening around the ears. "These people make you pay *à l'Anglaise* every time they hear you talk English," he said. "I don't like to be always paying for that. It's irritating. And I irritate them, too, in revenge, letting them know they are cheating. Maybe one cause of it is that these little businesses are always changing hands. About a year ago I was in a little bar behind the Bourse. Six months later I saw the proprietor at Toulon, where he had bought another bar, and the other day I saw him at Nice, where he had just taken over a third after selling out at Toulon. I prefer going to an honest bourgeois brasserie. And even then you've got to look out for the waiters if they think you're a greenhorn. Just yesterday one of them brought my friend change for a fifty after he had given him a hundred-franc note. My friend doesn't speak French, and when I called the bluff he had it all ready for me right on the tip of his tongue like that bistro woman: 'Pardon. I've made a mistake!'"

Curiously, the song kept singing in Ray's head:

> "Everybody's doing it,
> Everybody's doing it. . . ."

"I get along with the little bistros, all right," said Ray. "They take me for Senegalese and treat me right. But whenever I'm with fellows speaking English they've got to pay for it just like you. I never make any trouble when the others pay, especially American fellows. They don't know, the price is ridiculously cheap to *them,* coming from a dry country. But when *I've* got to pay for it, I kick like hell. I'll be damned if I'm going to be a sucker for these hoggish *petits commerçants.* I know it's the dollar complex these people have that makes them like that, but I'm no dollar baby. I don't ever see enough francs, much less dollars. And they can get bloody insulting sometimes when you call their hand. For instance, I found out the woman who did my laundry was overcharging Banjo and the boys whenever they could afford to have their clothes done. The next time they were getting their laundry I went with them to straighten it out, and she got mad and shouted, 'Dollah, dollah,' and refused to do any more for us. What the hell do we boys know about dollars?"

"The only time they'll lose anything is when they do it to insult you," said the white. "They lose more than they gain by such pettiness. Some months ago we picked up a couple of toffs and they took us for a spree down the coast. We stayed a little time in Antibes. One night my friend telephoned me from a café in the square and the proprietor himself told the waiter to charge him two francs. He happened to mention it and I knew the cost was half a franc. The next morning I went and asked the fat old thing why he had overcharged my friend. He tried to make out that it was a double call, which wasn't true, of course, and would only have amounted to a franc in any case. I left it like that. It was enough for me to see the proprietor in an embarrassing position. I get a devilish lot of fun out of them and their sous. And that's why I am always correcting their subtraction and addition. But of course we never went back to *that* café while we stayed in Antibes."

"I wish they wouldn't figure against us poor black boys when *we* speak English," said Ray. "The trouble is you Europeans make no color distinction—when it is a matter of the color of our money."

"You mean the French," said the young man, his

Anglo-Saxon pride suddenly bursting forth. "You don't find anybody in England playing such penny tricks."

"Oh, well, you've got a different method, that's all," said Ray. "I've got a very definite opinion about it all. When I was in England I always felt myself in an atmosphere of grim, long-headed honesty—honesty because it was the best business policy in the long run. You felt it was a little hard on the English soul. It made it as bleak as a London fog and you felt it was an atmosphere that could chill to the bone anybody who didn't have a secure living. I wouldn't want to be broke and be on the bum there for a day, and you wouldn't, either, I guess."

"You bet I wouldn't," the young man laughed, "judging by where I am now."

"In America it's different," Ray continued. "I didn't sense any soul-destroying honesty there. What I felt was an awful big efficiency sweeping all over me. You felt that business in its mad race didn't have time to worry about honesty, and if you thought about honesty at all it was only as a technical thing, like advertising, to help efficiency forward. If you were to go to New York and shop in the popular districts, then do Delancey Street and the Bowery afterward, you'd get what I mean. Down in those tedious-bargain streets, you feel that you are in Europe on the shores of the Mediterranean again, and that their business has nothing to do with the great steam-rolling efficiency of America.

"But in Germany I felt something quite different from anything that impressed me in other white countries. I felt a real terrible honesty that you might call moral or religious or national. It seemed like something highly organized, patriotic, rooted in the soul—not a simple, natural, instinctive thing. And with it I felt a confident blind bluntness in the people's character that was as hard and obvious as a stone wall. I was there when the mark had busted like a bomb in the sky and you could pick up worthless paper marks thrown away in the street. There were exchange booths all over Berlin—some of them newly set up in the street. I saw Americans as heedless as a brass band, lined up to change their dollars in face of misery that was naked to the eye at every step. Yet I never felt any overt hostility to strangers there as I do here.

"When I was going there the French black troops were in the Ruhr. A big campaign of propaganda was on against them, backed by German-Americans, Negro-breaking Southerners, and your English liberals and Socialists. The odd thing about that propaganda was that it said nothing about the exploitation of primitive and ignorant black conscripts to do the dirty work of one victorious civilization over another, but it was all about the sexuality of Negroes—that strange, big bug forever buzzing in the imagination of white people. Friendly whites tried to dissuade me from going to Germany at that time, but I was determined to go.

"And I must tell you frankly I never met any white people so courteous in all my life. I traveled all over Prussia, from Hamburg to Berlin, Potsdam, Stettin, Dresden, Leipzig, and I never met with any discourtesy, not to mention hostility. Maybe it was there underneath the surface, but I never felt it. I went to the big cafés and cabarets in the Friederickstrasse, Potsdammer Platz, and Charlottenburg, and I had a perfectly good time. I went everywhere. I've never felt so safe in the low quarters of any city as I have in those of Berlin and Hamburg. One day I went to buy some shirts after noting the prices marked in the shop window. When the clerk gave me the check it was more than the price marked, so I protested. He called the manager and he was so apologetic I felt confused. 'It's not my fault,' he said, 'but the law. All strangers must pay ten per cent more.' And he turned red as if he were ashamed of the law. Yet I never liked Germany. It was a country too highly organized for my temperament. I felt something American about it, but without the dynamic confusion of America."

They had reached Joliette, where the Britisher said he must turn back.

"Come on, let's have a look at the Dollar boat," said Ray.

"No. I have an important engagement with my friend."

XII. Bugsy's Chinese Pie

"WHAT'S his gag, pardner?" asked Banjo.

"He's a regular guy. I just got a hundred francs outa him."

"How come? Why didn't you put me next, too? Is he rough-trade business?"

"Oh no! They're bums just like us—he and his friend. You know I don't pal around with rough-trade business, though I appreciate them."

"Youse one nuts of a black beggar, pardner. But wha'd'y'u mean bums like we is? You ain't telling me they ain't sitting on a independent bank roll?"

"No, they ain't. They're dickey bums, just panhandling through life like us, without any ambition for a steady job. But they only bum the swells. The one that just left us pulls the gentleman stuff, and his partner hands them the raw colonial brass. It's the gentleman stuff that does the best business, however."

"Gawd-an-his-chilluns! What a wul'! But how they make it, all dressed up fine and dandy like that?"

"Why, Banjo, you stiff poker! That's the best way to bum among swell people. The sprucer you are and the slicker your tongue, the surer your chances. Why, those fellows make a thousand francs when we can only make five. When one of those fellows bums a tourist, he'll feel ashamed if he can't hand him a fifty or a hundred franc note, the same way you and I feel ashamed when a bum singer does his stuff in a bistro and we haven't got a copper to put in the hat. Well, it was a lucky thing I bumped into him and got this hundred francs. I was jim-clean. Went up to the agency expecting a little dough from the States, but I didn't get a cent. I would have had to spend tomorrow in coal or grain."

"No, you wouldn't, either, pardner. I got me two hundred francs."

"And your suit out, too! How'd you makem?"

"Ways a doing it, pardner. Even you' bestest friend you can't let in on *ehvery* thing you do. Whenevah time youse jim-clean, though, don't go making you'self blacker than you is working in the white man's coal. Jest tell you' pardner how you is fixed. I guess I c'n handle that coal better'n you kain."

"But you don't have to, mah boy. You've got your banjo to work for you."

"And youse got you' pen. I want you to finish that theah story you was telling about and read it to me. I think you'll make a good thing of it. Ise a nigger with a long haid on me. I ain't dumb like that bumpitter Goosey. I seen many somethings in mah life. Little things getting there and biggity things not getting anywhere. I done seen the wul' setting in all pohsitions, haidways, sideways, horseways, backways, all ways. Ef I had some real dough I'd put it on you so you could have time to make good on that theah writing business."

They did not find the other boys in the Joliette Square. They looked for them in the cafés of the place and spied them at last in a side street before a hotel restaurant where stranded sailors were always housed by the American consulate. Malty, Bugsy, Ginger, Goosey, Dengel, and the little Irish fellow. They formed a semi-circle around a woman of average size.

It was a Negro woman, Banjo and Ray found, when they got up to them. She was brown like oak, and was wearing a nigger-brown skirt and a black blouse with white cuffs and collar, to which was attached a broad white tongue, and in her hand she held a Bible. She had that week arrived directly from New York and she was telling the boys about it.

"I got a message fwom the Lawd. He dreamed me in a vision and said, 'Take up you' Bible and hymn-book and go. Go far and fureign to a place fohgot of Gawd whar theah's many black folks and white folkses all homeward bound for hell.' And I told that message to the sistahs and brotherin of mah chierch and we-all of us prayed ag'in, and that prayer was answered foh me to git ready and come along to this heah Marcelles, and heah I is."

She showed Ray her American passport, in perfect order, visaed by the French consul in New York. "But did you know anything about Marseilles before?" he asked, feeling uneasy under her strange, holy-rolling eyes.

"Nosah, not a thing until the Lawd him dreamed me. And oh-h-h, how right it was! Oh-h-h, how right it was!" She clasped her hands and looked ecstatically to heaven. The boys glanced uncomfortably at one another and round about them. Was she going to throw that holy stuff right there?

"The Lawd dreamed me to come and warn yo'-all. I know why all you young niggers jest loves it so around heah without thinking a you' souls' salvation. I done seen it all the fust day I landed, mah chilluns. H-m-m-m-m! What a life! I ain't blind, and ef I didn't close mah eyes against sich a grand parade of sinfulness as I nevah seen befoh, it was because the Lawd done whisper to me: 'Keep you' eyes wide open, Sistah Geter, so you c'n see it all, and don't miss anything that'll make mah message the stronger.' "

No printed word could record the voluptuous sound

of Sister Geter's "H-m-m-m-m!" Banjo asked her how she had located Joliette and the Seamen's Hotel, and she said the American consul had arranged it.

"The consul him send you heah foh preaching!" Banjo exclaimed.

"He done puts me heah foh bohd and lodging. He didn't put me heah foh no preaching, for them's jest as ungodly up theah in need a saving as yo'-all is down heah. I went straight up theah as I landed and jest' lay mah Bible down on the desk befoh that high and mighty white man, and I told him that the Mightiest One had done send me on this jierny for to preach the gospel word.

"And he done started in to tell me that I'd had to go right on back home by the fust boat sailing, for Marcelles was no place for me. And don't ask me ef I didn't done get him told jest as Jesus wanted me to. I told him how he was in need a saving jest like anybody else, and that he was nothing more than a sinner, and that no pohsition wouldn't nary save him even ef he was our own President hisself and not jest standing heah foh him same as the President is standing foh Gawd and our country.

"Yessah chilluns, I done gived him his share of the message same as yo'-all gwina git yours, foh Gawd is no respecter of high pohsitions, and befoh I done finish got him told I seen that the spirit had laid strong hands on him, for he was looking at mah papers and a counting mah money and gitting a man to come and fix me up heah whar I is."

"But, ma," said Ray, "if you've really come on salvation business, down here is too righteous for you. You should go up to the Bum Square where the world hangs out."

"Sure. That's the place. Tha's the hell where all

them li'l' ofay devils am monkeying, ma," Banjo declared in a rollicking, rakish accent.

"I'm scared they might grab me," Sister Geter replied, inclining her head on her shoulder in a slightly suggestive way of worldliness, while a smile centering on her full brown nose brightened her features, and just for a moment she seemed flirtatious. Just for a moment, but it did not escape the prehensile sense of Banjo, who quickly nudged Ray behind and winked. But just as quickly also did Sister Geter become her missionary self again.

"Did you leavem all a you' money up theah at the consulate, ma?" Ginger asked.

"Why, no. I done change a few dollars in them heah French francs to carry me along for a little while."

"You know, ma," said Ginger again, "wese all good boys. We all loves Big Massa Gawd and ain't doing anything wicked, but wese jest stranded heah; can't get a broa—a boat; and wese always hard up and hungry, so ef you c'n hulp us out a li'l' bit with a li'l' money fust——"

"Oh *La-a-a-awd!* Save you' poah chilluns Lawd, Lawd! Save them fwom sarving the devil and drifting to hell so far away from home, Lawd!"

Sister Geter had thrown the holy stuff, gagging Ginger before he could finish, and was performing on the pavement just as if she were back home in a Protestant revival state. She brought a crowd of French folk running up in no time. Shop-keepers, restaurateurs, bar people, chauffeurs, seamen, dockers, girls, and touts—the colorful miscellany that makes the Place de la Joliette always a place of warm interest. And following the crowd, four policemen from the square were precipitating themselves toward the scene. The beach boys fled.

There were piles upon piles of boxes on the pier, and dozens of dockers were wheeling them across planks into the hold of the ship. Taxicabs dashed in with passengers, taxicabs dashed out, and taxicabs were waiting. Private detectives stood talking with port police, and black, brown, and white guides were buzzing about. White beach fellows prowled up and down in their smelly rags, looking up to the decks like hungry dogs. The black fellows, less forward, stood a little way off. Two white American sailors in sports clothes were conversing with a ship's officer. One of them had been in hospital, the other had missed his ship, and both of them were being put up by the consulate against repatriation.

It was a splendid pattern of a ship, a much more impressive thing in its bigness than the memory of the President after whom it was named. Its world-touring passengers crowded the decks tier upon tier. There were elderly people who seemed not to be enjoying the trip, but there were many others, young men and women who were bubbling over with high spirits.

Over above them all, poised high up on the funnel of the great liner, was the brazen white sign of the dollar. It was some dockers pausing, pointing and spitting at it, that drew Ray's attention as he stood at one side with his companions. And immediately, too, a reaction of disgust was registered in him. He could understand the men's gesture and apprehend why that mighty $ stood out like a red challenge in the face of the obstreperous French bull.

Even though the name of the man who bossed the line was Dollar, thought Ray, it was at least bad taste for him to be sending that sign touring round the world in this new era of world finance. An idea flashed upon Ray, and for a moment he wondered if he could capitalize it by patenting a plan of giving the dollar lessons in diplomacy, but it was immediately driven from his mind by the charming voice of a young lady calling from the deck: "Boy! boy!"

She was gesturing toward the black boys, and they all started forward, but Bugsy was ahead of the others. She was a tall fair girl, between brunette and blond, and wore a reddish-gray traveling dress in which she was as striking as a Fifth Avenue shop's cut of a French model.

"Boy," she said, looking down on Bugsy, "are you from Dixie?"

"Yes, miss."

"And the others, too?"

"Yes, miss, wese all Americans."

"Listen at that nigger," Banjo said to Ray, "playing straight for a hand-out."

"I thought yo'-all were American boys," said the girl. "But what yo'-all doing so far away from home?"

"We works on ship, miss," said Bugsy; "we-all waiting on ship now."

"Are yo'-all having a good time while you're waiting?"

"Not so bad, miss, although wese all of us broke all the time."

"Isn't it wonderful!" she said, aloud, yet more to herself. "These cullud boys here just like they were back home! . . . Say, boy, will you get me a paper—an American paper?"

But before Bugsy could say yes, a white South African fellow on the beach had put himself in front of him and offered his services.

"You want a paper, lady? I'll get it and anything you want. I know the town better——"

"She ain't asting you foh nothing. It's me she done ask!" Bugsy was up in the face of the little white, who was just his size, with twitching hands, his knuckles rapping his antagonist's breast.

"Stand off, you bloody kaffir—*nigger!*" said the white.

Bugsy palmed him full in the face. "You want fight? Fight, then."

The South African staggered back a little, steadied himself, and came back at Bugsy. He was game for it. Bugsy ducked the drive to his jaw and closed in. With a swift movement of his right foot he sent the South African down on his back and was down upon him with fist and knee.

"That's not fair fighting; that's not fair," the South African cried.

"Wha's not fair? Ise fighting, tha's what Ise doing," retorted Bugsy.

Some dockers had gathered around, and one of them pulled Bugsy up. The South African, mad with anger, rushed him, but Bugsy stepped aside, and if it had not been for one of the large ropes attaching the ship to the pier, the white boy would have fallen into the water. He came back sparring at Bugsy, who maneuvered a clinch. The South African drove his fist low-down into Bugsy's belly. Bugsy retaliated with a double butt. That broke off the clinch, and suddenly he dove down between the South African's legs and, lifting him by the feet into the air, he sent him away off sprawling on his back. It was nothing less than a miracle that the boy's skull missed the iron pillar on the pier. That ended the fight.

Bugsy looked toward the deck and saw not the fair passenger, but a Chinese cook in native dress of blue pantaloons and yellow jacket, with a large apple pie in his hand. To Bugsy's surprise the Chinaman bared his Oriental teeth, rather dirty, and handed him the pie, patting him all the while on the shoulder:

"Tek pie. Me give. You fight good. Me love to see you fight like that. Tek pie."

The Chinaman patted Bugsy again and hurried back with his quick jerky steps up the gangway, leaving him happy with his American pie, but still rather astonished by the gesture and not in the least understanding what it was all about.

The Irish boy was at Bugsy's elbow. Bugsy turned to him.

"He say I don't fight fair. Nuts! Fighting is fighting. In England when they oncet get you down they kick you all ovah. I didn't even lift mah foot at him."

The Irish boy laughed. "Don't worry about him. Perhaps he had an idea you was putting on a sparring match for the benefit a them tourists."

In the meantime Banjo had superseded Bugsy in the favor of the gracious young lady.

"I'll get that theah paper for you," Banjo said.

"Be sure you get American and not English," she had moved a little down the gangway and pretended not to have seen the fight. She gave Banjo a dollar.

Banjo held the dollar in a tentative, humorous manner and said: "But I gotta go way up yonder uptown to get it, miss, and I'll have to take a taxi, and that alone'll cost a dollar."

"Will it?" Her eyes took in Banjo's strutting elegance in a swift glance. She smiled and said: "Well, here's another dollar for yourself and five francs. You can get the paper with that. It's all the French money I've got. . . . What part of the South you from?" she asked as Banjo reached for the money.

A moment's hesitation, too slight for her to remark, and he said, "Norfolk, miss."

"Norfolk! Why, I'm from Richmond and I know Norfolk very well. What part do you come from? I have relatives there. Do you know the Smith family?"

"Sure, miss. I useta work as a chauffeur foh one a

them. That they one was . . . he was . . . I think he was. . . ."

"Was it Mr. Charlie?"

"Egsactly, miss. I done drove Marse Charlie's car and——"

"Did you never hear him mention his cousins, the Joneses of Richmond?"

"Sure thing, miss. Him and his wife and all a the family was always talking about them Joneses. I knows Richmond mahself, miss. I useta live there on Wellington Street——"

"Now isn't it just too extraordinary for anything to see all you boys from back home here! How do you find it?"

"Tough enough, miss, while wese waiting to get a job on a ship, but sometimes fellahs like oursel's working in our line will hulp us out some when a boat is in, and when it is a big liner like this we hang around for any little job going that a passenger might want done."

"Give me back those two dollars." The girl opened a richly-variegated bead bag and, taking the two dollars from Banjo, she handed him a five-dollar note, saying: "Divide that up among you-all and get me what papers you can with the five francs. Those published in Paris will do, but be sure they're American."

Banjo pulled his hat off and made a fine darky acknowledgment. The fight was finished. The girl, indicating the South African, asked, "Is he American, too?"

"No, miss," replied Banjo, "he's British."

"Oh!" she exclaimed, casually, and went back up on deck among the passengers, who had also followed the fight with neutral amusement.

On the l'Estaque road Banjo caught a tramcar going to Joliette. He boarded it and, arriving in the square, he bought copies of the Paris editions of the *New York Herald* and the *Chicago Tribune*. He got another tramcar going back toward the pier, and thus eliminated taxicab fare. Five dollars at forty francs apiece to be divided up among us, he mused. That'll give twenty-five francs apiece to mah buddies and fifty for this good-luck darky that done pulled the trick off.

After delivering the papers he caught the tramcar again and stopped off at a café on the Quai d'Arenc, where his pals were waiting for him. The Irish boy was not there. He also had struck something good and had taxied off with a passenger who wanted to be shown the *quartier resérvé*.

The boys had already emptied a few bottles of wine, and Ray had paid for them before Banjo got there.

"Wha' you wanta blow you'self foh?" Banjo demanded. "You know I'm the best plugger of the gang all this week, hitting nothing but bull's-eye pim on the head ehvery time."

He gave the boys twenty-five francs apiece. Dividing up was a beach boys' rite. It didn't matter what share of the spoils the lucky beggar kept for himself, so long as he fortified the spirit of solidarity by sharing some of it with the gang. The boys were hungry, and, besides the general handout, Banjo paid for some food. So much and so quickly did the boys eat, that the *patrone* had to send out for bread. Joined together were two long green tables of sausage and ham sandwiches, bottles of red wine, filled and half-filled glasses.

"Foh making grub palatable," said Malty, "I ain't seen no place equal to this that c'n do so much with a piece of meat and a li'l' vegetable, 'cep'n' it's way home yonder where I was bohn; but ——"

"Don't talk crap about home cooking in them monkey islands," Banjo interrupted. "The onliest thwoat-tickling cooking like French cooking is black folks' cooking back home in Dixie."

"You don't know anything about the West Indies, them, breddah," said Malty. "Mah mudder could cook you a pot a rice and peas seasoned with the lean of corned pork that'd knock anything you got in Dixie stiff cold."

"Chuts! Rice is coolie grub," said Banjo. "I ain't much on it 'cep'n' when I want a change a chop suey. I would give all the rice and peas in the wul' foh one good platter a corn pone and chicken ——"

"Corn pone!" sneered Malty. "Tha's coon feeding ——"

"You said it, then," cried Goosey, "and I wish yo-all would say corn bread instead of corn pone. Corn pone is so niggerish."

"Mah mammy useta call it corn pone," said Banjo, "and tha's good enough foh me."

"I was gwineta say," continued Malty, "that I had moh'n was good foh mah belly a that theah corn pone when I was way down in Charleston and Savannah, and it couldn't hold a candle against our owna banana pone."

"Banana-what-that?" exclaimed Banjo. "You mean banana fritters."

"Not ef I knows it, buddy," Malty laughed. "Banana fritters is made from ripe banana. But I said banana pone, which is made from green banana grated with cocoanut and spice and sugar and baked in banana leaf. I ain't nevah find nothing moh palatable than that in any place in all the wul'. And that is black folks' eating, too. You nevah find it on any buckra table."

"I've eaten it," said Ray. "It sure is great stuff."

"Kuyah!" exclaimed Malty, happy to be backed up, "you eat it in Haiti, too."

"Sure. And I ate it in Jamaica. I was there for two

years when I was a kid. We had a little revolution and the President that was ousted was exiled to Jamaica with his entourage. My father was among them and that was how I happened to go."

"Yo'-all got me ways off what I was a gwineta say at the beginning," said Malty, "and that was that the Frenchies am A number one in the kitchen, but they ain't gotem on the bread."

"I like French bread," said Goosey. "My teeth are good."

"And my own is good, too, yaller," said Malty, "but French bread is no good foh sandwich."

"I don't like French bread, anyhow," said Bugsy. "It's like a rotten pimp up in the Ditch—all crust and no guts to it."

Bugsy's witticism brought a roar of laughter and spurred Banjo to a pronunciamento on the touts of the Ditch.

"What do them poah ofay trash in the Ditch know about doing the stuff in the big-style way it's done back home?" declared Banjo. "Why, them nothing up there can't even bring you a change a suit outa what them gals is giving them! Why, they can't eat a decent meal! But a man who is subsequential to a three-franc throw, says I, ain't got no business to wear a pants. I nevah seen such a lotta mangy p-i in all mah life. A fellah doing that back home gotta show himself a man ehverytime. Him gotta come strutting swell and blowing big. He's gotta show he ain't nobody's ah-ah business. I knowed a fellah named Jerco in Harlem. Hi-eee! but he was one strutting fool. I remember one night I was with some white guys in a buffet flat in Harlem. But they was cheap skates and only buying beer for the house. The madam sent out to find Jerco, and when that nigger blowed in theah them cheap ofays jest woke right up. The piano-player was half asleep. Jerco brushed him one side and made that piano cry a weeping 'blues.' He ordered whisky and he ordered wine. It wasn't no time before he had the whole house going and the ofays coming across the right way. There was a li'l' dog sleeping under a table. Jerco woke him up and told the madam to feed him. And when the dog finished eating he started to dance. And that was how the 'dog-walk' started."

This time the boys' laughter shook the place so hard that it knocked over a bottle which carried a glass to the floor, both of them breaking. The *patrone* called "Attention!" and came from behind the counter to pick the pieces up. Banjo offered to pay, but she refused to let him. She was laughing herself, although she did not understand.

Bugsy's Chinese pie was splendid stuff after the sandwiches. And when the boys finished it, they left the café, going through the docks toward Joliette. It was too late for them to sleep on the breakwater after their feed. So they straggled along, remarking the ships in the docks. There was a new Italian ship, a fine thing, moored where they were building the American-style concrete warehouse.

The boys stopped to admire her and the building. A little farther on they came upon a small pinch-faced white boy with a hunk of bread so hard that he was softening it under a hydrant to be able to eat it.

"Look at that poah kid!" said Banjo. "Starving, and we just done ate moh'n we could finish! Oh, Gawd! what a life! Some stuffing till they're messing up themsel's all ovah, and some drinking cold water to kill pain in the guts. . . . Heah! Come heah, kid!"

"Wachu gwina do? Don't give the white bastard a damn thing!" Bugsy cried.

"Shet you' trap, ugly mug," said Banjo.

The boy saw Banjo beckon, and went to him. He did not understand English. Banjo gave him five francs, and the boy said "Merci" and started toward a little buffet shed near by.

"Youse a bloody sucker, you," said Bugsy. "A white person can always make a handout, where you kain't."

"I don't give a low-down drilling about that," replied Banjo. "The kid was hungry and I done give him a raise. I know more'n you do, perhaps, Bugsy, that being black ain't the same as being white, but— Ain't I right, pardner?"

Banjo not finding words to express exactly what he felt, broke off and appealed to Ray.

"Sure you are. I was going to give the kid something mahself, but you were before me."

"Last week," said Banjo, "when Malty tried to bum a Englishman on that P. & O. boat, the bloody white hog said that he didn't wanta talk to no black fellows. Today I kid a cracker gal outa five dollars for the bunch. It's a funny life and you got to take it funny."

"Youse a regular sore-back nigger," remarked Bugsy. "I done said it some moh times and I'll say it again, you nevah know when an American black man gwine show himself a white man's nigger."

"I'll slap the sass outa you, you mean little cocoanut-dodger," cried Banjo, "ef you call me any white man's nigger," and he gave Bugsy a poke in his jaw that sent him sprawling.

Bugsy got up frothy at the corners of his mouth, which was always a biological peculiarity with him, but now in his wrath it was more pronounced. He opened a large pocket knife and cried, "I'll cut you all ways and don't miss you throat."

"Try it, nigger," said Banjo, quietly enough. "Because you lick that theah South African Jew boy, you think youse got a chance against me?"

But the other boys put themselves between them and disarmed Bugsy. In the scuffle Ray's wrist was cut and bled a great deal.

To Ray the incident recalled another, almost identical affair that happened in London. It was some time after the report of the Amritsar massacre had demonstrated that the mind of the world, shock-proof from the deeds of the great war, nevertheless could still be moved by tragic events. One evening Ray was strolling through a square with two Indians when a one-armed man stepped out of the shadow and begged alms. Evidently he was ashamed, for his hat was pulled down to hide his face. One of the Indians gave a harsh refusal, adding, as they walked on: "It is his kind the British use to make our people crawl before them in India."

Ray felt ashamed. Ashamed that the man should be forced to beg. Ashamed of the refusal. Ashamed of himself. Ashamed of humanity. Instinctively he felt that the man who begged was not of the hateful type that does the sentry duty of the British Empire. Yet he could not feel that his Indian friend was wrong. He never gave alms in public himself, even when he could afford it. It made him feel cheap and embarrassed. But he would have liked to give something to that one-armed man. And he had not dared.

He hated the society that forced him into such an equivocal position. He hated civilization. Once in a moment of bitterness he had said in Harlem, "Civilization is rotten." And the more he traveled and knew of it, the more he felt the truth of that bitter outburst.

He hated civilization because its general attitude toward the colored man was such as to rob him of his warm human instincts and make him inhuman. Under it the thinking colored man could not function normally like his white brother, responsive and reacting spontaneously to the emotions of pleasure or pain, joy or sorrow, kindness or hardness, charity, anger, and forgiveness. Only within the confines of his own world of color could he be his true self. But so soon as he entered the great white world, where of necessity he must work and roam and breathe the larger air to live, that entire world, high, low, middle, unclassed, all conspired to make him painfully conscious of color and race.

Should I do this or not? Be mean or kind? Accept, give, withhold? In determining his action he must be mindful of his complexion. Always he was caught by the sharp afterthought of color, as if some devil's hand jerked a cord to which he was tethered in hell. Regulate his emotions by a double standard. Oh, it was hell to be a man of color, intellectual and naturally human in the white world. Except for a superman, almost impossible.

It was easy enough for Banjo, who in all matters acted instinctively. But it was not easy for a Negro with an intellect standing watch over his native instincts to take his own way in this white man's civilization. But of one thing he was resolved: civilization would not take the love of color, joy, beauty, vitality, and nobility out of *his* life and make him like one of the poor mass of its pale creatures. Before he was aware of what was the big drift of this Occidental life he had fought against it instinctively, and now that he had grown and broadened and knew it better, he could bring intellect to the aid of instinct.

Could he not see what Anglo-Saxon standards were doing to some of the world's most interesting peoples? Some Jews ashamed of being Jews. Changing their names and their religion . . . for the Jesus of the Christians. The Irish objecting to the artistic use of their own rich idioms. Inferiority bile of non-Nordic minorities. Educated Negroes ashamed of their race's intuitive love of color, wrapping themselves up in respectable gray, ashamed of Congo-sounding laughter, ashamed of their complexion (bleaching out), ashamed of their strong appetites. No being ashamed for Ray. Rather than lose his soul, let intellect go to hell and live instinct!

XIII. Bugsy Comes Back at Banjo

THE Cairo Café in Joliette was packed full. An aged girl, her pale, tired features grotesque under the paint, was pounding out on the piano a tragic imitation of Raquel Meller's song:

"Mimosa! Mimosa!
Elle n'a pas regarde chere petite,
Mais elle a vu bien plus vite
Que son coeur palpite,
Et qu'il lui tend les bras,
Mimosa! Mimosa!"

A slightly built Algerian rattled the drum and banged the cymbals. Young men, rigged out in fashionable regalia, burning colors from shoes to cap, danced with the girls of the quarter and with one another. Some wore proletarian blue. Egyptians, Maltese, Algerians, Tunisians, Syrians, Arabians, and Chinese bobbing up and down in ungainly jerks.

Chinese and Arab men are awkward in modern dances. They have nothing of the natural animal grace and rhythm of Negroes jazzing.

Although the Cairo was a colored bar, the Negroes hardly ever went there. Negroes and Arabs are not fond of one another—even when they speak the same language and have the same religion. There is a great gulf, of biological profundity, between the ochre-skinned North-Africans and the black dwellers below the desert.

The Negro's sensual dream of life is poles apart from the Arab's hard realism.

Bugsy, passing the Cairo, saw Latnah inside and entered. Since his misunderstanding with Banjo, the wiry little fighter was walking very much by himself. And he enjoyed it. Bugsy was happiest when he was breathing some militant resentment. He did not speak to Latnah, not knowing with whom she had come nor what she was doing, but went to the bar and called for a glass of lemonade-menthé.

Latnah spoke to him. Although she was sitting at a table with white girls and brown men, she was really alone. She knew the proprietor, who was a brown man, and had stopped for a word with him. And then she had sat down and stayed, to listen, perhaps, to the language familiar to her, which Banjo mockingly called the Arabese.

Latnah called Bugsy and shifted, without getting up, to a small unoccupied table in the corner parallel to the one from which she moved. Bugsy went over to her, taking his drink.

"What you doing heah, taking that thing away from Banjo?" he asked her.

"Banjo!" Latnah sneered. "Me no never see him. Long time him no come sleep. Banjo dirty man and no good friend."

Bugsy was very glad that Latnah was piqued and ready to hear him unburden himself about Banjo.

"You jest now finding out he's a dirty spade and ain't no good?" he said. "I knowed it long time. If Banjo had a had plenty a money he'd never speak to a cullud person. I know that."

"But why?" Latnah demanded. "He black man."

"That ain't nothing. Him is crazy 'bout white folks.

He's a Alabama nigger or cousin to one, and jest bohn foolish about that white skin. I tell you he'll sooner give a white beach-comber a raise than one of his own color. And you know it's easier for a white man to bum a good raise than us to. A white man can bum off his own color, and he think him is doing a colored man a favor when he pay him the compliment a bumming him, but often when we start bumming a white man, all we get outa him is 'damned dirty nigger' and his red moon in our face."

"I know Banjo little mad, but I no think he love white more than colored. No, he just like everything without thinking. He *Negre;* he can't love the white."

"You don't know that nigger like I does. He ain't lak me and you. He is a sore-back nigger and sure got white fevah. I done listen at him talking and I knows he ain't got no use foh your kind. . . . Why, did you evah see him when he made that big raise off a them boys with the music on that City Line boat? You bet you didn't. And now you ain't seeing him, either, since Taloufa done paid and got his suit out and gived him a big raise befoh going away——"

"Oh, Taloufa gone away?"

"Sure. He done take his tail away from this bum hussy." (Bum hussy was one of Bugsy's names for Marseilles.) "And all the money he done leave Banjo that nigger is spending in Boody Lane on that kelt that he done wasted all his duds on when he come here first. Same one that wouldn't nevah so much as look at him when he done run through all his money and got him messed up in a fight."

"He with her again?" Latnah asked.

"Sure. Ef you go 'long up to that there rendezvous café near Boody Lane Ise sure you find them theah together."

The thought of Banjo having money and spending it on that girl, together with Bugsy's intimation that this was Banjo's real preference, made Latnah crazy with anger.

"I no understand good," she said. "I go with white man, but only for money. White race no love my race. My race no love white."

"Banjo ain't like us. Him is a sore-back nigger," said Bugsy, vindictively. "Them that likes white folks riding them all the time."

So, thought Latnah, he no like my kind. He no man. He no good. He no got no pride of race. Me give him sleep. Me give him eat. Me give him love. Me give him money for go buy that thing. Even my money he took and went off laughing and sailor-rocking like that, away from me to spread strange joy. She had never been jealous of his change of pillow. That she understood, Orientwise. But for him to lose good money to those things in the Ditch, and for what? For the benefit of their two-legged white rats. Banjo an ofay-lover. She was seething with that deep-rooted sexual resentment that the women of the colored and white races nourish against one another—a resentment perhaps even more profound among the women than among the men of the species, because it is passive, having no outlet for brutal expression.

While Banjo had temporarily got up strutting and looked good to the Ditch again, his first flame had fallen far down the scale to a box in the Ditch. After quitting her *maison d'amour* for picnic days with Banjo, she had found another when the strutter's funds were exhausted. But she did not remain very long in the new place. Banjo's grandiose way of doing things must have stirred to life dead romances in her and spoiled her for the discipline of the shuttered places. However, the change was not advantageous even if she lived now in more natural light, seeing more of the street, for she was merely a "leetah" girl and down at the very bottom.

And now, in her changed estate, she did not withhold a smile from Banjo passing by more dandified than ever and looking his handsomest. Banjo, who never bore rancor for any length of time against anybody or anything, fell again.

"Chère Blanche!" That was her name, and some one had chalked it up on the rough, weather-beaten gray door of her dark little hole-in-the-wall.

Bugsy, of course, had Banjo wrong. Banjo was no ofay-lover. He simply would not see life in divisions of sharp primary colors. In that sense he was color-blind. The colors were always getting him mixed up, shading off, fading out, running into one another so that it was difficult to perceive which was which. Any pleasing color of the moment's fancy might turn Banjo crazy for awhile.

Bugsy was wrong indeed. Banjo would put no ofay before Malty, much less Ray. If he had Latnah tangled up and lost in the general color scheme, it was because she was a woman, and he took all women as one—as they came—roughly, carelessly, easily.

Banjo with Ray was at the little bar not far from Boody Lane. They were playing American poker with a red-skinned tout from Martinique, and a group of Corsican and Provençal touts were playing a French game at another table. Chère Blanche had deserted the sill of her box, where she was a fixture on the lookout night and day now, and was talking to the *patrone* at the bar.

Two girls came in, one of them whistling Carmen's

song. The sharp features of the whistling girl were brown as an Arab's, but she was Provençal. She wore a flaring pink frock and her face was smeared with rouge. She was an old and hard habitant of the Ditch, but her companion, who was new to it, was very pretty, pink-rosy and young, between fifteen and sixteen. She had just a little rouge on her lips and she had on a black frock, as if she were mourning somebody; but that was camouflage. She had not a yellow card to live the life of the Ditch, for she was too young to get one. And so she was being chaperoned and cautiously initiated into the ways by the older girl. She had been only two weeks down there, having run away, so they said, from some country place. She was very much admired, naturally, for her youth and fresh prettiness among the old girls gave her the air of a little princess among scrub-women. But there was not a latent spark of interest in her eyes. She was thin, and already a fever color was supplanting the rose of her cheek, and from the bones the flesh was sagging unpleasantly.

The boys of the Ditch who were not touts gossiped about her all the time. They said that if the police caught her they would send her away to some place of confinement and keep her there a good many years, giving her time enough to reflect. But such gossiping was merely slum sentimentality, for the ways of the Ditch were open to all eyes and police eyes, like touts' eyes, were keen to see what they wanted to see and blind to what they wanted not to see.

It was just a month since a very interesting couple had been pounced upon and borne away. A boy of seventeen and a girl of sixteen from a little tourist town. They had come into the Ditch with something of the verve of the black beach boys. She, boy-bobbed, wearing a cerise frock, and he like a romantic apache in black, a red cloth around his neck, a bright cap pulled down sideways on his face and often a flower, fixed always in the corner of his mouth. The girl was usually reading *Le Film Complet, Mon Ciné,* and moving-picture novelettes. In the bistro where they lolled out each day they were amorous of each other in a curious way—like stage folk apparently forgetful of the audience—an amorousness that was as different from the monkey exhibitions of the runted touts and their ladies as a good glass of red wine was from the camouflage absinthe-and-water of the Ditch. It may have been that that young couple brought something into the scene which made them impossible to the poor old actors there. Anyway, the police were soon on to *them.*

The girl who was whistling ruffled Ray's kinky black mat. "Pay me a drink?" she asked.

"Sure; but what will you do for it?" he demanded.

She shrugged. "What is it you want?"

"You might sing what you were whistling. Do you know the words?"

"Putain! C'est ça? Sure I know 'Carmen.' I see it every season. I never miss it. 'Carmen,' 'Bohême,' 'Mignon' . . . I love them all. But 'Carmen' the most. I saw it three times one season, the artiste who played Carmen was so wonderful."

"Let's hear you sing it. I love it, too," said Ray.

The girl went to the counter, drank an apéritif sec, and began singing:

> "L'amour est un oiseau rebelle . . ."

Her voice was rather hoarse and soiled, incapable of holding a note or ascending very far, but her acting was superb as she side-stepped about the bistro, posing and gesturing with a cigarette between her fingers. It was her manner when she whistled that had piqued Ray to ask her to sing. She was Carmen incarnate in her acting. What a hip-shaker she was!

Comic opera was ever a thing of great joy to Ray. It gave him such a perfect illusion of a crazy, disjointed relationship of all the arts of life. Singing and acting and orchestra and all the garish hues. Fascinating *mélange* of disorder. No one part ever equal to the other. Like life . . . like love. All the world on a stage just wrong enough to be right.

Ray recalled the first time he had ascended to the gods to see Geraldine Farrar in "Carmen" at the Metropolitan in New York. Geraldine certainly did not act that Carmen stuff as brazenly well as this girl. Going down from colored Harlem to the opera then was a stealing away from his high home of heavenly "blues" and rag-time to taste some exotic morsel brought from a faraway other land of music. The pals of his milieu tapped their heads knowingly at his going among the ofay gods to throw away a dollar or two. There were so many charming things at a dollar or so a throw in Harlem. He felt a little lonely going, but was compensated afterward by the blood-tingling realization of how much the composite life of Harlem was like a comic opera. He had traveled far since those days, yet no scene had ever conveyed to him such a sensuous impression of a comic opera as Harlem.

A little lusting for opera in the Ditch was a different thing. It was quite easy to find a companion of a sort in a bistro ready for a trip to the gods of the opera. And Ray never had that feeling, as he had had it in Harlem, of going out of his own warm environment into a marble-cold world of dilettantism.

For a change, a slight operatic tune in the Ditch was not an exotic thing. Such airs flowing through the alleys were as natural as rain water washing down the gutters. It was often a delicious experience for Ray suddenly to hear a girl whistling or singing such a fascinating old favorite as "Connais tu le pays ou fleurit l'oranger . . ." or "Oui! On m'appelle Mimi . . ." or a fleeting fragmentary lilt from "La Flute Enchantée." It was nonetheless lovely if the melody was broken by a volley of bullets tearing down some dark alley and scaring the Ditch to cover. That enhanced the color of the place as a theater. That endeared the Ditch to him. There was nothing artificial about that. It was as strikingly natural as the high-heeled fancy shoes and the pretty frocks of popeline de soie and crêpe Marocain and all the voluptuous soft feminine stuff parading there in the mud and slime and refuse. The poor overplucked chickens who loved to jazz all night to American rag-time and the music-hall hits of Mistinguett also had an ear for other kinds of music—even as Ray.

> *" 'L'amour est enfant de Bohême,*
> *Il n'a jamais connu de loi;*
> *Si tu ne m'aimes pas, je t'aime!*
> *Si je t'aime, prends garde a toi!' "*

The girl flicked her skirt in Ray's face, and, laughing, ended her song. At that moment Latnah entered the bistro. She had abruptly left Bugsy at the Cairo bar to come to the Ditch. Chère Blanche was familiarly posing against Banjo. Latnah rushed up to her and said in French: "You haven't done him enough harm when you robbed him and got him in trouble. Now you run after him again. You no good, you damned mean slut. That for you."

She slapped the girl in her face. The girl screamed and started toward her, but Latnah caught her flimsy frock at the neck and with one fierce jerk, ripped it apart so that it fell at Chère Blanche's feet. And that was all her clothing. She gathered the pieces about her and fled from the café.

Banjo grabbed Latnah's wrist. "What in hell-fire you come here messing with the gal foh?"

"You fool!" cried Latnah. "Gal no love you. Because you got good clothes now and little money and she thrown out of the *maison fermé* and got no friend, not even a dirty maquereau wanting her, she running after you again."

"You lemme manage mah own self and don't come poking you' nose in mah business, for I don't want no black woman come messing me up."

"I no black woman."

"You ain't white."

"But I no nigger like you. So what Bugsy say is true, eh? You prefer help ofay than colored boys. You no proud of race, no like your own color. You no good then. You no come no more my house, no speak no more to me. Me finish."

"I don't care. You know why I went with you? I did that to change mah luck."

"I no understand."

"You don't?" Banjo explained. "When I was up against it, as if the ofays hadda done hoodoohed me, I thought that by changing color I might change mah luck."

Now Latnah understood. It humiliated her. She crumpled under Banjo's jibe. He had spoken in a bantering way, but his words were cruel; they ate into her.

"By-by, mamma." Banjo touched her shoulder playfully—"and don't nevah you pull off no moh of that hen-scratching stuff on me."

"Touch me again and I stick you!" She whipped her little dagger out of her bosom.

Banjo saw the silver-headed thing and recoiled quickly as from the sudden menace of a rattlesnake. His eyes and mouth popped open, his face wearing horror like an African mask.

XIV. Telling Jokes

THERE was one Southern black on the beach whom Banjo and his boys hated to see and always avoided. He had come to Marseilles from a North-African port, where he had been paid off on a foreign ship. When he arrived at Marseilles, like the boy of the "Don't-light-it-afire" story, he was highly disdainful of the beach boys and would have none of them; but he allowed himself to be picked up by some insectile Corsican *voyous* who made their headquarters in a sewer hole of a hotel-bistro of the Ditch. When his money was gone he went to the American consulate, and it was arranged for him to be returned home by an American freighter. But when the day came for him to ship he refused to go. He had got a little money somewhere. He lived on it for a few days. After that was gone he again returned to the consulate for help, but the clerk in charge of the seamen's department would have nothing to do with him.

Then he tried to get in with the beach boys, but they would not have him. Not merely because he had scorned their company at first, but because he was a dead thing with no spark in him of the vagabond flair for life which was the soul of the beach existence. The boys called him Lonesome Blue.

Lonesome Blue had been excited by the boys' talk of raiding the good wine of the docks. And one fine afternoon he hiked down and bunged out a barrel on the breakwater, right under the eyes of the police. He was arrested and got prison for three months and a writ of expulsion from the country effective ten days after he was released.

If you have the hard luck to get expelled from France, the department of the Sûreté Générale does not worry itself about the manner of your going. The order is, Get out! and you yourself must find the way. Because of this, many criminals merely change their names and the scene of their activities in order to remain in the most fascinating of European countries. Some of them stay in the same place, if it is, like Marseilles, big enough to hide in, having faith in their cleverness to escape the toils of the police. Ginger, for example, having got into difficulties, had been sentenced to do a little time and then to be deported. That was long, long ago. But on coming out of jail he had destroyed the expulsion paper and was still enjoying Marseilles. That is not such a simple thing as it sounds, for the police are ever on the lookout for evaders, for whose arrest they get a premium of some ten francs per head. Ginger had been caught in many a "rafle," but his little store of colloquial French and his good-natured wit had got him through the examination every time.

Poor Lonesome Blue was tongue-tied and witless. Since his first imprisonment, he had twice been in jail for disobeying the expulsion orders, and he had made souvenirs of the papers for the benefit of the police. He had just been let out again and entered the African café on seeing Banjo and the boys, who had assembled there after lunch.

"Here is ole Lonesome Blue again," cried Banjo. "Always exposing himself when you least expect, scarifying like a haunts."

"Why don't you get outa it, mah boy?" said Ginger.

"Seeing as youse messed up you'self in this Frenchman's town, why don't you ketch you a broad and get outa it? Look how you stand."

Lonesome Blue was in a crumpled tangle of rags, his toes poking through a poor proletarian pair of Provençal *pantoufles,* his face scabby and wearing a perpetually soured expression, as if some implacable, invisible demon had a clutch on the back of his neck.

"Youse a sick nigger," said Banjo. "You look in a bad way to me, lak somebody done got a passport for the boneyard."

"You don't have to tell me that. I know it," replied Lonesome Blue. "I know it without you saying it. Only Gawd knows how I feel," he finished with a belly-deep groan.

"Gawd won't hulp you a damn sight mohn the debbil will, nigger," retorted Banjo. "You better cut out the preaching Jesus stuff and get you a broad foh going back home. And when you git back you take you'se'f to a hospital and get some shots, for if you ain't got the sip I ain't nevah seen none."

"Wha' you wanta drink?" Ginger asked.

"Not a damn thing to drink with our gang," said Banjo. "Ain't none of us gwine encourage Lonesome Blue to lay around heah and die. If we got any money, let's give it tohm. But let him keep to himself until he's so lonely that he'll sure get right outa this Frenchman's town. I don't know what youse hanging around here foh. The consul ain't evah gwine to do anything for you again, and the police will git a hold a you everytime them ten days am finished."

"That's the truth," said Goosey. "I quit my ship and have never gone to any consul since. And I don't intend to. When the consul put you on that ship, Lonesome, it would have been better you had gone. You made a big mistake."

"A nigger is a bohn mistake," declared Banjo, laughing. "When Gawd made the white man, he put a little stuff in his haid for him to correct his mistakes. And so when the white man invented writing and pencil, he put an eraser on that pencil to rub out mistakes. But Gawd nevah gived the nigger no brain-stuff foh'm to correct his mistakes, and so the nigger kaint invent anything to correct his mistake.

"For when Gawd was making the first nigger, a bluebird jest fly down into the Tree of Life and started singing that the wul' was ready and waiting foh the love a Gawd. And the tune was so temptation that Gawd lost his haid and set down the golden bowl with the nigger's brain in it. And the serpent was right there. And he ups and et the nigger's brain and put a mess a froth in the golden bowl. And that stuff for the nigger's brain gived the serpent the run of the earth. . . .

"And when Gawd done took up his work again, he took the froth in the bowl and dumped it into the nigger's brain and finished his job. And that's why you find the world as it is today. The debbil ruling hell and earth, the white man always getting by and there, and the nigger always full a froth or just dumb like this heah Lonesome Blue."

All the boys had a rollicking laugh in which they were joined by Kid Irish, who had come in while Banjo was holding forth, accompanied by a fleshy young man, a Jew, who made a living as a guide and a seller of sex post cards to tourists. The Jew had arrived from Toulon, whence he had followed the American squadron, that had just put in at Marseilles.

"But, Lawd Gawd," said Ginger, "imagine what we niggers woulda been today if Big Massa hadn't a made a mistake. Why, if we am as we is from a mistake, what wouldn't we be if we had been made right from the start? We woulda had Gawd and them angels in glory and all nuts."

The boys roared out again and Goosey said: "That story you told was raw niggerism, Banjo, and you ought to be ashamed to tell that on the race before a white person."

"Eh-eh-ehieeee!" Malty laughed. "Can't the race stand a joke?"

Whereupon the Jew said he knew a better one than Banjo's and volunteered to tell it if the boys didn't mind.

"Sure. Speak up, kid," said Banjo. "There ain't no ladies here objecting, except Goosey. And ef he don't like it he can take his box outa here."

The Jew said: "I guess you all heared about 'Shuffle Along,' the colored show that had such a long run on Broadway. I seen it about six times. Gee! there was some swell-looking colored goils in it. I used to see real money guys waiting just to get a glimpse of them coming out of the theater. Well, what I'm going to say is about two of the goils and I'm telling it straight as I heard it.

"One night two of the show girls was walking home together, and they saw a white man lying in the gutter. They didn't know whether he was hurt or drunk, and they woulda liked to help him, but they were goils and colored (you all understand), so they couldn't do anything for him.

"'It's really too bad to leave him be like that,' says one of the goils, 'but we've gotta, because some white person might see us helping him and think something bad of us. Let's go on our way, dearie.'

"And as they walked off the other goil she says:

'Too, too bad poor white man fallen so low. Seems to belong to some dickty family, too. Did you notice his clothes? And such a handsome profile.'

" 'Profile!' says the other goil. 'It wasn't no profile you see, honey, but his flask a liquor in his pants.' "

The joke went over the heads of all the boys excepting Ray and Goosey. Ray smiled and remarked that most of the stock "Negro" jokes were of Jewish origin, but Goosey scowled and cursed under his breath.

"That makes me remember," said Ray, "I read in a colored newspaper that one of those 'Shuffle Along' girls was fired from the company for keeping a date with a white man."

"Served the damn wench right," said Goosey.

"Oh, I know a good one meself," said Kid Irish.

"I think we've had enough of colored jokes," said Goosey.

"Enough you' grandmammy!" cried Banjo. "Quit you' bellyaching blah and get along from here. A joke is a joke——"

"Yes, but white people don't make jokes like that about themselves," maintained Goosey. "Especially the one-hundred-per-cent Yankees. You fellows don't know anything about the race movement. Ray knows better, yet he holds in with you. You don't know why the white man put all his dirty jokes on to the race. It's because the white man is dirty in his heart and got to have dirt. But he covers it up in his race to show himself superior and put it on to us. The Yankees used to make jokes out of the Germans. Then when the Germans got strong enough to stop that, they got it out of the Irish and Jews. When the Irish and Jews got too rich and powerful in politics, they turn to Italian and Negroes."

"That ain't right on the Irish, me man," said Kid Irish. "There's barrels o' Irish jokes going around."

"If the Yankee can't afford a joke and the Negro can, then the Negro is the bigger and richer man," said Ray.

"That's poetical," replied Goosey. "The weak and comic side of race life can't further race advancement."

"You talk just like a nigger newspaper," said Ray.

"Niggah from you, Ray!" exclaimed Goosey, "and with white folks among us! I expected that from Banjo or Malty, but not from you."

"Yes, nigger," repeated Ray. "I didn't say 'niggah' the way you and the crackers say it, but 'nigger' with the gritty 'r' in it to express exactly what I feel about you and all coons like you. I know you think that a coon is a Negro like Banjo and Ginger, but you're fooling yourself. They are real and you are the coon—a stage thing, a made-up thing. I said nigger newspaper because a nigger newspaper is nothing more than a nigger newspaper. Something like you, half baked, half educated, full of false ideas about Negroes, because it can't hold its head up out of its miserable purgatory. That's why we—you—the race—can't get beyond the nigger newspaper in the printed word. That's why an intelligent man reads it only for the comic—the joke that it is. You talk about niggerism. Good Lord! You're a perfect example of niggerism. Sometimes you get me so worked up with your niggery bull, I feel like giving you a poke in your stupid yaller jaw."

Swept by a brain-storm, Ray was gesticulating in Goosey's face.

"Get your monkey-chasing hand out of my face, black nig—man," cried Goosey, getting hot. "Because you're a man without a country, you have no race feeling, no race pride. You can't go back to Haiti. You feel there's no place for you in Africa, after you've hung around here, trying to get down into the guts of the life of these Senegalese. You hate America and you despise Europe.

You're just a lost sore-head. You pretend you'd like to be a vagabond like Malty and Banjo here, but you know you're a liar and the truth is not in you."

"Aren't you happy you've got a country and a flag to go back to?" asked Ray, now quieting down.

"When it comes to myself, I'm not studying those United Snakes," retorted Goosey.

"Holy Gees!" cried Kid Irish. "Don't start a riot among ye, or if youse going to, wait and let me deliver meself first."

"Sure. Go on with it, bud," said Ginger. "Ray, how come you make Goosey get you' goat like thataway?"

Ray laughed, puzzled himself at his little flare-up.

Kid Irish said: "There's four people in me story, so that makes it a square joke.

"There was two Irish friends from Galway. They were very poor and they went to America to make their fortune. The oldest friend was engaged to be married. When the two partners reached New York they soon got jobs and they lived together. The oldest one became a policeman and his friend got a job as a bartender. They had an apartment in San Juan Hill in a district where there were many niggers——"

"Negroes," corrected Goosey.

"Yes, Niggerows. Excuse me," said Kid Irish. "The policeman started in to save to send for his girl. But after a year he didn't have enough money. So his friend offered to help him and proposed they should all three housekeep together to save expenses when the girl came. She arrived and was married to the policeman, and the three of them took a flat in the same quarter. And of course in time the bride got in the family way.

"The husband was very happy and he and his friend began saving more than ever so that after the birth they would all go back to Ireland. But the strangest thing happened, some funny freak o' nature, for when the baby was born it was black. The husband said he didn't want the baby and he wasn't going to stay in New York; he was going back home and he couldn't take the bride with him. The friend said he would go back home, too. So they bought steamship tickets to go back to Ireland and left the bride and the strange infant. But the friend was awfully sad about the whole business, and when they were on the pier, waiting to board the ship, he broke down and cried as if his heart was going to break.

"And the husband said to him: 'Cheer up! The way you carry on they would think it was you and not me that was married to her.'

"And his friend replied: 'I just can't help it, seeing how it took two Irishmen to make one nigger.' "

The boys roared as Kid Irish stopped. Goosey liked that joke and joined in the laughter.

Banjo got up, jigging round the café, chanting the popular melody: "It takes a long, tall brownskin."

"What about going down to the docks, fellahs?" asked Ginger. "There's a good broad in. I know the crew."

"I'm game for anything," said Malty.

"Let's give Lonesome Blue some money, between us," said Banjo, "for I just ain't gwine to have this rear-end facer trailing us."

They found five francs for Lonesome Blue, and as he was limping off from the café Ray called after him:

"Wait for me. I'm going with you."

"Whereat?" demanded Banjo. "You're going with us."

"No, I'm going to police headquarters or to the American consulate with Lonesome. If they expel him, why don't they send him home to America? This jailing of a man again every ten days after he is out seems the most abominable thing to me. And a man like Lonesome. Sick and nutty and not able to help himself. How can a civilized government do that? Is there no international law for deportées?"

"I tell you, pardner, as you best friend," said Banjo, "if I was you I'd keep away from all them gov'ment people, whether theyse French or Americans. I ain't nevah fooled round them. What you want to go and get mixed up with them for, all on account of this dumb Alabama darky——"

"I ain't from Alabam'——"

"You look like you is, all the same," Banjo said to Lonesome Blue.

"All the same, I am going to see what I can do," insisted Ray. "We don't want to see him die off like a dog around here, like that old man in Joliette."

Ray went off with Lonesome Blue.

The old man in Joliette was a half-crippled, white-head fixture who came on crutches every morning to squat in the Place de la Joliette near the fountain where the coal workers stripped to the waist to wash themselves after work.

When the black beach boys bummed food they brought him some, pieces of bread and scraps of meat. And sometimes the coal workers gave him coppers. Banjo would get food for him and give it to one of the boys to take to the old man. But Banjo always steered wide of the spot where he sat. Banjo lived entirely on his strength and was scared of contacts with any Negro that had lost the one thing a vagabond black had to live by.

The old man was a used-up British seaman. Looking down on the square from a hilly street is the British Mediterranean Mission to Seamen, which operates under the patronage of His Britannic Majesty, the Archbishop of Canterbury, and other distinguished personages. Floating above it is a blue flag bearing a white angel flying to the aid of seamen. And nearly every day a cock-eyed white servant of His Majesty's mission passed by the disabled old black seaman in the square to visit the in-coming ships and distribute tracts and mission cards to able-bodied sailors. One morning the old man could not come to the square, for he had died in his sleeping-hole on the breakwater.

XV. White Terror

SIMULTANEOUSLY with the American squadron, an American freighter and two large English ships, one from South Africa and another from India, had arrived in port. There were also a number of British tramps at anchor for some days. There was much changing of dollars and pounds and ten-shilling notes in agencies and cafés by sailors, officers, and tourists. The guides were as busy as could be showing the new arrivals about. For the chauffeurs of the docks it was a picnic day. All the night places were excited with anticipation of new guests. The *boîtes de nuit* had sent delegations of cocottes down to the docks to greet the newcomers with cards of invitation.

Some of these cards were decorated souvenirs, and, like many of the cabarets, bore the flags of the great shipping nations and advertised British ale and whisky and American cocktails. . . .

It was twilight and Ray was hurrying along the Rue de la République toward Joliette where he was to meet Banjo, as he had promised. Besides its usual peripatetic exhibition of youths in proletarian blue, cocottes, Arabs, Senegalese, soldiers, and sailors with red pommels on their caps, the street parade included groups of British seamen and white-capped sailors from the destroyers.

In the Place Sadi Carnot, Ray was accosted by a staggering seaman with a card in his hand.

"Is this the—the—Bru—Bru—Bru—Brutish-Amurican Bar?" he asked in a drunken stutter, punching with his finger a card that he held.

Ray looked at it. An advertisement of the British and American Bar with its delightful symbolic trade-mark—a Union Jack and Stars and Stripes united upon a Tricolor. It also bore a plan of Marseilles, with a long red line like a serpent indicating the route from the quays to the establishment in the Place de la Bourse.

"No," said Ray, "this is not the British-American Bar, but you keep straight on until you reach the end of this street. Then you are at the Vieux Port and anybody will show you the Bar."

"Thank yer, mite," and the seaman staggered onward, repeating, "Bru — Bru — Bru — Bru—Brutish-Amurican Bar. . . ."

On the same street, where the Boulevard des Dames crosses it, Ray had another rencontre, this time a surprising one—three American Negro seamen from an American freighter, one of whom was a waiter he had known on the railroad.

Ray's old friend insisted that he should turn back with them. They went to the Senegalese Bar. Banjo was there, having returned from Joliette by the short way. Ray introduced the seamen to him, the *patron,* and a handsome Senegalese boxer.

The acquaintance between Ray and the railroad waiter, now turned ship's steward, was slight. They had never worked on the same dining-cars, but had met each other casually at the railroad men's quarters in Philadelphia. Yet they met now and acted like old and dear friends. Meeting like that was so unique, it stirred them strangely.

The seamen stood drinks. They said they would like to go to some place where they could amuse themselves. Banjo suggested a place in the Ditch, but they wanted something of the better sort. All three of them were well dressed. The boxer thought the British-American Bar would be all right. So the whole party decided to go. Banjo was in such an exciting, merrymaking mood that he won the admiration of the boys and was the target of most of the questioning. The atmosphere of the Senegalese Bar had won them immediately. It was run by a Negro and catered to colored men and they agreed that it was the best they had seen in any foreign port. When the proprietor talked English to them they felt proud that he had emigrated to America and made enough money there to return to France and start a business. . . . And Banjo! So gay and dressy on his hand-to-mouth existence without ever worrying about anything. That was marvelous!

"You find it all right over here, eh?" one of the newcomers asked him. "The froggies treat you better than the hoojahs, eh?"

"Well now, that's a question I wouldn't know how to answer noneatall," said Banjo, "for it all depends on which way you take it. There ain't no Canaan stuff sweeter than this heah wine and honey flowing in this place, but otherwise speaking, the Frenchies them have the same nose like a Jew, and ef you don't smell a money they can't use you."

"Hi! now you're saying that thing," Ray laughed.

"All the same, you've got more freedom here," said the seaman; "when you have money you can go any place you got a mind to."

"Sure can," said Banjo. "Theah's moh freedom, all right, if you know how to handle it. But some a them niggers come here, boh, am as funny and dumb jes' like that thing. They get in every way except the right way. They ketch the wrong end of the stuff. They ketch the pohliceman's billy, they ketch the jail-house, and what not ketch? Oh, Lawdy! ask not me!"

"Maybe the good liquor makes them crazy after boozing so long on moonshine corn," said a seaman.
"And mos'n a them don't even know how to use it right," said Banjo. "They come here wanting whisky and gin, and when I tell them to drink French wine, that's the best stuff to feel good on, they say it's sour dago red. Can you beat that?"
"Don't be too hard on them, Banjo," said Ray. "They got to learn."
"Learn!" sneered Banjo. "Them kind a babies nevah learn anything. A real traveling guy has got a preambulating nose for the bestest thing in any country whenever it is accommodated to him, but there's many people running round the world that nevah shoulda been outa them own home town."
For certain reasons, arrived at from a wide knowledge of the eccentricities of civilization and experience personal and impersonal, Ray felt no eagerness to transfer the party to the British-American Bar on such an evening. He was really rather reluctant, but because he preferred not to deaden in any way the keen anticipation of the evening's pleasure for his comrades, he said nothing.
The atmosphere of the cabaret, when the boys got there, was heavily charged with contrary foreign influences and they were greeted by an extraordinary salvo of shrill female laughter as they entered. The Senegalese was irritated and said he did not like the atmosphere and the reception. Ray told him he did not think it was mocking laughter. Ray was never on the lookout for hostile hints; his mind was too rich of sane, full living for that. But there was no obtuseness there to prevent him from making immediate note of any such tendency. He had often remarked that white people were never more contemptibly vulgar than when a Negro

entered a white place of amusement. If it were not a hostile exhibition of bad manners, as in America, it would be an imbecile theatrical demonstration, as often happened in Europe. It was as if the black visitor could not be seen in any other light but that of a funny actor on the stage.

He had never known black people to act like that when white persons entered a Negro place of pleasure. On such occasions Negroes could assume a simple dignity as remote from white behavior as primitive African sculpture is from the conventionalism of a civilized drawing-room. He had never remarked a vulgar gesture. Primitive peoples could be crude and coarse, but never vulgar. Vulgarity was altogether a scab of civilization.

The boys squeezed together round a table and had some drinks. The Senegalese was right. None of the girls wanted to dance with them. It was purely a matter of good business. Ray understood and he was glad to get away from the place. Cockney was not a musical accent to his ears, nor was there any æsthetic pleasure in the sight of those white caps on hard-boiled, over-shaved heads. But it hurt him that these black boys, coming off the ship after a long hard trip should tumble into this.

Not far from the British-American Bar was another. The head waiter was a boxing enthusiast and was friendly with Ray and the Senegalese. Ray told the boys to wait for him in the square while he went to the bar to talk to the head waiter. It was a more expensive bar than the British-American.

The head waiter was at the bar when Ray entered. He was glad to see Ray and offered him a drink, but he wasn't pleased to hear what Ray wanted for his comrades. He wished it was any other time, for the *boîte-de-nuit* was full of American and British officers spending plenty of money, drinking champagne. He was sure there would be trouble. There had been before when there were colored men in the bar and English and American customers—especially Americans. Once that bar had been ordered closed for six months because of a colored-white incident. He was for the boys, all right, for he was one of them himself, but if they did come in there might be a fight and it would spoil the boss's business.

Business! Prejudice and business. In Europe, Asia, Australia, Africa, America, those were the two united terrors confronting the colored man. He was the butt of the white man's indecent public prejudices. Prejudices insensate and petty, bloody, vicious, vile, brutal, *raffiné,* hypocritical, Christian. Prejudices. Prejudices like the stock market—curtailed, diminishing, increasing, changing chameleon-like, according to place and time, like the color of the white man's soul, controlled by the exigencies of the white man's business.

Back in the square with his comrades, Ray said he knew of one other place where he had been a few times with the two gentlemen bums, but he felt sure it would be no different from the rest on a night like that.

"Damn the white man's bars!" he said. "Let's go back to the Ditch."

"When I enlisted in the army during the war," said Banjo, "mah best buddy said I was a fool nigger. He said the white man would nevah ketch him toting his gun unless it was to rid the wul' of all the crackers, and I done told him back that the hullabaloo was to make the wul' safe foh democracy and there wouldn't be no crackers when the war was 'ovah and ended,' as was done said by President Wilson, as crackers didn't belong in democracy. But mah buddy said to me I had a screw loose, for President Wilson wasn't moh'n a cracker. He was bohn one and he was gwineta live and die one, and that a cracker and a Democrat was one and the same thing. And mah buddy was sure right. For according to my eyesight, and Ise one sure-seeing nigger, the wul' safe foh democracy is a wul' safe foh crackerism."

"I was just waiting for one of those Americans to make a move against us," said the Senegalese boxer. "I would like to murder one of them. I have my gun."

"No good that," said Ray, who, although he was always ready to defend himself in the jungles of civilization, was dead set against stupid violence.

"It's just about two years," said the Senegalese, "that some Americans caused a black prince to be thrown out of a cabaret in Montmartre, and Poincaré made a declaration against it. He said Americans cannot treat Negroes in France the way they do in America."

"That won't prevent discrimination, though," said Ray, "so long as the pound is lord and the dollar is king and the white man exalts business above humanity. 'Business first by all and any means!' That is the slogan of the white man's world. In New York we have laws against discrimination. Yet there are barriers of discrimination everywhere against colored people. Sometimes a Negro wins a few dollars in a test case in the courts. But no decent Negroes want to go to court for that. We don't want to eat in a restaurant nor go to a teashop, a cabaret, or a theater where they do not want us, because we eat and amuse ourselves for the pleasure of the thing. And when white people show that they do not want to entertain us in places that they own, why, we just stay away—all of us who are decent-minded—for we are a fun-loving race and there is no pleasure in forcing ourselves where we are not wanted.

"That's why the amusement side of the life of the Negro in America is such a highly-developed thing. And in spite of the deep differences between colored and white, it is the most intensely happy group life of Negroes in any part of the civilized world."

"You're right," said one of the visitors. "I have been in many a poht, all right, and I've spread joy some, but when it comes to having a right-down good time, there ain't any a them that's got anything on Harlem. Well, whar we going?"

"It's rotten luck," said Banjo, "for you-all to hit this town when it is lousy with crackers. It ain't always like this. But the Ditch is all right, though. Everything is down theah. And I nevah crave to leave it for any other show."

The boys had shuffled off along up the Canebière, talking.

"Sure the Ditch is all right," said Ray. "I was just thinking how we fellows traveling around like this learn a whole lot a things. A sailor ought to be the most tolerant person in the world, he has seen so much. And I think he is in his rough way, from all I've seen of sailors knocking around port towns. Except the white American sailor. He sees everything, but he learns nothing. And I don't think he's capable of learning. He carries abroad with him everything that should be left back home. Everything that is mean, hard-boiled, and intolerant in American life.

"Well, if we can't learn anything from the traveling representatives of American culture, we might learn from other people. I'll tell you something about these sailors. A few months ago I was visiting Toulon, when this same squadron arrived. Now on the Boulevard de Strasbourg at Toulon there is a tavern where the young officers always dance. Many of the better class of cocottes go there. The common French sailor is not allowed in there. But when the American sailors came they were given the run of the tavern. Why? Because they had plenty of dollars to spend—the pay of an American sailor turned into francs is probably as much as the pay of a French lieutenant. I'm not sure.

"Some hundreds of low cocottes came to Toulon for the American sailors. And they all flocked with them to the tavern. I was interested to know what the young French officers would do. Of course, they couldn't stand the changed atmosphere of the place. And they just stopped going there! There was a little exclusive dancing-place in an out-of-the-way street, and I saw a few of them dancing there with their girls.

"After all, they were officers with a right to kick. But they didn't. They just separated themselves from the *canaille.* They knew what a little extra good business meant to a French *commerçant.* You know in America, with our high wages and the dollarized standard of living, we have no idea of money value and economy in the ordinary European sense. But that is something else. All I want to say is that I learned something helpful from that incident at Toulon. Something that made me sure of myself and stronger in my own worth."

"I get you," one of the seamen said.

"You do?" asked Ray. "There are different ways of growing big and strong, for individuals as well as for races."

When the boys reached the Place de la Bourse again they were suddenly surrounded by a troop of painted youths who, holding hands, danced around them with queer gestures and queerer screams, like fairy folk in fables.

"Here they are!" laughed Ray. "If there's a British-American bar over there, there's none here."

"A regular turn-out foh the deep-sea stiffs," commented Banjo. "Ain't nothing missing in this burg."

"They ought to give them yellow cards, too," said the Senegalese.

"Pourquoi?" asked Ray.

"Pour la santé publique, comme les filles. Et voyez, ils sont toujours en concurrence avec eux. Ce n'est pas juste."

Ray laughed. "Justice, like equality, *mon vieux,* does not exist in the mathematics of life. It's a man's world, you might say a white man's world and . . . 'a man's a man for a that.' "

Two sailors, arm in arm, their white caps set far back on their heads, came out of the British-American Bar and moved in a slow drunken roll across the square, chanting, as if they were rooting for a team: *"We are Americans. . . . We are Americans. . . ."*

The African Bar was jammed full when the boys got back there. Smoke hung in gray chunks in the hot, strong-smelling air. Under it the player-piano was spitting out a "Charleston" recently arrived in Marseilles, while Martinique, Madagascan, and Senegalese soldiers, dockers, *maquereaux*—and, breaking the thick dark mass in spots, a white soldier or docker—were jazzing with one another and with the girls of the Ditch.

A Senegalese, squeezed up against the bar, with his wrist in a sling, called to Banjo as the boys pushed themselves in:

"Hey! you see American sailor?"

"I seen plenty a them, but I don't pay them no mind," said Banjo. "Wha's matter with you' hand?"

The Senegalese related to the boys how a gang of American sailors had rushed a bistro-dancing in Joliette, where colored and white of the quarter were amusing themselves, and tried to break it up. He had got a sprained wrist, but for revenge he had landed a sailor a butt that skinned his forehead and clean knocked him out.

"How did it finish up?" Ray asked.

"The police came just when the *patron* got out his revolver."

"Oh, Lawd!" Banjo began in a Negro prayer-meeting tone. "It's a hellova life and all Gawd's chilluns am creatures of the debbil, but, oh, Lawd, lawdy, don't let a cracker cross mah crossings in this Frenchman's town."

The boys pushed into the dance.

XVI. The "Blue Cinema"

RAY had met a Negro student from Martinique, to whom the greatest glory of the island was that the Empress Josephine was born there. That event placed Martinique above all the other islands of the Antilles in importance.

"I don't see anything in that for *you* to be so proud about," said Ray. "She was not colored."

"Oh no, but she was Créole, and in Martinique we are rather Créole than Negro. We are proud of the Empress in Martinique. Down there the best people are very distinguished and speak a pure French, not anything like this vulgar Marseilles French."

Ray asked him if he had ever heard of René Maran's *Batouala*. He replied that the sale of *Batouala* had been banned in the colony and sniggered approvingly. Ray wondered about the truth of that; he had never heard any mention of it.

"It was a naughty book, very strong, very strong," said the student, defending the act.

They were in a café on the Canebière. That evening Ray had a rendezvous at the African Bar with another student, an African from the Ivory Coast, and asked the Martiniquan to go with him to be introduced. He refused, saying that he did not want to mix with the Senegalese and that the African Bar was in the *bas-fonds*. He warned Ray about mixing with the Senegalese.

"They are not like us," he said. "The whites would

treat Negroes better in this town if it were not for the Senegalese. Before the war and the coming of the Senegalese it was splendid in France for Negroes. We were liked, we were respected, but now——"

"It's just about the same with the white Americans," said Ray. "You must judge civilization by its general attitude toward primitive peoples, and not by the exceptional cases. You can't get away from the Senegalese and other black Africans any more than you can from the fact that our forefathers were slaves. We have the same thing in the States. The Northern Negroes are stand-offish toward the Southern Negroes and toward the West Indians, who are not as advanced as they in civilized superficialities. We educated Negroes are talking a lot about a racial renaissance. And I wonder how we're going to get it. On one side we're up against the world's arrogance—a mighty cold hard white stone thing. On the other the great sweating army—our race. It's the common people, you know, who furnish the bone and sinew and salt of any race or nation. In the modern race of life we're merely beginners. If this renaissance we're talking about is going to be more than a sporadic and scabby thing, we'll have to get down to our racial roots to create it."

"I believe in a racial renaissance," said the student, "but not in going back to savagery."

"Getting down to our native roots and building up from our own people," said Ray, "is not savagery. It is culture."

"I can't see that," said the student.

"You are like many Negro intellectuals who are bellyaching about race," said Ray. "What's wrong with you-all is your education. You get a white man's education and learn to despise your own people. You read biased history of the whites conquering the colored and primitive peoples, and it thrills you just as it does a white boy belonging to a great white nation.

"Then when you come to maturity you realize with a shock that you don't and can't belong to the white race. All your education and achievements cannot put you in the intimate circles of the whites and give you a white man's full opportunity. However advanced, clever, and cultivated you are, you will have the distinguishing adjective of 'colored' before your name. And instead of accepting it proudly and manfully, most of you are soured and bitter about it—especially you mixed-bloods.

"You're a lost crowd, you educated Negroes, and you will only find yourself in the roots of your own people. You can't choose as your models the haughty-minded educated white youths of a society living solid on its imperial conquests. Such pampered youths can afford to despise the sweating white brutes of the lower orders.

"If you were sincere in your feelings about racial advancement, you would turn for example to whites of a different type. You would study the Irish cultural and social movement. You would turn your back on all these tiresome clever European novels and read about the Russian peasants, the story and struggle of their lowly, patient, hard-driven life, and the great Russian novelists who described it up to the time of the Russian Revolution. You would learn all you can about Ghandi and what he is doing for the common hordes of India. You would be interested in the native African dialects and, though you don't understand, be humble before their simple beauty instead of despising them."

The mulatto student was not moved in his determination not to go to the African Bar, and so Ray went alone. He loved to hear the African dialects sounding around him. The dialects were so rich and round and ripe like soft tropical fruit, as if they were fashioned to eliminate all things bitter and harsh to express. They tasted like brown unrefined cane sugar—Sousou, Bambara, Woloff, Fula, Dindie. . . .

The *patron* of the African Bar pointed out men of the different tribes to Ray. It was easy to differentiate the types of the interior from those of the port towns, for they bore tribal marks on their faces. Among civilized people they were ashamed, most of them, of this mutilation of which their brothers of the towns under direct European administration were free; but, because tattooing was the fashion among seamen, they were not ashamed to have their bodies pricked and figured all over with the souvenirs of the brothels of civilization.

It was no superior condescension, no feeling of race solidarity or Back-to-Africa demonstration—no patriotic effort whatsoever—that made Ray love the environment of the common black drifters. He loved it with the poetical enthusiasm of the vagabond black that he himself was. After all, he had himself lived the rough-and-tumble laboring life, and the most precious souvenirs of it were the joyful friendships that he had made among his pals. There was no intellectual friendship to be compared with them.

It was always interesting to compare the African with the West Indian and American Negroes. Indeed, he found the Africans of the same class as the New World Negroes less "savage" and more "primitive." The Senegalese drunk was a much finer and more tractable animal than the American Negro drunk. And although the Senegalese were always loudly quarreling and fighting among themselves, they always made use of hands, feet, and head (butting was a great art among them) and rarely of a steel weapon as did the American and West Indian Negroes. The colored touts that were reputed to be dangerous gunmen were all from the French West Indies. The few Senegalese who belonged to the sweet brotherhood were disquietingly simple, as if they had not the slightest comprehension of the social stigma attaching to them.

At the African Bar the conversation turned on the hostile feeling that existed between the French West Indians and the native Africans. The *patron* said that the West Indians felt superior because many of them were appointed as petty officials in the African colonies and were often harder on the natives than the whites.

"Fils d'esclaves! Fils d'esclaves!" cried a Senegalese sergeant. "Because they have a chance to be better instructed than we, they think we are the savages and that they are 'white' negroes. Why, they are only the descendants of the slaves that our forefathers sold."

"They got more advantages than we and they think they're the finest and most important Negroes in the world," said the student from the Ivory Coast.

"They're crazy," said the *patron*. "The most important Negroes in the world and the best off are American Negroes."

"That's not true! That can't be true!" said a chorus of voices.

"I think Negroes are treated worse in America than in any other country," said the student. "They lynch Negroes in America."

"They do," said the *patron,* "but it's not what you imagine it. It's not an everyday affair and the lynchings are pulled off in the Southern parts of the country, which are very backward."

"The Southern States are a powerful unit of the United States," said Ray, "and you mustn't forget that nine-tenths of American Negroes live in them."

"More people are murdered in one year in Marseilles than they lynch in ten years in America," said the *patron.*

"But all that comes under the law in spite of the comedy of extenuating circumstances," said Ray, "while lynch law is its own tribunal."

"And they Jim Crow all the Negroes in America," said the student.

"What is Jim Crow?" asked the Senegalese sergeant.

"Negroes can't ride first class in the trains nor in the same tramcars with white people, no matter how educated and rich they are. They can't room in the same hotels or eat in the same restaurants or sit together in the same theaters. Even the parks are closed to them ——"

"That's only in the Southern States and not in the North," the *patron* cut in.

"But Ray has just told us that ninety per cent of the Negroes live in those states," said the student, "and that there are about fifteen millions in America. Well then, the big majority don't have any privileges at all. There is no democracy for them. Because you went to New York and happened to make plenty of money to come back here and open a business, you are over-proud of America and try to make the country out finer than it is, although the Negroes there are living in a prison."

"You don't understand," said the *patron.* "I wasn't in the North alone. I was in the old slave states also. I have traveled all over America and I tell you the American Negro is more go-getting than Negroes anywhere else in the world—the Antilles or any part of Africa. Just as the average white American is a long way better off than the European. Look at all these fellows here. What can they do if they don't go to sea as firemen? Nothing but stay here and become *maquereaux.* The Italians hog all the jobs on the docks, and the Frenchman will take Armenians and Greeks in the factories because they are white, and leave us. The French won't come straight out and tell us that they treat us differently because we are black, but we know it. I prefer the American white man. He is boss and he tells you straight where he can use you. He is a brute, but he isn't a hypocrite."

The student, perplexed, realizing that from the earnestness of the café proprietor's tone there was truth in what he said, appealed to Ray in face of the contradictory facts.

"You are both right," Ray said to the student. "All the things you say about the Negro in the States are facts and what he says about the Negro's progress is true. You see race prejudice over there drives the Negroes together to develop their own group life. American Negroes have their own schools, churches, newspapers, theaters, cabarets, restaurants, hotels. They work for the whites, but they have their own social group life, an intense, throbbing, vital thing in the midst of the army of whites milling around them. There is nothing like it in the West Indies nor in Africa, because there you don't have a hundred-million-strong white pressure that just carries the Negro group along with it. Here in Europe you have more social liberties than Negroes have in America, but you have no warm group life. You need colored women for that. Women that can understand us as human beings and not as wild over-sexed savages. And you haven't any. The successful Negro in Europe always marries a white woman, and I have noticed in almost every case that it is a white woman inferior to himself in brains and physique. The energy of such a Negro is lost to his race and goes to build up some decaying white family."

"But look at all the mulattoes you have in America,"

said the student. "White men are continually going with colored women."

"Because the colored women like it as much as the white men," replied Ray.

"Ray!" exclaimed Goosey who had entered the café, "you are scandalous and beneath contempt."

"That's all right, Goosey. I know that the American Negro press says that American colored women have no protection from the lust and passion of white men on account of the Southern state laws prohibiting marriage between colored and white and I know that you believe that. But that is newspaper truth and no more real than the crackers shouting that white women live in fear and trembling of black rapists. The days of chivalry are stone dead, and the world today is too enlightened about sex to be fooled by white or black propaganda.

"In the West Indies, where there are no prohibitory laws, the Europeans have all the black and mulatto concubines they need. In Africa, too. Woman is woman all over the world, no matter what her color is. She is cast in a passive rôle and she worships the active success of man and rewards it with her body. The colored woman is no different from the white in this. If she is not inhibited by race feeling she'll give herself to the white man because he stands for power and property. Property controls sex.

"When you understand that, Goosey, you'll understand the meaning of the struggle between class and class, nation and nation, race and race. You'll understand that society chases after power just as woman chases after property, because society is feminine. And you'll see that the white races today are ahead of the colored because their women are emancipated, and that there is greater material advancement among those white nations whose women have the most freedom.

"Understand this and you will understand why the white race tries so hard to suppress the colored races. You'll understand the root of the relation between colored women and white men and why white men will make love to colored women but will not marry them."

"But white women marry colored men, all the same," said Goosey. "White women feel better toward colored people than white men."

"You're a fool," replied Ray. "White men are what their women make them. That's plain enough to see in the South. White women hate Negroes because the colored women steal their men and so many of them are society wives in name only. You know what class of white women marry colored men."

"There are Negroes in America who had their fortunes made by white women," said Goosey.

"There *are* exceptions—white women with money who are fed up. But the majority are what I said a while ago. . . . Show me a white woman or man who can marry a Negro and belong to respectable society in London or New York or any place. I can understand these ignorant black men marrying broken-down white women because they are under the delusion that there is some superiority in the white skin that has suppressed and bossed it over them all their lives. But I can't understand an intelligent race-conscious man doing it. Especially a man who is bellyaching about race rights. He is the one who should exercise a certain control and self-denial of his desires. Take Senghor and his comrades in propaganda for example. They are the bitterest and most humorless of propagandists and they are all married to white women. It is as if the experience has over-soured them. As if they thought it would bring them closer to the white race, only to realize too late that it couldn't.

"Why marry, I ask? There are so many other ways of doing it. Europe can afford some of its excess women to successful Negroes and that may help to keep them loyal to conventional ideals. America 'keeps us in our place' and in our race. Which may be better for the race in the long run.

"The Jews have kept intact, although they were scattered all over the world, and it was easier for them than for Negroes to lose themselves.

"To me the most precious thing about human life is difference. Like flowers in a garden, different kinds for different people to love. I am not against miscegenation. It produces splendid and interesting types. But I should not crusade for it because I should hate to think of a future in which the identity of the black race in the Western World should be lost in miscegenation."

Six distinguished whites entered the café, putting an end to the conversation. They were the two gentlemen bums, three other men and one woman. The woman saw Ray and greeted him effusively with surprise.

"Oh, Ray, this is where you ran away to hide yourself, leaving all the artists to mourn for their fine model."

"But she is American," the Ivory Coast student, pop-eyed at the woman's friendly manner, whispered to the *patron*.

"Sure," he answered, in malicious triumph. "Did you think there were no human relations between white and black in America, that they were just like two armies fighting against each other all the time?"

Ray did not know who the woman was, whether she was American or European. She spoke French and German as readily as she spoke English. He had met her at the studio of a Swiss painter in Paris (a man who carried a title on his card) when he was posing there, and she had made polite and agreeable conversation with him while he posed. Later, he saw her twice at cabarets in Montmartre, where he had been taken by bohemian artists, and she had not snubbed him.

The gentlemen bums were as surprised as the Ivory Coast student (but differently) when the woman greeted Ray. They had met the group and were going through the town with them. The leading spirit of the party had desired to stop in the bar when he was told that it was a rendezvous for Negroes.

He was a stout, audacious-looking man, a tireless international traveler, who liked to visit every country in the world except the unpleasantly revolutionary ones. The accidental meeting was a piquant thing for Ray, because he had heard strange talk of the man before. Of celebrations of occult rites and barbaric saturnalia with the tempo of nocturnal festivities regulated by the crack of whips. A bonfire made of a bungalow to show the beauties of the landscape when the night was dark. And a splendid stalwart, like one of the Sultan of Morocco's guards, brought from Africa, as a result of which he had been involved in trouble with governmental authorities in Europe.

Certainly, Ray had long been desirous of seeing this personage who had been gossiped about so much, for he had a penchant for exotic sins. Indeed, a fine Jewish soul with a strong Jeremiah flame in him had warned Ray in Paris about what he chose to call his cultivation of the heathenish atavistic propensities of the subterranean personality. The Jewish idealist thought that Ray had a talent and a personality so healthily austere at times that they should be fostered for the uplift of his race to the rigorous exclusion of the dark and perhaps damnable artistic urge. But . . .

Well, here was this bold, bad, unregenerate man of whom he had heard so much, and who did not make any deeper impression than a picturesque woman of Ray's acquaintance, who carried her excessive maternal feelings under a cloak of aggressive masculinity.

The two other men were Americans. The party was bound for any place in the Mediterranean basin that the leader could work up any interest for. They were spending the night in Marseilles and wanted to see the town. The gentlemen bums had taken them through Boody Lane where they had had their hats snatched and had paid to get them back. The hectic setting of Boody Lane with the girls and painted boys in pyjamas posing in their wide-open holes in the wall, the soldiers and sailors and blue-overalled youths loitering through, had given the party the impression that there were many stranger, weirder and unmentionable things to see in the quarter.

"I tell them there is nothing else to show," said the Britisher, speaking generally and to Ray in particular. "Paris is a show city. This is just a rough town like any other port town, where you'll see rough stuff if you stick round long enough. I can take you to the *boîtes de nuit,* but they're less interesting than they are in Paris."

"Oh no, not the cabarets. They bore me so," said the woman. "We're just running away from them."

She was tall and of a very pale whiteness. She seated herself on a chair in a posture of fatigue. Ray remembered that strange tired attitude of hers each time he had seen her. Yet her eyes were brimful of life and she was always in an energetic flutter about something.

"There's nothing else here," the Britisher apologized to the leader of the party, "but the *maisons fermées* and the 'Blue Cinema' and they are all better in Paris."

"The 'Blue Cinema,' " the leader repeated casually. "I've never seen the thing. We might as well see it."

He ordered some drinks, cognac and port wine, which they all had standing at the bar. A white tout drifted into the bar. Three girls from Boody Lane followed. Another tout, this time a mulatto from the Antilles, and after him two black ones from Dakar. More girls of the Ditch. The news had spread round that there were distinguished people at the café.

"We'll go and have dinner and see the 'Blue Cinema' afterward," said the leader.

Sitting on the terrace, a Senegalese in a baboon attitude was flicking his tongue at everything and everybody that passed by. He reclined, lazily contented, in a chair tilted against the wall. One of the girls, following the party as they came out, called him by name and, leaning against the chair, fondled him. He smiled lasciviously, his tongue strangely visible in his pure ebony face.

Ray, turning his head, saw in the face of the woman the same disgust he felt. Those monkey tricks were the special trade-marks of the great fraternity of civilized touts and gigolos, born and trained to prey on the carnal passions of humanity.

A primitive person could not play the game as neatly as they. During a winter spent at Nice, he had found the cocottes and gigolos monkeying on the promenade more interesting to watch than the society people. The white monkeys were essential to the great passion play of life to understudy the parts of those who were holding the stage by power of wealth, place, name, title, and class—everything but the real thing.

And as there were civilized white monkeys, so were there black monkeys, created by the conquests of civilization, learning to imitate the white and even beating them at their game. He recalled the colored sweetmen and touts and girls with whom he had been familiar in America, some who lived in the great obscure region of the boundary between white and black. Following as they did their own shady paths, he had never been strongly repelled by their way of living, because it was a rôle that they played admirably, scavengers feeding on the backwash of the broad streaming traffic of American life. They were not very different from the monkeys of the French Antilles who carried on their antics side by side with the Provençals and Corsicans and others of the Mediterranean breed. They had acquired enough of civilized tricks to play their parts fittingly.

But not so the Africans, who were closer to the bush, the jungle, where their primitive sex life had been controlled by ancient tribal taboos. Within those taboos they had courted their women, married and made families. And so it was not natural for them, so close to the tradition of paying in cash or kind or hard labor for the joy of a woman, to live the life of the excrescences attaching like mushrooms to the sexual life of civilization. Released from their taboos, turned loose in an atmosphere of prostitution and perversion and trying to imitate the white monkeys, it was no wonder they were very ugly.

After the dinner the younger American created a problem. He was of middle build, wearing a fine New York suit, reddish-brown stuff. He was the clean-shaven, clean-cut type that might have been either a graduate student looking at the world with the confident air of one who is able to go anywhere, or a successful salesman of high-class goods. He wore no horn-rimmed glasses to hide his clear-seeing eyes, and his jaw was developing into the kind common to the men who are earnest, big, and prosperous in the ideals of Americanism.

"But this 'Blue Cinema,' what is it, really?" he demanded.

"I suppose it is a cinematic version of the picture

cards the guides try to sell you in the street," the leader answered. "You don't have to go, you know."

"Oh, I'd like to see the thing, all right," replied the young man, "but—are there colored or white persons in the picture?"

"White, I suppose. The colored people are not as advanced and inventive as we in such matters. Excepting what we teach them," the leader added, facetiously; "they often beat us at our game when they learn."

"But she isn't going, is she?" The American indicated the young woman. "They won't let her in a *maison de rendezvous*."

"Most certainly I am. Am I not one of the party? There isn't anything I am not old enough to see, if I want to. Do you want to discriminate against me because I am a woman?"

"They'll let her in in any place if we pay the price," said the Britisher.

"But she can't go if he is going." The young man looked at Ray.

"Oh, Ray!" The young woman laughed. "That's what it's all about. You needn't worry about him. He has posed in the nude for my friends and he was a perfectly-behaved *sauvage*." She stressed the word broadly.

"That's all right," said Ray to the young man. "I am not going if you go. I am full of prejudices myself."

"Well, good night," the young man said. Abruptly he left the party.

"My friend has done his bit for the honor of the Great Nordic race," the remaining American remarked.

Nobody thought that the "Blue Cinema" would be really entertaining. The leader was blasé and desired anything that was merely different. But they were all curious, except the gentlemen bums, who had seen the show several times as guides and were indifferent. It was very high-priced, costing fifty francs for each person.

The fee of admission was paid. In the large dim hall they were the only audience. . . .

Before the first reel had finished the leader asked the young woman if she preferred to go.

"No, I'd rather see it out," she said.

There was no brutal, beastly, orgiastic rite that could rouse terror or wild-animal feeling. It was a calculating, cold, naked abortion.

The "Blue Cinema" struck them with the full force of a cudgel, beating them down into the depths of disgust. Ray wondered if the men who made it had a moral purpose in mind: to terrify and frighten away all who saw it from that phase of life. Or was it possible that there were human beings whose instincts were so brutalized and blunted in the unsparing struggle of modern living that they needed that special stimulating scourge of ugliness. Perhaps. The "Blue Cinema," he had heard, was a very flourishing business.

He was sitting against a heavy red velvet curtain. Toward the end of the show the curtain was slightly agitated, as if some one on the other side had stirred it. He caught the curtain aside and saw some half a dozen Chinese, conspicuous by their discolored teeth and unlovely bland smiles, standing among a group of girls in a kind of alcove-room which the curtain divided from the cinema hall. The woman of the party saw them, too, before Ray could pull the curtain back, and gave a little scream. The Chinese there did not surprise Ray. He knew that they were hired to perform like monkeys. There were other houses that specialized in Arabs, Corsicans, and Negroes when they were in demand.

As they were leaving the lady president of affairs

appeared and suggested their seeing also the tableaux vivants.

"Oh no, the dead ones were enough," replied the leader.

"Why did you scream?" the leader asked, roughly, when the party was in the street again.

"It was my fault," said Ray. "I pulled the curtain back and she suddenly saw a roomful of people behind it."

"That was nothing. I saw them, too, as you did, but I didn't scream." He turned on her again. "You say you want to go to any place a man goes and stand anything a man can stand, and yet you scream over a few filthy Chinese."

"I'm sorry," she said. "It was out before I could check myself."

"I suggested leaving in the beginning, but you insisted on staying it out; I didn't expect you to scream. Did you enjoy it?"

"It was *so* ugly," she said, adding: "I think I'll go to the hotel. You men can stay, but I'm finished for to-night."

The leader laughed and asked the American to take her home.

"Oh, I don't need an escort. I'll just take a taxi," she said.

"You'd better not go alone. The taxis are not safe this time of night," said Ray.

"I don't care whether you need an escort or not. *I* am taking you to the hotel," said the American.

They walked to the main street and Ray hailed a green Mattei taxicab. "They are run by a big company and are safe," he said. "The unsafe ones here hang around the shady places—just as in New York and Chicago. Some of the private drivers are touts, and as you never know which is which, I always recommend my friends to ride with the Trust."

"Where shall I find you fellows afterward?" the American asked.

"Where now?" said the leader. "After this 'blue' refinement I should like to go to the roughest and dirtiest place we can find."

"I think Banjo's hangout down Bum Square way is just the place we are looking for," said Ray.

"That's the place," the Britisher agreed.

They told the American how to find it.

"Whether it is blue or any other color of the rainbow, the cinema is for the mob," said the leader. "It will never be an art."

"I don't agree," said Ray. "Pictorial pantomime can be just as fine an art as any. What about Charlie Chaplin?"

"He's an exception. A conscientious artist with a popular appeal."

"All real art is an exception," said Ray. "You can't condemn an art wholesale because inartistic people make a bad business of it. The same condition exists in the other arts. Everybody is in a wild business race and the conscientious workers are few. It's a crazy circle of blue-cinema people, poor conscientious artists, cynical professionals and an indifferent public."

"You know I like the cinema for exactly the reverse of its object," said the leader. "Because it's about the easiest way to see what people really are under the acting."

Ray laughed and said: "The 'Blue Cinema' was just that," and he added: "Some of us don't need the cinema, though, to show us up. We are so obvious."

In the Bum Square they ran into Banjo with his instrument.

"Where you coming from?" Ray asked.

"Just finish performing and said *bonne nuit* to a kelt."

The leader was curious to know what "kelt" meant.

Banjo and Ray exchanged glances and grinned.

"That's a word in black freemasonry," explained Ray, "but I don't object to initiating you if Banjo doesn't."

"Shoot," said Banjo.

"In the States," said Ray, "we Negroes have humorous little words of our own with which we replace unpleasant stock words. And we often use them when we are among white people and don't want them to know just what we are referring to, especially when it is anything delicate or taboo between the races. For example, we have words like ofay, pink, fade, spade, Mr. Charlie, cracker, peckawood, hoojah, and so on—nice words and bitter. The stock is always increasing because as the whites get on to the old words we invent new ones. 'Kelt' I picked up in Marseilles. I think Banjo brought it here and made it popular among the boys. I don't know if it has anything to do with 'keltic.' "

"Oh no," said the leader. "Kelt is a real word of Scottish origin, I think."

"That might explain how Banjo got it, then. He used to live in Canada."

The party went to Banjo's hangout and the whole gang was there drinking and dancing.

The American joined them very late, worried about his younger friend. A panhandling Swede had accosted him in the Bum Square and told him that he had seen his friend in Joliette, helplessly drunk and getting into a taxicab with a couple of mean-looking touts. The American had gone at once to his friend's hotel, to Joliette, and then had searched in all the bars of the quarter, but could not obtain any information about him.

The next day he was found in a box car on a lonely quay beyond Joliette, stripped of everything and wearing a dirty rag of a loin-cloth for his only clothing. The sudden and forced reversal to a savage state had shocked him temporarily daft.

XVII. Breaking-up

WHEN the dawn came filtering down through the Ditch, Ray left the party and staggered through Boody Lane to find his bunk. Dengel and Ginger had left the place before him, knocking their heads together in a drowsy roll. Malty had sprawled in a corner over a table. The bistro man helped him to a room upstairs. Banjo was full and tight as a drum, but he kept right on playing and drinking as if he were just beginning a performance. Goosey was tired out, but he was curious about the distinguished company and his desire to keep up with it kept him awake. The gentlemen guides had tried to persuade Ray to go with the party to an all-night café off the Canebière for a big breakfast, but he had declined. All the nourishment Ray needed then was to lay his body down and rest.

Boody Lane showed no stir of life as he passed through it. All the holes in the wall and the cafés were closed. Not a dog, not a cat prowled through the alley. A strange clinical odor rose from the heaps of rubbish in the gutters, communicating to his wine-fogged senses an unpleasant sensation as if he were in quarantine. He had remarked that strange odor in the Ditch at regular intervals and he could not account for it. The big hospital was just on the hill above. That could not be the source of the smell, he argued, for he had often walked through the street right under the hospital without detecting it.

Ray's head was pounding with the tom-tom of savage pain and his brain was in a maze, reacting against himself. For weeks he had been purposelessly boozing and lazing and shutting his mind against a poem in his heart and a story in his head, both clamoring to be heard. There was no reason why he shouldn't do something, and yet he couldn't do anything.

He could not sleep, although he was so tired. The racket in his head left him unstrung. The drinking-bout after the cinema was a stupid thing, he knew. Couldn't expect anything but a mess from mixing myself up like that. Every time he dozed off he woke up with a broken dream of some vivid experience, as if his real self did not want to go to sleep.

However, repose was so good, even though sleep played the imp, that he had no idea how many hours he had lain there until Banjo broke into the room, demanding if he was going to sleep through the night after sleeping all day.

"You can carry on sleeping forevah," said Banjo. "I'm gwine to leave you-all. I'm gwine away to the Meedy."

"Which Midi and who are you going away with?" Ray asked. "You're right in the Midi now, don't you know that?"

"Oh, I gwina away to the real Meedy down the coast whar the swell guys hang out at."

Ray guessed at once that the leader of the party had proposed to take Banjo along, and he said: "You'd better stay here in Marseilles. It's no use you running off with those people. They're no good for you."

"Ain't nothing bad foh mine, pardner. I was bohn on the go same like you is, and Ise always ready for a change."

"Where they taking you?"

"Nice, Monte Carlo, some a them tony raysohts. I don't care which one. But I'm going there and don't you fear. You hold mah place for me in Boody Lane till I come back, mah friend."

"Boody Lane in your seat. You're a damn fool to go. What about the orchestra? Aren't you going to fool with that any more?"

"The orchestry! What you wanta remember it now for? You'd fohgotten it as well as I and everybody did, becausen theah was so many other wonderful things in this sweet poht to take up our time. All the same, pardner, Ise jest right in with the right folkses now to hulp me with an orchestry."

"Help my black hide. You'll get nothing but a drunken bath outa those people, and it's better you get that way in the Ditch than where you're going. They can't help themselves, much less you. You can think about an orchestra, but they can't think about anything. They don't want to. I know it's no good your going with them. I'm sorry I introduced you to them."

"Hi, pardner, what's eating you? You jealous of a fellah just becausen they done took me instead a you?"

"You big bonehead. He wanted me to go, and it was after I refused he asked you. I know those people. I'm sure I can stand them better than you by being a charming, drunk, unthinking fool. But I couldn't stand them sober and thinking just a little bit. You won't be able to stand them drunk or sober. I know it. You'll cut a hell of a hog before you know what's happening.

"How do you think I've been traveling round so much without having any money? I wasn't a steady seaman like you. I did it by getting on to people like those for a while. I could carry on—*for a while.* But I aways got tired and quit. I can't see you carrying on with them for any time at all—can't imagine you ever being funny with that big lump of a buffalo."

"Well, I'm gwina try it, all the same, pardner. I know them folks mahself just like you does. I been around Paree with one a them once, a dandy hoojah. Didn't I tell you about it?"

"Yes, but he was different."

"Why don't you come with us, and ef we didn't like it we could come back together?"

"I don't want to go and they wouldn't want two of us, crazy. One black boy is just odd enough for a little diversion. But what do you want to quit us for? What about Latnah?"

"You know she is mad at me. Nearly stick me with a dagger. I leave her to Malty and you."

Perhaps Banjo did not know how great his influence was over the beach boys. His going away with his instrument left them leaderless and they fell apart. And as a psychological turn sometimes foreshadows a material change, or *vice versa,* even in obscure isolated cases, the boys felt that something was happening and realized that it was becoming very difficult for them to gain their unmoral bohemian subsistence as before.

They did not know that the Radical government had fallen, that a National-Union government had come into power, and that the franc had been arrested in its spectacular fall and was being stabilized. They knew very little about governments, and cared less. But they knew that suddenly francs were getting scarce in their world, meals were dearer in the eating-sheds and in the bistros, and more sous were necessary to obtain the desirable red wine and white, so indispensable to their existence.

However, some of them had an imperfect commonsense knowledge of some of the things that were taking place in the important centers of the world, and that those things were threatening to destroy their aristocratic way of life. Great Britain's black boys, for example. They observed that colored crews on British ships west of Suez were becoming something of a phenomenon. Even the colored crews on the Mediterranean coal ships, of which they had a monopoly in the past, were being replaced by white crews. The beach boys felt the change, for the white crews would not feed them the left-over food.

The beach boys were scattered and broke. Goosey and Bugsy had joined a gang of Arab and Mediterranean laborers and were sent by a municipal agency to work in an up-country factory. Ray had no money. He owed rent on his room and could not obtain any money by either begging, beseeching, versifying, or story-telling.

Latnah solved the situation by proposing that she, Ray, and Malty should go to the vineyards to work. The agencies wanted hands. The pay was about thirty francs a day, with free board and lodging and plenty of wine. They could save their wages to return to Marseilles. The harvesting would last about a month.

Ray jumped at the idea. He had been just about fed up with the Vieux Port when he met Banjo. The meeting and their friendship had revived his interest. Now that Banjo was gone and the group dispersed, the spell was broken and he felt like moving on. He tried to get Ginger to go along. But Ginger, as an old-timer on the docks, preferred to stay and take his chances with Dengel.

THIRD PART

XVIII. Banjo's Return

IT WAS high, hot, golden noon. Blackened from head to foot, clothes, hands, neck, face, a stream of men from the coal dock filed along the Quai des Anglais, across the suspension bridge, and into the Place de la Joliette. There was no telling blond from dark, yellow or brown from black.

The men were half-day workers. They circled round the fountain in the square, stripped to the waist, and splashed water over their bodies. From the cleansing process emerged two black busts, and one was Banjo's.

He was remarked by Ray, who had returned with Malty and Latnah from the vintage and were seated at a table on a café terrace across from the fountain, drinking tumblers of beer.

"There's ole Banjo working in coal," said Ray.

"Whar?" asked Malty. "Oh, he done find the Ditch again, eh? Couldn't banjo it enough foh them ofays. He musta come back jim-clean and broke-up foh gone working in coal."

"Something musta happened to him," said Ray.

Latnah gave a cattish giggle. "Coal good for him," she said. "He very good look working in coal." She giggled again.

"What's matter with coal, Latnah?" asked Ray. "I've worked in it, too, and I'm not ashamed, for it's better than bumming if you can stand it."

Banjo was passing without seeing them, on his way to a little tramp bistro. His air was rather melancholy. Ray called to him, and immediately he brightened up and came swaggering up to them.

"So you're back here again," said Ray. "I told you you wouldn't like it. What was the matter you quit?"

"Because I wasn't any monkey business," replied Banjo.

"What do you mean, monkey business?" asked Ray.

"Just what I done said and no moh. I was tiahed of it befoh stahting in. It wasn't no real man's fun with them people like it was with that cracker that done blow me to such a swell time in Paree. It was like a ole conjure-woman business with debbil fooling in hell that didn't hit mah fancy right noneatall, so I jest haul plug outa it and here I is. If Ise gwine to be monkey business it sure is moh nacheral foh mine in the Ditch."

Banjo had returned to the Vieux Port about a fortnight after he had left it, to find the group dispersed.

One evening when he was playing at the Rendezvous Bar, he fell in with two Senegalese whom he had not known before. They invited him to a bistro in a narrow, shady lane near the St. Charles Railroad Station, where many Arabs and Negroes and white touts lived. The Senegalese ordered plenty of wine and expensive cognacs and liqueurs. They treated some bistro girls to drinks. They danced while Banjo played.

After midnight one of the Senegalese left the bistro—to arrange a little affair, he said. When he did not return in half an hour the other Senegalese went in search of him. None of them ever returned. The *patrone* of the bistro said Banjo would have to pay for the drinks, and the amount was a hundred and ten francs. He had on the suit that Taloufa had redeemed for him and looked prosperous, but he had only two francs in money.

The woman seized his instrument and thus Banjo lost his magic companion.

"Imagine them two cannibals playing me a cheap trick like that," commented Banjo. And he laughed. "The cannibals them learning the dirty li'l' ofay tricks quick enough. I've been made a fool of by many a skirt, but it's the first time a mother-plugger done got me like this and, by Gawd! they had to come black like the monkey them is to do it. Yessah-boy."

With the loss of his musical instrument, Banjo determined to get himself a job. He went hustling, and far down the docks toward Madrague he found Dengel, who had shifted his hangout to a freighter that was undergoing repairs and manned by Senegalese. Dengel was in his usual state and looked as if liquor was oozing from his skin in a soft moisture of perspiration. Banjo learned from him that a crew of black men, some of whom knew Ginger when he was an able seaman who never funked any work, had got him drunk and stowed him away with them. That was the only way of getting Ginger to leave his beloved breakwater.

Banjo told Dengel he was hunting for a job and wanted him to help.

"What for a job?" demanded Dengel.

"Because I've got to work. I ain't got no money. I done lost mah banjo. I ain't got nothing left, so I jest nacherally gotta find anything that looks some'n' like that hard-boil' ugly-mug baby they calls a job."

"Job no good. Good job no easy find," said Dengel. "Why you no keep on as you use to?"

"Kain't no moh. Gang's all broke up and gone the cardinal ways that every good thing dead must go."

There were two Senegalese section bosses on the docks who hired the majority of the Senegalese when there was work for them. One of them was always in a boisterous semi-drunken state. The other was a fine, upstanding specimen of black man with strong white teeth and clear eyes, a full, gorgeously-carved mouth, and smooth-shining ebony skin. His name was Sarka. Banjo had seen him a couple of times at the African bar. But he did not often frequent the Vieux Port quarter. He was married and lived in a more respectable proletarian district of the town. Banjo got Dengel to arrange a meeting between him and Sarka at the Rendezvous Bar.

Banjo took with him to the bistro his suitcase with a few chic articles of toilet in it. He had heard that the boys who had jobs often had to grease the palm of the section boss. Having been used to that in the United States, he was prepared to meet it. He had a few sous for wine and he relied on Dengel to help out his sparse French vocabulary.

With an apologetic gesture Sarka turned up his palms in reply to Banjo's demand for work. He didn't think it was possible. Work! It was difficult nowadays. There was a new law passed about strangers working in France. Banjo didn't know that, eh! The hectic post-war period when there was more work than men to do it was passing now. Strangers who wanted work had to show a special permit.

The new law did not in any way affect those dock workers who were strangers. The majority of the little bosses were Italians and when men were wanted to load and unload ships, they took the men that were at hand. When work was scarce the strangers yielded place to the favorite sons, of course. And the favorite sons were naturally Italians, who were strangers in the unnaturalized sense, but not foreigners in the generally accepted sense.

Banjo chinked glasses with Sarka and Dengel, gulped down some red wine, and turned to occupy himself with his suitcase. He fished up a striped silk shirt and handed it to Sarka. Sarka's eyes gleamed bigger and whiter in his jolly, handsome face. He had seen American seamen with those shirts that opened all the way down, just like the B.V.D.'s that one could put on without ruffling the kinks in the hair after combing them. He was eager to possess one. Now it was his without cost —a silk one!

"Pour moi?" asked Sarka.

"Oui, vous," responded Banjo, his forefinger punching Sarka's heart. And then he nearly knocked him over with a gorgeous oblique-striped necktie, of the kind that college boys flaunt in America.

"Mais non!" exclaimed Sarka, and affectionately his hand sought Banjo's shoulder.

"Oui, oui, vous take," Banjo grinned. *"Vous, moi, amis, bons amis."*

"Toujours amis," agreed Sarka. *"Demain, vous venez me chercher aux docks. Travail."*

Thus Banjo opened a way to work on the docks. And Sarka, who hoped to go to America some day, began learning English words from him. Some British West Africans of the Ditch asked Banjo to introduce them to Sarka. He did, and they, too, got work. Soon Sarka's gang was English-speaking and he was saying to his men: "Get down," "Come up," "Time to begin," "Stop," and a few more boss words.

At the African Bar it was gossiped that Sarka had taken on the English-speaking hands in place of the Senegalese because he touched a five-franc graft every day from each of them. Besides, they were always swilling wine together in the evenings and it was the gang that paid. Banjo was Sarka's friend and chief man, of course, and the gossip excluded him from the daily graft, but it was well known that he had given a bribe of fancy stuff to gain Sarka's good will.

Dengel told Banjo all about the gossip and Banjo replied: "I ain't worrying about them niggers' evil lip. They c'n talk their jawbone loose. Ise used to niggers talking. What's giving a man a shiert? Back home wese every jackman used to scrambling foh buying jobs. Peckawoods and niggers. It's all the same. A shiert! Five francs! That ain't no money. I done buy moh jobs than I can count up in the States. I buy them offen white mens and I buy them offen niggers. Them was big-money days when every man was after the other fellah's skin. Oh, Lawdy! Life is a game a skin; black skin, white skin, sweet skin and all skin and selling one another is living it."

Sarka did not boss his new gang very long. There were cross-currents of rivalry and jealousy on the docks between Italians, Arabs, Maltese, and Negroes. Sarka got into a knife fight with two Italians, and when they were separated, he and one of his opponents had to be rushed to the hospital, dangerously wounded and streaming blood. It was that that sent Banjo down to working in coal.

The coal worker is a grim, special type of being, whether he is underground or under water or above ground. On the docks there was always an easy chance to work in coal. But the jolly beach boys never turned to coal when poor panhandling and hunger obliged them to think of a temporary job. Coal that made them blacker than they were and the flesh-eating sulphur were the two principal commodities they avoided. A cargo of grain or fruit was preferable when an overflow of cargoes in port gave them a chance. Coal was not in the line of the regular dock workers either. And so this general aversion saved derelict foreign drifters who wanted to work from starving on the docks.

The irresponsible, care-free Banjo became a steady worker in coal. Every morning he roused at five o'clock, got into his coal rags, and hustled down to Joliette to get into the first line of workers. Sometimes he had a full day's work, sometimes a morning's work, sometimes an afternoon's work, sometimes no work at all. Days when he did nothing he sat drinking in a little bistro near Chère Blanche's box in the Ditch. Reacting against the trick of the Senegalese that cost him his instrument, Banjo had made up with her again. So much messy fuss about skin color, he reasoned, and this life business ain't nothing but a skin game with all the skins doing it—black, yaller, white . . . what's the difference!

Even the wine he drank afforded him little pleasure. He never got tipsy now in the exciting, guzzling manner of the free banjo-playing, panhandling days. As casually as ever he had returned to hard labor again and remained doggedly at it. Thirty and odd francs a day. Food, wine, a pillow at Chère Blanche's. He existed now as if those glad camaraderie days had never been.

Ray found Banjo's new condition exasperatingly melancholy and tried to talk him out of it. Days of drifting without purpose, not knowing what tomorrow might bring them, were altogether better, Ray argued, than the dirty-drab contentment in which Banjo was now burying himself. But Banjo had undergone a complete metamorphosis.

"The gang's done broke up, pardner, and I done lose mah instrument. Good fun like that kain't last forevah. Everything works out to a change."

"But Malty and I are here. We can get together again."

"I don't think. I don't feel habitually ambitious and musical no moh."

"But you used to be so different. Why, the way you used to talk and act, living the way you talked! When I had the blues so bad and felt like chucking everything, it was you who made me screw up the courage to keep plugging on. The way you were your own big strutting self and to hell with hard life and hard knocks and one hard hussy in the Ditch. Now you're nothing but a poor slave nigger in coal for *une putaine blanche*."

"I was fed up with everything and just had to have some human pusson close to me, pardner. I ain't back home where I could find a honey-sweet mamma, so I just had to take what was ready and willing. Life is a rectangular crossways affair and the only thing to do is to take it nacheral."

XIX. Lonesome Blue Again

EVERYTHING works out to a change." Banjo had said a right pretty thing. The grand rhythm of life rolled on everlastingly without beginning or end in human comprehension, but the patterns were ever changing, the figures moving on and passing, to be replaced by new ones.

So the life of the Ditch remained, but for Ray the aspect was changed. It was gray now. And he was thinking of moving on and taking with him the splendid impression that the beach boys' lives had left him in that atmosphere. He would go away now while that impression was gorgeously intact, before the place palled on him. He never liked to stay in a place beyond the point where there was something to like about it. Though the Ditch was dirty and stinking he had preferred it to a better proletarian quarter because of the surprising and warm contacts with the men of his own race and the pecuniary help he could get from them at critical times. Their presence had brought a keen zest to the Ditch that made it in a way beautiful.

So Ray was preparing to move on, although he had not many preparations to make. His baggage had consisted of some books and manuscripts of which he was now unfortunately relieved. Before going to the vintage he had boxed them up and left the box in care of the manager of the Seamen's Mission. He thought that that was the safest procedure. But when he returned from the vintage the box could not be found and the cock-eyed manager could not account for it. White beach-combers had stolen it with the books and the manuscripts, which included all the new things that Ray had done and was trying to do.

"That's where I get plugged up for fooling with Christian charity," commented Ray. "I've never believed in the thing and yet I went messing with that damned mission with the Archbishop of Canterbury's angel flying over it. Better I had left my stuff in the African pub."

"Get you ready, hand and foot, and let's beat it away from here," Ray apostrophized his members. Every day he thought of going, but he hesitated, and a week had flashed by since his talk with Banjo. He had had money enough to take him a long way when he returned from the vintage, but it was now considerably reduced. There was no ship in sight with an easy place. Well, whatever it was, he was decided about going.

One morning he went down through the docks to the breakwater, desiring to get certain aspects of it fixed in his memory before leaving. Returning at noon, he came upon the apparition of Lonesome Blue in Joliette Square.

Ray had not seen Lonesome Blue since the day at the Senegalese café when the boys were telling jokes. That afternoon he had gone with Lonesome to police headquarters and seen the assistant chief about his case. That official had told Ray that the police had nothing to do about an order of expulsion but to arrest and prosecute the delinquent again if he did not put himself beyond the frontiers of France. Ray tried to get a written statement to that effect to take to the American consulate, but the official said that that was a generally understood thing.

From police headquarters he went to the American consulate with Lonesome. The French official was right.

They knew all about the regulations controlling deportés. Ray saw the chief clerk who was in charge of shipping and seaman's affairs. The chief clerk was a Britisher of that typical breed, overbearing to common persons and crawling to superiors, that a mere British subject has to buck up against all over the world.

This gentleman recognized Lonesome immediately and vented a low-down growl, such as a vicious hound might make at a mangy mongrel daring to approach his presence.

"Hm. Yer back heah again, eh?" he said to Lonesome. "What do yer want? I swear I'll do nothing more for yer and I don't want you to come back to this office." He brought his fist down on the desk.

Ray told him that he had brought Lonesome there because the man was ill, helpless, and daft. He had been to police headquarters and asked why the boy was continually arrested and punished in prison for violation of the expulsion law when he seemed incapable of acting for himself, and they had told him that his case was the affair of the American consular authorities and not theirs. The chief clerk told Ray that Lonesome Blue had refused without reason to go on the first ship he put him on months ago, and he would do nothing further for him. He had too many pressing cases and other business to give any further attention to Lonesome, who had left the United States on a foreign vessel and did not really merit the same treatment as an American seaman on an American vessel.

The clerk was long and lean, with the appearance of a woman who had suffered and grown gaunt and spidery from never having a man. His lips were tightly compressed, too repellently thin and slight to utter a hearty laugh. He was just the little-official type that is punch-pleased when some poor devil fails to comply with instructions given, gets into trouble, and affords the opportunity to say, "I did *my* duty." The wretchedest thing about him was his voice, which was a sort of unnatural amalgam between a cockney whine and the English gentlemanly accent, and it grated up and down Ray's nerves like a saw against a nail.

"But why did you come here?" he asked Ray. "Why are yer interested in this?"

It was on Ray's tongue to say that he was there only in the interest of common decency, but he checked that, remembering that his purpose was not to be cleverly sarcastic, but to try to get Lonesome Blue back to the United States, where he might have a chance to pull himself together among his own people. And so Ray was humble and begged the clerk to give Lonesome another chance, because he was sorry for his first mistake. The clerk remained obdurate, and Ray went with Lonesome to see one of the consuls.

He was ushered into the presence of the chief and he explained Lonesome's case. Quite different from his underling, the consul was attentive and courteous. He reiterated that Lonesome Blue's initial blunder was a serious one, that seamen's affairs were dealt with entirely by the chief clerk, but he would speak to him and see that the fellow was given another chance.

Ray thanked the consul and left Lonesome Blue in the office. He did not see him again before going to the vintage and thought that he had been shipped home. Now, here he was like an apparition, swaying strangely and mournfully in the square like a fading tree without roots in the soil.

Ray's first impulse was to make a détour and pass by without speaking, but he checked it and went over to him. Lonesome showed no signs of surprise or pleasure when Ray addressed him and asked what he was still doing in Marseilles. He was lifeless, existing mechanically because the life-giving gases still gave him sustenance. The pimples on his face had developed into running sores and the texture of his skin was ash gray. His clothes were like rags eaten at by rats. The suit was originally Ray's who had received it second-hand from an American friend. It was too large for him and he had given it to Lonesome. The soles of his shoes kept contact with the uppers by being corded round his ankles.

"Where were you all this time?" asked Ray.

"In prison again for two months. The day you left me at the consulate the shipping-master gived me twenty francs and tells me to come back every day until he got a ship for me. I went and got me a room in the Ditch and that same night the police comes and gits me right theah in the hotel. It was the fierst time they done took me out of a hotel. That was jest my hard luck. The time they done gived me for the last expulsion was up and I couldn't explain them nothing that the consul was gwineta send me back home this time, for I ain't acquainted with the language, and so I jest nacherally had to go right on back to that awful prison."

"Well, this time you must ask the consul for some kind of paper so that the police will keep off you until you find a ship," said Ray.

"I don't know about getting anything moh out a them people," said Lonesome. "I been up theah this morning and the shipping-master bawled me out and said he thought I was dead or gone away, and if I kain't find a ship or stow away like any other no-count sailor, I must die, but he ain't agwineta do nothing moh foh me. And he chased me outa there. Maybe ef you would go back up theah with me again that 'u'd hulp some."

"I don't know. I hardly think so," said Ray. "I think I'll try a letter this time."

That was the best and last plan he could think of. In a talk, interrupted by questions and answers and perhaps extraneous matters, he might miss presenting the most important points that would help. He hadn't the lawyer's manner of presenting facts verbally. And in this case circumstance and condition did not permit him the lawyer's privilege. In a letter he would review Lonesome's case from his initial mistake of refusing to go home the first time he was sent, his subsequent getting into trouble and prison, and the many sentences he had served since, practically all for the same offence. He would say that the chief clerk was right to be angry, but he would show that the man was ill, he had suffered, he was sorry, and was begging for another chance to be sent back to the country of whose ways and language he had some understanding.

Ray thought the letter might have a little more influence if it wore the obvious respectability of this age, so he decided to typewrite it. He went to a typewriter agency and hired the use of a machine. Instead of giving his address in the Ditch he borrowed the decent one of his friend, the gentleman bum. The hotel clerk there knew him and would take care of any reply.

He got the letter done and gave it to Lonesome Blue, and he waited for the result at the African Café. In the late afternoon Lonesome came to the bar with twenty francs, a good pair of second-hand shoes, a serviceable old suit that had been given to him at the Consulate, plus a changed manner.

"I give that there letter a your'n to one a them consuls," he told Ray. "I don't know which one, causen I don't know them differently. And he went up to that shipping-master's office and gived him all that was coming to him, indeed he did. I was outside, but I was sure listening, and I heared the shipping-master said I hadn't acted like a knowed I was a colored boy for quitting a ship after he done put me on it and when there is many skippers as don't want no colored mens. And the consul said he didn't care about that, I was American and had to be sent on back home."

Ray told Lonesome that it wasn't just because he was American that the consul had spoken like that. It was because his was a special case for there were many stranded Americans abroad, white ones, that consuls did not worry themselves about.

"Oh, I knows all about that," Lonesome said. "It's a new day now foh cullud folks. I been reading the cullud newspapers and there is a big organization foh cullud people called the Unia movement of Negroes. Ain't you heared none of it? I thought you was keeping up with race progress, youse always so indiligence-talking. Theyse got to treat us better now all ovah the wul'. The Unia movement will makem, chappie."

"Look here, Lonesome," said Ray. "I always knew that you were the damnedest foolest nigger-head that ever was crazy. It is not because of any organization that the consul is going over the chief clerk's head and giving you another chance. Let me tell you this, as you don't seem to know it. The two go-getting things in this white man's civilization are force and cunning. When you have force or power you make people do things. When you haven't you use cunning.

"You're the poorest kinky-head I ever did see. I put my nicest manner in a letter to get you out of this damned fix you're in, you come shooting off your mouth full a bull about the Unia movement. Don't think I like frigging round officials. I hate it. The movement you need is something in your block to move you away from here.

You're too damnation dumb for this Frenchman's town, which is about the meanest place for any fool who's got no more in his bean than in his block——"

"Oh, quit you' lecturing and let's drink up this twenty francs," said Lonesome.

"No, damn you. I drink with fellows on the beach who are regular fellows, but not with anything like you. I'd drink up the last franc with Banjo, but not you. You'd better take that money and get you a room and report to the consul every day until you get a ship."

Ray left the café with something of the mixed feelings of Banjo and the chief clerk at the consulate toward Lonesome. He felt that it was men like Lonesome, stupid, and utterly repulsive in their stupidity, who made petty officials the mean creatures of bureaucracy that they were.

He hated with all his soul the odor of bureaucratic places, and right then he felt intensely hostile toward Lonesome as the cause of his coming in contact with them. He was no welfare-worker and had rather wanted to do as Banjo had advised—leave Lonesome alone. But he was unable to rid himself of the insistent thought that, as he was qualified, it was the decent thing for him to do it. He pondered the fact that his education and a different culture had made an attitude that was positively logical for Banjo inhumanly cowardly for him. Banjo's back was instinctively turned away from the Lonesome trail that leads you straight along to the Helping-Hand brotherhood of Christian charity with all its sanctimonious cant. And though Ray sometimes had to follow the Lonesome trail a little, he felt deep down in his heart that Banjo's way was the better one and that he would rather lose himself down that road and be happy even to the negation of intellect.

"I think I'll leave this burg this very evening," Ray

said aloud to himself. He felt a forceful urge to go, and go at once, as if he feared that something else would happen to dampen the hot, hectic, riotous rooting and scramble of the Ditch that he wished to preserve. He wanted always to think of it as he personally preferred it.

He went to his lodging and paid up his rent and put his things in a hand-bag. In the evening he returned to the African café, looking for Malty and Banjo and Latnah, to have a farewell drink. They were not there, but Lonesome Blue was, drinking up his twenty francs with a group of Portuguese blacks and Senegalese whose company the beach boys spurned because it was said that they lived off the garbage thrown from the big liners.

Lonesome was singing that hideous cockney song, "Show me the way to go home." He waved his glass at Ray and said: "Come on, nigger, and join the gang and quit playing youse a white man because you got a little book larnin'."

Ray turned his back on Lonesome and went outside, smiling sardonically at himself. A sharp gust of wind blew through him, a warning that cold weather was coming soon. He buttoned up his coat and thought of a serviceable jersey that he possessed and of an overcoat that he possessed not.

He walked on aimlessly. Before the Monkey Bar a crowd was collected in admiration of a new jangling jazz, and in the Bum Square he came upon Malty, who told him that Banjo was taken suddenly ill and was dying.

XX. The Rock of Refuge

IN HIS little *chambre noire* in a lodging-house of the Ditch Banjo was bearing his pain. His kidneys were not functioning and his belly was as tight as a drum and hard as a rock. He sat on the little bed, hunched up in a clenched resistance, as if trying to hold the pain back from laying his body out. Sometimes he would lie down on his side, his back, his belly, sometimes slide to the floor, but always in that hard, huddled posture. Sometimes in his shiftings he could not repress a deep-down groan, but he bore his punishment bravely like a man—one who knows that he must take the consequences of spurning the sheltered, cramping ways of respectability to live like a reckless vagabond, who burns up his numbered days gloriously and dies blazing.

"We got to get him into hospital," Ray said to Malty.

He rushed out to find a taxicab. He found one in the Rue de la Loge whose chauffeur he knew. He had once been a sailor at Toulon and Ray had become acquainted with him during a winter he spent there. He had been of service to Ray in giving him the low-down in that interesting sailor town, and Ray had returned it by teaching him the right English phrases for his frequent pick-up trips to Nice and Marseilles, where he met the right sort of tourists that helped eke out his wage pittance.

He had finished his compulsory service and was now, among other things, a chauffeur at Marseilles, where his

English was invaluable to him as a chauffeur-guide on the docks and in the town. He greeted Ray familiarly when they met, but they were no longer friends. For Ray was always with the beach boys and the Senegalese and the chauffeur belonged to the touting set of the Ditch who hated the beach boys and the Senegalese, especially as their special field was being invaded and disorganized by the blacks.

Ray and Malty helped Banjo from the third floor down the dim, narrow, frowsy staircase and into the taxicab. The hospital was near a church on the hill above the Ditch. Ray left Banjo in the taxicab and entered the admission bureau. At the desk was a pale, thin woman with a nose sharp-pointing upwards. She was eating a sandwich. Ray told her about Banjo's illness and that he would like to get him into the hospital. She replied in a familiar, condescending way and asked where Banjo came from. Banjo had declared that he was French, but as he had nothing to prove that and as his accent was so unmistakably Dixie, Ray said that he came from the United States. She asked Ray if he had a paper from the American consul sending Banjo there. Ray said no. She told him that Banjo could be admitted only by an order from the consul or the local police. Ray thought it was better to go to the police. He had had enough of the consulate with Lonesome Blue's case.

But at the police station they wanted proof of Banjo's residence in Marseilles. Banjo had nothing to show but a dirty picture card that a stowaway pal had sent him from Egypt. What the police wanted was an identity card and that no beach boy could get.

"The man is dying for want of medical attention," said Ray to the police officer. "You won't let him die because he hasn't got an identity card."

The police officer reddened and gave Ray a permit for Banjo's admittance to the hospital.

When they returned the lady of the admission bureau had something more to say before she passed Banjo in. "You know, Sidi," she said to Ray, "our hospitals here are all filled up with strangers, so that there is little place for French citizens. The consuls send us patients, but the foreign governments never pay for them. It is the French taxpayer who must pay."

The boys had helped Banjo into the entrance and he was sitting patiently and silently on the lower step. While the woman was talking and before she had made out the necessary paper, a medical student came down the stairs and spoke to Ray. They had met in a café frequented by students. He was attracted to Ray, as he also wrote a little.

The woman, seeing that Ray was acquainted with a superior of the hospital, completed the formality of Banjo's admittance with dispatch and politeness.

The student was going home, but he turned back and conducted Ray and Banjo to the emergency ward, into an atmosphere so full of kindliness, courtesy, and solicitous attention that the irritation of getting there was immediately wiped off the boys' minds. There were two nurses, an interne, and another medical student. Banjo was put on an operating table and given first aid, which relieved him a little. The student stayed until that was finished. Afterward Banjo was conducted to a regular ward. The doctor said he would have to undergo a real operation.

Ray stayed with him until he was settled. As soon as Banjo was relieved, a little of the old vagabond color came back to him and he said, "I thought I was Canaan bound by a hellova way."

"You thought right, maybe," said Ray. "The little

street leading up here is called Montée du Saint Esprit, which means Going up to the Holy Ghost."

"Don't mention that theah hauntsing name, pardner, because I ain't noneatall ready for him yet."

Ray told Banjo about Lonesome Blue.

"That haunts back in this sweet poht again!" he exclaimed. "No wonder I done fallen ill, foh that nigger is hard luck. Don't ask me how, but I know he ain't nothing else."

Banjo, like the other beach boys, was superstitious. Things they saw and people they met and shook hands with. The food they ate. They could tell on getting up of a morning whether their day would be lucky or unlucky, by the kind of thing or person they first met. Certain types of people, like Lonesome Blue, always brought trouble. Their superstitions were logical reactions.

As for Lonesome Blue, Ray fully sympathized with Banjo's belief that he was a bringer of bad luck.

When Ray left the ward the chauffeur was gone, although he had not been paid. A couple of days later Ray saw him and asked how much was owed. The chauffeur replied: "Nothing at all. You were my good comrade once and now you help a comrade who is sick and you are poor. I don't demand anything for the taxi."

He invited Ray into a café for a drink and told him that he was going to get married in a short time. The chauffeur had a girl in Boody Lane from whom he got money, and he mentioned another in one of the *maisons fermés*. The girl he was going to marry came from the country. He boasted that she wore her hair long and did not use rouge.

One day Ray saw them on a café terrace in the Rue de la République and he was introduced. The girl was all the chauffeur had said besides being heavy, simple and possessed of no noticeable charm. Ray supposed that the chauffeur after dealing so much in ready-made attractive girls desired for a wife a type that was radically different. He was buying a piece of ground and a cottage in one of the suburbs and wanted Ray to ride out with him and his fiancée to see it, but Ray declined, pleading a rendezvous.

The chauffeur told Ray with the frankest gusto that, besides his legitimate trade, he had an interest in Boody Lane and a Maison Fermé and that he was employing all the tricks he knew to obtain his cottage and lot and settle down to a respectable married life.

He was merely one illustration of the sound business sense inherent in the life of the Ditch.

There was no mistaking the scheme of life of the Ditch, that bawdiness was only a means toward the ultimate purpose of respectability. And that was why it was so hard on simple seamen and beach boys who came to it with romantic ideas as a place of loose pleasure.

Ray decided that he could not think of going away without seeing Banjo through his operation. He had shared the boys' pleasures and it was merely decent for him to share their troubles and do what he was individually capable of doing to help.

He had wanted very much to leave taking intact the rough, joyous, free picture of the beach boys' life in the regimented rhythm of the Ditch. He felt that time, circumstance, and chance had contributed to fill it full of a special and unique interest that he would never find there again, and he wanted the scene to remain always in his mind as he had reacted to it.

But life is so artistically uncompromising, it does not care a rap about putting a hard fist through a splendid plan and destroying our dearest artifice. So the unwelcome reappearance of Lonesome Blue was the beginning of a series of events that enlarged and altered greatly the impression of the Ditch that Ray had hoped to preserve.

"As them doctors am gwina cut me up, pardner," said Banjo, "I guess you'd better write back home foh me." Facing the prospect of an operation, with, on one hand, his Canadian army discharge certificate which made him in a sense British, and, on the other, the fact of his deportation to France as a French citizen, Banjo's thoughts at last reluctantly turned to America as home. His parents were long ago dead. He had only an aunt in a Cotton-Belt town. She had raised him and a brother who had died in adolescence. Banjo gave Ray that aunt's address. He had last seen her in 1913 and did not know whether she had moved or was dead or alive.

Banjo also asked Ray to let Chère Blanche know that he was in the hospital. Ray did so, but Chère Blanche never stirred from her post to visit him. Latnah would not go to see him, either. She swore that she was finished with him because he was a man who had no race pride. But Malty got money from her with which good things were bought for Banjo.

The boys kept him supplied with cigarettes and sweets, although the beach was not a place of plenty now. Wine was not allowed. Ships were few and they were having the most difficult of panhandling times. But Ray was in good luck. He had sold a poem, and a friend of poets had liked it so much that she had sent him a gift of money.

One Sunday, a week after Banjo had been admitted to hospital, Ray and Malty took him a chicken dinner. Ray had bought the chicken and Latnah had cooked it. She protested weakly when Ray said he was taking a part of the dinner to Banjo, but she did not try to prevent him, and it was she who provided a bowl.

The Hôtel Dieu (so the hospital is named) presented the aspect of a gloriously macabre picnic on this Sunday noon. It loomed like a great gray Rock of Refuge on the hill above the Ditch. The ultimate hope of salvation for the afflicted. Below it was a church with a wooden Christ nailed to a cross in the yard. Across the street opposite the church was the police force. Patients who were not bedridden flocked out on the two tiers of verandas. Girls of the Ditch with bandaged eyes and broken mouths and noses, and touts with knife wounds and arms in slings, hobbling on crutches, all victims of the bawdy riot; hollow-cheeked youths limping by; poor pimply children of leaky, squinting eyes; ulcerous middle-aged men and women, and old ones learning to creep again. From the beds against the windows, red naked stumps of arms and legs were stuck up like grotesqueries. Into this scene entire proletarian and bawdy families, as well as friends, had come to share the sacred Sunday dinner with the patients. Their children were with them and each group gathered around the bed of the patient to gorge and guzzle red wine amid the odors of ether and iodine.

Banjo enjoyed his chicken feed and asked what was new in the Ditch. Malty told of some Indian seamen (coolies, he called them) who had come straggling down to the African Café from one of the love shops the night before. They complained that all their money was taken away from them and that they were turned out of the place. They had approached the police in the street, who pretended they could not understand them. So they had gone to the African Bar to ask if any of the blacks would interpret for them.

"I acks them," said Malty, "why they 'lowed them kelts to get holt a that good money a theirns. And the best explanation one (they all speaks a turr'ble jabberway) he says because the kelts was such good spohts, kidding and laughing with them."

"Laugh," said Ray. "Nobody in this Ditch knows how to laugh. These people can't laugh. They smirk at the color of money and the fools think that is laughing. They can't laugh, for their mouths are too tight and their lips too thin. We Negroes can throw a real laugh because we have big mouths."

"That can be true," said Malty, "but them Indians ain't much different to me. When they show their teeth it's like a razor blade. I don't like it noneatall and I don't trust no coolie laughing."

Malty's metaphor was striking. He had often felt even more physically uncomfortable among Indians. Next to Negroes, the Asiatic people with whom he always felt at ease and among whom he always loved to be, were the Chinese.

"I can't forgive the mean cruelty of this Ditch," continued Ray. "Why the licensed houses with the police marching up and down before them if the seamen can't have any protection? Are the places licensed for the benefit of the touts or the clients? Men coming off a ship after days and weeks at sea must need women. And the Ditch is the most natural place for the average seaman. I can understand a man getting in a pickle by a bad pick-up on the street. But when he is robbed in the licensed places I ask what's the good of them? You might as well have no licensed place at all, as in John Bull's and God's own, so that if you get caught in a sex trap you could take it as a private affair and not blame it on the authorities, as the fellows do that get bitten here."

"Ain't all the fellahs blaming nobody, pardner?" laughed Banjo. "This heah Lincoln Agrippa, otherwise Banjo, is one no-blame business. Of cohse, someathem houses is jest a trap-hole and them pohlice no better'n a gang a cut thwoat p-i's. But it's the mens them that make the stuff such hard business. I know more about it than you does, pardner, 'cause Ise been moh low-down rough-house than you. And you don't know nothing of all what a pants-wearing bastard will do between welching on a bargain and running off and not coming across. Tha's why the womens carry guns in them ahmpits and keep a lot a touts foh protecting them. You mustn't fohget that their business ain't no picnic. It is hard labor."

Ray could not reply to this. He felt that there was something fundamentally cruel about sex which, being alien to his nature, was somehow incomprehensible, and that the more civilized humanity became the more cruel was sex. It really seemed sometimes as if there were a war joined between civilization and sex.

And it also seemed to him that Negroes under civilization were helplessly caught between the two forces. There was an idea current among the whites that the blacks were over-sexed. He had heard it coarsely from ordinary whites and he had spoken frankly with intelligent-minded ones about it. He had also got it from things written by white people about the black.

But from his experience and close observation of Negro sex life in its simplicity in the West Indies and in its more complex forms in American and European cities, Ray had never felt that Negroes were over-sexed in an offensive way and he was peculiarly sensitive to that. What he inferred was that white people had developed sex complexes that Negroes had not. Negroes were freer and simpler in their sex urge, and, as white people on the whole were not, they naturally attributed over-sexed emotions to Negroes. The Negroes' attitude toward sex was as much removed from the English-American hypocritical position as it was from the naughty-boy exhibition manner of the Continent.

Even among rough proletarians Ray never noticed in black men those expressions of vicious contempt for sex that generally came from the mouths of white workers. It was as if the white man considered sex a nasty, irritating thing, while a Negro accepted it with primitive joy. And maybe that vastly big difference of attitude was a fundamental, unconscious cause of the antagonism between white and black brought together by civilization.

The beginning of the cold season brought the boys straggling back to Marseilles. Ginger had made his way back from Cardiff to Rouen, from Rouen to Bordeaux, and he had taken ten days, he said, to walk from Bordeaux to Marseilles. Goosey left Bugsy at the factory, going away with a white fellow. He had wanted to go to Paris. He got as far as a town near Lyon, where he found a job as kitchen man in a hotel. But under the new law the proprietor could not keep him unless he could obtain French papers. There was an American consul in the town and Goosey went and asked his help in procuring the necessary papers. The consul was a colored man, but Goosey did not know it, because he was so near white. (It was Ray who told Goosey when he returned to Marseilles that the consul was Negroid, for he had read about him and seen his photograph in an American Negro publication.) The consul could not get the coveted papers for Goosey, and, faced with the fact that he could get nowhere without them, he returned to Marseilles. He was discouraged and became ill on the way back. Arriving at Marseilles, he had just enough strength to drag himself to the American consulate, from which he was sent to the hospital. He was placed in a ward below Banjo.

The turning of the weather was detrimental to the boys, whose scanty clothing was suitable for summer only. It also dampened their ever-bubbling gayety. But they all agreed that Marseilles was the most convenient port for them. The only one missing from the group was Bugsy. Nobody knew whether he had left the factory or was still there.

One Saturday, when Ray went to the hospital, Banjo told him that he expected to be operated on the next week. As Ray was leaving, Banjo asked him almost casually if he ever saw Chère Blanche. Ray said he had not seen her since he took her his message, because he did not pass frequently through Boody Lane, but he had heard that she was still in her box.

"What do you expect, Banjo? I told you to lay off her, because I knew she would treat you a second time just as she did the first. Those people in the Ditch—they can't afford to have a heart."

"I knowed she was no angel," said Banjo. "But as she done come and made up with me without me chasing after her a second time, she coulda leastways come and see me once. Is that theah Latnah still hanging around?"

"Yes, she is," said Ray, "but everything is different, you know. The gang doesn't hang together as we used to. And you know Latnah is mad at you. Would you like to see her?"

"Well, I wouldn't mind befoh fixing mahself foh that cold steel business," said Banjo.

"I'll tell her," Ray said.

Latnah went to see Banjo with flowers.

"Now ain't this showing some'n'!" exclaimed Banjo. "The whole ward'll think wese crazy. Everything comes heah. Eats and drink and the whole shooting family, but it's the first time this place got gifted with flowers."

They made up to each other.

"Quand on est malade, on ne garde pas la rancune," said Latnah.

Banjo assented. "It's a sure thing I ain't making no preparation for the boneyard, for I jest ain'ta gwina die. But being as Ise gwineta get down and under the knife, it does make me feel better for all of us to be as we uster befoh. It was a bum business we getting mad at each other ovah a no-'count kelt."

"It was no that made me angry," said Latnah, "no she herself. I was mad when Bugsy tell me you like white more than colored and that you were so lucky getting money, and every time you get it you waste all with the white and don't remember friends. And she after you again jest because you make a big raise——"

"That Bugsy is the meanest monkey-chaser I evah seen," cried Banjo. "Bugsy hate white folks like p'ison and all a them look the same to him without any difference. He got mad at me 'causen I done gived five francs to a poah hungry white kid. But all the stuff he been handing out about me is bull. Of cohse I know mah limentations and I know I kain't nevah wear that there crown of glory as a pure-and-holy race saint. But I know what I is, what I feel, and what I loves, and I ain't nevah yet fohget that Ise cullud and that cullud is cullud and white is some'n' else."

"I no could imagine you really love the white more than the colored," said Latnah.

"Chuh! How could I evah love white moh'n colored?" cried Banjo. "White folks smell like laundry soap."

And Banjo and Latnah laughed so contagiously that all the white patients in the ward joined them without suspecting in the least that they were laughing at themselves.

XXI. Official Fists

SOME time after the operation Banjo left the hospital. Latnah volunteered to put him up until he felt strong enough to rough it.

Ray had suggested to Banjo that when he came out of the hospital he should go straight to the American consulate to inquire for mail, as that was the address he had given his aunt when he wrote to her. When Banjo presented himself at the consulate he found two letters from his aunt, and one contained a ten-dollar note neatly folded in a bit of newspaper. He was also given ten francs and sent to a Seaman's Hotel, where his board-and-lodge would be paid by the consulate until a boat was found for his repatriation. He was not subjected to any questioning as to how he had come to Marseilles or how long he had been there.

Banjo changed the ten dollars and gave the boys of his group ten francs a piece. To Ray he gave fifty and kept a hundred for himself. They celebrated the evening big. Banjo, Ray, Malty, Latnah, Dengel, and some others who had recently landed on the beach; a stripling of a mulatto mess-boy, who was also put up in Banjo's hotel, waiting for a ship; a Central American from one of those complicated little Tangier-like places, who was working all the consulates of the Latin republics as well as the British and American; an Egyptian black and three British West Africans. Bugsy was still missing, and Goosey was not with the gang.

Goosey had left the hospital before Banjo, but his illness had scared him into careful retirement. He had entered the hospital coughing and feverish, and had come out quite emaciated, like a skeleton with his nigger-brown suit hanging loose on him. The consul had put him in the same hotel where he sent Banjo, but Goosey did not get all that without being lectured for his obstinacy in quitting his ship when he was warned not to.

The gang fed at an Italian feeding-place. There was a grand pouring of red wine, plenty of black and green olives, pickles, and tiny salt fishes and *saucisson,* macaroni and tomato sauce, and veal à la Milanaise. From feeding they went to the African Café, with the roses of the Ditch in their wake. Music was supplied by a tinpanny pianola and half of the night was jazzed away to its noise. All through the feverish coughing-spitting jazzing there was restless movement of feet between Boody Lane and the bistro, and when the hot tumult was falling note over note from its high crescendo, the jazzers pairing off, Latnah did not find her Banjo. Chère Blanche had not vamped him this time, however, as his emotions were as indifferent to her now as to Latnah. Banjo was stuck in another hole of the Ditch.

Banjo bought a second-hand instrument at a bargain. He got it at one-half the amount that he owed at the restaurant where his original companion was held. He redeemed his clothes from the Mont de Piété. He made sweet music for the boys again, but the old spontaneous, care-free happiness was not in the new gang.

For one thing, Banjo was no longer a homeless drifter. He was safe. He had no need to worry about his keep. He would soon be sent back home. It was splendid that he had a few francs to help the boys during the cold days when ships were scarce and panhandling was worthless. But he could not share his eats at the hotel with them. If he ate outside, he could not let one of them have the benefit of his hotel meal. And he could not take any of them up to his room. When the mistral blew the freezing Atlantic gusts into the Mediterranean and it was too shivering cold in the box car for the boys, Latnah would sneak some of them up to her box on the roof and Ray allowed others the floor of his *chambre noire,* which he shared with the Egyptian who worked as a watchman on the docks. But Banjo could not help.

One afternoon Goosey, with Ray, Latnah, and Malty, was sitting on the terrace before his hotel when a tall, slim black boy with straight jet-shiny hair came up to them. He looked like a Somalie. The boy was one of the gang with whom Goosey and Bugsy had gone to work in the up-country factory. He spoke to Goosey and told him that Bugsy was very ill in a lodging-house in one of the alleys back from Boody Lane. They had both come back just that week to the Ditch. He had told Bugsy to go to the hospital, but he had refused, saying he didn't like a hospital for he was afraid that they might make away with him there. The boy had been getting milk for him, which was all that he would take. But he had talked all night long the night before. The boy had been to the docks for a half a day's work, and when he went home in the afternoon he had found Bugsy very quiet and strange. He thought he ought to be compelled to go to the hospital, and so he had come to ask Goosey's help.

The boys and Latnah started off for the Ditch. On the way they picked up Banjo. Bugsy was lying in one of those little *chambres noires* that are among the distinctive human contributions to Mediterranean cities of blessed sunlight and beautiful sea and blue sky, where the tourists go for health and play. You find them in

Marseilles in all the third and fourth class hotels. Rooms built, it would seem, particularly to exclude the sun. Rooms without windows open to the air and only a transom hole giving on the corridor. If you are too poor to take a room with a window, you might be able to afford one of these. They are suffocating enough in the center of the city, but in the Ditch, where the great army of dock workers live, and where the air is always humid and the alleys are never free of garbage, they are fetid dens.

The good sun of the Midi was splendid outside, but it was gloomy night in Bugsy's room. Banjo turned on the thin electric light and there he was on the dirty bed. Strange and quiet he was indeed, as the boy had said. He lay there like a macabre etched by the diabolic hand of Goya. With clenched fists and eyes wide open, as if he were going to spring at an antagonist, even if he were God himself. He finished with life as he had lived it, a belligerent, hard-fisted black boy.

Latnah tried to close his eyes, but only one would stay shut, and so she tied a handkerchief over them. He had no clothes but the rags he had died in. The boys contributed things to bury him. Goosey gave his blue Charleston pants, Ray an extra blue coat that he had, Banjo a shirt and socks. The boys got together at the African Café, and subscribed the cost of the funeral—fifth class or a class near to it. The cost was only one hundred and twenty francs, including the priest.

Latnah wanted a wreath. Ray objected. Why a wreath? It was nonsense and wasteful. Latnah insisted that it would look lovely to give what was once Bugsy a wreath of flowers. Why not a wreath? Why not, indeed? thought Ray. And he collected the money for a wreath. Nonsense and waste he had said. But nonsense was often pretty. Who shall gauge or determine the true spirit that lies between the proudest or humblest outward show and the inward feeling? And he really had no rooted objection to waste. Why not waste money on a tradition of flowers as on wine or non-utilitarian ornaments? Think of the fortunes the seamen wasted in the Ditch and the sums the beach boys bummed and spent for the pleasure of drinking, when there were even poorer people than they who might have used that money for necessary nourishment. No, he did not resent waste. He always loved to read of millionaires spending gorgeously. There was something sublime about waste. It was the grand gesture that made life awesome and wonderful. There was a magical intelligence in it that stirred his poetic mind. Perhaps more waste would diminish stupidity, which was to him the most intolerable thing about human existence.

So Bugsy had his wreath of flowers and the boys got together behind his hearse and marched to the cemetery. American, West Indian, Senegalese, British West African and East African blacks and mulattoes, a goodly gang of them, and one little brown woman.

A few days after Bugsy's funeral Ray moved to a nice little hotel in the center of the town. He had a small, cheerful room, very clean, and a window overlooking a garden through which the morning sun poured. Just then he was beginning to do some of the scenes of the Ditch and he felt lifted out of himself with contentment to sit by a sunny open window and work and hear sparrows chirping in the garden below. It was a solitary delight of the spirit, different from and unrelated to the animal joy he felt when in company with the boys in the Ditch.

He had arrived at this state by one of those gestures that happened to spur him on at irregular periods when thought was in abeyance and he was mindlessly vegetating. A temperamental friend in Paris had sent him another life stimulant by the hand of a young American, who had decided to stay in Marseilles for awhile, and had persuaded Ray to move to a respectable quarter where they could keep in touch with each other. . . .

Ray had made the little move, although feeling that it would have made small difference if he had finished with the town in the Ditch. He would have to make a bigger move before long. Where, he didn't know. Some point in Africa, perhaps, or back to Paris, or across the pond, following Banjo.

Soon Banjo and Goosey would be leaving. Two white fellows had been sent back and it was their turn next. Goosey was still rather weak, and reluctant and sad about returning. But Banjo was worried about nothing. He stayed on in the hotel and was happy to be taken care of. He ate and drank a plenty, bought wine for the gang with his extra francs, told big stories, and played the banjo.

One morning the Egyptian with whom Ray had roomed invited Goosey, Banjo, and Malty to take lunch on the ship of which he was watchman. It was an American ship and the steward was a Negro. The Egyptian had told the steward about the boys and the steward had said he would like to have them down to lunch. Goosey declined the invitation, saying that he did not feel up to walking down to the docks.

Banjo and Malty went. In the Joliette Square they met Dengel and a British West African and invited them along. But when they got to the ship an officer refused to let them go aboard and posted a man to see that they did not. The officer said to the white seaman: "Don't let any of them niggers on here." Calling the boys "niggers" made them angry.

The West African cried out to the officer that he would show him what "niggers" could do if he came on the dock. "We know all you Americans hate Negroes," he said, "but you're not in America. This is France."

The boys stood on the pier, frankly contemptuous. They had money among them, and as Banjo could go back to his hotel to eat, they did not really care about the ship's food. In the meantime, unknown to them, the officer had sent a man to inform the police. They had just moved from the ship and were sauntering farther down the dock when two policemen on bicycles overtook them. The boys were taken to the police station on the Quai du Lazaret and given a merciless beating. Each of them was taken separately into a room by the policemen, knocked down and kicked. Then they were turned loose.

Banjo took the matter humorously. Sitting in a café that evening with Ray and the young American, whose name was Crosby, he said: "Ise lame all ovah. They didn't do nothing if they didn't bruise us with knuckle and boot heel, but they know their business so damn good you'd have to use one a them magicfying glasses to find the marks.

"They got us jest where they wanted, so we couldn't do nothing. And they dusted us, pardner. Fist and feet they dusted us good and proper and didn't miss no part but the bottom of our feets."

Ray and young Crosby thought that the case should be reported. It seemed incredible to them that the boys should be so brutally treated without any charge against them, without a hearing, when they were innocent of any illegal act. Was it because they were friendless black drifters?

"I ain't doing nothing at all about it, nor noneathem others, either," Banjo said. "I done told you that time with Lonesome Blue, pardner, that them official affair ain't nevah no good to get mixed up with. I jes keeps away from them. Especially the pohlice. I do mah stuff, but Ise always looking out foh them in every white man's country and keeping a long ways off from them, 'causen them is all alike. We fellahs done drink up a mess a good wine down them docks without paying anything for it. If we ketch a li'l' hell this day—well, you can't get away with the stuff all the time."

"Get away with the stuff nothing," said Ray. "You fellows didn't do anything."

"But we *have,* though, pardner. Wese done a lot and didn't get caught."

Often Ray had heard the Senegalese say that the police treated them like cattle because they considered them mere blacks. But he had no proof that that was a general attitude. Nearly all the Negroes lived in the Ditch or contiguous to it, and amused themselves there. And as the life of the Ditch was so bloody brutal, the police could not be gentle. Every week there were *rafles,* and every ordinary person in the Ditch was searched, white, brown, and black. The touts and girls and bistro-keepers always knew in advance when a *rafle* would take place. Therefore the only people that were taken in the combing were newcomers to the Ditch, mostly seamen who carried blackjacks or revolvers to protect themselves against the touts. Ray had become used to being searched in the Ditch. The police were never polite, but he didn't expect them to be. With the identity-card regulation and the frequent *rafles* the French police had unlimited power of interference with the individual and Ray had arrived at the conclusion that he had really had more individual liberty *under the law* in the Puritan-ridden Anglo-Saxon countries than in the land of "Liberté, Egalité, et Fraternité."

That evening he went with Crosby to see the second

half of the Crystal Palace show. Afterward they looked in on two *boîtes de nuit,* which they did not like, and then went to a big café, where they sat on comfortable cushioned benches and talked. Crosby was younger than Ray. A young poet who had the fanatical faith of youth in the magic of poetry, he argued with Ray about his marked absorption in prose. Ray contended that it seemed a natural process to him that youth should pass from the colorful magic of poetry to the architectural rhythm of prose.

They parted after midnight. Crosby's hotel lay west of the Canebière and Ray's to the east. The east was more respectable in Marseilles than the west. The mail had arrived in the late evening, bringing the Paris morning newspapers. Ray took his way to his respectable quarter in his most respectable rags, armed with respectability—in the form of the Paris editions of the *New York Herald Tribune,* the British *Daily Mail* and *Le Journal.*

He was thinking about Banjo and the boys and of their beating-up and philosophically wondering if the boys had not done something to deserve the beating—something that Banjo had not revealed in telling about it—when passing two policemen in the street leading to his hotel (one leaning against the door of a house and the other standing carelessly on the pavement), he was suddenly grabbed without warning. The policemen started to search him roughly and thoroughly.

Ray protested. What was it and what did they want of him? he demanded. He had his papers and would show them immediately. This he was proceeding to do when the bigger policeman stunned him with a blow of his fist on the back of the neck. He forthwith arrested Ray, handcuffed him, and took him to the police station in the bawdy quarter. The handcuff was a special chain kind that could be tightened and loosened at will, and the policeman took great pleasure in torturing Ray on the way to the jail. There the two police wrote out and signed a charge against him. Ray also made a signed statement. The police quarters stank much more than the dirtiest den of the Ditch with that odor peculiar to jails. Ray was locked up all night and in the early morning was told to go.

As to the why of his arrest and brutal treatment Ray could obtain no answer. He went home and wrote a statement of his case to the prefect. A couple of days later he received a notice to call at police headquarters. Crosby, who was particularly worked up over the incident, accompanied him. He was a Western-state lad of radical persuasion. His great-grandfather had been a frontiersman, an Indian-fighter in the struggle to win the West for civilization. His mother, a Southern woman, came from one of the proudest of the slave states.

At police headquarters Ray repeated his statement to an investigating inspector, who confronted him with the two policemen. They contradicted his story, asserting that Ray had tried to obstruct them in doing their duty, but he maintained his statement and further accused them of lying.

The inspector was naturally partial to his men. He read the statements again and then asked Ray what he wanted. Ray hesitated, and Crosby said, "Justice." The inspector turned and said savagely he was not talking to him. The word "justice" had been the first to suggest itself to Ray, but as he did not believe in that prostitute lady who is courted and caressed by every civilized tout, he had not pronounced her name.

The inspector then admitted that if Ray prosecuted the case on the statement he had made, the policeman who had struck him would lose his job. Did he want to prosecute or not? Crosby was nudging him to prosecute, but Ray declared that what he really wanted was to know why he had been beaten and arrested. Was it because he was black? The inspector replied that the policemen had made a mistake, owing to the fact that all the Negroes in Marseilles were criminals.

"Oh!" Ray said, this was the first time he had heard that Doctor Bougrat was a Negro. The police clerk who had taken Ray's statement hid a grin behind his palm.

(The Doctor Bougrat case had provided the excitable Provençal city with one of its most notorious crime sensations. The man had been a soldier during the war and was seriously wounded in the head. He was a drug addict and a hard drinker. One day the body of a cashier who had disappeared with an unimportant sum of money was found hidden in his office in a state of decomposition. Doctor Bougrat declared that the man had died accidentally after an injection. He was indicted for murder and sentenced to life imprisonment and banishment. The case had particularly impressed Ray from the way the public reacted to it. The newspapers tried the doctor and called him a murderer and a thief and charged him with every criminal activity before the case went to the courts. And on the day when the crime was reconstituted, according to French procedure, in the doctor's office, an enormous crowd gathered in the street and along the Canebière *prolongee* and the army of touts and prostitutes who lived by the plunder of tourists and seamen joined their voices to that of the respectability of the city in calling for Bougrat's blood: "Lynch him! Lynch him!")

As he accepted his dismissal and started to go, Ray turned to the inspector and said that when he was a boy the French book that had moved him most was Victor Hugo's *Les Misérables*. Javert, typifying the police, had been particularly fascinating to him, and judging from the inspector's statement about the Negroes of Marseilles the French police had not changed since those days. But had grown a little worse.

Crosby's sense of injustice was strong. He resented the inspector's insulting manner toward him and he reproached Ray for not following up the case.

"But I didn't want to," protested Ray. "Do you think I want to mess my time up fooling with the stinking law, just for a policeman to lose his job? Twenty-five francs a day and a family! That most sacred of French things—a family on twenty-five francs a day. Can you wonder they are what they are? When I wrote to the prefect I didn't write for revenge, but for knowledge."

"But what good is that?" said Crosby. "You only wasted your time, since you had a chance to prosecute and didn't. You haven't gained anything."

"Haven't I? Don't you think it was revenge enough for me that you, an American, half-Southerner, had to protest to a French official about French injustice to a Negro? The French are never tired of proclaiming themselves the most civilized people in the world. They think they understand Negroes, because they don't discriminate against us in their bordels. They imagine that Negroes like them. But Senghor, the Senegalese, told me that the French were the most calculatingly cruel of all the Europeans in Africa.

"You heard what the inspector said in explanation. To me the policeman's fist was just a perfect expression of the official attitude toward Negroes. Why should I prosecute *him?*"

"I think you've got a little Jesus stuff in you," Crosby said.

"I don't have any Jesus stuff, nor the stuff of any other Jew—Moses or Jeremiah or St. Paul or Rothschild."

"You don't like Jews!"

"Not any more than I do the Christians. You mustn't forget that the Christians were made by the Jews. Christian morality is the natural child of Jewish morality. When I think of the Jews' special contribution as a people to the world I always think of them as obsessed by the idea of morality. As far as I have been able to think it out the colored races are the special victims of biblical morality—Christian morality. Especially the race to which I belong.

"I don't think I loathe anything more than the morality of the Christians. It is false, treacherous, hypocritical. I know that, for I myself have been a victim of it in your white world, and the conclusion I draw from it is that the world needs to get rid of false moralities and cultivate decent manners—not society manners, but man-to-man decency and tolerance.

"So—if I were to follow any of the civilized peoples, it wouldn't be the Jews or the Christians or the Indians. I would rather go to the Chinese—to Confucius."

"That's a long way," remarked Crosby.

XXII. Reaction

IN THE evening Ray and Crosby had dinner together. Afterward they sauntered along the Canebière. The metropolitan newspapers had arrived and a few proletarian enthusiasts were marching up and down the street, crying: *"Humanité! Humanité!"* Ray bought one, saying: "Let me try contact with the printed animal. It may be better than the natural."

They went into a café where Crosby had made a few student acquaintances. The waiter came over to serve them and he said familiarly to Ray, "How is everything, Joseph?"

"Don't call me Joseph," said Ray. "I'm not a damned servant like you."

Crosby, shocked, looked incredibly at Ray, as if his ears had belied him.

"What shall I call you, then?" asked the waiter, still pleasantly and using the familiar French *tu.*

"Don't *tutoyer* me, either," Ray said. "I don't know you and I don't want to. You speak to me as you do to any other stranger."

The waiter turned sullenly away.

"Good God! Why were you so hard on him?" said Crosby. "He only meant to be friendly."

"Not in the way you think," replied Ray. "'Joseph' is the common French name for male servants in general, just as 'George' is for Negro servants in America.

He meant to be friendly, yes, the way a child is with a dog."

"But the way you jumped on him, saying you were not a servant like him. I was astonished . . . for you have worked as a servant yourself."

"That's no reason why I should be sentimental about stupid servants, Crosby. In fact, my experience puts me in a better position than you to understand and discriminate. I worked as a menial because I was obliged to, and I gave good service and was treated fairly enough without being either familiar or sycophantic. I was not a menial born like this fellow. Some people are born menial-minded and they are not limited to any one class of society. In America there are good darkies who find their paradise in domestic service. But there are Negroes who do it strictly from necessity and they are as different from the good darkies and your Swedish and Irish servant cows as I am from this slimy garçon. I think you're a sentimental radical, Crosby——"

"I thought *you* were a proletarian," he cut in.

"Sure. That's my politics. But you never have asked me why I prefer Proletarian to Liberal, Democrat or Conservative."

"Well?"

"Because I hate the proletarian spawn of civilization. They are ugly, stupid, unthinking, degraded, full of vicious prejudices, which any demagogue can play upon to turn them into a hell-raising mob at any time. As a black man I have always been up against them, and I became a revolutionist because I have not only suffered with them, but have been victimized by them—just like my race."

"But you have no real faith in the proletariat," said Crosby. "Then what can you expect from proletarian politics?"

"I've never confused faith with politics. I should like to see the indecent horde get its chance at the privileged things of life, so that decency might find some place among them. I am not fond of any kind of hogs, but I prefer to see the well-fed ones feeding out of a well-filled trough than the razor-backs rooting all over the place. That's why I am against all those who are fighting to keep the razor-backs from getting fat and are no better doing it than fat swine themselves."

"If that's how you feel, your opponents may consider it their duty to protect the pearls from the razor-backs."

"Pearls are accidental things. You don't find one in every oyster and there may be many among the razor-backs that the fat swine are trampling on while they pretend to be protecting the few in their hands."

"Your being politically proletarian from hatred's got me stumped," said Crosby. "I thought you loved the proletariat."

"I love life—when it shows lovable aspects."

"The docks, for example, you seem so fond of them. And that day I went down with you I heard the white dockers *tutoyer* you and you didn't mind."

"Oh, that was different! That is the dockers' natural language. They take me as one of them and don't worry about distinctions. But this *garçon* does all the time. He has one way of talking to the girls who sit here a long time to sell themselves and pay him a fat tip for it; he has another for me and another for his respectable clients. He *tutoyer* me just like the herd of petty officials of the departments—the post office, the hospital, the identity-card bureau, even in the stores. When I ask them not to *tutoyer* me, they become angry cats and want to scratch. You see, that's their way with the Senegalese. They do it in the manner of the Southerners who 'nigger' the blacks in Dixie. In England all the common working-people say 'darky,' but it is friendly; you feel that, and don't mind. But all the educated people say 'nigger' and I loathe them."

"But perhaps they, too, don't know better."

"Well, they ought to. What's all this modern education for, then? Is it to teach something of real decency in dealing with all kinds and classes of people or is it just to provide polite catch-words for the most-favored classes to use among themselves?"

The unpleasant incidents of the week, all crowding together upon him, had got Ray into an inside-boiling mood. Crosby rather irritated him because he could not readily comprehend his reactions. His white face and the privileges of his white inheritance in a white universe—all fenced him off from that goblin world that did its mocking dance around Ray.

Crosby felt, naïvely, that in Europe, where there was no problem of color, Ray would be happier than in America. Ray refused to accept the idea of the Negro simply as a "problem." All of life was a problem. White people, like red and brown people, had their problems. And of the highest importance was the problem of the individual, from which some people thought they could escape by joining movements. That was perhaps the cause of that fanatical virus in many social movements that frightened away sane-thinking minds.

To Ray the Negro was one significant and challenging aspect of the human life of the world as a whole. A certain school of Negro intellectuals had contributed their best to the "problem" by presenting the race wearing a veil with sanctimonious Selahs. There was never any presentation more ludicrous. From his experience, it was white people who were the great wearers of veils, shadowing their lives and the lives of other peoples by them. Negroes were too fond of the sunny open ways of living, to hide behind any kind of veil. If the Negro had to be defined, there was every reason to define him as a challenge rather than a "problem" to Western civilization.

As they were talking, a student acquaintance joined them at their table. The newcomer had shown a friendly regard for Ray. He had been in Paris and had heard black jazz players, and as he had liked the jazz musicians and Josephine Baker, whom he had seen at the Folies Bergère, he wanted also to like Ray. Upon seeing *Humanité* in Ray's hand, he suddenly bristled and slammed down the *Action Française* on the table before him.

For the first time Ray noticed in the lapel of the student's coat a fleur-de-lys button.

"Why do you read that?" he demanded. "It isn't French! Why don't you read a French newspaper?"

"Such as? *Humanité* is printed in French."

"But it is not French, all the same."

"I suppose you'd like to choose my French reading for me. Do you want me to read the *Action Française?*"

"I didn't say that, but you might at least read a newspaper that is really French, like the *Petit Parisien* or *Le Journal.*"

"I hate *Le Journal,*" said Ray. "The best thing in it is the *Contes du Jour,* but I am tired of all of them smirking over a woman deceiving her husband or bourgeois lover with a gigolo. That has no meaning after Maupassant."

"Well, you'd do better to read the *Action Française* than *Humanité*. You're literary, and the editor, Daudet, is our greatest living *littérateur*. He writes the best and wittiest things about French writers, living and dead. If you read the *Action Française* you'll be keeping in touch with the best things in French literature."

"Perhaps," said Ray. "I really read the *Action Française*—sometimes, but I can't stand the paper when your

Daudet makes political propaganda over the suicide or murder of his fifteen-year-old boy. That makes your *Action Française* an obscene thing for me. You know, although the Anglo-Saxon countries are so hypocritical, no editor or political leader could do that in England or America and put it over on his public. Maybe it is because the Anglo-Saxon publics are less intelligent and more sentimental than the French. Anyway, you couldn't play party politics with them on such a morbid issue."

"But you think that way because you don't understand French politics," said the student. "The boy's murder was a political act. The police murdered him. You don't know the French police."

"Yes, I do, too," said Ray, "and I think they are the rottenest in the whole world."

"Don't talk like that about our police," said the student. "It is not nice. Why do you say that?"

Crosby laughed and Ray said, "Because that's just how I feel."

"I don't think you appreciate the benefits of French civilization," said the student, angrily. "We're especially tolerant to colored people. We treat them better than the Anglo-Saxon nations because we are the most civilized nation in the world."

"You use the same language that a hundred-per-cent American would use to me, with a little difference in words and emphasis," replied Ray. "Let me say that for me there is no such animal as a civilized nation. I believe there are a few decent minds in every nation, more or less, yet I wouldn't put them all through the test of Sodom and Gomorrah to find out. It is better to believe! You're right when you say you're more tolerant toward colored people in your country than the Anglo-Saxons in theirs. But from what I have seen of the attitude of this town toward Negroes and Arabs, I don't know how it would be if you Europeans had a large colored population to handle in Europe. I hope to God you won't ever face that. You Europeans have a wonderful record in Africa and I suppose you're all proud of it. The only thing lacking is that the United States should have a hand in it too. And I hope she will. In spite of her traditional attitude toward black folks she may become as embarrassing to Europe in Africa as she is in China."

The student abruptly left the table, and Ray felt happy that he had angered him. He was just crammed full of the much-touted benefits of French civilization—especially for colored people. His acquaintances, from workman to student, always parroted that, although he missed the true spirit of it in their attitudes. The cocotte was strikingly conscious of it, newspapers were full of it, and certain clever writers insisted that Paris was the paradise of the Aframerican.

Ray looked deeper than the noise for the truth, and what he really found was a fundamental contempt for black people quite as pronounced as in the Anglo-Saxon lands. The common idea of the Negro did not differ from that of the civilized world in general. There was, if anything, an unveiled condescension in it that was gall to a Negro who wanted to live his life free of the demoralizing effect of being pitied and patronized. Here, like anywhere (as the police inspector had so clearly intimated by his declaration) one black villain made all black villains as one black tout made all black touts, one black nigger made all black niggers, and one black failure made all black failures.

Exceptions were not considered. Ray would have considered the white world an utterly contemptible thing from its attitude toward the black if it were not for his principle of stressing the exception above the average.

The white mind in general approached the black world from exactly the opposite angle. He often pondered if an intellectual life could have been possible for him without that principle to support it.

Supposing he were to react to French or any other civilization solely from the *faits divers* columns of the newspapers. For one crazy month of the past summer he had read of nothing but crazy crimes: young couple dispatching their grandparents with a hatchet for a meager inheritance; mother holding her children under water until they were drowned; father seducing daughter at the time of her first communion; murderer shooting up street; and all the sordid *crimes d'amour et de la passion* that were really *crimes d'argent*.

It could have been easy for him, a black spectator of the drama, to seize upon and gloat over these things as evidences of the true nature of this civilization if he had allowed them to warp and rob him of his primitive sense of comparative values and his instinct to see through superficial appearances to the strange and profound variations of human life.

But life was more wonderful to savor than to indict. Leave the indictment to the little moral creatures of civilized justice. They had their little daggers sharpened for the victims who were white, and when they had the good luck to find a black victim, they made a club of him to slay the whole Negro race.

Ray had been specially entertained by one of these slaughterings, resulting from a terrible crime committed by a crazy Senegalese soldier and for which the entire black race was haled before the bar of public opinion.

It was authorized by a radical paper supporting the radical government under whose régime the West African Negroes were being torn out of their native soil, wrenched away from their families and shipped to Europe to get acquainted with the arts of war and the disease of syphilis. It was such an amusing revelation of civilized logic that Ray had preserved it, especially as he was in tacit agreement with the thesis while loathing the manner of its presentation:

"Un tirailleur sénégalais, pris d'on ne sait quel vertigo, a fait, à Toulon, un affreux carnage.

"On s'évertue maintenant à savoir par quelle suite de circonstances ce noir a pu fracturer un coffre et s'emparer des cartouches avec lesquelles il a accompli le massacre.

"Qu'on le sache, soit. Mais la question me semble ailleurs. Il faudrait peut-être se mettre la main sur le cœur et se demander s'il est bien prudent d'apprendre à des primitifs à se servir d'un fusil.

"Je n'ignore pas qu'il y a de belles exceptions; qu'il y a des 'nègres' députés, avocats, professeurs et que l'un d'eux a même obtenu le prix Goncourt. Mais la majorité de ces 'indigènes' à peau noire sont de grands enfants auxquels les subtilités de notre morale échappent autant que les subtilités de notre langue. La plus dangereuse de ces subtilités est celle-ci:

"Tu tueras des êtres humains en certaines circonstances que nous appelons guerre.

"Mais tu seras châtié si tu tues en dehors de ces circonstances.

"Le Sénégalais Yssima appartient à une catégorie humaine où il est d'usage, paraît-il, quand on doit mourir de ne pas mourir seul. Le point d'honneur consiste à en 'expedier' le plus possible avant d'être soi-même expédié.

"Si cela est vrai, on voit oú peuvent conduire certaines blagues de chambrées. Pour tout dire franche-

> ment, il n'est pas prudent de faire des soldats avec des hommes dont l'âme contient encore des replies inexplorés et pour qui notre civilisation est un vin trop fort. Sous les bananiers originels, Yssima était sans doute un brave noir, en parfaite harmonie avec la morale de sa race et les lois de la nature. Transplanté, déraciné, il est devenue un fou sanguinaire.
>
> "Je ne veux tirer de cet horrible fait divers aucune conclusion. Je dis que de semblables aventures (qui ne sont d'ailleurs pas isolées) devraient nous faire réfléchir sérieusement. . . ."

Suddenly and strangely Ray felt a hard hatred for Crosby that seemed inexplicable, and yet was not. He had fallen into a mood in which the whole white world of civilization appeared like an obscene phenomenon. And Crosby sitting there by him was a freak because he was not indecent. He was too fine a type, something too real for Ray's frame of mind. His presence became unbearable.

"I am going back to the Ditch," Ray said. He frowned at Crosby and left him without any word of explanation.

He went to his hotel and got his bag and returned to the Ditch. It was moving out of the Ditch that caused the policeman to take me for a criminal nosing round the quarter of respectability, thought Ray. Better had I stayed down here with Banjo and the boys where the white bastards thought I ought to be. They always searched me like a criminal down there, but they never beat me up. I moved away from there and got myself messed up. It was all through Crosby persuading me to go respectable. Whenever I get mixed up with nice people I always catch it. Better to know nice people, if I must know them, in books, and me for living my own vagabond life. Maybe I would have felt better if the knuckle-dusting frogs had beaten me up by mistake down here. He felt that somebody ought to be blamed, ought to be hated, for what had happened to him, and he worked himself up against Crosby.

XXIII. Shake That Thing Again

RAY returned to the Ditch, and at the African Bar Banjo was treating Malty, Ginger, Dengel, and some West African boys. Banjo had received notice from the consulate to prepare to leave in a day or two. Ray was boisterously welcomed. Girls and their touts were dancing to the continuous racket from the pianola. Banjo suggested that the gang should go to his old hangout, where he would play and they could kick up their own racket.

The long back room in the rear of the bistro was the boys' for spreading joy. Banjo revived "Shake That Thing" for the party. Malty joined him blowing a little horn or whistling, while the boys kept up a humming monotone of accompaniment as they danced.

> Old folks doing it, and young folks too,
> The young folks learning the old how to do,
> Shake That Thing, Shake That Thing.
> *I'm getting sick and tired, but* . . . OH, SHAKE THAT THING!

Front and rear the bistro was jammed—girls and touts and beach boys. The girls helped themselves liberally to the boys' wine on the tables. Dengel, who rarely danced, was dogging it with a boy from Grand Bassam. A vivacious girl pointed at them and cried: "Look at that Dengel dancing. I thought he didn't do anything but booze."

She cut in between them and, her feminine curiosity rising over her passion for gain, she ignored the boy from

Grand Bassam, who was new to the Ditch and supposed to have money, and, taking hold of Dengel, said "Dance with me." Tall and very slim, Dengel looked like a fine tree fern. He bent over to the girl in that manner of swaying inebriation peculiar to him, and executed an African jig so wildly that space had to be cleared for them. Surprised at Dengel's rough wildness, the girl laughed and shrieked and wiggled excitedly.

When Banjo stopped playing, she rushed up to him and asked for the same thing again. Just at that moment a tout entered and whispered something to the Jelly-roll *patrone* of the bistro, who held up her hand and called: "Listen! If any of you have guns or any other weapons, give them to me, for there's going to be a *rafle* tonight."

The touts handed over their guns and knives to her. Of the colored men, only a mulatto, a Martiniquan, had a revolver, which he gave to the woman. She put the weapons in a drawer of the counter and locked it. A boy who was a stranger to the quarter asked her; "You always know when the police are going to operate down here?"

"Sure. That's understood," she said. She was near the entrance, and stepping out into the narrow alley she said, with a raucous laugh, "That for the police."

She reëntered the bistro heaving with laughter and, patting one of the Senegalese who was standing white-eyed by the door, said: *"Tu as vu le clair de lune?"*

Hearing that the police were coming, Ray felt that he could not stand being handled by them again just then. He might do something crazy and get into serious trouble. So he quietly slipped off. Just as he reached the corner the police entered the bistro. He had to cut across Boody Lane to reach the Bum Square, and as he was passing he saw a policeman coming out of one of the holes-in-the-wall and finger-wiping his long mustache as if he had just finished the most appetizing *hors-d'œuvre* in the world. Maybe.

In the Bum Square he met Latnah. Her manner was strangely preoccupied. Ray asked her if she knew the boys were celebrating in the Ditch. She knew, but did not care to go.

"I think you're blue like me," said Ray. "Maybe what we need to fix us up is a pipe dream."

"You do that, too?" Latnah asked.

"I do anything that is good for a change. All depends on the place and the time and the second person singular?"

"Then I have stuff," Latnah said. "We go."

They went up to her little place. She spread the colored coverlet on the floor and threw down two little cushions for pillows. She brought out a basket of oranges and dates. And they sat down together on the rug. A little brass plate, lamp, tube and, the iodine-like paste strangely fascinating in its somnolent thickness. Latnah prepared for the ritual.

"Take fruit. It good with fruit," she said.

"I know that," Ray replied.

"You know all about it," she smiled subtly. "I think is leetle Oriental in you."

"Maybe. There's a saying in my family about some of our people coming from East Africa. They were reddish, with glossy curly hair. But you have the same types in West Africa, too. You remember the two fellows that used to be at the African Bar during the summer? They looked like twins and they were heavy-featured like some Armenians."

"I think they were *mulattres,*" said Latnah.

"No, they weren't mixed—not as we know it between black and white today. Perhaps way back. I heard they were Fulahs."

"We all mixed up. I'm so mixed I don't know what I am myself."

"You don't? I always wonder, Latnah, what you really are. Except for the Chinese, I don't feel any physical sympathy for Orientals, you know. I always feel cold and strange and far away from them. But you are different. I feel so close to you."

"My mother was Negresse," said Latnah. "Sudanese or Abyssinian—I no certain. I was born at Aden. My father I no know what he was nor who he was."

Latnah picked an orange clean of its white covering and handed a half of it to Ray. He put his tube down and slipped a lobe into his mouth. The incense of the rite rose and filled the little chamber, drifting on its atmosphere like a magic canopy. Drowsily Ray remembered Limehouse and those days of repose in the quiet dens there.

Latnah must have captured his thoughts psychically, for she suddenly said, "It no never haunt you?"

"No. I remember it as one of the strange and pleasant things in my life, just as another person might recall any interesting event. But when I quit I just put it out of my mind—forgot it and started in living differently."

"You beaucoup Oriental," said Latnah. "Banjo never touch anything strange like us. *Il est un pur sauvage du sang.*" She sighed.

Ray locked her to him in his elbow. Peace and forgetfulness in the bosom of a brown woman. Warm brown body and restless dark body like a black root growing down in the soft brown earth. Deep dark passion of bodies close to the earth understanding each other. Dark brown bodies of the earth, earthy. Dark . . . brown . . . rich colors of the nourishing earth. The pinks bring trouble and tumult and riot into dark lives. Leave them alone in their vanity and tigerish ambitions to fret and fume in their own hell, for terrible is their world that creates disasters and catastrophes from simple natural incidents.

A little resting from the body's aching and the mind's trouble in sweet dreaming. Ray's hankering was for scenes of tropical shores sifted through hectic years. Salty-warm blue bays where black boys dive down deep into the deep waters, where the ships shear in on foamy waves and black youths row out to them in canoes and black pilots bring them in to anchor. Cocoanut palms like sentinels on the sandy shore. Black draymen coming from the hilltops, singing loudly—rakish chants, whipping up the mules bearing loads of brown sugar and of green bunches of bananas, trailing along the winding chalky ways down to the port.

Oh, the tropical heat of earth and body glowing in the same rhythm of nature . . . sun-hot warmth wilting the blood-bright hibiscus, drawing the rich creaminess out of the lush bell-flowers, burning green fields and pasture lands to crispy autumn color, and driving the brown doves and pea doves to cover cooing under the fan-broad cooling woodland leaves.

But he dreamed instead of Harlem . . . the fascinating forms of Harlem. The thick, sweaty, syrup-sweet jazzing of Sheba Palace. . . . Black eyes darting out of curious mauve frames to arrest the alert prowler . . . little brown legs hurrying along . . . with undulating hips and voluptuous caressing motion of feminine folds.

XXIV. The Chauffeur's Lot

AT NOON the next day Ray went out, treading on air. His nature was buoyant. He went to a little Italian restaurant and fed. In the early afternoon he joined Goosey and Banjo on a café terrace.

His chauffeur friend, passing by, hailed him. He said he was going out to look at his suburban place and asked if Ray would like to go. Ray said he wouldn't mind going, but that he was with Banjo and Goosey. The chauffeur said that he would take them all if they wanted to go. They did, but Goosey objected that the ship might arrive and the consul call for them.

"That won't make no difference," said Banjo. "No ship ain't nevah gwine out the same day it put in at this heah hallelujah poht."

"Yes, the Dollar Line boats do, too," said Goosey.

"Well if it does the skipper has got to wait on us, his bum passengers, believe me," said Banjo. "Come on, pardner, let's go."

Ray rode beside the chauffeur. The suburban route was melancholy. Before he went to the vintage he had gone out to another country place, and it had been refreshing then all along the way to see trailing bramble roses in the ripened green grass and marigolds and irises blooming in truck gardens of cauliflowers, and bunches of tempting grapes hanging from the fences. Now there was nothing but dead and rotting leaves everywhere and some withered blackberries.

The chauffeur's place was like any of the common suburban lots owned by the great army of the lower middle class of modern cities. A cottage of three rooms and a kitchen, a young chestnut tree near the gate and a large fig tree in the rear.

Of the lots on either side of him, the chauffeur told the boys that one belonged to a bistro-keeper and the other to a policeman. Ray thought his neighbors were just right and told him so. The chauffeur smiled. He was proud of his neighbors, too. The other lots were worth a little more than his, he said, for they had their water supply and he hadn't yet.

Banjo asked him how much he had paid for his place.

"Eleven thousand francs," the chauffeur replied, and that he was still making periodical payments on it.

"Sometimes we have evening parties up here," he told Ray.

"What kind?" Ray asked.

"If I pick up a tourist and a girl who want to take a joy-ride I bring them out here. Anything to help pay for the place. One night I had a gang, and it would have been fun to have you. But you're so changed now from when I knew you at Toulon—always with the Senegalese —I didn't trouble."

"That's all right," said Ray. "Change is my passion. Can't stay in one rut forever. Got to pull out and find something new."

Goosey had detached himself from them and was in the act of digging under the fig tree.

"What you doing there, you?" Banjo called.

They went up and found Goosey filling a little squat glass jar with earth.

"What you doing with that theah dirt?" asked Banjo.

"To keep as a souvenir," said Goosey.

"Oh, my Gawd, what a nigger, though!" Banjo horse-laughed. "It's you should be making pohms and not Ray, for youse the sweetest cherry-diver I evah did see."

Goosey held his jar of earth against his heart.

"It's the soil of France," he said. "I couldn't make it, all right. I was outa luck, but I can always remember that I was here."

"Kain't you remember without that theah flask a dirt?" asked Banjo. "Better you tote back a flask a real Martell cognac on you' hip, for that you won't find back home in Gawd's own, but you'll find plenty a dirt. Dirt is the same dirt all ovah the wul' cep'n' for a li'l' difference in color, maybe."

"Leave him alone," said Ray.

"You don't understand this thing, Banjo," said Goosey, angrily, "so it's better you shut up."

The chauffeur had been listening with sentimental interest and now he said to Goosey: *"Vous avez raison. La France, c'est le plus joli coin du monde."*

"How do you know that?" said Ray. "You have never been out of it."

"Yes I have," responded the chauffeur. "I've been to North Africa and Spain and Italy and Constantinople. You forget I was a sailor."

"Le's quit arguing about dirt and find the first café where we can have wine," said Banjo.

Later in the afternoon they all returned to the Vieux Port. After a parting drink with the boys the chauffeur drove off. Ray looked after him contemplatively and thought how differently he felt toward him now in comparison with the days when he knew him at Toulon. The chauffeur's life at Toulon had been about the same kind of animal-cunning existence that it was at present.

He had once recounted to Ray how he had been arrested in a raid, when the police took from him a miniature ledger in which he kept a check-and-balance account of all the extra change he made, the places and persons (when he knew their names) that contributed to it.

The affair had been very amusing for Ray, just as it had been amusing for him to give the chauffeur all the tips and hints and cues he knew that he could follow up to gain something. In his picturesque uniform, old and overworked symbol of a free and reckless way of living, the chauffeur's ways of eking out his means of enjoying life did not seem at that time unbeautiful.

Living the same life now with more freedom, he appeared loathsome to Ray. Perhaps it was what he was living for that made the difference. For as to *how* he was living . . . there were many luxury-clean people who had become high and mighty by traffic in human flesh. As a Negro Ray was particularly sensible to that fact—that many of the titled and ennobled and fashionable and snobbish gentry of this age have the roots of their fortunes in the buying and selling of black bodies. And had he any reason to doubt that the landlords of Boody Lane and the Ditch as a whole were collecting that prostitute rent to live respectably and educate their children in decency?

What made the chauffeur so unbearably ugly to him now was that he was trafficking obscenely to scramble out of the proletarian world into that solid respectable life, whence he could look down on the Ditch and all such places with the mean, evil, and cynical eyes of a respectable person.

"Just imagine that chauffeur paying eleven thousand francs foh that place!" said Banjo to Ray. "Only eleven thousand! I coulda bought it with what money I landed here with and have something left ovah."

"You could, all right, and yet you couldn't," said Ray. "You and I were not made for that careful touting life.

Did you ever meet, back home, a black p-i that was saving up off his women to marry respectable? Or a brown sob-sister chippy whining that she was doing that to support an old mother? You bet you and I never did meet any of the black breed like that. They were all true-blue sports in the blood.

"That chauffeur will marry with a clear conscience from his scavenger money. He may chuck up the chauffeur job and buy a café—become a respectable *père de famille*—a good taxpayer and supporter of a strong national government, with a firm colonial policy, while you and I will always be the same lost black vagabonds, because we don't know what this civilization is all about. But my friend the chauffeur knows. It took over a thousand years of lily-white culture to make him what he is. And although he has no intelligence, he has the instinct of civilization, Banjo, and you and I just haven't got it."

"I can't make out nothing, pardner, about that instinking thing that youse talking about. But I know one thing and that is if I ain't got the stink of life in me, I got the juice."

Passing through the Place Sadi Carnot, the boys saw Sister Geter being conducted down a side street by a policeman.

"I wonder if they've arrested her?" said Ray. "Such a long time since I've seen her, I thought she'd gone home." He was hesitating about going to see what was up, but Banjo said, "Let's find out, anyway, what theyse doing with her, pardner."

"She might start that 'Black Bottom' stunt on us again," objected Goosey, "and then—good night!"

"Oh, come on. She kain't make no moh 'Black Bottom' than her nacheral," said Banjo.

The boys caught up with Sister Geter and the policeman and Ray spoke to her. The policeman asked Ray if he knew her and what she was doing raising such a racket in the streets. He couldn't understand her, for she did not speak French. Ray told him that she was an evangelist. The policeman let her go and said he had only walked her away so that the big crowd that was collecting round her in the square should disperse. The people thought she was a high priestess of fetich Africa and would work *magie noire.* He told Ray to tell her not to preach in the streets. Sister Geter walked with the boys toward Joliette.

"I thought you were gone away," Ray said, "so long since I never saw you."

"No, chile, Ise right here deliv'ring that holy message. The Lawd Him done sent me heah with His wohd in mah mouf, and I ain't thinking about moving nowheres else tell Himself gimme another marching order. I been preaching that message right along. Sometime the pohlice com'n' moves me along jest like that one done did. But they nevah hold me no time. They look at mah bible and turn me loose."

"But the people kain't understand what you're preaching to them, since you don't talk French," said Goosey.

"What you know 'bout understanding reeligion, yal' boy?" demanded Sister Geter. "I belongs to the Pentecostal Fire Baptized Believers and I ain't studying no lang-idge but the lang-idge of faith. I was fire-baptized in the gift of tongues and when I deliver this heah Gawd's message" (she tapped nervously on the bible and humped herself up, while the boys glanced apprehensively at one another, thinking 'Black Bottom') "people heahs what I say and jest gotta understand no matter what lang-idge they speaks."

"Funny I didn't run into you again," said Ray. "I was away for a little over a month at the vintage, but I've been a long time back."

"Yo'-all don't see me, mah chilluns, 'causen you don't want to. For yo'-all know prexactly what's holding you heah in this mahvelous poht, and that Ise a-preaching against all the most deadliest sins, and theah's none moh deadly than fohnication. Ise warning you'-all now and straight that Gawd's sure agwina git you for all them sins youse sweetening on and looking so good on it."

"We ain't so bad as you thinking, ma," said Banjo. "Wese a hard-hustling bunch a regular fellahs. It's them sweetmens back down in the Ditch you should go preaching to."

"Yo'-all needs it, too. Mah message is foh you to take it and use. Git converted, git salvation, change you' ways a living in sweet sin. For if you don't the Lawd him will git hold a you and wrastle with you and throw you down on a bed a tribulation and give you the biggest shaking you evah did get."

Banjo began softly whistling, "Shake That Thing."

They had arrived in the Place de la Joliette before the Seamen's Bar.

"Let's go in here for a drink a soda-pop," said Banjo.

Goosey and Ray grinned.

"Take a glass with us, ma?" Banjo asked.

"No. I ain't putting mah feets in no gin shop with Gawd's Wohd in mah hand. I sweahs off gin and any drink that's sold in a bottle evah since I was fire-baptized, and tha's seven years gone now."

"But there might be a sinner in here needing conversion, ma," said Ray. "The Salvation Army folk don't mind going into a saloon."

"Maybe it's because they loves the smell a the gin they done sweahs off," replied Sister Geter, "but I doesn't."

She waddled away.

The boys went into the Seamen's Bar and there was

Home to Harlem Jake drinking with a seaman pal at the bar. He and Ray embraced and kissed.

"The fust time I evah French-kiss a he, chappie, but Ise so tearing mad and glad and crazy to meet you this-away again."

"That's all right, Jakie, he-men and all. Stay long enough in any country and you'll get on to the ways and find them natural."

Ray introduced Banjo and Goosey.

"I guess youse the two gwine back home with us," said Jake. "I heard the skipper say some'n' about it when he got back from the consulate."

"Well, chappie," Jake said to Ray, "we just got in last night and wese pulling out tomorrow, so wese all gwina get together and spread some moh joy in this heah sweet poht tonight. What it takes to pay I've got, and I'm gwina blow mahself big foh this hallelujah meeting-up. Whachyu say?"

"I say O. K.," replied Ray. "But how come you here? You remember you told me you were never going to fool with the sea again?"

"I did say that, yes. But some moh things done happen to me after you quit Harlem, chappie."

Jake told Ray of his picking up Felice again and their leaving Harlem for Chicago. After two years there they had had a baby boy. And then they decided to get married. Two years of married life passed and he could no longer stick to Chicago, so he returned to Harlem. But he soon found that it was not just a change of place that was worrying him.

"I soon finds out," he said, "that it was no joymaking business for a fellah like you' same old Jake, chappie, to go to work reg'lar ehvery day and come home ehvery night to the same ole pillow. Not to say that Felice hadn't kep' it freshen' up and sweet-smelling all along.

She's one sweet chile that sure knows how to make a li'l' home feel good to a fellah. But it was too much home stuff, chappie. So it done gone a year now I think that I just stahted up one day and got me a broad. And now it's bettah. I don't feel like running away from Felice no moh. Whenevah I get home Ise always happy to be with her and feel that Ise doing mah duty by Ray."

"Ray?" exclaimed Ray.

"Sure, the kid. I done name him after you. Not that I want him to be like you in many ways. But Ise gwina give him what I neveh had and tha's an edjucation. And p'raps he'll learn to write pohms like you. He's a smart-looking kid."

"You're a thousand times a better man than me, Jake. Finding a way to carry on with a family and knuckling down to it. I just ran away from the thing."

"You! You din't leave Agatha a li'l' one, did you?"

"I leave more things than I want to remember," replied Ray. "Come on, let's have another drink and get outa here."

Banjo and Goosey hurried off to the consulate to see what orders were there for them and Jake and Ray were left alone to gab about Harlem before and after Prohibition. Jake had found Harlem wonderfully changed when he returned from Chicago. The Block Beautiful had gone black and brown. One Hundred and Twenty-fifth Street was besieged and bravely holding out for business' sake, but the invaders, armed with nothing but loud laughter, had swept around it and beyond. And higher up, the race line of demarcation, Eighth Avenue, had been pushed way back and Edgecombe, Jerome, Manhattan, St. Nicholas, and other pale avenues were vividly touched with color. The Negro realtors had done marvels.

In Chicago, Felice had begun reading the *Negro*

World, the organ of the Back-to-Africa movement, and when they came back she was as interested in Liberty Hall as in Sheba Palace. She had even worried Jake to take a share in Black Star Line.

"Let's get on to it too, dad," she had said. "There can be some'n' in it. Times is changing, and niggers am changing, too. That great big nigger man ain't no beauty, but, oh, lawdy! he sure is illiquint."

But Jake had resisted Felice's new enthusiasm and it was only a few months after their return to New York that Liberty Hall lost Leader Marcus to the Federal jail.

At supper time the boys came together again in the Bum Square. Banjo, playing the square game according to the standards of the bum fraternity, had rounded up all the beach boys he knew to meet Jake and be treated to drinks or hand-outs. They went to the African Bar. Ray introduced Jake to the proprietor and the two chatted a little about Harlem. Jake stood a round of drinks for the picturesque black rabble.

Banjo, Goosey, Ray, and Jake were going to sup together. Ray suggested they should eat at an Italian chop-house in the quarter where he sometimes fed when he was flush with francs. The cooking there was always well done and moderately spiced as he loved cooking to be, and the wine one grade removed from the *vin rouge ordinaire* was superb for the price and mellow to the palate. And the proprietor could concoct the most delicious zabione.

But when the boys came to the restaurant, Jake objected to feeding there because it was next door to a *cabinet d'aisance*—so much next door that if you were a little gone in your cups you could easily mistake one entrance for the other.

"By the britches of Gawd, chappie!" cried Jake, "what

done happen to you sence you show Harlem you' black moon. After me telling you that I want to blow to the swellest feed there is, you bring me to a place with a big W. C. sign ovah it. I remember when you was a deal moh whimscriminate. When you couldn't eat the grub on the white man's choo-choo 'causen you was afraid the chef cook done did nastiness to it as he swoh he would. And now——"

"But just look at that!" cried Goosey. "There's the whole family setting down to eat right in there."

Yes. At the lower end of the shop, flanked on either side by cabinets, the family dinner was spread. A long loaf of bread, two large bottles of red wine, and a great basin of soup with a ladle in it. And around the table sat husband and wife, a girl of about fourteen years, a boy a little less, and a shrunken gray grandmother. Clients were coming and going and the family were swallowing their soup amid the sounds and odors of the place, while the wife occasionally vacated her seat to attend to business.

"But don't they have a *home?*" demanded Jake. "Sure they ain't sleeping theah, then why does they wanta feed in it?"

"I wouldn't let nobody see me do that work, much less eat in there," said Goosey. "These people don't know any shame."

"Shame you' trap," said Jake. "It ain't no being ashame'. Can we niggers cry shame about any kind a work to make a living in this big wul' of the ofays? It ain't doing the work, but what you make it do with you. You remember, Ray, when you and me was on the road together? When you done finished with that theah pantry hole and I got outa that steaming grave, we couldn't even stomach them lousy quahters. We was crazy to go any place we could fohgit the whole push."

"That was seven years gone, Jake," said Ray. "And in seven years many things can change to nothing according to law. You haven't changed any. You're a good black American. Too American. We had a fellow in our gang called Bugsy. He died here—died with his eyes wide open. He was the toughest black boy I ever knew. Yet when he found out he'd been eating horse meat in his cook-joint, thinking it was beef, he cried ——"

"He was a real nigger. I woulda puked," said Jake.

"One day," continued Ray, "one of my nice liberal friends ran into me here and I happened to tell him about Bugsy and the horse steak. And he was so surprised that a Negro should have prejudices—especially such a delicate sort."

"Ain't a bumbole thing delicate about a man being particular what he's putting away in his guts," said Jake.

"All the same, Jake, this place, that family. You're in the most civilized country in the world, and you aren't civilized enough to understand."

"I ain't what's that?" demanded Jake.

"You heard exactly what I said, ole-timer."

"Well, whether I is or ain't, you take me away from here and show me the swellest house-of-many-pans foh feeding in this heah poht of the frogs. Ise got enough a them francs to blow fifty face-feeders with the few dollars I done change. I don't know what done happen to you in the seven years we ain't seen one anether. But foh the sake a good ole friendship, chappie, I hope you ain't no stink-lover."

"What kind a place you want?" asked Ray. "I don't want to go to one a those places with a lotta stiff, hard-faced people stuffing themselves, and flunkies that don't know what to do with you because you aren't like them."

"And I didn't mean one a them sort," said Jake. "I

mean a clean place where we can get good eats and jolly one another and be nacheral without anybody being offended."

They went to the other side of the Vieux Port on the Quai de Rive Neuve where the restaurants specialized in sea foods. A waiter brought them a basket of fine fish and told them to choose. Soles, dorades, loups, mullets—some alive and twitching. Jake insisted on having champagne. And when the smiling head waiter submitted the wine list he chose an expensive brand, Duc de Montebello, because, he said, "the name sounded lak a mahvelous mouful."

The boys had a gorgeous time feeding and sampling the sparkling liquor and swapping jokes, except for one little snag, which they swept grinning over. At the third table across from them there was a party of two women and three men, and one of the men, who looked like a middle-aged salesman, kept throwing phrases at the boys in English: "It's good here, eh? . . . You like drink fine champagne. . . . I know many blacks. I been in America. . . . You get good treatment here. Eat good, sleep good. . . . *Les filles.*" He smirked and leered nastily at them and Ray told him in French:

"We don't know you and we don't want you to butt into our party."

A look of mean hatred came into the man's face and he replied, "You are not polite."

"I know," said Ray. "When we don't let you condescend to interrupt us, we're not polite, and if any of us had tried to do the same thing with your party we would be impertinent blacks."

The man's party paid their bill and left the restaurant a little after the incident.

Then Goosey remarked: "You didn't have to trip him

up so hard, Ray. You know in New York we couldn't eat in a white restaurant like this."

"I don't give a white damn for that," said Ray. "If we can't eat downtown we can eat better in Harlem. I wouldn't give Aunt Hattie's smoky cook-shop for all the Childs restaurants white-washed like a tomb. I guess that puss-faced Frenchman was thinking just like you. But all the same, if they let us into their white places, they've got to treat us naturally like other guests. This black boy won't stand for any condescending crap."

"Mah pardner is right, Goosey," said Banjo. "For all you' bellyaching talk about race, youse a white man's nigger in the bottom. You got you' haid so low down behind that white moon, believe me, that you kain't see nothing clear."

The Bum Square was a close, busy, bustling place when the boys returned there. There were many ships in port—American, English, Norwegian, Italian, and others—and all the common seamen had come to the quarter for amusement. It was like a pit with all things in it—men, women, aged, infirm, boys, touts showing their girls with ghoulish gestures, children, dogs, and cats—all boiling in desire. But there was no free, wild bubbling over. It was a boiling as of purchased food put in a caldron and carefully fed with fire to a certain point. A boiling exhibition for a strong smell of change was in the Bum Square. Loveless eyes told and hounds' voices barked without words the price of the circus—boxes, balcony, gallery, parquet, pit, front and rear.

Automatically the piano-panning jumped madly out of the Anglo-American Bar to clash rioting in the square with that of the Monkey Bar.

"Gawd's love!" exclaimed Jake. "Ain't no wonder you fellahs stick in this sweet mud. Fust place I evah feel mahself in a jazzing circus some'n' lak Harlem. It shoh smells strong."

"Not like Harlem, though," said Ray. "Harlem's smell is like animals brought in from the fields to stable. Here it's rotten-stinking."

Jake grinned. "You remember you' send-off feed in ole Aunt Hattie's cook-shop, chappie? You ain't fohgit how I done told you there was no other place like Harlem in the white man's wul'. And now foh putting a li'l' Harlem stuff in this jazzing."

A young girl went by them, limping with a pathetic, half-resentful, half-terrified look in her eyes and a fever-hot color in her cheeks.

"See that gal?" Banjo said. "Jest a few months back she hit this Ditch the cutest thing in it. Comed from the country, they said, and, oh, Lawdy! if it wasn't a rushing wild. And then blip-blap it was the hospital next and look at her now."

They went to the Ditch to a bistro full of brown and black and Mediterranean seamen, automatic music, strenuously jazzing girls, loud, ready-made laughter, and vigorous swilling of liquor.

Ray's friend, the chauffeur, was there, drinking and surrounded by an admiring group of pale touting youths. Ray went over to him for a moment. The chauffeur asked him to join the party, but Ray pointed out that he was with Banjo and Jake. He glanced a little inquiringly at the boys. The chauffeur smirked and said: "They are all my boys. They do everything you want them to do. Steal, murder, love in all ways, lie, and spy."

The boys' features wore a sickly smile as they listened to the chauffeur boosting them. Ray rejoined his group. A little later Latnah came in with Malty and Dengel. Latnah, peeved, unreconciled to Banjo's going away, although she had not uttered a word about it, sat rather apart on the edge of the group. The girls of the circle glanced resentfully at her. They could never like the little brown woman. Although quite unobtrusive, the superiority of her difference from them was too eloquently obvious.

The chauffeur left his place and went over to where Latnah was sitting. Standing behind her, he put his arms around her.

Latnah said, "Take you' dirty hands off me and leave me alone."

The chauffeur laughed and said, "I am boss of everything here."

"Except me," replied Latnah. "I'm not like your Arab wench."

This Arab girl was different from the Arab-black one. She was honey-colored, with flaky-soft shining coal hair, deeply curled. Her mouth was not cruel, but her eyes were mad. She was one of the chauffeur's women.

The chauffeur said: "Don't mention her any more. I'm through with her. We had a big row and I am finished."

Latnah smiled and said, "You've got enough of her, eh?"

The chauffeur attempted to caress her again, but Latnah's hand shot threateningly to her bosom and he backed away from her.

"You'd better leave that woman alone," said Banjo.

Right then the Arab girl marched into the café. She bent down with a funny gesture, brought a revolver up from under her skirt and emptied it into the chauffeur. He crumpled to the floor, and she fell upon him and began keening: "I didn't mean to kill him. . . . I didn't mean to kill him."

XXV. Banjo's Ace of Spades

A FUNERAL was winding its way through the Ditch. It was not the chauffeur's, but a policeman's. He had been shot a day before the chauffeur by a Ditch-dweller just let out of prison. In the Ditch they said it was a story of revenge. It was a large funeral. All the big city officials were there or represented, black-bearded, gray-haired men, black-clothed, decorated, beribboned and medaled. The most important ones had orated valiantly over the corpse, praising the valor and virtues of the force.

Obseques solenelles.

A full turnout of the force. And dutiful comrades in service actively making the way clear for the mourning officials and the immense crowd. Wreath-covered hearse and carriages following, chockful of flowers. From the church on the hill above the quarter, slowly, pompously, and solemnly the mournful army went marching through the Ditch and all the girls along the way crossed themselves and all the touts uncovered.

Directly in the line of march, Ray was sitting on the terrace of the African Bar. Not wanting to salute, nor be conspicuous by not saluting, a show stinking with insincerity and more loathsome to see than the obscene body of a crocodile, he got up and went inside, turning his back on the lugubriously-comic procession.

When the noble company had passed far and away out of the Ditch, Ray started off for Joliette to find Banjo and

Goosey and give them the farewell hand. But in the Bum Square he met Goosey, who had spent all the morning hunting for Banjo. He had the consular letter from the captain of Jake's ship on which they were to go home. But Banjo was missing. He had not returned to the hotel after last night's feasting and merrymaking. Goosey had gone by all the familiar box-holes of the place, but Banjo was not to be found in any.

"Only thing to do is go back to Joliette and wait for him at the hotel," suggested Ray. "Then if he doesn't show up in time, you'll have to go alone."

They went to the hotel in Joliette and waited on the terrace over a couple bottles of beer. And when the impatient Goosey was becoming unbearably fidgety as the time of the boat's departure approached, Banjo came rocking leisurely up to them.

"Good God, man, get some American pep into you and don't act so *African,*" cried Goosey. "Don't you know we've got to move by the white folks' schedule time now? You think the skipper's going to wait on us?"

"Don't excite you'se'f, yaller boy. Go you' ways without me. I ain't gwine no place."

"Not going!" cried Goosey. "After the consul paid for your board and lodging and gave you a free passage back home? You sure joking. You remember Lonesome Blue?"

Lonesome Blue had finally disappeared from the scene. When a ship was found for him he had vanished. The police could not have picked him up again, for he had been furnished papers that gave him immunity. Nobody knew where he had gone.

"Remember you'self, you," said Banjo. "I ain't studying you nor Lonesome nor no consuls when I done finish make up mah mind. There is many moh Gawd's own consuls than theah is in Marcelles and this heah Lincoln

Agrippa, call him Banjo, has got moh tricks in his haid than a monkey."

Goosey looked bewildered and scared of going alone. He was shocked by Banjo's sudden desertion and felt cheated of his strong support. His lower lip hung down in a mournful way.

"Well, I guess I've got to go back alone," he said. "I've been sick near death's door and would have been in the boneyard like Bugsy if the consul hadn't helped me out. I'm going home."

"Sure gwine back this time, eh?" Banjo grinned aloud. "Won't take no chances telling another skipper to chase himse'f. Yo' gwine back home to what you call them United Snakes after you done sweahs offer them. You was so bellyaching about race I knowed you'd bust. Ise a gutter-snipe as you said, all right, and mah pardner done bury his brains in the mud and we ain't singing no Gawd's own blues——"

"That hasn't got a thing to do with my going back," said Goosey. "I still hold to my opinion. I know what my race has got to buck up against in this white man's world, if you don't know and Ray with his talent don't want to. I know what I was running away from and if I couldn't make it over here——"

"Couldn't make the point of mah righteous nose!" exclaimed Banjo. "Red-nigger, you kain't make nothing at all but the stuff you was made foh. You done got carried ovah heah by accident. And a li'l' French luck carried you along upstate. But you done flopped so soon as you got left on you' own, 'causen you ain't got no self-makings in you. Get me? You go right on back to them United Snakes that you belongs to with you li'l' pot a French dirt."

"And you'll hear from me, too, some day," said

Goosey. "Some day you'll hear about me orating for my race and telling them about the soil of liberty."

With a kind of prayerful gesture Goosey held up his sacred souvenir.

"And you think we don't care a damn about race, eh?" Banjo turned seriously on Goosey. "Listen and hear me, Goosey. You evah seen a lynching?"

"No."

"I guess you hadn't. Well, I seen one down in Dixie. And it was mah own li'l' brother. Jest when he was a-growing out of a boy into a man and the juice of life was ripening a pink temptation kept right on after him and wouldn't let be until he was got and pulled the way of the rope. You didn't go through the war, neither?"

"No, I didn't."

"I knowed. Because you was too young. I did because I was jest young enough. I was in Kenada when I joined up and I remember a buddy a mine calling me a fool for it. I remember he said that he would only wanta fight if they was calling him to go to Dixie to clean up foh them crackers. But I joined up all the same, and went through that war, for I was just crazy for a change. And the wul' did, too. And one half of it done murdered the other half to death. But the wul' ain't gone a-mourning forevah because a that. Nosah. The wul' is jazzing to fohgit."

"Except the bloody politicians," said Ray.

"They ain't in our class, pardner. Yessah. The wul' is just keeping right on with that nacheral sweet jazzing of life. And Ise jest gwine on right along jazzing with the wul'. The wul' goes round and round and I keeps right on gwine around with it. I ain't swore off nothing like you. United Snakes nor You-whited Snakes that a nigger jest gotta stand up to everywhere in this wul', even in the thickest thicket in the Congo. I know that theah's a mighty mountain a white divilment on this heah Gawd's big ball. And niggers will find that mountain on every foot a land that the white man done step on. But we niggers am no angels, neither. And I guess that if evah I went down in the bushes in the Congo, even the canninbals them would wanta mess with mah moon if I leave me careless, and if I runned away to the Nothanmost pole, the icebugs would squash me frozen stiff if I couldn't prohtect mahself. I ain't one accident-made nigger like you, Goosey. Ise a true-blue traveling-bohn nigger and I know life, and I knows how to take it nacheral. I fight when I got to and I works when I must and I lays off when I feel lazy, and I loves all the time becausen the honey-pot a life is mah middle name.

"You got a li'l' book larnin', Goosey, but it jest make you that much a bigger bonehead. You don't know nothing when to use it right from when you should fold it up and put it away like you does a dress suit after a dickty party. You got a tall lot yet to larn, Goosey boy. You go right on back to them theah United Snakes and makem shoot a li'l' snake-bite wisdom into you' and take somathat theah goosiness outa you' moon."

The noisy honk-honking of a horn dispersed an idly-gossiping group in the middle of the streets as a taxicab dashed through them and swerved to a stop before the hotel. Out of it jumped Jake.

"I done took it in mah haid to come and get you fellahs," he said. "Because after that theah goodest of time last night, I got to thinking you-all might be feeling too sweet in you' skin to get outa it for that unrighteous sea change. So here I is with taxi and everything to make sure you-all don't get left."

"Youse one most faithfully buddy," Banjo grinned. "But Ise jest finish explaining to Goosey heah that Ise most gratiate to the consul foh hulping me this far along, but I ain't gwine no further. And I was a-telling him like a wise old-timer to dust his feets and make that boat alone befoh it miss him, foh this nigger ain't gwine no place."

"Ain't going!"

Jake grinned. Banjo grinned. Ray grinned. Goosey only was glum. Jake understood Banjo too thoroughly to ask any questions. He enjoyed the situation. For a moment he felt strangely moved to throw himself in with Banjo and send Goosey back alone to the ship. But the next moment he reflected that he was no longer a wild stallion, but a draft horse in harness now with the bit in his mouth and the crupper under his tail, and—that he liked it.

The taxicab slowly trailing them, the boys crossed down the street and into the Seamen's Bar, where they stood at the counter, *à l'Américaine,* for the final drink together.

"When is you coming back to look us over?" Jake asked Ray.

"When the train puts me off," said Ray. "I like this rolling along, stopping anywhere I'm put off or thrown off. Like Banjo. I may get off to see you one a these days if the train pass your way."

"Well, when youse tired a rowling, if evah a broad evacuate you on any a them Gawd's own beach, you point you' nose straight foh Harlem. And if it is even in the middle of the night you get theah, we'll put out that elevator runner that lodging with us and make room to take you on."

They drove from the Joliette square down the docks to the ship, where they said good-bye. As Goosey went up the gang-plank after Jake, Banjo called out again:

"Go'-by, Gawd blimey you, Goosey, and don't fohgit what I done told you. Put it in you' flute and blow it."

Banjo and Ray wandered casually along the docks. Workmen were busy completing the big new American warehouse. The hand trucks were noisy on the paving stones with the shifting of boxes and barrels and the loading and unloading of ships. The eternal harvest of the world on the docks. African hard wood, African rubber, African ivory, African skins. Asia's gifts of crisp fragrant leaves and the fabled old spices with grain and oil and iron. All floated through the oceans into this warm Western harbor where, waiting to be floated back again, were the Occident's gifts. Immense crates, barrels, cases of automobiles, pianos, player-pianos, furniture; sand-papered, spliced, and varnished wood; calico print, artificial silk; pretty shoes and boots; French wines, British whiskeys, and a thousand little salesmen-made goods. Composite essence of the soil of all lands.

Commerce! Of all words the most magical. The timbre, color, form, the strength and grandeur of it. Triumphant over all human and natural obstacles, sublime yet forever going hand in hand with the bitch, Bawdy. In all relationships, between nations, between individuals, between little peoples and big peoples, progressive and primitive, the two lovers spread and flourish together as if one were the inevitable complement of the other.

Ray was wondering if it could have been otherwise—if it were madness to imagine the gorgeous concourse of civilization, past, present and to be, without these two creatures of man's appetites spreading themselves together, when Banjo said:

"Wha's working on you, pardner?"

"Me? Oh, just when are we going to get outa here?"

"Fed up with the ole poht, eh, scared of it gitting you now?"

"No fear. I've got this burg balled up with a mean hold on 'em."

"Nuts is good dessert, pardner, but I ain't seen no monkey antics yet."

"You will when the exhibition is open."

A Peninsular and Oriental boat had entered a basin farther up the docks and the boys rounded some warehouses to reach it. When they got there they found Malty and Ginger panhandling. The crew was Indian.

"Ain't nevah nothing doing on a coolie-jabbering boat," said Malty, deprecatingly, "but it ain't costing us nothing noways to hang around."

"The A-rabs am the best of them people for a handout on a broad," said Banjo.

There was a company of British soldiers on board and on the upper decks groups of tall, svelte, dignified Indians were conspicuous among the European passengers.

A knot of Senegalese were gathered a little way off to themselves, with their eyes on the galley. Three Indian boys of the beach were signaling to the Indian cooks against the railing above. The cooks seemed unheeding, looking down unsympathetically on the dark rabble beneath them. At last one of them went to the kitchen, returning with a paper packet which he threw down to the three Indian boys. The packet burst, scattering a mess of curried food in the dust. With nervous eagerness the boys seized the packet and scraped up the food from the ground.

The knot of Senegalese began stirring with excitement as their eyes turned the other way from the boat and saw a little cart rumble by them. It bore two scavenger-like whites and came to a halt near the gangway. They had come to get the garbage of the great liner, that was not dumped overboard, but brought into port and sold for the feeding of pigs.

Kitchen boys, two to each can, toted the garbage down the gangplank to dump it in the cart. The rank stuff was rushed and raided by the hungry black men. Out of the slime, the guts of game and poultry, the peelings of vegetables, they fished up pieces of ham, mutton, beef, poultry, and tore savagely at them with their teeth. They fought against one another for the best pieces. One mighty fellow sent a rival sprawling on his back from a can and dominated it until he had extracted some precious knuckles of bones with flesh upon them. Another brought up a decomposed rat which he dashed into the water, and wiping his hand on the sand, dived back again into the can. There were also two white men in the rush. A small Southern European was worsted in the struggle and knocked down, while a big Swede, with the appearance of a great mass of hard mildewed putty, held his own.

"Look at the niggers! Look at the niggers!" the passengers on deck cried, and some of them went and got cameras to photograph the scene.

Once when Ray was badly broke he had gone with Bugsy to sell an American suit and shirt to a young West African called Cuffee. Many of them, British and French black boys, clubbed together in a big room that took up half of a floor, for which each paid two francs a day. They were cooking when Ray got there; the smell of the stuff was good and he was hungry. They offered him some, but Bugsy whispered to him not to eat, because he had seen them picking over the garbage of the docks.

The Africans did not understand the art of panhandling as did the American and West Indian Negroes. When they could get no work on the docks they would not beg food of any ship that was not manned by their own countrymen speaking their language. Seamen who came in with money would help their fellows ashore. But outside of their own primitive circle the African boys were helpless.

"Ain't you ashamed a you' race?" Banjo asked Ray.

"Why you think? We've been down to the garbage line ourselves."

"Not to eat it, though. I'd sooner do some'n' inlegal and ketch jail."

"It's just a difference a stomach," said Ray. "Some stomachs are different from others." He remembered the time he had worked as a waiter in hotels and how the feeding of certain of the guests was always an interesting spectacle for him. They were those pink-eared, purple-veined, respectable pillars of society who in a refined atmosphere of service always stirred up in him an impression of obscenity. Their bellies seemed to him like coarse sacks that needed only to be filled up and rammed down with a multitude of foodstuffs.

It was a long way from them to these stranded and lost black creatures of colonization who ate garbage to appease the insistent demands of the belly. At night they would go to the African Bar and dance it away.

"Taloufa is right heah with us again," said Malty.

"Taloufa back in this burg?" exclaimed Banjo.

"You betchyu he sure is. And ef you got anything foh helping him, git it ready, for he ain't nothing this time more'n a plumb broke nigger."

The boys found Taloufa at the Seamen's Bar in Joliette, with his guitar, and a bow of colored ribbons decorating it, broke but unbroken. He was talking to an Indian, a thin, gray-haired man.

"I thought you were in England," said Ray.

"Wouldn't let me in," replied Taloufa.

"How you mean wouldn't let you in?"

From a set of papers in his pocketbook Taloufa extracted a slip and handed it to Ray.

The paper bore Taloufa's name and fingerprint and read:

> "The above-named is permitted to land at this port on condition that he proceeds to London in charge of an official of the Shipping Federation, obtains document of identity at the Home Office, and visa (if required), and leaves the United Kingdom at the earliest opportunity.
>
> (Signed)....................
>
> Immigration Officer."

When Taloufa arrived in England, the authorities would not permit him to land, but wanted him to go home direct to West Africa. Taloufa did not want to go there. Christian missionaries had educated him out of his native life. A Christian European had uplifted him out of and away from his people and his home. His memory of his past was vague. He did not know what had become of his family.

He tried to convince the authorities that he had a right to land in England. He had friends in Limehouse and in Cardiff. He had even a little property in the shape of a trunk and suitcase and clothes that he had left behind when he failed to return from his last American voyage. Nevertheless, he was permitted to land only to see about his affairs and under supervision.

Colored subjects were not wanted in Britain.

This was the chief topic of serious talk among colored seamen in all the ports. Black and brown men being sent back to West Africa, East Africa, the Arabian coast, and India, showed one another their papers and held sharp and bitter discussions in the rough cafés of Joliette and the Vieux Port.

The majority of the papers were distinguished by the official phrase: Nationality Doubtful.

Colored seamen who had lived their lives in the great careless tradition, and had lost their papers in low-down places to touts, hold-up men, and passport fabricators, and were unable or too ignorant to show exact proof of their birthplace, were furnished with the new "Nationality Doubtful" papers. West Africans, East Africans, South Africans, West Indians, Arabs, and Indians—they were all mixed up together. Some of the Indians and Arabs were being given a free trip back to their lands. Others, especially the Negroes, had chosen to stop off in French ports, where the regulations were less stringent. They were agreed that the British authorities were using every device to get all the colored seamen out of Britain and keep them out, so that white men should have their jobs.

Taloufa, under supervision, had crossed from England to Havre, had gone to Paris and, his money exhausted, had come to Marseilles to get a ship in any way he could. The Indian conversing with him was a unique case. Gray-haired, with a fine, thin, ancient, patient face, he was brown and brittle like a reed. He had left India as a ship's boy when he was so small that he could not recall anything of his people or his home. He had been a steward on English ships for years, before and all during the war.

One day, he said, he came in from a voyage and the medical officer for the local Seamen's Union put him on the sick list and took him off his ship. He said he was not ill, but he knew that the union officials were replacing colored seamen with white by any means. He went to a reputable private doctor and received a certificate attesting that he was not ill. He took it to the local official of his union, but that official ignored him. He had already put a white man in the Indian's place as steward. In a fit of anger the Indian foolishly tore up his union card and left the local office.

Weeks and months passed and he did not get another job. One day he was persuaded to take a place on a boat that was going out to stay in service in the East. But when he reached Marseilles, where the crew was to sign on, the steward changed his mind about going to the Far East on a "Nationality Doubtful" paper. Then he came up against the fact that he could not get back into England where he had lived for over forty years. He was six weeks on the beach in Marseilles. He had a pile of foolscap correspondence with the British Home Office. He was a "Nationality Doubtful" man with no place to go.

This was the way of civilization with the colored man, especially the black. The happenings of the past few weeks from the beating up of the beach boys by the police to the story of Taloufa's experiences, were, to Ray, all of a piece. A clear and eloquent exhibition of the universal attitude, which, though the method varied, was little different anywhere.

When the police inspector said to Ray that the strong arm of the law was against Negroes because they were all criminals, he really did not mean just that. For he knew that the big and terror-striking criminals were not Negroes. What he unconsciously meant was that the police were strong-armed against the happy irresponsibility of the Negro in the face of civilization.

For civilization had gone out among these native, earthy people, had despoiled them of their primitive soil, had uprooted, enchained, transported, and transformed them to labor under its laws, and yet lacked the spirit to tolerate them within its walls.

That this primitive child, this kinky-headed, big-laughing black boy of the world, did not go down and disappear under the serried crush of trampling white feet; that he managed to remain on the scene, not worldly-wise, not "getting there," yet not machine-made, nor poor-in-spirit like the regimented creatures of civilization, was baffling to civilized understanding. Before the grim, pale rider-down of souls he went his careless way with a primitive hoofing and a grin.

Thus he became a challenge to the clubbers of helpless vagabonds—to the despised, underpaid protectors of property and its high personages. He was a challenge of civilization itself. He was the red rag to the mighty-bellowing, all-trampling civilized bull.

Looking down in a bull ring, you are fascinated by the gay rag. You may even forget the man watching the bull go after the elusive color that makes him mad. The rag seems more than the man. If the bull win it, he horns it, tramples it, sniffs it, paws it—baffled.

As the rag is to the bull, so is the composite voice of the Negro—speech, song and laughter—to a bawdy world. More exasperating, indeed, than the Negro's being himself is his primitive color in a world where everything is being reduced to a familiar formula, this remains strange and elusive.

From the rear room of the café came sounds of music, shuffling of feet, shrill feminine cackle, and Malty's deep, far-carrying laughter. Banjo was at his instrument again. Presently Malty dashed in.

"For the love a life, Taloufy, come on in heah and play that holy wonderful new thing you done bring back heah with you."

"Wait a minute——"

"Wait you' moon! You come right along and make that mahvelous music and fohgit the white man's crap."

Taloufa followed Malty with his guitar. His new piece was a tormenting, tantalizing, tickling tintinnabulating thing that he called "Hallelujah Jig" and it went like this:

"Jigaway, boy, jig. . . . jig, jig, jig, jig, jig, jig, jig
Jig, jig, jig, black boy . . . jig away . . . jig away. . . .

"Lay off the coal, boy, and scrub you' hide,
Jigaway . . . jigaway.
Bring me a clean suit and show some pride,
Jigaway . . . jigaway.

"Step on the floor, boy, and show me that stuff
Jigaway . . . jigaway,
Strutting you' business and strutting it rough,
Jigaway . . . jigaway.

"Show me some movement and turn 'em loose,
Jigaway . . . jigaway,
Powerfulways like electric juice,
Jigaway . . . jigaway.

"Up the ole broad, boy; good nite to the bunk,
Jigaway . . . jigaway,
What you say, fellahs? I say hunky-tunk,
Jigaway . . . jigaway.

"When the lights go out until the stars fade,
Jigaway . . . jigaway,
For that's the bestest thing in the life of a spade,
Jigaway . . . jigaway.

"Jigaway, boy, jig, jig, jig, jig, jig, jig, jig, jig,
Jig, jig, jig, black boy . . . jig away . . . jig away. . . ."

Above the sound of the music the Indian was emphasizing the necessity for all colored people to wake up and get together, for, he said, although Indians belonged to the white stock according to science—the white people, particularly the British, were treating them like black people.

But Ray could not hear any more. The jigaway music was pounding in his ears. The dancing and singing and sugary laughter of the boys. It filled his head full and poured hot fire through his veins, tingling and burning. Such a sensual-sweet feeling. There was no resisting it.

"Pardon me," he said to the Indian, and hurried into the rear room.

Slowly the Indian gathered up his bundle of foolscap, methodically assorting the letters according to date. Then he went to the partition and looked in on the boys. Against the glass pane he looked like an ancient piece of broken bronze, a figure from an Oriental temple leaning among indifferent objects in the window of a dealer in antiques.

It was dismaying to him that those boys with whom he had just been conversing so earnestly should in a moment become forgetful of everything serious in a drunken-like abandon of jazzing.

"Just like niggers," he muttered, turning away. "The same on the ships. Always monkeying and never really serious about anything."

Yet the next day Taloufa stowed away safely for America, leaving the Indian on the beach, making his pathetic appeals to the English gentleman's Home Office.

"It was Taloufa bring that cargo a good luck," declared Banjo. "It's the same with humans like with them stars ovah us. Good and bad luck ones. Now Lonesome Blue was sure hard luck. But Taloufa is a good-luck baby."

It was indeed in every way a cargo of good luck that the boys were handling. They were no longer "on the beach." A wealthy shipowner from the Caribbean basin, profiting by the exchange rate, had bought a boat, which he was overhauling to take back to the West Indies. And the boys were on the boat.

It was a formidable polyglot outfit. The officers represented five European nations. The crew were supposed to be Caribbean. Malty was chosen to find and recommend the men. He got his gang in first, including Dengel, who wished to cross the Atlantic by any means.

"Though youse French," Malty told him, "you masticate that Englishman's langwitch bettah than a lottah bush niggers back home."

Malty also took West African boys, a "colored" South African, a reed-like Somali lad, and another Aframerican besides Banjo. They were all "going on the fly" and none of them was thinking of staying with the boat after the trip, but rather of getting to Cuba, Canada, and the United States. Ray worked with them, but said he was not going to sign up, as the very thought of returning to the Caribbean made him jumpy.

Ray teased Banjo about going as a seaman to the West Indies so soon after he had turned down a free trip to the United States. He predicted that Banjo would follow his nose to the States in quick time, for he would find the islands too small and sleepy for him.

"I'm gwine along with the gang, pardner, and tha's a different thing from going back with Goosey. This heah is like a big picnic for all of us. If youse wise, you'll join in with us."

The boys scraped, scrubbed, painted. They got only twenty francs a day, although the regular wage for such work was over thirty francs. But they were beach boys and not union men. And the union bosses had no knowledge of what was going on on the little boat. There is sometimes much free-for-all work on the docks. However, the boys did not allow *their* work to push them hard. They made shift to get through it. It would be different when they signed on. Then they would get the union wages of British seamen.

The African Café, The Rendezvous Bar, The bistro-cabaret in the Rue Coin du Reboul—all of them nightly did well with the boys. The Ditch looked at them differently, for they measured up to and above the "leetah" standards.

At last the boat was shipshape and ready to sail. The day came when the boys were called to sign on. Ray could have had an easy place, but he would not take it and he watched Banjo sign a little wistfully. They all had the right, under British Seamen's Regulations, to take part of their month's wages in advance. Each of the boys availed himself of this, that he might buy needful articles. Banjo took a full month's wages.

They cashed their cheques with a seamen's broker in Joliette. That night they had a big celebration. But Banjo was not with them. Nor had he used any of his money to buy new things. He invited Ray to go with him to a quiet little café in Joliette, and there he announced that he was not going to make the trip.

"And Ise gwine beat it outa this burg some convenient time this very night, pardner. Tha's mah ace a spades so sure as Ise a spade. You come along with me?"

Not going on the ship. . . . Beat it. . . . Come along with me.

"But you've signed on and taken a month's wages," protested Ray. "You can't quit now."

"Nix and a zero for what I kain't do. Go looket that book and you won't find mah real name no moh than anybody is gwine find this nigger when I take mahself away from here. I ask you again, Is you going with me?"

Ray did not reply, and after a silence Banjo said: "I know youse thinking it ain't right. But we kain't afford to choose, because we ain't born and growed up like the choosing people. All we can do is grab our chance every time it comes our way."

Ray's thoughts were far and away beyond the right and wrong of the matter. He had been dreaming of what joy it would be to go vagabonding with Banjo. Stopping here and there, staying as long as the feeling held in the ports where black men assembled for the great transport lines, loafing after their labors long enough to laugh and love and jazz and fight.

While Banjo's words brought him back to social morality, they brought him back only to the realization of how thoroughly he was in accord with them. He had associated too closely with the beach boys not to realize that their loose, instinctive way of living was more deeply related to his own self-preservation than all the principles, or social-morality lessons with which he had been inculcated by the wiseacres of the civilized machine.

It seemed a social wrong to him that, in a society rooted and thriving on the principles of the "struggle for existence" and the "survival of the fittest" a black child should be brought up on the same code of social virtues as the white. Especially an American black child.

A Chinese or Indian child could learn the stock virtues without being spiritually harmed by them, because he possessed his own native code from which he could draw, compare, accept, and reject while learning. But the Negro child was a pathetic thing, entirely cut off from its own folk wisdom and earnestly learning the trite moralisms of a society in which he was, as a child and would be as an adult, denied any legitimate place.

Ray was not of the humble tribe of humanity. But he always felt humble when he heard the Senegalese and other West African tribes speaking their own languages with native warmth and feeling.

The Africans gave him a positive feeling of wholesome contact with racial roots. They made him feel that he was not merely an unfortunate accident of birth, but that he belonged definitely to a race weighed, tested, and poised in the universal scheme. They inspired him with confidence in them. Short of extermination by the Europeans, they were a safe people, protected by their own indigenous culture. Even though they stood bewildered before the imposing bigness of white things, apparently unaware of the invaluable worth of their own, they were naturally defended by the richness of their fundamental racial values.

He did not feel that confidence about Aframericans who, long-deracinated, were still rootless among phantoms and pale shadows and enfeebled by self-effacement before condescending patronage, social negativism, and miscegenation. At college in America and among the Negro intelligentsia he had never experienced any of the simple, natural warmth of a people believing in themselves, such as he had felt among the rugged poor and socially backward blacks of his island home. The colored intelligentsia lived its life "to have the white neighbors think well of us," so that it could move more peaceably into nice "white" streets.

Only when he got down among the black and brown working boys and girls of the country did he find something of that raw unconscious and the-devil-with-them pride in being Negro that was his own natural birthright. Down there the ideal skin was brown skin. Boys and girls were proud of their brown, sealskin brown, teasing brown, tantalizing brown, high-brown, low-brown, velvet brown, chocolate brown.

There was the amusing little song they all sang:

> "Black may be evil,
> But Yellow is so low-down;
> White is the devil,
> So glad I'm teasing Brown."

Among them was never any of the hopeless, enervating talk of the chances of "passing white" and the specter of the Future that were the common topics of the colored intelligentsia. Close association with the Jakes and Banjoes had been like participating in a common primitive birthright.

Ray loved to be with them in constant physical contact, keeping warm within. He loved their tricks of language, loved to pick up and feel and taste new words from their rich reservoir of niggerisms. He did not like rotten-egg stock words among rough people any more than he liked colorless refined phrases among nice people. He did not even like to hear cultured people using the conventional stock words of the uncultured and thinking they were being free and modern. That sounded vulgar to him.

But he admired the black boys' unconscious artistic capacity for eliminating the rotten-dead stock words of the proletariat and replacing them with startling new ones. There were no dots and dashes in their conversation—nothing that could not be frankly said and therefore decently—no act or fact of life for which they could not find a simple passable word. He gained from them finer nuances of the necromancy of language and the wisdom that any word may be right and magical in its proper setting.

He loved their natural gusto for living down the past

and lifting their kinky heads out of the hot, suffocating ashes, the shadow, the terror of real sorrow to go on gaily grinning in the present. Never had Ray guessed from Banjo's general manner that he had known any deep sorrow. Yet when he heard him tell Goosey that he had seen his only brother lynched, he was not surprised, he understood, because right there he had revealed the depths of his soul and the soul of his race—the true tropical African Negro. No Victorian-long period of featured grief and sable mourning, no mechanical-pale graveside face, but a luxuriant living up from it, like the great jungles growing perennially beautiful and green in the yellow blaze of the sun over the long life-breaking tragedy of Africa.

Ray had felt buttressed by the boys with a rough strength and sureness that gave him spiritual passion and pride to be his human self in an inhumanly alien world. They lived healthily far beyond the influence of the colored press whose racial dope was characterized by pungent "bleach-out," "kink-no-more," skin-whitening, hair-straightening, and innumerable processes for Negro culture, most of them manufactured by white men's firms in the cracker states. And thereby they possessed more potential power for racial salvation than the Negro *litterati,* whose poverty of mind and purpose showed never any signs of enrichment, even though inflated above the common level and given an appearance of superiority.

From these boys he could learn how to live—how to exist as a black boy in a white world and rid his conscience of the used-up hussy of white morality. He could not scrap his intellectual life and be entirely like them. He did not want or feel any urge to "go back" that way.

Tolstoy, his great master, had turned his back on the intellect as guide to find himself in Ivan Durak. Ray wanted to hold on to his intellectual acquirements without losing his instinctive gifts. The black gifts of laughter and melody and simple sensuous feelings and responses.

Once when a friend gave him a letter of introduction to a Nordic intellectual, he did not write: I think you will like to meet this young black intellectual; but rather, I think you might like to hear Ray laugh.

His gift! He was of course aware that whether the educated man be white or brown or black, he cannot, if he has more than animal desires, be irresponsibly happy like the ignorant man who lives simply by his instincts and appetites. Any man with an observant and contemplative mind must be aware of that. But a black man, even though educated, was in closer biological kinship to the swell of primitive earth life. And maybe his apparent failing under the organization of the modern world was the real strength that preserved him from becoming the thing that was the common white creature of it.

Ray had found that to be educated, black and his instinctive self was something of a big job to put over. In the large cities of Europe he had often met with educated Negroes out for a good time with heavy literature under their arms. They toted these books to protect themselves from being hailed everywhere as minstrel niggers, coons, funny monkeys for the European audience—because the general European idea of the black man is that he is a public performer. Some of them wore hideous parliamentary clothes as close as ever to the pattern of the most correctly gray respectability. He had remarked wiry students and Negroes doing clerical work wearing glasses that made them sissy-eyed. He learned, on inquiry, that wearing glasses was a mark of scholarship and respectability differentiating them from the common types. . . . (Perhaps the police would respect the glasses.)

No getting away from the public value of clothes, even for you, my black friend. As it was, ages before Carlyle wrote *Sartor Resartus,* so it will be long ages after. And you have reason maybe to be more rigidly formal, as the world seems illogically critical of you since it forced you to discard so recently your convenient fig leaf for its breeches. This civilized society is classified and kept going by clothes and you are now brought by its power to labour and find a place in it.

The more Ray mixed in the rude anarchy of the lives of the black boys—loafing, singing, bumming, playing, dancing, loving, working—and came to a realization of how close-linked he was to them in spirit, the more he felt that they represented more than he or the cultured minority the irrepressible exuberance and legendary vitality of the black race. And the thought kept him wondering how that race would fare under the ever tightening mechanical organization of modern life.

Being sensitively receptive, he had as a boy become interested in and followed with passionate sympathy all the great intellectual and social movements of his age. And with the growth of international feelings and ideas he had dreamed of the association of his race with the social movements of the masses of civilization milling through the civilized machine.

But traveling away from America and visiting many countries, observing and appreciating the differences of human groups, making contact with earthy blacks of tropical Africa, where the great body of his race existed, had stirred in him the fine intellectual prerogative of doubt.

The grand mechanical march of civilization had leveled the world down to the point where it seemed treasonable for an advanced thinker to doubt that what was good for one nation or people was also good for another. But as he was never afraid of testing ideas, so he was not afraid of doubting. All peoples must struggle to live, but just as what was helpful for one man might be injurious to another, so it might be with whole communities of peoples.

For Ray happiness was the highest good, and difference the greatest charm, of life. The hand of progress was robbing his people of many primitive and beautiful qualities. He could not see where they would find greater happiness under the weight of the machine even if progress became left-handed.

Many apologists of a changed and magnified machine system doubted whether the Negro could find a decent place in it. Some did not express their doubts openly, for fear of "giving aid to the enemy." Ray doubted, and openly.

Take, for example, certain Nordic philosophers, as the world was more or less Nordic business: He did not think the blacks would come very happily under the super-mechanical Anglo-Saxon-controlled world society of Mr. H. G. Wells. They might shuffle along, but without much happiness in the world of Bernard Shaw. Perhaps they would have their best chance in a world influenced by the thought of a Bertrand Russell, where brakes were clamped on the machine with a few screws loose and some nuts fallen off. But in this great age of science and super-invention was there any possibility of arresting the thing unless it stopped of its own exhaustion?

"Well, what you say, pardner?" demanded Banjo. "Why you jest sidown theah so long studying ovah nothing at all? You gwine with a man or you ain't?"

"Why didn't you tell me before, so I could have signed on like you and make a getaway mahself?"

"Because I wasn't so certain sure a you. Youse a book fellah and you' mind might tell you to do one thing and them books persweahs you to do another. So I wouldn't take no chances. And maybe it's bettah only one of us do this thing this time. Now wese bettah acquainted, theah's a lotta things befoh us we'll have to make together."

"It would have been a fine thing if we could have taken Latnah along, eh?"

"Don't get soft ovah any one wimmens, pardner. Tha's you' big weakness. A woman is a conjunction. Gawd fixed her different from us in moh ways than one. And theah's things we can git away with all the time and she just kain't. Come on, pardner. Wese got enough between us to beat it a long ways from here."

Marseilles-Barcelona, 1927-28.

Books by Claude McKay
available in paperback editions
from Harcourt Brace Jovanovich, Inc.

BANANA BOTTOM
BANJO
A LONG WAY FROM HOME
SELECTED POEMS OF CLAUDE MCKAY